Praise for the F

"Grace Draven's exciting romantic fantasy features characters who are fresh and original. Their problems and triumphs will keep you reading into the night."

—#1 *New York Times* bestselling author Charlaine Harris

"Fierce and captivating, *Phoenix Unbound* is the story of a gladiator and a fire witch fighting for their freedom against an empire that wants them enslaved. With impossible odds, breathtaking battles, terrifying magic, and an unlikely love, this book is a must-read. Grace Draven is a master of romantic heroic fantasy."

—#1 *New York Times* bestselling author Ilona Andrews

"Fabulous. Quite possibly Grace Draven's best book yet. I couldn't put it down, and I didn't want it to end!"

—C. L. Wilson, *New York Times* bestselling author of *The Sea King*

"Must-read fantasy. . . . A wonderful story—full of romance, captivating characters, and a fantasy world that's beguiling." —*USA Today*

"Draven's outdone herself with this magnetic heroine and a magical world readers will be eager to return to."

—*Publishers Weekly* (starred review)

"Grace Draven has outdone herself with *Dragon Unleashed*! She's deepened and enriched the world established in *Phoenix Unbound*, spinning new twists and turns on an already magically compelling mythology. An epic tale of deception and greed that tests the bonds of family loyalty, *Dragon Unleashed* is also deftly woven romance that burns with sexual tension, then becomes swooningly delicious. With an original, sexy take on dragon shifters and a smart, self-contained healer, *Dragon Unleashed* kept me mesmerized and longing for more. This may well be Draven's best book yet."

—Jeffe Kennedy, award-winning author of *The Orchid Throne*

"With exquisitely drawn characters and superb worldbuilding, *Phoenix Unbound* once again proves Grace Draven's mastery of fantasy romance. This is exactly the kind of sweepingly romantic adventure story that I've been yearning for—and I can't wait for more."

—Meljean Brook, *New York Times* bestselling author of the Iron Seas series

"A tale of heartbreak and triumph, Grace Draven's *Phoenix Unbound* is truly exceptional. Be prepared to fall under the spell of these fierce, passionate characters and to root for them with all your heart."

—Amanda Bouchet, *USA Today* bestselling author of the Kingmaker Chronicles series

"Daring adventures, solid worldbuilding, and a sizzling romance make this first book in the Fallen Empire series a winner. Fans of fantasy and romance will be eagerly anticipating the next title. . . . Highly recommended."

—*Library Journal*

"Grace Draven is one of the finest romantic fantasy writers out there. . . . Tense, gripping, and entirely believable, [*Phoenix Unbound*] hooked me from the first page."

—*New York Times* bestselling author Thea Harrison

"Grace Draven weaves a spellbinding book that [is] impossible to forget. . . . I can't give this book enough praise. I came into it with stupidly high expectations, and it exceeded them all."

—Laura Thalassa, author of the Four Horsemen series

"Stunning! This book entices and mesmerizes to an astonishing degree. Like an intoxicating elixir, the more I read, the more I craved."

—*New York Times* bestselling author Darynda Jones

"When it comes to fantasy romance, Draven is in a class by herself. . . . A phenomenal start to what is sure to be an amazing series."

—RT Book Reviews

ACE BOOKS BY GRACE DRAVEN

THE FALLEN EMPIRE SERIES

Phoenix Unbound
Dragon Unleashed

DRAGON UNLEASHED

GRACE DRAVEN

ACE
NEW YORK

ACE
Published by Berkley
An imprint of Penguin Random House LLC
penguinrandomhouse.com

Library of Congress Cataloging-in-Publication Data

Names: Draven, Grace, author.
Title: Dragon unleashed / Grace Draven.
Description: First edition. | New York: Ace Books, 2020. | Series: The fallen empire
Identifiers: LCCN 2019042633 (print) | LCCN 2019042634 (ebook) |
ISBN 9780451489777 (paperback) | ISBN 9780451489784 (ebook)
Subjects: GSAFD: Fantasy fiction.
Classification: LCC PS3604.R385 D73 2020 (print) |
LCC PS3604.R385 (ebook) | DDC 813/.6—dc23
LC record available at https://lccn.loc.gov/2019042633
LC ebook record available at https://lccn.loc.gov/2019042634

First Edition: June 2020

Printed in the United States of America
1 3 5 7 9 10 8 6 4 2

Cover illustration by Arantza Sestayo
Cover design by Adam Auerbach
Book design by Elke Sigal

To Patrick, my best friend as well as my spouse.
Yes, love, the book is finished.

To Hasna Saadani, who once gave an unknown book by an unknown author a chance and reviewed it, then recommended it. You altered my trajectory. Thank you.

DRAGON UNLEASHED

CHAPTER ONE

If there was one thing Malachus had learned about humans during his long life span, it was that they were first and foremost thieves. They stole anything and everything, nailed down or not, from jewels and livestock to women and children. And if battlefields and graves were any true indicators, the dead were no more safe from their larceny than the living.

The Sovatin monks who'd fostered him as a child never truly prepared him for the scope of humanity's predation upon itself. Though human as well, the monks lived isolated from the depredations of the so-called civilized. Malachus never forgot the grief on their faces—the horror—at discovering their sacred necropolis destroyed beyond repair by treasure seekers. It was his first real taste of humanity as a whole, and he found it revolting. It was also the impetus for him to become a sought-after bounty hunter with a reputation feared throughout Winosia's prefectures.

His martial training combined with his true nature gave him an edge, one that made grave robbers and slavers question whether pursuing their professions was worth the risk of becoming the quarry in his hunt.

This hunt was different, more personal, and his prey far wilier than he'd anticipated, slipping through his fingers countless times over numerous leagues and a treacherous sea. Either they possessed extraordinary luck or they knew what he was and how to outmaneuver him. Now, far away in an unfamiliar country, Malachus's luck had run dry.

The pair possessed a treasure he would move mountains to regain, and they had fled across the Raglun Sea to these lands. The ship Malachus had sailed on to follow them had almost caught up to theirs, the mother-bond calling to his soul with a war drum's beat. But fickle gods had churned the waters into a raging cauldron and flung his ship far off course. An experienced captain and crew had saved the ship and those on board, sailing the beaten vessel into harbor with broken masts and ripped sails. Malachus's quarry had long since vanished into the interior, moving westward.

He'd managed to track them from the coast to this forest, guided by the internal beacon connecting him to the artifact he hunted. His mother-bond, which was all that remained of his mother, his birthright, and his ability to reclaim his true heritage.

Malachus stood at the tree line and gazed upon the fields before him that stretched to the base of the distant black-striped mountains. A wide road snaked toward a miasma of dust in the distance, a steady stream of wagon and foot traffic traveling its length. According to those he'd spoken with when he first came ashore, a great market, promising all manner of goods available for sale, had sprung up where once a Kraelian garrison had stood. He suspected his prey was there. He stabbed the damp earth in front of him with the point of his sword, wishing it was the belly of one, or both, of the thieves. He needed that mother-bond. Nothing more than a bit of bone at first glance, its value lay far beyond anything the pair might get from a buyer. After four hundred years of imprisonment in a human body, kept quiet by magic, his true form had grown restless, a dangerous prisoner, and a fatal one if he didn't set it loose in time. Even now, the force of his inevitable transformation surged through his bones and muscles, making the veins in his arms and neck bulge at times, and his head throb. It was certain that he'd have to slough off his human guise and embrace the draga one. Ignoring that imperative guaranteed death. He needed the mother-bond to safely initiate that change.

At his patient mare's inquiring whicker, he turned. She whuffled a second time when he stroked her neck.

"They're close, Batraza," he told the horse. "Likely trying to pawn what they pilfered."

Finding the thieves and the mother-bond would be easier in a contained market than trying to track them across leagues of unknown, and likely hostile, terrain. If he listened hard enough, he could hear hints of faraway voices. They were about a full day's ride from the dust cloud, and that was if he and Batraza didn't have to shelter from the summer storms that periodically doused the area.

For now the sky curved blue above him, and he eyed the clouds scudding by, noting those that gathered into thunderheads to linger in the distance. Malachus sighed, cleaning his blade before resheathing it. The ragged tips of Batraza's tail slapped against his arm as she swatted away the pesky gnats that swarmed in clouds around their heads and tried to fly up their noses. Unlike other horses, she didn't lay her ears back in warning or try to bolt when Malachus drew near her. That, as much as her preternaturally long life span, made her as strange as her rider.

Malachus offered her the treat of a withered apple he had fished from the depths of one of the bags attached to the saddle, and swung nimbly onto her back. The two turned away from the road toward an open space where the tree line curved in a horseshoe shape around gently swaying grassland.

Time and solitude allowed Malachus to plan his next move as he tracked the mother-bond to the shores of the far-flung Krael

Empire. Sometimes he felt more hound than human or draga, his nose either to the ground or to the wind as he searched for his legacy. The blue sky overhead rapidly gave way to blackening thunderheads fissured with lightning. A few bolts broke free to strike the ground, and Batraza pranced beneath him, nervous at the storm's approach. Malachus guided her deeper into the trees before dismounting. She leaned against him as he cast a spell the monks had taught him to calm her so she wouldn't bolt when he left her to return to the open curve of grassland on foot.

Rain blew in with a howl and then a roar, slanting sideways as the storm gusts drove it across the landscape like an overseer wielding a whip. Malachus tilted his face to the sky and let the deluge pummel him, washing away his frustration along with the layer of travel dirt he'd acquired since his last bath.

A shimmer of light illuminated the shield of his closed eyelids, followed by a boom of thunder. Within the sheltering trees, Batraza whinnied her fear. Malachus murmured, "It's all right, girl. Just a little light and noise, nothing more. You're the safest you can be where you are."

As quickly as the storm blew in, it passed. Thunder rumbled in the distance, chasing walls of rain that galloped across the forest before bashing into the mountain range. Black clouds splintered by lightning trailed behind, and Malachus crossed his fingers in the hope that his height and singularity on the flat ground might lure one of those crackling tongues of light toward him. Lightning always loved the draga, even those disguised as humans.

A bright bolt forked out of one of the clouds to strike him. He convulsed with the shock wave of power that hammered through his muscles and boiled the blood in his veins. For a moment, his heart seized before restarting with a double-time beat. Every hair on his body stood up, and the smell of charred cloth filled his nostrils. Still, he kept his feet as the lightning anchored him to the earth and exploded images across his mind's eye.

A market teeming with people against the backdrop of a ruined fortress, his mother-bond haloed in shimmering light and resting on a square of purple cloth. A woman's pretty face and somber gray eyes. An older man with similar features and the same gray eyes. And most important, the two thieves he'd tracked this far. All those depictions flashed before him in the time it took for the lightning to pin him to the ground, burn bright, then burn out.

Released from the lightning's lethal hold, Malachus staggered before falling to one knee. He breathed deep, fire in his lungs and agony in his bones. Smoke wreathed him and the burnt grass around him. A wispy tendril meandered from a thumbnail-size burn hole on the top of his right boot. The wetness of rain-soaked ground seeped through his sole. The lightning that exited his body had left a matching burn hole there.

Any other man would be a smoking husk by now, but Malachus was not a normal man any more than Batraza was a normal horse. His magic made the mare unique just as Malachus's mother's heritage made him peculiar. Batraza was a horse that wore the guise of magic. Malachus was magic who wore the guise of a human.

He'd need to repair his boot, but the damage had been worth it. The lightning had revealed a great deal. The valuable piece of his mother's skeleton still moved westward, pausing briefly as if teasing him with its nearness.

While most of the images the lightning had shown him were obvious location markers and hints, the one of the woman with the solemn features puzzled him. She might well be a buyer interested in possessing the mother-bond—and woe betide her if she was—or she might be traveling with the thieves he tracked, unknowing that they carried a lodestone that put a relentless hunter on their trail. The man she resembled was a mystery as well, though Malachus had no doubt that he, too, was somehow tied to the mother-bond. The lightning wouldn't have shown them otherwise.

He stood, soaked to the skin, and shook off the last remnants of the sky's blistering kiss before returning to Batraza. She snorted and rolled her eyes when Malachus drew closer, stamping a hoof as if to admonish him for leaving her alone among the trees.

"Peace, Bat," he said in his most soothing tone and gathered the reins before swinging into the wet saddle. The storm's power had fizzled. To the west, the clearing sky took on a golden hue, overpainting the blue as the sun regained dominion over the clouds.

Malachus guided the mare out of the forest. If they traveled without stopping and avoided the road's heavier traffic, they'd reach the market by the following nightfall. A new moon meant a blacker-than-usual night. He could enter the market without much notice, just one of many travelers journeying toward the temporary city. Though he wasn't human, he wore the form of one no different from all of those who trekked toward the ruins.

They reached the market after the vendors closed shop and the encampment surrounding it settled down for the night. That suited him fine. He found it far easier to navigate new surroundings without throngs of people milling about to trade, socialize, or steal.

The sickle moon hung midway in the night sky as he circled the camp perimeter, ringed by hundreds of tents and wagons as well as livestock pens guarded by a few people and a fair number of dogs. The air was redolent with the scent of humans and animals, mud and wet felt—unpleasant except for the drifting scents of cooking spices and herbal teas simmering over fires. Those teased his nostrils, and his empty stomach rumbled in response. Malachus nodded briefly to the watch who silently observed him as he rode past pens and clusters of tents, inciting the dogs into frantic barking or frightened yelps if his gaze lingered too long on them. The mother-bond's draw hummed along his senses like silver thread stitched into fabric. He guided Batraza along the market's edge and farther out still, where the grass grew undisturbed and untrampled and the light of torches no longer chased away the thick darkness. He brought the mare to a halt and breathed deep, allowing his senses to open wide, feel even more the hard draw of draga magic as he sharpened his focus on the thing that had driven him to cross deep seas and foreign lands to find it.

He'd camp for the night and renew his search in the morning. Reconnoitering in darkness had its benefits, but this was a large tent city populated with enough watchmen that someone would interpret his investigating as nefarious and try either to shoot him or to knife him. Confrontations never went unnoticed, and he didn't want to give any warning to his prey of his presence here. For all they knew, his ship had gone down in an angry sea and he along with it. He didn't want to disabuse them of the notion in case they'd made such a fortuitous assumption.

The spot where he chose to camp was no more than a patch of wet ground away from the meandering patterns of flattened grass that marked a well-traveled trek made by campers who wished to relieve themselves away from their living spaces.

The night sky stayed clear, and he counted the stars salting its expanse from his supine view on Batraza's saddle blanket. The mare grazed nearby, her lead rope staked within easy reach. Malachus listened to the sounds around him—the call of a night bird, the distant ululation of wolves, the rustle of some rodent hiding from predators looking to catch their dinner. Above those, the murmur and flow of voices, their words indistinct. Friendly conversations and hot arguments, the intense sensuality of moans during lovemaking, a woman's sweet lullaby to a fretful baby.

These were the things that reminded him there was more to humanity than its larceny, its petty cruelties. His understanding, and the empathy that came with it, was a fragile thing, even after decades of living among humans outside the monastery. He looked like them, but they possessed dark depths he'd never fully comprehend, nor did he want to. The sounds he listened to now, of mundane lives lived in peaceful hours, softened his attitude a small bit. It wouldn't last. It never did.

His thoughts settled once more on the gray-eyed woman the lightning had shown him earlier. Attractive, but he had known sublime. Dignified, but he had met majestic. There was nothing about her appearance that strayed from the conventional into the remarkable, yet her image remained emblazoned in his mind. He saw it overlaid across a spectacle of starlight and behind his lids when he closed them. It was more than a suspected connection to his mother-bond. He wanted to know her name, hear her voice, learn what lay behind those eyes the color of dove's wings. His fascination with her made no sense, but Malachus didn't question it. His spirit understood his instinct better than his mind did, and he couldn't shunt its message aside. The lightning had shown her to him for a reason.

He drifted into a fitful slumber, wondering how her misty eyes might change when she laughed and how that laughter might sound.

CHAPTER TWO

Halani searched the crowd from her spot at the stall she manned alongside Gilene, hoping to catch a glimpse of the Savatar clansmen everyone in the Goban market was talking about, including her. She'd bought a shawl for her mother, Asil, from a Palizi trader, when word of the nomads' arrival spread like a brushfire through the market. Asil was somewhere in the crowd with Talen and Dennefel, scouting the many stalls for to what to buy and resell later for a profit. Knowing her mother, Asil would race back to their own stall and demand Halani go with her to find the Savatar and admire those who had challenged the Empire and actually won.

Instead of hunting for her mother, she'd returned to the stall to help Gilene and share the latest market gossip. Not everyone expressed excitement over the Savatars' arrival. Gilene's reaction to the news surprised Halani. A stillness fell over her, as if she'd just spotted a hunter with his bow trained on her. Her voice was thick with conflicting notes of both dread and hope when she said, "Are you sure?"

Halani nodded. "They're roaming through the market now. Word is their leaders are honored guests of the Goban chief who controls this territory."

She considered climbing onto the table for an overhead view of the crowd and possible glimpse of the new arrivals but settled instead for standing on tiptoe and craning her neck to see over the crowd.

A piercing whistle whose modulations Halani instantly recognized cut through the marketplace's dull roar. A summons from Hamod, one that never failed to make her bristle. She wasn't a dog, and her uncle's assurances that the whistle was simply more effective than trying to shout didn't soothe her indignation. She was tempted to ignore it, but Hamod used the whistle judiciously. He needed her.

She spotted him through a gap in the crowd, standing with a group of traders. One held something wrapped in a scrap of violet silk.

Halani groaned and silently cursed. She offered Gilene an apologetic smile. "Probably another statue Uncle wants me to look at. I'm better than he is at spotting a fake. I'll have to leave you again for a moment."

Gilene returned Halani's smile with a thin one of her own, gaze sweeping the crowd as she replied. "It's all right. See to your uncle. We'll switch places when you return."

Halani hesitated. She'd known Gilene for less than a year, nursed her through two bouts of illness, and shared a wagon with her. Life had not been kind to Gilene. She'd almost died in the grotesque Flowers of Spring ritual and ended up separated from her husband, Valdan, still not knowing if slavers had killed him. A quiet, reserved woman who worked hard and rarely laughed, she was unfailingly kind to Asil and grateful to Halani for her aid. Her dark eyes cached a hoard of secrets, and she minded her own business so well even Hamod felt comfortable enough offering her a place among his free traders. But Gilene's response to Halani's revelation regarding the Savatars was strange. The air around her practically vibrated with a kind of harrowing anticipation, as if she half expected the Savatar to charge in on their horses and attack the market.

Were Hamod's whistles not growing more commanding, Halani would have stayed at the table. She gave a pained sigh and left the stall to shoulder her way through the throng.

The Goban marketplace's already lively atmosphere turned frenetic as rumor spread of the Savatars' arrival. To those who had lived in the shadows of the destroyed garrisons, they were heroes. To the free traders gathered here, the Savatar clans were the hammer that broke the Trade Guild's hold on the Golden Serpent. Gossip and retellings of the siege at Kraelag had reached epic proportions, until it was no longer a battle between the Empire army and barbarian steppe clans, but a clash between gods. A true goddess did make an appearance, one who left destruction in her wake, a city burned to the ground, and an empire shaken to its foundations by what she'd wrought. The Savatar called her Agna and, according to rumor, beseeched her aid in their bid to crack open Kraelag's defensive walls. The goddess had done so and more, leaving nothing to pillage and an empire that lost its sense of identity along with its corrupt capital.

Hamod's caravan had stopped several leagues away from the city, away from Kraelag and the invading armies. Halani had seen the black smoke billowing skyward in the distance. Only later did they get details of the siege, and those were recounted by an ill, traumatized Gilene, who told of a fortuitous escape from the terrible fate of a Flower of Spring thanks to the Savatar invaders, whose goddess had made a Flower of Spring of everyone who didn't flee Kraelag, immolating everything in holy fire.

Even Halani, a storyteller who understood how the most mundane events achieved grandiose proportions with time and numerous retellings, wanted to see a Savatar clansman, majestic on his horse, who didn't wait for the rapacious Empire to attack his homeland but brought the battle to the Empire's very gates himself. Unfortunately, it was time to play the guessing game of "real or fake." Halani had not lost yet, and her uncle counted on it.

The cluster of men standing with him was a motley lot. She recognized one, a free trader from Okeshen Flat Nose's caravan. Halani couldn't remember his name, but she remembered his hands, quick to grope any woman unfortunate enough to walk within reach. The one time he'd tried it with Halani, she'd broken his fingers with a pair of iron tongs. He caught sight of her striding toward them, went wide-eyed, and abruptly abandoned their group.

Conversation among the remaining four men stuttered to a halt as they watched the man flee before turning to see what had sent him racing away like a scared rabbit.

She didn't recognize those who stayed with Hamod. One wore the garb she'd seen on many of the Goban men attending the market gathering here: vests with three-quarter-length sleeves over ivory shirts whose hems were almost as long as a woman's frock. Wide sashes cinched the two garments close to the waist. The shirt and tunic had split sides that revealed loose breeches tucked into boots strapped to the legs with leather ties.

Halani's attention moved to his compatriots. Their garb was rougher, stranger, proclaiming them outlanders. Nor did they look like merchants. More like mercenaries who'd found another way to earn a coin or two beyond sell-swording. Their cheap hunting armor had seen better days, and they didn't bother concealing the weaponry they carried. She ran a practiced eye over the sheaths that covered their knives as well as the bow and quiver one wore across his back. Hamod and his folk dealt in all manner of goods, and while Halani wasn't an expert in sharp steel and armor, it didn't take a great deal of expertise to tell her these men either scavenged the dead on a battlefield or bought their garb and weapons from a vendor who traded in goods Hamod turned his nose up at and refused to sell.

One of the men held a square of the purple cloth she'd glimpsed earlier, within its folds a piece of ivory. She resisted rolling her eyes. If she had a silver *belsha* for every bit of bone she'd examined to determine its value, she'd be a rich woman. If this went like previous transactions of its ilk, she was about to get an earful of boasts and lies regarding the bone's origin. Which was no doubt of far humbler roots than what these two planned to tout.

Most bone traders dealt in common ivory bits they tried to pass off as something more exotic. Dog, cat, and snake skeletons were sometimes fused together in twisted new incarnations and peddled as remains of rare or mythical beasts worthy of the high price the bone merchants charged for them.

Hamod was a wily trader and taught everything he knew to his niece. Charming, sly, and armed with a repertoire of half-truths, he could sell a beggar his own rags back to him given enough time, and spot a costly trinket in a midden heap at a hundred paces. Never an easy mark, he still deferred to Halani on some things, like determining the authenticity of an artifact. Hamod graced her with a jovial smile that didn't reach his eyes or hide the avaricious gleam sparkling in his pupils—a telltale sign that whatever these men had told or shown him, it had caught his interest in the worst way. The Goban merchant seemed more a curious onlooker, while the two mercenaries—and she grew more certain of their profession the closer she got to them—appeared ready to bolt at the first sneeze, their gazes never settling for long on one person or one spot, shifting constantly to scan the busy market's bustling crowd as if searching for someone.

Hamod didn't introduce her. As free traders, they came in

contact with all sorts of people, honest and unsavory alike. None of the men had looked at Halani with anything resembling lust, but Hamod chose not to reveal anything about his niece.

He gestured to the silk cloth the one man held. "Take a look," he said, "and tell me what you think."

The mercenary-trader passed the ivory to Halani with a willingness that surprised her, dropping it into her open palm as if he found the thing repulsive to the touch. A rush of vibration shuddered up her arm, and she swallowed a gasp at the sensation. Cold, prickly, pulsing.

The bone's weight surprised her as well. Its shape hinted that she held the end bit of a claw. She ran her thumb over its interior curve, careful not to slice her flesh on its outer edge or prick her finger on its pointed tip. Good gods! If merely a fragment, then whatever this once belonged to, the creature had been gigantic. Several more passes of her thumb revealed a new discovery. A shape not naturally made by bone growth was engraved into the claw's flat plane at the spot where the arc was widest. Here, too, the sharpest sensations punctured her fingers like needles dipped in ice water. She held the claw bit up to the sun, seeing nothing. Wait. She peered a little closer. Was that a glow around the perimeter of the engraved shape? Halani blinked, and it was gone, though the needle pinpricks remained as strong.

"Our friends here say it's from a draga." That greedy light in Hamod's gaze grew from a sparkle to a blaze the longer she held the bone fragment in her hand.

Despite the odd vibration still coursing through her hand and her arm, Halani only raised a doubtful eyebrow. "Is that so?"

How many times had she heard such a fanciful boast told by a trader working easy marks in a crowd eager to part with their coins? Real draga bones, even the fragments, were hard to come by, mostly sold to rich collectors.

Plenty of gossip ran the breadth and length of the Krael Empire that Empress Dalvila once had the complete skeleton of the fabled Golnar suspended from her bedchamber's ceiling. Halani had never seen it for herself or known of anyone who had, but such notions made for good storytelling fodder. Now those rumors would remain only hearsay. Golnar's bones had burned with the rest of the palace, even the legendary strength of draga-kind unable to withstand the destroying power of god-fire.

"It's true," the second mercenary-trader said in response to her skeptical look. "Draga through and through. If you can find some way to grind it into powder and sell it in small quantities, you'll be rich. Draga bone is magic."

"If that's so, then why would you want to sell it to us, knowing you'll get far less from a fellow trader than you would from a regular buyer?"

Hamod's scrutiny switched from her to the two men, and he eyed them with the same skepticism. "Good question."

She and Hamod had done this before, teamed up to work over a difficult seller: one playing the role of eager, unwary buyer, the other the reluctant miser unwilling to buy a dram of wine unless he could get the entire barrel it came from thrown in for the price. This time was different. Halani wondered why these two would want to give up something with significant value by selling it to a free trader, that notorious group of merchants who refused to serve the Guild and obtained their goods to sell by questionable means.

The two men shared a glance before the second one spoke. "We know others want it, but trade isn't our calling. We're hired swords who bought the draga bone for a good price from a man eager to get rid of it himself. Now we know why. Those who covet it will do anything to have it. It's not worth it to us to keep it, and it's getting in our way of hiring on for other work."

In other words, they or the previous owner stole it, and someone with clout wanted it back. Halani estimated that half of what the man just spouted was truth and half was so much horseshit. At the moment she couldn't quite tell which of the two was the greater. Once more she ran the pad of her thumb over the claw's flat curve, distracted by the magic suffusing her body. She was surprised no one yet had commented on her hair standing on end. Every strand felt as if it were vibrating, and her eyelids twitched involuntarily.

The sensation was both strange and familiar. Familiar in that it carried the hum of earth magic, a tune all its own that shared some similarities with the music she sensed in everything born of soil, rock, and tree. Music that hummed to a lesser degree in the herbs she harvested for healing salves and in the grave dirt she dug when raiding a barrow. Those vibrations were gentle tones of varying pitch. This . . . this was a roar.

Hamod's thin veneer of casual boredom began to fracture as Halani stood there, weighing the man's words and stroking the ivory. The calculating gleam in his eye warned her that no matter what argument she used to convince him not to make the sale, it would fall on deaf ears.

I think we should return whatever this bone is to those who took it, walk away, and not look back.

They were the words she wanted to say but didn't. Her uncle reveled in the embrace of the mistress that ruled him best—greed. Instead of sound argument, Halani employed a weapon she rarely used on the wily Hamod. She lied.

"It's an interesting piece," she said, adopting a regretful sigh. "But it looks like any old bone one might pick off a large animal carcass."

The dismay on the men's faces might have been comical were Halani not so focused on fooling her uncle. She held out the bone to the man who'd given it to her. He took a step back as if she offered him a live viper.

Hamod reached for the artifact, only to have Halani hold it away from him. She surprised herself, but something instinctive told her that to surrender it to him meant he wouldn't give it up, no matter her false assurances that the bone was nothing special.

His eyes narrowed before he gave the two men a thin smile. "Give me a moment. Sometimes we differ on those items we think will interest our buyers." That was no more true than her assertion about the bone fragment, but she didn't argue when Hamod pulled her to the side out of earshot of the traders and gave them his back so they couldn't see his scowl.

"Don't lie to me, girl," he said. "To them, fine. We can bargain for a better price if we insist it's fit only for the midden heap."

She'd never been able to fool Hamod. He was, and always would be, a master of mendacity.

"I'm sorry, Uncle." She glanced down at the bone on its bed of silk. "Whatever creature this belonged to, no good can come from owning it. It has the feel of a lodestone about it. Its purpose is to lure someone or something to it."

Hamod's scowl melted away. "You learned all that just from holding it?" At her nod, a triumphant smile danced across his lips. "Then it's definitely magical and should fetch a decent price."

"Maybe," she hedged. Her gaze settled on the two mercenaries waiting nearby. "But look at those men. You heard what they said. It's coveted. Even if I didn't sense anything from this piece, I'd wager it isn't just coveted, it's hunted, and they no longer want any part of that chase. Theirs is a desperate honesty. They've tried to sell it before and had no takers. Something about it is warning people away." Hamod's gleeful expression clouded with doubt, then cleared, and he shrugged.

"If it's fake, I'll bid low and grind the bone into powder. We'll sell it as a cure for baldness, or you can make a cream. We'll tout it to the crones trying to recapture their youth." He chuckled at her disapproving glare. "Stop looking like a shriveled apple. You know as well as I that we've fed our group more than once on the backs of other people's vanity."

Halani hated it when he used practicality to justify some of his ethically questionable actions. "What if it is valuable? Bone from a truly rare creature?" The hum along her skin assured her that the bone was anything but ordinary.

Hamod's eyes gleamed. "Then we count this our lucky day, and if someone else wants this pretty back, they can buy it or fight for it." As free traders, their caravan was heavily armed, wary of strangers on the road, and its members unhesitating in defending themselves. But in this Hamod was wrong.

"We may not have the numbers to keep it from whoever is searching for it."

Again, that maddening, unconcerned shrug. "Then we'll deal with them if that day comes. I doubt it will, and I know more than a few people in Domora who'd be happy to part with a full purse to possess such an artifact to show off to their wealthy friends." He held out a hand, crooking his fingers. "Now, hand it over so I can get to bargaining, and you can get back to the stall and help Gilene."

As if uttering the woman's name summoned it, a female voice

bellowed above the noise of the crowd, bringing the market to a halt. "Azarion!" Halani turned toward the commotion, startled to see Gilene's absent husband, Valdan, stride through the crowd toward the trader tables where Gilene manned their booth.

No longer the ragged, injured dye merchant Hamod's caravan had come across on a dusty road at the edge of the forest, Valdan wore the trappings of a leader. Bearded and dressed in the garb of a Savatar horse nomad, he was still the handsome man Halani remembered. His piercing green gaze rested solely on Gilene, who stared back, eyes wide and bright with tears. Hamod used the distraction to snatch the bone fragment out of Halani's hand and returned to the two skittish traders.

Torn between curiosity over the drama playing out between Gilene and her husband and wanting to harangue her uncle more, Halani paused amid the crowd. She pressed her palms together, striving to recapture a remnant of the magic hanging over the bone like an invisible mist.

A ghost of ancient earth swirled between her fingers, a memory of pain and regret, of desperation, and of hope. But most of all a silent but plaintive call to be found and united. With what? With whom?

The sudden, more physical tug on her elbow brought her out of her ruminations. Her mother stood next to her, weathered features creased by a wide grin. She pointed to Valdan as he approached the table Gilene stood behind. "Look, Hali! Valdan isn't dead," she said in her high, childish voice. "Come with me. I want to tell him hello!"

A cluster of Savatar lined up behind him like a human redoubt. They were an intimidating group of men and women dressed in light armor and carrying a myriad of weapons. None looked as if they'd welcome a gleeful Asil skipping through their ranks to offer greetings. Nevertheless, Halani rarely refused her mother's wishes and followed her back toward their stall.

A flicker of movement close to the table caught her attention, and she spotted a pack of cutpurses as young as six, but no older than twelve, easing closer to the pile of goods stacked toward the back of the stall as well as the unguarded items on the table itself. "Bollocks!" she snapped. With Gilene and Valdan seeing only each other and the Savatar watching only them, the stall was easy pickings for small, fast thieves. They'd be cleaned out in moments.

Asil's eyes widened. "What?

Halani pointed in the cutpurses' direction as she raced toward them. Asil shot past her, far fleeter and more nimble than her aged appearance suggested. She reached the table just as one of the older, bigger juveniles snatched a tooled leather pouch from the table's corner and bolted into the thick of the crowd.

He didn't get far. One of the Savatar women abruptly straightened her arm from her side, clotheslining the runner. He struck the unexpected barrier so hard, he ricocheted off her vambraced forearm, feet flying out from under him before he landed on his back. The bag he held tumbled through the air and was snagged by Asil. The thief's compatriots scattered in all directions. Halani suspected they'd managed to make off with a fan and one of the hideous hats Dennefel loved to make and Hamod insisted they try to sell. It could have been much worse. Winded but not incapacitated, the downed thief sprang to his feet and fled, kicking up his heels even higher when the Savatar woman lunged toward him as if to give chase.

Halani reached her mother's side in time to overhear her praise the woman.

Asil's cheeks were red, and her eyes danced, as if preventing an impromptu raid on their stall had been great fun. "You're very strong," she said, admiration in her voice.

The Savatar inclined her head and returned a similar compliment in heavily accented Common tongue. "And you're very fast."

Halani skirted around the Savatar barricade to straighten the table and move some of the items most in danger of being snatched to a more inaccessible spot.

"Oh, Halani, I'm sorry! I'm so sorry!" Gilene no longer stared into her husband's face as if seeing a vision. She tried to help Halani move the trade items to a safer spot. Halani shooed her away.

"Stop fretting." She nodded toward Valdan. "I think you have a good excuse for the distraction. Besides, I left you here to man the stall alone. Cutpurses always look for lone sellers in the markets."

"I'm to blame," Valdan said behind her. "I'll pay for the loss of anything taken, Halani."

She offered him a smile. "We're very glad to see you alive and well. Gilene isn't one to wear her feelings for all to see, but I know she pined for you and worried."

Even at second glance, his appearance still startled her. He had introduced himself to their caravan more than a year ago as a dye merchant attacked by raiders who had nearly killed him, injured his wife Gilene, and stolen their supplies and horse. When Hamod told Valdan he had the look of a steppe-man about him, Valdan said he was the child of a Kraelian woman and an Empire soldier of Nunari blood. At the time, his stories and explanations seemed believable, and neither he nor Gilene had given Hamod reason to think otherwise during their stay with the caravan.

Looking at him now, thinner, haggard but still handsome, and garbed in the raiment of high rank among an entourage of Savatar who showed him obvious deference and Gilene surprising reverence, Halani was certain this man was no simple dye merchant.

Asil jumped between them before he could reply. "Valdan, you're not dead!" she crowed, so obviously delighted by the fact that Valdan and the rest of his companions laughed.

He reached for one of her hands, giving it a squeeze. "No, Asil. I'm not dead, and as before, I owe you and your daughter a life debt." His gaze traveled to Gilene, standing behind Asil, the look in his eyes so scorching, Halani sighed inwardly. No man had ever stared at her in such a way—as if everything and anything of value to him resided within her. His next words to Asil only confirmed her thoughts. "You've given back to me that which I treasure above all else in the world."

The Savatar woman who'd thwarted the cutpurse spoke, this time in a language Halani didn't understand, though she recognized a few Nunari words in the rapid speech and was sure she again heard the word "Azarion."

He replied in kind, heavy green gaze still on Gilene. He switched to Common tongue then. "You'll come with me? With us? We've taken the grounds just west of the garrison ruins for our camp."

Gilene nodded, expression radiant. She turned to Halani. "Do you mind? I can stay until the market closes. I don't wish to abandon you."

Halani laughed. "First, you don't need my permission. I'm not your keeper. Second, if I were you and my exceptionally handsome husband, who I feared might be dead but who turned up alive and well, asked me to go with him to his camp, all you'd get from me is a wave and an assurance that you might, *might* see me the next morning."

"I knew there was a reason why I liked you the moment I met you, trader woman." Valdan touched his forehead in a gesture of respect. "Is your uncle here?" Halani nodded. "Tell him he and all his kin are invited to sup with us tomorrow just after sunset. I have gifts to offer and an explanation to give. Look for the round black tents with flags at their peaks. That will be our encampment."

The invitation extended, he wasted no time in scooping Gilene into his arms and hugging her close before walking away from the stall. The Savatar reformed their redoubt into a pathway, each one bowing as he passed, some murmuring the words "*ataman*" and "*agacin*," while others reached out tentative hands to touch Gilene as if they were supplicants in the presence of something sacred.

Valdan halted and turned when Halani called to him. "Your name isn't Valdan, is it?"

Asil's confused "It isn't?" tail-ended her question. It had been Gilene who'd put the question in her mind. Gilene, whom Halani overheard also calling Valdan "Azarion," and she doubted the word meant "husband" in Savatar.

His answering smirk confirmed her suspicion even before he replied. "Tell Hamod he's a guest of Azarion Ataman of Clan Kestrel." He turned away with Gilene, who gave a short wave before they both disappeared ahead of the line of Savatar who fell in behind them.

Halani didn't have the luxury of watching them leave. Doing so would put her right back in the unfortunate position of fending off a new pack of cutpurses. She left the task to Asil, who stared at the retreating Savatars, a puzzled frown knitting her brow.

"So his name is Valdan Azarion or Azarion Valdan?"

Her daughter shrugged. "I don't know, Mama. It sounds like we'll know more tomorrow. Here, come help me redo the table. The gods only know how many customers we lost with all the commotion that just happened here. We'll never hear the end of it from Uncle."

The two women spent the remainder of the afternoon putting the table and stall to rights and hawking their goods. Halani patiently answered Asil's repeated questions regarding Gilene and Azarion.

Talen, another of the free trader women from Hamod's caravan, appeared at the stall just as the masses were beginning to thin and business had slowed to a trickle. Her puzzled gaze swept over the pair. "Where's Gilene?"

Halani blew a stray strand of hair out of her eyes and arched her back to relieve the ache there. "Now, that's a story to tell." She removed her apron and passed it to Talen. "Can you man the stall with Mama until the market closes? I need to find Uncle and deliver a message, and I promised to drop off a bottle of that perfume made in Askartown to a rug merchant two lanes over."

Talen tied the apron to her waist, disgust pinching her features. "They know that stuff is nothing but mule piss boiled with rose petals, right?"

"I told them. Twice. The merchant's wife doesn't care. He said she'd bathe in the stuff if she could afford enough of it."

"I swear, people will buy anything if you pour it in a fancy bottle and give it a fancy name."

"And I thank the gods for them," Halani replied. "We eat another day." She hugged Asil, who kissed her cheek in return. "Help Talen, Mama, and don't wander off. I'll see you back at camp." She tucked the bottle of rose-scented mule urine into a small velvet bag she looped onto her wrist and set out for the rug merchant's stall and then to find Hamod.

She dreaded what other mischief he'd gotten up to since she left him with the strange claw. Her worry didn't stem from a fear he'd been gulled into buying something worthless or counterfeit. That ivory was authentic, whatever it was. Possessed of a power with all the markers of earth magic, it both fascinated and troubled Halani.

Navigating the numerous lanes created by the hundreds of

stalls and tables presented less of a challenge once the crowds had thinned as the day wore down. Halani delivered the perfume to the delighted rug merchant's wife and paused at a fruit seller's stand to buy a bag of stone fruit, as richly purple as the cloth that covered the sorcerous ivory. She intended it for the caravan's cook, Marata, who would work his own magic and turn the plums into a delectable tart or pudding.

She paused at one more stall to admire a stack of leather-bound books, carefully turning the blank parchment sewn into the binding, imagining what mysterious things a scribe might write on the pristine surface. Halani set the journal down. Such goods weren't for the likes of her. She could neither read nor write. Purchasing a journal made no sense.

As the sun dipped below the horizon, merchants began closing down their stalls. Halani walked a few more of the market paths, noting which sold goods the caravan needed to resupply their stores, which goods could be resold at more distant markets for profit, and which held those small indulgences she and the other caravan women might want to purchase for themselves or their children.

Except for the stalls selling ale and spirits, most of the market had closed by the time she abandoned her browsing and headed back to Hamod's camp. A few people wished her a good evening as they passed. Others hurried by, pretending not to see her. Those wearing the official badges of Guild traders raked her with disdainful gazes. She was a free trader, not subject to Guild regulations and, thanks to the Savatar and Goban people, no longer barred from trading on the profitable Golden Serpent.

Halani returned their contempt with a sunny smile, nimbly dodging the stream of saliva one Guild trader spat at her. She expected nothing different and didn't dwell on it until a voice behind her made her freeze midstep.

"Do you wish for him to apologize for his rudeness?" She pivoted to face the speaker, discovering a man taller than average height leading a sleepy-eyed horse by its reins. He tilted his head toward the trader striding away from them. "I can make him do so."

Her defender was handsome, though not in the way some might think of male beauty, like Gilene's husband with his refined features. This man's face was sharper, harsher, with a beakish nose and a thin-lipped mouth creased on either side by unforgiving lines. His eyes reminded her of the ink Galedrin scribes made from oak and walnut galls—a brown so rich and dark, it looked black in certain lights, with streamers of sunlight swirling in its depths. His attractiveness was more memorable than traditional. His clothing and accented Common reminded her of the two mercenary-traders Hamod had dealt with earlier in the day, though he dressed far better than they.

The similarities alarmed her. Halani wasn't a believer in coincidence, and while this market had drawn people from all parts of the Empire and territories outside its reach, she hadn't seen many dressed like him or the trader pair. She had warned Hamod the engraved claw was sorcerous, and she didn't think it too far-fetched that this man's appearance in the Goban market wasn't a matter of chance.

He waited for her answer, unconcerned that the Guild trader had put a fair distance between them by now. To Halani's mind, he wasn't worth the trouble of chasing down just to extract an empty apology. Such a thing offered momentary satisfaction followed by days of petty retributions. She wanted no trouble from the Guild.

She bowed briefly. "I thank you, but no. He means nothing to me; therefore, his opinion means nothing. Besides, an apology only has value when it's sincerely given."

And she didn't want to be in a stranger's debt. He might mean well, a noble gesture toward someone he considered unjustly wronged. Or his offer might come with expectation of repayment, something Halani had no intention of giving.

"A wise way to look at it," he said and returned her bow. "Then I wish you well, madam, and bid you good evening."

He led the horse past her, and Halani stiffened, hearing in her spirit a hum of earth magic, purling like a wave toward the shoreline with a tune she'd never heard until now. As if he heard the same from her, he paused, turned, and stared at her for several moments, saying nothing.

The nearby shout of a drunkard demanding a refill from one of the pub stalls snapped Halani out of her stupor. She retreated without returning the farewell, seeking a different way to the caravan camp, hoping the stranger wouldn't follow her. He didn't, though she felt the heavy weight of his gaze on her back long after the market stalls hid her from his view.

Hamod. She had to warn Hamod, of what she couldn't say. A man with a horse and the feel of sorcery about him? Garbed like the traders who so wanted to get rid of the engraved claw? Her uncle might scoff at her suspicions, but he might not. He didn't always listen to her advice, but he trusted her instincts enough to take them into account. Halani picked up her pace until she jogged along the paths, urged to greater speed by the certainty that if Hamod had purchased the ivory, he'd brought trouble to their camp.

CHAPTER THREE

The Spider of Empire perched on her throne, swathed in gauzy silks that did more to enhance her nudity than to cover it. Most of the colorful fabric spilled in a waterfall over her right shoulder, hiding the fact that she no longer possessed her right arm.

She crossed her legs, idly tapping the air with one foot as she pinned her best henchman with a flat stare. "If I thought you might be anything other than bored with it all, I'd invite you to the entertainment I have planned for later."

As Dalvila's favorite go-to minion for everything from a pie delivery to an assassination, Gharek had learned long ago not to show emotion to his liege and give her the opportunity to use it against him. She already had him by the balls as it was. The gods only knew what that "entertainment" entailed. Sex, torture, a combination of the two. He hadn't heard any screaming when the guards escorted him into the receiving chamber to wait, but it only meant Dalvila hadn't yet left a victim on her bedroom floor, insensate, insane, or in pieces.

"How may I serve you, Your Greatness?" The right voice modulation, that sweet-spot combination of interest and willingness without overt fawning, took practice and years for him to get it just right. And it had saved his life more than once when dealing with the Spider.

She motioned to a slave kneeling on the lowest step of the dais on which her throne sat. The man knee-walked up the remaining treads, carrying a large tome in his arms, which he carefully deposited on the small table next to the empress. A brief touch of his forehead to the marble floor, and he knee-walked backward down the steps to resume his former place. Gharek was impressed with the man's dexterity in keeping his balance. Had he fallen, Dalvila likely would have punished him for the offense.

Dalvila casually flipped the book open, turning pages as if time stopped to await her pleasure. She finally closed the book and returned her attention to Gharek. "This book was taken out of Midrigar by a pair of thieves. Or one thief at least. The other didn't survive the race to the gates." Gharek quashed the urge to roll his eyes. Only the stupid and the greedy braved haunted Midrigar to steal artifacts. Even the desperate knew better. There were worse things to suffer than death, and they lurked in the ruined city, waiting for foolish prey that always, always fell into their trap. "The book must be of great value for someone to risk so much in obtaining it."

"That, or there are those who'll filch anything not nailed down."

She tapped the book with the tip of one brightly painted nail. "This is an alchemist's grimoire from the age of Emperor Vorhesian. Within it, recipes for an elixir and a salve I intend to have. The elixir grants long life and youth. The salve heals all wounds and even restores missing limbs. Both are made of gold and draga blood."

Were this anyone except the empress telling Gharek such a thing, he'd scoff at them, advise they toss such nonsense into the nearest fire and stop wasting his time. This was not just anyone, so he waited, holding his tongue.

Dalvila searched his features with a serpent's gaze, looking for any mockery there. Finding none, she relaxed in her seat and continued. "I have plenty of gold. I need a draga, and I want you to get one for me."

You must be fucking joking, he wanted to snap at her. Whatever bizarre game she'd chosen to play with him this warm summer afternoon, she was the only one to find it amusing. Gharek, on receiving her summons, had assumed she had an assignment for him. Kill and get rid of a general who dared to question her, drown a woman she perceived as a rival for the terrified affections of a lover she'd probably hang in a fortnight once she tired of him. She'd once sent Gharek on a journey halfway across the Empire to bring back a culinary delicacy whose name he still couldn't pronounce and which she declared disgusting after taking one bite. He'd dispatched her rivals, garroted her rebellious commanders, and delivered sugarcoated sweets to her without complaint and with alacrity and efficiency, earning her admiration if not her trust. Dalvila trusted no one. It was why she still held the throne in an iron grip, even after her husband, the emperor, was reduced to an ash heap in Kraelag's god-fire conflagration.

Unfortunately for Gharek, she'd just set him up to fail. The only question was how long he could stave off the foregone conclusion of his execution with false promises and lies. "My understanding is the dragas were hunted to extinction in the Empire long ago, though I know your spies to be skilled in uncovering information. Have they found one hiding in your territories?"

Her thin smile warned him he trod dangerously close to the bootlicking she found so annoying and which had gotten more than one courtier's head removed from his shoulders. "Not yet, but I expect we will soon." The sweet chime of her laughter at his raised eyebrows didn't fool Gharek. She sounded the same when she laughed at someone's disemboweling. "And you're right about my spies. I hire the best, and I send them even farther afield than

I send you on occasion." She glanced at the book, the flare of some emotion enlivening her empty blue eyes for just a moment before dying. "The Empire might not have dragas, but some of the kingdoms across the Raglun Sea do. They hide there in plain sight, disguised as humans most of the time, but dragas will be dragas, and some people have witnessed them transform and fly, raid farms to take cattle and sheep or steal treasure."

He could believe that, though he wondered just how truthful these witnesses were and how much was simply storytelling twaddle more entertaining than accurate. Surely the empress's spies didn't believe every font of nonsense that reached their ears? Surely the empress didn't believe everything her spies told her.

Something in his expression must have given away his doubt, for Dalvila's gaze once more turned serpentine. "You believe me a fool, Gharek?"

The fact that his stomach made no sound as it plummeted to the floor at her words surprised him, but not enough to make him speechless. "Not at all, Your Greatness," he replied smoothly. "If you say there are dragas in the kingdoms across the Raglun Sea, I believe you. Wholeheartedly. I need only to understand what you wish for me to do with this information."

If Dalvila told him the moon was blue and covered in fish scales, Gharek would find a way to believe that, too. His life depended on it. His daughter's life depended on it.

Satisfied with his answer, she settled back in her lofty chair once more. "Draga bones, at least fake ones, show up in the markets as regularly as lice infestations. I think even one of my handmaidens had a set of teeth made for her husband from bits of draga bone. But it's dead bone, of no real value except to a collector." Her sublime features took on a demonic avarice that almost made Gharek take a step back. "I have a spy planted in the Maesor market, one who's heard rumors that someone has arrived on our shores in possession of a mother-bond to sell. A real mother-bond with the glow mark of a living offspring still on it." The old draga tales had mostly faded over time, with the exception of the tale of the Sun Maiden, and even that one expounded more on the exploits of the hero Kansi Yuv than on the draga he fought and slew. Dalvila was right that draga bones were popular trade items, even the fake ones, but the Maesor market wasn't an average market, and nothing sold there was fake, nor was it cheap. He'd never heard of a mother-bond, but if someone believed they could sell it on the Maesor, it was both highly valuable and highly outlawed in the Empire.

Dalvila smiled her venomous smile. "I forget sometimes that you come from gutter-rat stock instead of nobility so probably never had access to the libraries." Gharek didn't flinch at her offhand insult. She spoke the truth. He'd earned his current place in Empire society; he hadn't been born to it. "Dragas," she said, "are creatures of magic. Not only were they said to have wielded sorcery; it was in their very nature. Woven into their veins, their blood, and their bones. A mother-bond was a draga offspring's birthright bequeathed to it by its dam. The dam bit off a piece of her body, bespelled it, and used it to force her hatchling into the guise of a human child to protect it from being hunted and killed while it matured. Once it reached adulthood, it used the mother-bond to reclaim its true state and all the power that belongs to a draga, including the sorcery that makes its blood so valuable."

"The long life and wound healing you mentioned," he said. Gharek dared not refer directly to Dalvila's own maiming injury or even glance at it. To do so courted death.

The empress's features froze, and his heartbeat froze with it. "Thanks to those Savatar mongrels, I don't even have Golnar's bones to display any longer. I want that mother-bond, and I want the draga it belongs to." Rage seethed in her voice, still burning as hot as the old capital where she'd lost her husband, her arm, and her dignity.

Kraelag, once the Empire's capital and crown jewel, still burned in places, months after the steppe savages laid siege to its gates and summoned their equally savage goddess to destroy it with holy fire. Even the famous bones of the draga Golnar hadn't withstood the tidal wave of flame that reduced the capital to charred rubble and scattered heaps of molten rock and metal. The emperor had died while his empress had survived, though not unscathed. A Savatar archer, under the command of a Savatar general who had once been the Empire's most famous slave gladiator, had fired an arrow from an impossible distance and struck the empress. Not a kill shot, at least not an immediate one.

Dalvila had barely survived. The wound to her shoulder had poisoned, turning putrid. Each lancing performed by the court leeches only made it worse. As the infection spread and the empress sickened, her closest advisers turned to other measures.

All within the summer palace and half of Domora, the Empire's new capital, heard Dalvila's shrieks as her surgeons sawed off the rotting limb and cauterized the mutilated flesh and exposed bone left behind. In the days that followed, court nobles who had escaped the destruction of Kraelag maneuvered for positions of power while the empress hovered at death's threshold.

To the relief of some and the disappointment of many more, Dalvila survived. Her surgeons' brutal actions had saved her, and she repaid their efforts in kind. Gharek had witnessed that repayment firsthand. Dalvila had ordered the three men brought before her, all in a show of pomp and praise. Still pale and drawn, she thanked each man with flowery plaudits uttered in the sweetest voice, before ordering them bound and forced to their knees before her.

The court held its collective breath, no one daring to come to the surgeons' defense as they questioned the reason for their punishment and begged for mercy. The empress only smiled.

Sometimes Gharek still dreamed of her reply, syrupy and completely devoid of any humanity, any compassion.

"You enjoyed the sound of my agony. Now I will enjoy the sound of yours."

The court torturers in her employ knew how to entertain the cruel and prolong the victims' suffering. They cut off the surgeons' hands first, then their forearms to the elbow, and finally the rest of their arms at the shoulder. And they didn't stop with one arm. The three men lost both arms, their screams echoing throughout the receiving chamber over and over until they could only squeak their agony.

The entire room reeked from the tide of blood mingled with vomit that spilled across the marble floor. The odor of burned flesh joined the stench as the torturers cauterized the wounds, dealing out even more torment to the poor wretches.

Once Dalvila had her fill of their suffering, she ordered the men removed from the room and released her captive courtiers to go about their business. Gharek had strode away from the shaking, gagging crowd filing out the doors, wondering what monstrous creature had birthed the empress from its grotesque womb, because it surely wasn't a human woman.

If the stories about the draga blood's benefits were true, and they actually managed to get their hands on and kill a draga, then the Empire faced a long and brutal future under Dalvila's reign. Gharek briefly pondered the logistics of taking his daughter and fleeing the Empire for a ship that sailed to those faraway kingdoms where dragas might rule the skies but this twisted creature held no sway over the land. He shoved the thought aside. Dalvila's quest for draga blood revived a dead hope inside him. If draga blood gave Dalvila her arm back, could it not also help his daughter?

"Do you know where the mother-bond is now so I can use it to lure this draga?"

She growled low in her throat. "No, unfortunately. My spies tracked two mercenaries arriving from Winosia who first boasted about what they had; then they went to ground somewhere near a market that sprang up around one of my garrisons." Her blue eyes burned with a cold fire. "It's possible they thought it too dangerous to keep and pawned it for next to nothing. That market is full of free trader bands. My spies thought it might be easy to find the mother-bond, or even the mercenaries themselves, among the free trader camps, but so far, nothing." Gharek wasn't surprised by the failure to glean information. Free traders were notoriously close-mouthed outside their own groups, an insular people who offered hospitality willingly enough but very little information. And it was a sure bet that if a free trader in possession of this mother-bond knew about the Maesor and how to get to it, he also knew not to share his real name with anyone interested in buying what he was offering to sell.

"An item like that won't sell in the regular marketplace, not even under the table and not for the price whoever has it will want for it. It's a guarantee they'll try to get into the Maesor to sell it. If they do, I can track them down, coax them to give up the mother-bond, and find a way to lure this draga to Domora," he told her. He wasn't one of her spies. Their value depended on their anonymity. Everyone knew Gharek as the empress's cat's-paw and feared him because of it.

"You won't have to lure it," Dalvila assured him. "The mother-bond is a lodestone for the offspring, one it's compelled to find if it wants to live. Find the mother-bond, and you'll have the draga in your lap soon enough."

"And once we do?" Gharek had faced and defeated numerous dangerous adversaries in his role as the empress's chief henchman. This would be a first of its kind, and an unknown that made him uneasy.

"We kill it and butcher it. I'll have the blood I need to heal and live long and a brand-new draga skeleton to replace the one I lost in Kraelag."

Either she'd purposefully misunderstood his question or assumed that such a massacre would be an easy thing to accomplish without much thought or planning. He dared not push for more information. Dalvila expected him to figure out the logistics of many of the tasks she wanted him to accomplish without much guidance from her. This was just another, albeit much more difficult, task.

He bowed. "As you wish, Your Greatness. I'll begin my search for this mother-bond immediately and report back to you as soon as I have something useful."

She shrugged a lopsided shrug. "Useful will be the mother-bond, Gharek." A darkness flitted through her eyes, spun up from the abyss where her soul should have been. Gharek stiffened. "How is your daughter? What is her name again?"

"Estred," he said, forcing the name through stiff lips.

He'd expected it, waited for it, and still her questions ripped the breath out of his chest. She twisted the knife, reminding him that for all his menace and sinister reputation, he had one vulnerability that made him as powerless and as weak as the lowliest street beggar.

"That's right," she nearly purred. "Estred. Who knew I might one day have something in common with a gutter rat's spawn?" The faint smirk hovering around her mouth disappeared, replaced by a scowl that nearly made her attending slave faint in terror. "I don't like the comparison, Gharek," she said in a voice that could have frosted the south-facing windows. "Bring me that mother-bond and the draga it belongs to. Don't fail me. If you do, it won't be just me you fail, and not only you who pays the price for it."

At her gesture of dismissal, Gharek bowed once more before strolling out of the throne room as if he didn't have a care in the world. Outside, the summer sun blazed down on his head. He felt none of it, only the cold grip of terror mixed with fury. Dalvila had given him a task and a warning. If he had to tear down all of Domora stone by stone, he'd find the free trader and the mysterious mother-bond, haul the draga by its tail back to the throne room single-handedly, and cheerfully butcher the thing himself in front of the empress. There would be no failure.

CHAPTER FOUR

The woman with the rain-cloud eyes was prettier in person than in the vision the lightning had shown to Malachus. She possessed a soft, round face framed by wisps of curly brown hair that had escaped her braid, and long dark lashes that almost hid the flash of alarm in her gaze as it swept over him.

He hadn't expected to find her this soon and certainly not by chance. Malachus had rubbed his eyes just to make sure he wasn't imagining things when he first spotted her standing in front of a fruit stall purchasing a bag of plums. He'd followed her after that, keeping enough distance away that she didn't sense his scrutiny.

There was a sense of purpose about her. The people who eddied around her meandered from one stall to another as if carried by the thinning river of humanity surrounding them. She, on the other hand, didn't waste time browsing, stopping at certain stalls only long enough to ask the vendors a question, inspect an item, then moving on without lingering. He might not have caught up with her had she not stopped long enough to buy the fruit.

She'd nimbly avoided the stream of spittle a man dressed in rich robes spat at her as he passed, neither pausing to confront him nor speeding up to avoid another possible spraying. And while she exhibited no anger at the act, Malachus's own temper flared at the unprovoked harassment.

He approached her as she stepped away from one of the market's higher-end stalls, one that sold blank journals bound in embossed leather and filled with lower-quality parchment instead of vellum. Her slender hand had stroked the book she held under the merchant's hawkish gaze before she put it down as if it were made of finely spun glass.

In his earlier musings, Malachus had assigned her a particular voice, one almost throaty and deep. When she replied to his inquiry, it was neither. Only a perfectly ordinary female voice lacking any raspy quality, and with overtones of mild surprise and a growing wariness the longer she spoke with him. Malachus wondered what about him beyond the fact that he was a stranger had spooked her. He had his answer as soon as he bid her good evening and led Batraza past her.

Sorcery, a familiar kind forged of earth and its eternal hymn, whispered across his skin. More than a hushed note, it had reached out to touch him, as if in recognition of a like entity. He paused, as did the woman, her eyes widening for a moment before she spun on her heel and strode away, lengthening her stride until she was nearly running back the way she'd come. Malachus watched the path she took until she turned a corner onto a smaller alleyway that led south from the market's center.

He had walked a little more than half the Goban market today, scouting its lanes and stalls in a north-to-south direction, moving in a zigzag from east to west and back again. To the casual observer, he was simply a visitor browsing the goods he could buy with the coin he possessed. So far the lodestone power of his mother-bond had stayed true and stationary. Either the thieves he tracked remained unaware he was hunting them, or they'd pawned the bone off to another unwary buyer in the market.

Images from the lightning had hinted that maybe the gray-eyed woman was one of those buyers, but if so, she didn't carry the mother-bond on her person. Malachus would have sensed it instantly.

Lightning was a gift from both air and earth, its ceraunomancy sharp in its imagery but not always accurate. When the bolt that shot through Malachus had shown him the woman, he'd assumed it had done so in relation to the mother-bond. Now he questioned his assumption. Whether she knew it or not, she was a servant of earth, just as he was. Judging by the brief glimpse he got of her wide eyes and alarmed expression, she knew and treated it as a secret too dangerous not to keep. Maybe the lightning had shown him her face simply because of a bond of common magic. If so, then searching out her camp in the market would be a waste of time. Still, he couldn't risk not following a path that might lead him to the mother-bond.

He turned Batraza around to follow her, senses open to the wispy threads of earth song trailing behind her. He lost her track not far into his search, the notes fading to silence. Malachus didn't fret. He'd find her again when he reconnoitered this part of the market tomorrow. Until then he'd use the time to take supper with a loquacious vendor hoping to sell him a costly bit of jewelry in exchange for information on a pair of traders who'd stopped at his stall to inspect his wares.

His luck so far favored him. If events continued in the same fortuitous vein, he'd have his mother-bond in hand in a matter of days and be on a ship returning home by the following week.

If only fate didn't have a twisted sense of humor.

Gedamon the jeweler had served a fine meal to his guests—if one disregarded the faintest whiff of a sleep nostrom in both the wine and the stew. Curious as to what the man hoped to achieve by drugging his supper companion senseless, Malachus pretended to drink the wine and blunted the drug's potency in the stew by using bread as a sop. His lips and tongue tingled from the effects, but he staved off the somnolence, adopting the behavior of a man teetering on the edge of unconsciousness. His host's eyes gleamed in the lamp's ambient light, and he subtly gestured to his wife while pouring a steady stream of distracting chatter into Malachus's ear.

Malachus watched with a slitted gaze as she crept toward the satchel he'd brought with him, her movements stealthy even as she pretended to clear away dishes and pick up items from the floor. She nudged the bag away from his side with her foot, moving by small measures so he wouldn't notice. The jeweler's voice rose in volume to cover the sound of her furtive movements. When she bent, ostensibly to move a tray of cups from one spot to another with one hand, the other reached for the satchel's flap.

Malachus set his goblet down with a *thunk*, uncaring that half of the drugged contents sloshed over the rim. "Madam," he said in a flat voice. "If you put your hand in there, I will break your husband's hands as punishment for putting you up to such mischief."

They froze at his words, and Gedamon's wife blanched, still bent with her hand on the flap. She darted a terrified gaze to her equally pale husband. He did a better job of mastering his shock and fear than she did, blustering his way through the tense moment by adopting indignation.

"Here now, get away from there, you foolish *atwiten*. What do you think you're doing?" She leapt away from the satchel as if it had tried to bite her and scurried behind Gedamon, hiding her face behind her shirt's draping sleeve. The jeweler turned an innocent look to Malachus and raised his hands as if shocked by her actions. "Forgive me, *serdah*. I don't know what to do with her sometimes."

Tamping down the urge to sling the dregs of contaminated wine in the man's lying face, Malachus pushed the goblet and the mostly uneaten food away from him. "Save your breath for an honest explanation," he said. "You're a rich man without the need to pilfer off someone else. There's nothing about my appearance to indicate great wealth, and you went through a lot of trouble here in the hope of searching my belongings and picking me over once you thought I was too stupefied to notice. You did all this for more than a chance at robbing me of a few *belshas*. Tell me why, and I'll be a lot more forgiving regarding your trickery."

He suspected he knew the man's answer before he gave it. Gedamon, goaded by his wife's elbow in his back and her furious whispering in his ear, proved him right.

"I swear, *serdah*, it was a chance thing. I'd seen you earlier in the day walking the market, dressed like the folk of the northern Winosia prefectures." He offered a strained smile. "I've visited there. Beautiful country." As if that somehow made him and Malachus compatriots of sorts. "Not long after, two men of similar dress stopped by my shop. I mentioned that if they were looking for their friend, I'd just seen you no more than an hour earlier."

Malachus groaned inwardly. There went any element of surprise. The jeweler had verified he was alive and well and not at the bottom of the sea. "What did they say? And did they buy anything from you?" Gedamon dealt in real gold, silver, and gems—not the cheap bits of tin and copper worn by most people. Malachus's blood sang with the feel of precious metals and jewels nearby, a tiny hoard that his hidden heritage recognized and yearned for. The smallest bauble came with a high price. If the thieves had bought something, it meant they'd sold the mother-bond, and he'd have to look for a new quarry. A vision of the gray-eyed woman flitted across his mind's eye.

Gedamon shook his head. "No," he said, adamant in his denial. "They didn't buy a thing, though they asked what you looked like and offered a . . . generous deposit on a ring if I'd invite you here and learn more about you."

"And you felt the need to drug me to do so?"

The merchant went even paler. "They said you were no friend of theirs, though they knew you. A wealthy nobleman's son in possession of an artifact prized by collectors of the rare, the magical, and the outlawed."

Malachus snorted. He truly wished his mother had thought to lay some sort of revulsion spell on the mother-bond she'd left with him. Maybe then fewer people would be so motivated to try to steal it.

If Gedamon only knew how he'd been tricked. Malachus was tempted to tell him except that the real joke was on Malachus. His mother-bond, so close now, yet still maddeningly elusive.

"What are you going to do now that you know?" The merchant's pupils were fully dilated with fright, his wife's gaze just as black as she peered over his shoulder at Malachus.

He rose and retrieved his satchel, opening it for good measure so the two could get a good look at the contents inside—clothing, a leftover bit of pastry wrapped in a handkerchief for later. He might have laughed at their disappointed faces were he not so annoyed. "I'm not going to do anything. For now." Let them sweat from their own fevered thoughts of what vengeance he might extract in the coming days. Their imaginings would most likely be far worse than anything he could think of even were he bothered to put in the effort.

With as much snaffling and pilfering as he'd witnessed and dealt with in the short day and a half he'd been at the Goban market, he was vaguely surprised to find Batraza still waiting for him outside the shop. He'd half expected to find her gone or at least her saddle disappeared. She whuffled a greeting to him, and he patted her neck. "Let's go, Bat. I've had enough of humanity for today. By the time this is over, I'll be desperate not to see another human being for a very long time."

Except for the woman in his vision. He'd like to see her again and intended to, even if only at a distance. The mother-bond remained somewhere in this market, likely still with the thieves who'd paid the unwitting Gedamon to delay and distract him from his hunt and buy them time to pawn the artifact and escape the market. There was no way they'd keep it now that the jeweler had confirmed Malachus was not only alive, but here.

Sleep was a luxury he couldn't afford tonight, and he sought out one of the makeshift stables hurriedly built to house horses for those riders who'd arrived without the benefit of clan or tribe corrals to shelter their mounts. Malachus paid the extra coin for a roofed stall away from the other horses and an extra bucket of feed before leaving Batraza in the stable master's care and returning to the market's dark, empty byways. He had a night in which to scout the area, working from the center out in a widening circle, guided by his senses, which he focused on finding the mother-bond.

He gave up at dawn, having worked his way out to the market's perimeter on its eastern flank. His coin had paid one night's boarding for Batraza. If he wanted more, he'd have to return and pay again before they led her out of the stall and put her and his tack up for auction to cover unpaid time. If there was a generosity of spirit in the Goban marketplace, it didn't exist at the stable yard.

The new stable master was happy to take another day's boarding fee from Malachus and even more pleased at receiving an extra tip to exercise the mare away from the other horses. Malachus wasted no time returning to the market, this time tracking from the western perimeter to the center, starting with the cluster of round black tents newly erected by the celebrated Savatar nomads.

Searching their encampment proved impossible. This was a military force more than a trader group, their presence here by invitation, according to the gossip running through the marketplace. They'd likely confine any buying and selling to the stalls in the market itself and treat any visits to their camp as not only suspicious but also unwelcome. He didn't linger. The Winosia thieves, if they had any sense, wouldn't approach this group.

Once more he tightened his search pattern, circling back toward the heart of the market. A familiar silhouette caught his eye, and he spotted the spare, haughty trader who'd spat at the gray-eyed woman the previous afternoon. The man wore different robes, displaying a wealth that should have had every vendor on this alleyway clamoring for his attention and business. Instead, they either stared at him with baleful gazes or turned their backs, pretending not to see him. Even the merchant manning the pastry shop at which he stopped to browse simply watched him with a deadpan gaze.

The same merchant turned a much friendlier face toward a petite older woman with gray hair, a lined face, and a young expression. She returned his smile with a grin before her eyes lit on the pastries showcased on the table, and her mouth formed a delighted O.

Malachus's stomach grumbled. He hadn't eaten since last night, and then only very little thanks to his host's predilection for drugging the food and wine he served. His belly clamored for sustenance, and the scents wafting from the pastry stall lured him with a magic as strong as the mother-bond's.

He also wanted a closer look at the haughty customer, who now stared down his nose at the woman as if she crawled with fleas.

Blithely unaware of the man's obvious contempt, she asked the vendor a few questions about his pies and cakes in a childish voice Malachus found both strange and charming.

"Hali liked the cake with the rose cream I brought her yesterday but not the spicy one. Do you have something else like the rose one?"

The vendor slid a decorated confection toward her. Covered in flowers shaped of sugarcoated dough dyed in pastel shades, the palm-size cake resembled a spring bouquet. "Take this to her. If she liked the rose flavor, she'll like this one." He pushed a second cake toward her. "And this is for you, Asil. No charge."

He chuckled at her soft squeal of delight. She picked up the first cake as if it were a sacred relic instead of a sweet.

Arrested by the sight, Malachus checked his more negative assumptions regarding people in general. He'd just witnessed a generous gesture with no expectation of reciprocal charity, reminding him that not all of humanity suffered from petty cruelty and miserly spirits. Then again . . .

Beside the woman called Asil, the richly dressed trader scowled. "I was here before this flea-bitten cuntmonger," he protested in waspish tones. As he said the words, he shoved Asil aside. Caught unaware, she staggered sideways, grasping for the table's edge with her free hand in an attempt to keep her balance. The table tilted with her, sending pastries sliding toward her and the ground.

Frantic to save his goods, the vendor scrambled to catch them before they tumbled off the table, leaving smears of icing, honey, and crushed fruit across the surface. Malachus leapt forward, caught Asil, and righted the table. The smirking trader gave a nasty laugh and turned to leave.

His pained yelp cut through the morning air, the sound abruptly choked to silence when Malachus snagged him, practically garroting him with the collar of his own robe.

"Not so fast, *serdah*." Malachus spun the trader around, hands still gripping the robes tight. The trader's expression had gone from sneer to fright, and he gaped at his captor, who offered a smirk of his own.

"You're an unpleasant piece of work, aren't you?" Malachus said in casual tones, as if he strangled everyone he met during conversation. "Spitting on women as they pass you in the street, shoving them about as they buy a cake for a friend, destroying a man's goods and labor because he didn't kiss your arse hard enough for a sale." He tightened his hold on the cloth so the man clawed at the suffocating collar. Malachus glanced at the woman, who gaped at him. "Are you well, madam?"

She nodded, her features creasing again with one of her open smiles. She raised the cake she still held, its decorations mostly undamaged except for one crushed flower. "I still have Hali's cake." Her grin gave way to a scowl, and she stuck her tongue out at the trader. "And I don't have fleas, you shit-eating Guild worm."

Malachus laughed, as did the pastry vendor and several onlookers. The trader reddened, either from embarrassment or from having his windpipe slowly compressed. He continued clawing at the constricting collar to no avail.

"How much for the damaged pastries as well as the two you gave Madam Asil?" Malachus asked the vendor. When the man quoted an amount, Malachus used his free hand to pat down the trader, finding his bulging purse of coins tucked tight into the belt that cinched his inner robes to his middle. He jerked the purse free and tossed it to the vendor. The trader squirmed even harder in his grip. "Count out the amount you're owed in restitution," he instructed the vendor. "I'm sure the *serdah* here can afford it and have plenty left over to continue his shopping."

A wheeze of protest escaped the trader's lips, and his eyes

bulged from their sockets at the sight of the vendor extracting a handful of coins from the purse.

"Are you going to strangle him?"

Malachus returned his attention to Asil, who split her scrutiny between him and the struggling trader. "I don't know yet," he replied. "Do you want me to strangle him?"

There was indeed something very childlike about this woman, in contrast to her aged appearance. A troubled look entered her gaze. "No. Hali would be cross with me if you did. She says the Guild is a boil on our arses as it is without borrowing trouble."

"She has the right of it there," the pastry vendor interjected behind her as he continued counting coins.

"Then we won't make your Hali cross," Malachus assured her. He gave the trader a hard shove, letting go of his robes at the same time so the man practically flew backward to land on his backside in the muddied pathway. Malachus caught the purse the vendor tossed him and flung it at the trader, who scrambled after it before one of the fleet cutpurses grabbed it. Humiliated, the trader glared at the trio with eyes brimming with a red-hot hatred. "You'll regret this," he snarled. "I'm a Guild factor, and the masters will hear what you've done to me."

As Malachus knew nothing of this Guild and couldn't care less, the threat bounced off him. Even the pastry vendor seemed unconcerned. "This is Goban territory now," the vendor said. "Not Empire. The Guild holds no sway here. Tell whoever you want whatever you want. No one cares." The Guild factor marched away then, shouting a string of blistering epithets at anyone in his path.

Judging by the look on Asil's face, someone did care. She still held on to her precious cake, her lower lip's telltale quiver betraying her worry. "I know Hali will still be cross," she said, her tone mournful.

Malachus opened his mouth to assure the distressed woman he'd be happy to accompany her back to her family, explain the circumstances, and shoulder the blame for inciting the Guild's wrath. He didn't get the chance.

A voice to his left spoke first, one he recognized from the day before, and his heart beat a little harder under his breastbone. "I'm not cross, Mama. I saw what happened. Nothing here was your fault."

He turned to see the woman the factor spat at approach them, her expression a mix of sorrow, fury, and gratitude. So this was Hali, whom Asil so obviously loved and held in esteem.

Asil offered the cake she held. "I wanted to get you something nice, but I smashed one of the flowers when I almost fell." Her eyes welled with disappointed tears.

Hali took the cake before gently enfolding Asil in a close embrace. "I'm a fortunate daughter to have you," she said softly. The taller of the two, she straightened and rested her chin on Asil's head before mouthing a "thank you" to both Malachus and the vendor. She leaned back to meet Asil's eyes. "I don't care if all the flowers got ruined, Mama. It will still taste wonderful, and you can share with me."

Fascinated by the interplay between this particular parent and adult child, with their uniquely reversed roles, Malachus motioned to the vendor. "Pack all those the factor ruined and paid for and give them to these two," he whispered. "If they have more family, they can share with them."

The other man nodded and set about wrapping up a dozen small cakes and hand pies in towels to send off with Asil and her daughter.

Once more Malachus found it difficult not to stare too long at the woman called Hali, seeing again her image as the lightning had shown it. The sense of his mother-bond hadn't changed with her proximity, though he again heard the notes of her magic sing to his spirit.

She must have sensed or heard hints of his power as well, for the grateful spark in her eyes took on the glitter of the same wariness he'd seen there yesterday. "My name is Halani, *serdah*, and I appreciate what you and Telkak here did for my mother," she said.

Halani, then. The longer formal version of Asil's more affectionate diminutive. Malachus liked it. A gracious name, it suited her.

Asil, no longer teary-eyed, planted her hands on her hips and gave Malachus an arch look. "And that arsewipe was a liar. I'm not a cuntmonger."

Halani gasped, her outrage ignited by Asil's revelation. "He called you that?" She hid her hands in the folds of her skirt, but not before Malachus saw them curl into fists. Her gray eyes no longer possessed that somber softness he found so beguiling, turning instead as hard and flat as unpolished steel.

Malachus offered Asil a short bow. "I believe you, madam. And for what it's worth, even if that were your profession, I suspect you'd have better taste than to choose his ilk as your customers."

Halani gave a delicate snort, and the vendor she referred to as Telkak guffawed. Asil offered him a sweet grin.

At first refusing the cloth-wrapped packages Telkak held out to her, Halani readily accepted them when he told her, "Take them. They're paid for with the factor's coin. That'll make them taste even better."

"Thank you, friend," she replied. "They will indeed." She met Malachus's eyes. "Twice you've offered and given us aid, and still I don't know your name so I may properly thank you, *serdah*."

"I'm Malachus, and no thanks necessary, madam. Some people are in desperate need of a comeuppance. I'm happy to oblige." He wasn't a hero by any stretch. Force-feeding the Guild factor a helping of his own contempt had been a pleasure.

"I like your name," Asil declared.

He grinned. "I'm glad you approve, Madam Asil. I like yours, too."

"Come, Mama." Halani nudged her away from Telkak's table and toward the street. "Uncle sent me to find you." She handed her gift of the flower cake back to Asil. "Hold on to this until we reach camp. It will be just for you and me. Marata can make tea, and we'll share the rest of the bounty with everyone." She thanked both men a third time, reminding Asil to do the same.

Malachus bowed in acknowledgment, watching the two women walk away until the growing crowd blocked them from view.

"That was a decent thing you did, *serdah*," Telkak said.

Malachus stepped to the side so that other customers could approach the table and place their orders. One of Telkak's assistants took over, leaving Telkak with a few free moments to chat. He joined Malachus. "A lot of folks will try and take advantage of Asil and those like her. I'm sure you figured out why quick enough. Her kin do a good job of protecting her, especially her daughter, but sometimes the most loving family can't shield them from arsewipes like that Guild factor."

Malachus frowned. "I saw him yesterday in the market. He spat at Halani when she passed him on the street. It was unprovoked. Do you know why he'd do it?"

Telkak eyed him curiously. "You're definitely an outlander if you need to ask such a question. Halani and Asil are part of a free trader band, merchants who refuse to join and abide by the rules of the Empire's Trade Guild. Until recently, the Guild controlled all trade on the Golden Serpent, the road cutting through all the territories under Kraelian rule, and they used the Kraelian army as their sword to strengthen their grip. It barred all free traders from working the Serpent. It's lucrative business. Keeping the free traders restricted to the drover paths and less traveled roads to do their trading stops them from rising in wealth and power."

"And stifles competition for the Guild."

"Just so." Telkak thrust his chin in the direction Halani and Asil went. "There's no love lost between the Guild and the free traders. The factor and the nest of wasps he reports to are probably spinning on their thumbs at no longer having the Serpent under their watch in these parts now that the Goban and Savatar destroyed this garrison and the other three that once held this territory for the Empire."

Telkak's explanation solved the mystery of the Guild factor's reaction to the women and shed light on some of everyday life in these unfamiliar lands. Malachus didn't ask about Asil's behavior. Anything from a head injury to emotional trauma to a mishap during her mother's labor might explain why Asil had the face and body of a woman old enough to bounce grandchildren on her knees but not the maturity of a grandmother. It was none of his business, though he was tempted to ask more about Halani.

Unless it led him to the mother-bond, such curiosity served no purpose. While he didn't regret coming to Asil's defense, it had taken away valuable time from his search. He eyed the table with its newest offerings of sweets. His stomach rumbled even louder in anticipation as he reached into his own coin bag for a *belsha* to purchase a pie.

Telkak stopped him with a shake of his head, chose two pies, and wrapped them himself before presenting them with a flourish. "Already paid for by His Royal Shithead himself," he said with a grin. "I heard your belly chatting you up while you were choking the life out of him and counted out an extra *belsha* or two to pay for your breakfast as well. Enjoy."

Malachus returned the grin, thanked Telkak for the food, and saluted him before leaving the stall.

He ate as he continued scouting the market, using the cloth Telkak had wrapped around the pies to clean his hands and later dunk into a barrel of rainwater. He wiped his face as the sun beat down on him and the crowd filling the market's streets.

The more sparsely populated outskirts offered a welcome respite from the heat and smells of sweating bodies packed too closely together. Here, on the southern side of the market, the ground didn't drain as well, and while the breeze cooled the air, it carried with it swarms of biting insects that bred by the millions in standing pools of water. Malachus adopted the same mode of dress as other travelers he'd seen in a bid to reduce the number of bites to his face, turning his kerchief into a face shield.

If the men he hunted wore the same, his task of finding them had just gotten a lot harder. By the same token, they'd have a harder time spotting him.

His search took him close to an encampment defined by numerous wagons parked nose to tail in a large ring. The wagons perched on large axles that raised the structures high enough off the ground that they required steps to reach their interiors. They were small homes on large wheels, complete with arched roofs, windows dressed in flower boxes, and ornately decorated doors. Some had the required steps folded down from the thresholds, while others lacked an entry without taking a running leap that guaranteed a painful face-plant if the door was closed. Temporary livestock pens occupied the protected space within the ring, with corrals for the bigger animals, such as the horses and oxen, hugging the outer perimeter.

A half dozen people moved about the camp, occupied with various tasks. The camp's size suggested that a greater population of people occupied the spot. He guessed the majority worked the market at whatever tables and booths they'd set up. Malachus retraced his steps, picking a path to the camp that was shielded from watchful eyes by the thick barricades of wild rye with its slender stalks and bristled flower heads, which grew taller than a man and hid one with ease.

The draga within him suddenly convulsed, and Malachus's breath crashed in his lungs as the beacon of his mother-bond went from a steady siren's song with only a general sense of place to a javelin of shrieking command, and it came directly from this camp. Overwhelmed by its forceful pull, he didn't hear or sense the danger behind him until too late.

Three rapid-fire *thwangs* teased his ear for a split second before powerful blows slammed into his body, striking his side, his hip, and just below his collarbone. The impacts hammered a shock wave of agony through him, leaving him with only the ability to gasp. He crashed to his side and rolled. A stuttered moan spilled past his lips, and his hands automatically reached for the arrow shaft sticking out from just below his collarbone, its fletching still shivering from the force of its penetration through skin and muscle.

He wrapped a hand around its length and tugged, nearly blacking out with the effort. Broadhead or bodkin tip, the arrowhead was buried deep. If he yanked it out, he'd likely bleed to death before the power of his magic could heal him. The frailty of his human body was as troublesome as the imprisoned strength of his draga one. Worse, a suspicious tingling spread from the injury points, oozing into his bones, turning them into water. Poisoned. His thoughts dragged as if caught in a river current. Whoever shot him had poisoned the arrowheads.

He concentrated on breathing slowly, hand moving to the arrow shaft extending from his side. Too low to puncture a lung but deep enough to penetrate other vital organs. It proved the most painful, trapping him on his opposite side and positioned in such a way that every twitch made the arrowhead bite even deeper into him.

The archer who shot him knew where to aim and where to hit, their accuracy admirable. The arrow shafts, crafted of animal bone, were far too strong for a man to break with his bare hands. But Malachus wasn't an ordinary man. He gripped the base of the arrow shaft where it sank into his chest and used his other hand to bend its length. His hands were numb, fingers struggling to obey his mind's command to curl around the shaft and grip. A low groan escaped his clenched teeth despite his best efforts to hold it in.

Voices, speaking in furtive whispers, drew closer. Malachus let his arms fall, closed his eyes, and relaxed his jaw so that his mouth fell partially open. He slowed his breathing, hoping his clothing and position made it difficult to discern the minute rise and fall of his chest. Part of him prayed whoever approached got close enough for him to take his vengeance, though he wondered if he could even lift his head now. Pain and nausea made it hard for him to stay silent, stay still.

"Is he dead?"

"Looks like it to me."

Malachus didn't recognize the voices, but the language he knew. These men were Winosian, like him. He'd tracked them across kingdoms and a sea, the latest "owners" of his mother-bond, who'd either bought or stolen it from the previous thief who'd absconded with it.

"I told you we shoulda never taken the bone from that old seer. And that ball sack Gedamon lied through his teeth. He was supposed to poison this fucker for us. At least enough to slow him down and give us a chance to get out of here."

"Shut it, Plunk," the other voice replied. "It don't matter now. He looks like crow bait to me."

"Maybe we should check him to make sure."

Yes, Malachus thought, staring through slitted eyes at the blurry outlines of the two men standing nearby. *Come a little closer.*

A gravid pause followed Plunk's suggestion before his companion replied in withering tones. "Feel free to walk over there, shithead, and check him yourself. I'll stay here and keep an eye out."

Plunk, obviously the less intelligent of the two, huffed. "Fine, I will, and if I come across his coin stash, the money is mine."

Malachus adopted a limp facade, becoming deadweight that Plunk shoved around, which forced Malachus to bite his cheek to suppress his shrieks until blood filled his mouth and trickled from one corner. The effect had an unforeseen and fortunate result. It, more than Malachus's limp body, convinced not only Plunk he was dead, but his companion as well, who now crouched beside him to scavenge his corpse.

It was then that Malachus struck.

The poison had seized his muscles, slowing him down so that every movement felt like swimming through mud, but he was fast enough to take the two men by surprise. He first attacked the one crouched closest to his head and with a bow slung across his back. Malachus jerked the knife the man held out of his hand, turned the blade, and rammed it through the archer's throat. He'd barely tumbled away with a soft gurgle before Malachus twisted, adrenaline and draga rage pumping through his veins along with the poison, so that for a moment he didn't feel the pain of the arrow wounds or the poison's effects. He scissored his legs over Plunk's shoulders to clamp his neck between his knees and twisted again. A dull snap sounded, and Plunk's full weight fell on Malachus, narrowly missing crushing the arrow embedded in his side and pinning him to the ground from the waist down.

Contorted in a way that threatened to crack his spine in six places and losing the range of his vision to a fuzzy darkness, Malachus shut his eyes against the battering of sunlight on his lids. The incapacitating numbness had spread so that he no longer felt the pressure of Plunk's dead body draped across him. Something scuttled across his cheek and over his brow, a spider maybe, or a water beetle deciding whether or not he was dead enough yet to feast on.

A thought drifted through his mind. The mother-bond's beckoning had come from the camp in front of him, not from his attackers, who'd sneaked up on him. They didn't have the mother-bond when they shot him. Someone else did. He spat out the blood in his mouth, a sluggish effort that managed to spill most of it down his chin.

Darkness swamped his senses, blotting out the last glows of sunlight filtering past his closed lids, drowning his vaporous musings of gray eyes and lightning, even smothering the mother-bond's infinite call to him. He was dying, and not in the way he'd feared—immolated or torn asunder by his heritage. Instead, he lay sprawled on wet ground, kept company in death by the murderous, the larcenous, and the treacherous. Had the poison not robbed him of the ability, Malachus would have laughed.

CHAPTER FIVE

The gods were kind to put Azarion and Gilene in our path those months ago." Hamod raised his cup of mare's milk in a toast to the pair where they sat together in spots reserved for the *ataman* and his favored guests. The tent, or *qara* as the Savatar called it, was crowded with clansmen and free traders. All raised their cups in response to the toast and cheered their chieftain and his consort in loud voices.

Halani hid her wry smile behind her cup. The previous evening Hamod had sung an altogether different tune when she'd delivered Azarion's message to him. Her uncle's features had darkened with a thundercloud of temper.

"That lying whoreson." He practically snarled the words. "I knew I recognized him. That fool's story of being the son of an Empire woman and Nunari soldier always made me wonder. He was the Gladius Prime!"

Halani had blinked at him, confused. Everyone in the Empire had heard of the Gladius Prime, though most had never seen him up close.

She finally interrupted his hour-long tirade. "Uncle, he was a valuable slave who'd escaped his masters. Once they realized he was gone, they'd have likely set soldiers, bounty hunters, and dogs on his scent to recapture him. Can you blame Azarion for lying to us about who he was? For the bounty he'd fetch, his own mother would've turned him over to his pursuers." She had no doubt Hamod wouldn't have thought twice about doing the same.

Hamod's scowl hadn't lessened. "It doesn't matter. When he lied to us and took advantage of our charity, he put all of us—you, Asil, everyone in this caravan—in jeopardy. Can you imagine what his masters might have done to us had they discovered we sheltered their most valuable property?"

He had a point. She knew very little of Azarion's past. A slave fighter who faced the bloodbath of Kraelag's infamous Pit—not once but many times—he'd found a way to break his shackles and flee. Halani applauded him for it and still didn't regret helping him and Gilene. Sometimes one took a stand for mercy, even when it involved risk to oneself. In this, she and her uncle differed vastly in their philosophies.

His resentment over Azarion's deception blunted a little after they'd arrived in the Savatar encampment, where Azarion, Gilene, and Azarion's clansmen hailed the free traders as heroes. Hamod had even cracked a pleased smile when Azarion showered their group with a mountain of gifts as thanks for bringing Gilene safely back to him, even if her return had merely been part of a fortuitous decision on Hamod's part to attend the Goban market and take advantage of the fact that the Golden Serpent was no longer restricted only to the Guild traders.

Reclined against a soft pillow placed on the *qara*'s carpeted floor, with her drink in hand and the remains of a sumptuous supper in front of her, Halani watched the Savatar repeatedly approach Gilene with small offerings and tokens to be blessed, their bows deep, their faces almost glowing with a reverence reserved for a devotee's worship. Gilene wore the look of the desperate: part cringe, part uneasy smile, as she graciously offered a few words to each person while gripping Azarion's knee with a white-knuckled hand.

A Savatar clansman sent to fetch Gilene's belongings had enlightened Halani regarding her friend's abilities. Hamod had nearly foamed at the mouth with the newest revelations. "An escaped gladiator slave *and* a fire witch among us?" He'd thrown aside the tack he'd been repairing and stomped to the new cask of ale they'd just purchased and had delivered to the camp. He downed two goblets full before speaking again, cheeks flushed with drink and fury. "I don't care if it's a gaggle of one-legged orphans begging us for a ride to the next town, that's the last time we offer succor to any more road travelers."

Halani wondered if he still felt the same after the generous munificence Azarion and his clan had just bestowed on them. They'd have to purchase another three provender wagons just to transport all the wealth bestowed by the clan chief.

Beside Halani, Asil popped a candied nut into her mouth and rolled her eyes in ecstasy. "I could eat an entire barrel of these, Hali. They're so good."

Halani slid the tray of sweets out of her mother's reach. "That's what I'm afraid of. You already ate plenty of the cakes Telkak gave us this morning. You're going to make yourself sick."

Asil stuck her lip out and huffed. "I bet Malachus would let me have another cake," she whined.

"Considering he wouldn't be the one to help clean you after you got sick, I'm sure he'd be most generous." Halani passed Asil a platter of bread to dunk in her refilled cup of salty milk tea. "Eat this. It's good."

Asil groused under her breath but accepted the food and was soon back to her jovial self, regaling Halani with everything she noted in the expansive *qara*, from the garb the Savatar wore and the way they dressed their hair to the interesting carvings etched into the birch poles that made up the tent's rigid framework.

Halani listened with half an ear, her attention split between watching Gilene and recalling the man who'd introduced himself as Malachus.

As often happened when the caravan stopped to trade in a town's market, Halani went searching for Asil at one of the stalls. Halani rarely admonished her mother for her waywardness. It didn't stop the behavior, and such distractions sprang from Asil's desire to please those she loved, especially Halani. This time it was to buy her daughter a tasty confection.

Telkak's display table of cakes was an irresistible draw to passersby.

Halani spotted Asil there. Her heart dropped into her stomach when she recognized the customer next to her mother—the nasty Guild trader who'd spat at Halani the day before and looked as if he was tempted to do the same to Asil.

Hackles raised, Halani marched toward the table, ready to do battle with those who would treat her mother badly. She didn't see Malachus until he suddenly appeared next to the Guild trader and almost strangled the man with his own robes.

Malachus didn't ask Asil if she wanted him to play defender, and by the time the confrontation was over and the Guild trader had stormed off with promises of retribution, Asil had stars in her eyes and extra pastries in her arms, courtesy of Telkak.

Even Halani, far more guarded than her overly trusting mother, offered a smile to this outlander who'd come to Asil's defense. This time she didn't speed off with Asil in tow, staying instead to thank him for his gallantry.

She liked his smile, an expression more open than his dark, enigmatic gaze. His Common was fluent but accented, much like that of the mercenary-traders but lacking a drawl theirs possessed.

He'd stayed in her thoughts the entire day, even while she and the other free trader folk enjoyed Savatar hospitality in Azarion's camp. Halani idly wondered if she'd see him again before they departed the Goban market to return to Empire territories.

The celebration in honor of Gilene's return lasted far into the night, until Asil had fallen asleep against a pile of furs and Halani feared she'd have to prop her own eyelids up with sticks to stay awake. Hamod and several of the free trader men matched their Savatar counterparts in numerous drinking challenges. No doubt several of their number would stay the night in the encampment, too inebriated to walk back to their wagons.

Sleepy and overheated, Halani escaped the *qara* for the cooler temperatures outside. It meant facing a barrage of bloodsucking midges, but she craved a respite from the celebrations, the noise, and the heat. Outside, a welcome breeze evaporated the perspiration gathered on her brow. The moon had sunk lower though the stars remained bright. She'd have to beg a couple of torches from the Savatar for the trek back to the caravan.

"Halani."

She turned to find Gilene headed toward her. Garbed in Savatar finery, she was a majestic sight, wearing her natural gravitas like a mantle.

Halani bowed. "*Agacin.*" She still found it hard to reconcile the reality of Gilene's sorcery. Fire, the greatest of all the elemental magics, flowed through this woman's hands.

Gilene paused midstep and her half smile faltered. "Don't," she said. "I've been called *agacin* so many times the past two days, I've almost forgotten the sound of my own name." She reached Halani, the light from nearby torches casting her slender shadow in sharp relief. "Why did you come outside?"

"To cool off and enjoy the quiet." Halani peered into the darkness with a frown. "Also to figure out how I'm going to get several drunk people back to our camp without someone breaking their neck in the fields."

Gilene chuckled. "You're all welcome to stay as long as you wish."

Halani appreciated the offer. She liked the Savatar, finding them fierce and boisterous, hospitable and generous. And she loved seeing Gilene with Azarion, the way he looked at her and she at him, as if they only existed for each other. But she missed the wagon she shared with Asil and her own narrow bed.

"Consider your offer accepted," she said. "You've saved me from a long, torturous lurch back to the camp with several stops in between so someone can fetch up their stomach."

This time Gilene flinched. "This will be a place of misery and despair by noon with all the moaning and groaning. I wouldn't blame you if you chose not to stay yourself."

The two women exchanged grins before Gilene turned serious once more. "May I ask you a question?" At Halani's nod, she gave a deep sigh and said, "Will you forgive me for lying to you and the others about Azarion? I know Hamod feels used and made a fool of, though such was never our intent. I fear you feel the same way."

Halani recalled Hamod's defense of his anger. She understood both sides. Life and circumstances often called for questionable choices. Desperation made people hard, willing to risk themselves and others to escape a terrible fate. While she wished Gilene and Azarion had been truthful, she didn't resent them for their deception. She would have done the same. The *ataman* and his fire witch were good people trying to make amends and show their gratitude.

She reached for Gilene's hand, twining their fingers together. "I'm not my uncle. There's nothing to forgive. I don't regret helping you two. Nothing bad came of it, and I made a friend."

Gilene visibly wilted before pulling Halani into her arms. The two women hugged. When they separated, tears glazed Gilene's eyes. "I'm glad," she said in a voice as fervent as her embrace had been. "I was afraid I'd lost your friendship. I have few, so they're precious to me."

Saddened by the hints of a lonely past revealed in Gilene's statement, Halani squeezed the other woman's arm. "We're friends and will remain so. Mama adores you too. She may hold it against Azarion for taking you from us."

"I'll miss you both when we go our separate ways." Gilene wiped at her eyes. "I pray we'll meet again."

"Me too." Halani doubted that would happen. Once Hamod and his group concluded their business at the Goban market, they'd return to the Empire and the familiar roads on which they typically traveled and traded. Gilene's future lay with Azarion and his clansmen over the Gamir Mountains and into the west, where the great steppe lay beyond the reach of the Empire's clutches, protected by geography and the great Fire Veil. The likelihood of her seeing Gilene after this was slim.

"Does he make you happy, Gilene?" She would worry less for Gilene if she were assured of her friend's happiness.

Gilene nodded, her features softening. "He does. We were adversaries once, then allies, then lovers, and now friends as well." Her widening smile made her almost beautiful. "He has my heart."

Lovers, then friends. A juxtaposition Halani hadn't expected but one that worked well for this couple. "It's obvious to all that you certainly have his."

They remained outside a little longer, chatting of inconsequential things, until Halani yawned thrice in a row. She gave Gilene an apologetic shrug. "I'm asleep on my feet. I need to get Asil and anyone else still able to stand and leave for our camp."

Hamod was too deep in his cups to make the walk back to their wagons, and Halani refused the offer to put him in a cart and drive him there. "I trust he's in safe hands here," she told Azarion. "Kursak or Marata will come for him later, once he's slept off some of the effects from all the wine and mare's milk he drank."

A dozen of their number stayed while the rest chose to join Halani. She held on to a groggy Asil, promising her she'd be in her bed in no time. They traveled in a loose-knit group, their path through the high rye grass illuminated by the torches they carried.

Kursak, her uncle's second and the caravan's wagon master when Hamod was absent, yelped a curse that made Halani and the rest of their group start. He bent, disappearing behind a wall of swaying grass. Beside him, Seydom moved the torch he carried to give better light to what Kursak inspected. His own "God's teeth, this isn't good" chased away Halani's drowsiness.

Alert now, Asil surged toward the two men to see what had captured their interest. Halani pulled her back. "Wait, Mama."

Her heart sped up when Seydom waved her over. "Halani, you need to see this."

After a stern command to Asil to stay put, she joined Seydom and Kursak, gasping at the sight that greeted her.

Three dead men sprawled in the grass, unseen and unnoticed until a traveler stepped on them as Kursak had. Halani swallowed back a second gasp when Seydom bent the torch closer for better light. She recognized all three men.

Crouched beside one with a knife through his throat, Kursak glanced up at her. "Looks like we've stumbled upon a botched robbery."

What they'd stumbled upon smacked of something more than a robbery. Two of the three had sold a magical draga bone to Hamod. The one wearing the knife in his neck lay on his back, a strung bow half hidden beneath him and a quiver of arrows beside him. His companion had collapsed in a heap across the third man's legs and lower torso. He displayed no obvious injuries, but his head was bent at an odd angle, and he watched the stars with an unblinking gaze.

An odd grief settled on her when Seydom's torchlight shone a little brighter on the last man, arrow shafts protruding from his body as if he were a grotesque pin-poppet. His features were slack, and his hand lay pale next to the entrance point of the arrowhead in his chest.

Malachus.

Kursak pointed to the mercenaries. "If I'm right, the one with the knife in him shot that one . . ." He gestured toward Malachus. "He and his friend took him for dead. Their last mistake. He wasn't dead enough. It looks like he took them both by surprise. Stabbed the archer and broke the other one's neck with his legs. He knew how to fight. The other two must have ambushed him."

Halani had witnessed death many times. She robbed graves and attended burials. Healed the sick, shrouded the dead, and comforted the living. And she never grew used to it. Deaths such as these were the worst, where violence ended a life. For her it was proof that men, by their very nature, brought the worst miseries on themselves.

Her throat ached and her eyes stung from a fierce need to weep. It made no sense that such feelings plagued her, but they did. Malachus had been kind to her, but most important, he'd defended Asil and turned her tears to smiles. He shouldn't have died this way.

The two mercenary traders looked lifeless, but she wanted to check for herself. No pulse beat under her fingers when she pressed them to their necks, nor did a breath tease her hand when she held it under their noses.

She hesitated in front of Malachus, that odd grief at his death weighing heavy on her. She should be relieved. Every instinct had warned her he was trouble. She'd known it from the first moment he'd spoken to her.

Both Kursak and Seydom reached to pull her away at her sudden inhalation. She shrugged off their touch, attention centered on the ground and the weak, thready song of earth magic playing there. Halani recognized the melody, unique to the man who'd come to her mother's aid.

"Wait." Her sorrow wavered toward hope as she pressed her fingers to Malachus's throat. A faint pulse knocked against her fingertips. "He's alive," she announced.

"What's happening?" Marata called out from where he and the others stood nearby, their view obstructed by the tall grass. Seydom waved them over, and soon they all huddled around the trio.

"Oh no, Malachus!" Asil dropped to her knees beside Halani and grabbed Malachus's limp hand. "It's Malachus, Hali." She turned a beseeching gaze on her daughter as if asking her to fix what was wrong with him.

"I know, Mama." Halani patted her shoulder and stared at Kursak, who stared back. "We can't just leave him here."

"This is the man Asil's been praising to the heavens all day?"

Halani nodded. "He did Mama and me a true kindness, especially Mama."

Kursak's cheeks puffed out on a hard exhale. "He's crow bait, Halani. If he isn't dead yet, he will be the moment we try to move him." He glanced at Asil still gripping Malachus's hand. "I'm sorry, Asil."

"Leaving him here for scavengers to gnaw on is no way to repay that kindness. And he still lives. We owe it to him to try and save him," Halani argued.

Hamod's fury would know no bounds if they brought Malachus into their camp, especially after his tirade regarding Azarion and Gilene, but Halani was willing to incur his wrath. She refused to leave an injured man to die in a field just to protect her uncle's questionable acquisitions.

Marata joined their conversation. "We're not far from the camp, and there are enough of us here to carry him." The camp cook was a big man and could easily carry Malachus by himself if they didn't have arrow shafts and injuries with which to contend.

Kursak shook his head. "That soft heart of yours will get you into trouble one day, Halani."

It already has, she was tempted to reply but stayed silent as Kursak rose and began relaying instructions for how to lift and carry Malachus.

"What about the dead ones?" Marata's wife, Talen, nudged the archer with her foot.

Compassion only extended so far to trump cold-blooded practicality.

"Strip them of any weaponry and valuables," Kursak said. "They won't be of any use to them now. We'll drag the bodies farther away from camp and leave them to the carrion eaters." He eyed Halani, one eyebrow raised. "Any objections?"

She shook her head. "None." Whatever feud there had been between Malachus and the two men, they'd taken him unawares and attacked from afar. This was no honorable conflict but the work of sell-swords. They didn't deserve a burial.

Assured by Kursak that he and the men drafted to help him would be careful with her newly acquired patient, Halani confiscated one of the torches and raced with Asil back to the camp to prepare one of the provender wagons as a sickbed.

Dawn was cresting the horizon, and those who'd stayed behind to guard the caravan while the rest attended the Savatar celebration waited beside Halani and Asil as Kursak, Marata, and two others carried Malachus into camp.

"Which wagon do you want him in, Halani?" Sweat dotted Kursak's face as he and the other men supported Malachus's weight between them. White as bleached bone and gray around the mouth, the injured man hung limp in their hold.

Halani wondered how he'd managed to survive this long. If she guessed right, those were broadhead arrowheads embedded in his flesh. The wounds didn't visibly bleed much, but inside, arteries sliced open by such arrows bled rivers into the body.

She pointed to the provender wagon behind her. "There. I've put down bedding inside and cleared space to tend him." They lumbered toward the wagon, grumbling when she harangued them: "Be gentle! He isn't a sack of potatoes."

Getting the man inside presented the trickiest part of their journey. It was a mercy he remained unconscious as the men practically wrestled him into the wagon. Once done, they retreated outside. Halani scampered up the steps and knee-walked down the aisle between Malachus's prone body and the wall. The bedding she'd laid down covered the rough floorboards, and she and Asil had cleared the wagon of everything stored in it to create enough room for her and an assistant or two to work.

"Is that all you'll be needing, Halani?" Seydom hovered at the wagon's entrance. "If you need him moved again, call one of us. He's a lot heavier than he looks."

Halani partially unlaced the man's tunic for a closer look at the entrance wound on his chest. An odd but recognizable whiff of something made her rear back with a frown. "Tell Mama to bring my small medicine chest. She knows which one."

Seydom bounded off the threshold to do her bidding, and she

returned her attention to Malachus, pressing her fingers to his neck once more to feel the stuttering pulse there. Assured his heart still beat, she inspected his wounds.

The arrowheads had penetrated deep and were surrounded by swollen, bloodied flesh. Before trying to remove them, she'd have to chop the shafts short with a hatchet. The initial wounding hadn't killed him outright, but if her nose was right, those arrowheads had been dipped in a lethal poison, which should have killed him even faster than the bloodletting.

Coin-size bloodstains marred his tunic and breeches where the arrowheads were lodged. The hip wound was the least grievous of the three. The one below his collarbone and the one in his side, far worse. Even if they managed to miss a vital organ, he might well bleed to death before Asil arrived with the medicine chest. Her mother climbed into the wagon, a small, intricately engraved chest tucked under one arm, a satchel stuffed with towels draped over her other arm. She shrugged off the satchel, dropping it at Halani's feet, and set the chest down nearby.

"I brought towels, Hali. Do you want me to boil water?" Asil was a precocious child trapped in an aging woman's body, but that arrested maturity didn't mean she was stupid, and she often acted as Halani's assistant when she cared for a sick or injured person.

"Thank you, Mama. You always know what to get even before I ask." The older woman preened under Halani's praise. "I'll need the towels and the hot water. And see if you can borrow Marata's sharpest hatchet and one of his blocks. These arrow shafts are made of bone. They're too tough to break by hand." She couldn't do anything about the poison but try to help his body overcome its effects. Had he imbibed a lethal elixir, she would have administered a purge, but this ran through the bloodstream instead of the belly. Asil wasn't gone long before Talen tapped on the doorframe to announce her presence and lifted an armload of linen for Halani to see. "I thought you could use some extra bedding and blankets."

Halani descended the steps to relieve Talen of some of her burden. "Thank you. Did Mama ask for a hatchet?"

The other woman nodded. "She's arguing with Marata right now over which is the sharpest to use." She peered into the wagon. "Do you have enough room in there for an extra person or do you want me to stay out here and pass the bedding to you?"

Halani motioned for Talen to follow her as she climbed back into the wagon. She dropped the bedding next to Malachus. "He's heavy, so I can use the help getting his clothes off. Seydom said to call him or one of the other men, but we'll manage fine between the two of us."

They knelt on either side of the unconscious man. Talen whistled her admiration. "He's handsome enough, even nearly dead. I wonder why someone tried to kill him."

Because they feared him. She kept the thought behind her teeth, but the idea refused to let Halani go.

She agreed with Talen's praise, but his looks were neither here nor there. Her task was to keep him alive. She slid her hands under his shoulders. "Here, help me lift him so I can get half his tunic off. I'll have to cut it away from the arrow shaft."

The two women gently lifted him into a partially reclined position. His head dropped forward, chin resting next to where the arrow shaft protruded from his chest just below his collarbone. Talen braced him against her knees while Halani cut away the fabric surrounding the wound. They eased the tunic off him, leaving his torso bare.

"Very handsome," Talen repeated, gaze lingering on his lean body.

Halani snorted. "Not too loud, Talen. I don't need Marata

turning my patient into stew meat with the hatchet just because his wife can't peel her eyes off him." Halani's humor soon evaporated as she got a closer look at two of the three wounds. One might require her to pull the arrow from bone, a bloody task requiring brute force, but not nearly as risky as removing one embedded in an internal organ, which she feared might be the case with the second arrow, in his side.

"If the poison those arrows were dipped in doesn't kill him, me trying to fish them out will probably do the trick." She changed positions, scooting down to his feet. "Boots off. Then his breeches."

They stripped him, tossing his garb into a corner before readjusting the bedding, which had twisted beneath him with their efforts.

Talen swiped at her brow. "Good thing he's unconscious. All that jostling would have left him screaming if he'd been awake."

"Thank the gods for small mercies, then." Halani stood up and leaned out the door to cool off. Asil had returned from arguing with Marata and now tended the fire she'd started nearby, watched by a small crowd of onlookers who'd gathered to gossip.

Halani scowled. "Mama, how much longer until the water boils?"

"Soon. Do you want the hatchet now?" At Halani's nod, she skipped to the wagon and handed her daughter the sharp-edged tool. "Marata says no nicks in the blade or you'll answer to him."

"You'd think that stupid hatchet is his favorite child." Talen squeezed past Halani to exit the wagon. "I'll tell him if he's that worried, he can come and chop those arrow shafts himself."

"Tell him I'll be careful," Halani replied. "And send Seydom to me. He's helped before when I've had to dig broadhead pieces out of someone." Asil had always been Halani's primary helpmate when it came to healing the sick or patching up the wounded, but she needed Seydom's strength for the worst parts of her surgeries.

Asil gave the fire one last check before joining Halani at the steps. "What now, Hali?"

The two women laid out supplies, including the medicine chest, towels, bandages, a support block, and the hatchet borrowed from Marata. Halani left the wagon long enough to bury three knives in the fire's hot coals and to mix a poultice of herbs. It oozed through her fingers as she swirled it by hand in the bowl. She closed her eyes and listened for the fading voice of the freshly cut herbs and the hymn of earth swirling under her feet. They were like threads once woven on the same loom, then cut. Halani pictured them thus and then herself capturing the trailing ends and tying them together, so that earth's deep magic infused the herbs within the poultice with power, with life. This was the foundation of her healing, what gave her salves and tinctures their potency, what made her an enemy of the Empire.

When she returned, she carried an additional knife with her, handing it and the poultice to Asil while she retrieved a thin length of silk from the chest.

"I hope I won't need this," she told Asil before laying the silk across the top of the chest. She reached for the hatchet and block just as Seydom entered the wagon.

"Glad you're here," Halani said and pointed to a spot next to Malachus. "Help us move him so I can mound the blankets beneath the block and wedge it under the arrow shaft." She pointed to the shaft protruding from his upper chest.

They managed to roll him in place without waking him. Every second he remained unconscious made her work easier. Halani lifted the hatchet and with one swift stroke chopped the arrow shaft down short enough to get most of it out of her way.

They repeated the process with the arrow in his hip and the more dangerous one in his side, and then Halani set the hatchet aside. “Well done,” she complimented her helpers. “Now for the messy work.”

“What if he wakes up while you’re cutting him, Hali?” Asil’s eyes clouded with worry.

The last time a patient had awakened while having a wound cleaned, he’d lashed out with a fist and blackened Halani’s eye. Bildu, the camp’s farrier, almost didn’t survive the incident. It had taken Marata and two others to pull an enraged Asil off him.

Halani tipped her chin toward Seydom. “Seydom is strong enough to hold him down if that happens. I’ll be fine, Mama.” She noted Seydom’s wary glance toward Asil. He’d been one of those who had wrestled Asil into submission and saved Bildu from a disemboweling.

Odd scars decorated Malachus’s nude body, beautiful in their way, with fernlike designs decorating his skin. Halani had seen her fair share of scars on her patients; she’d never seen any like these. “Hold the lamp a little higher, Mama.”

Asil did as she bade. “How do you think he got these?”

Seydom snorted. “We all saw those two men he killed. I’d be more surprised if he wasn’t scarred up.”

“You can ask him when he wakes.” Halani turned her attention to the arrow just below his collarbone first. She held the shortened shaft between thumb and forefinger and gave it a delicate twist, careful not to rotate it so hard that the sinew attaching the broadhead to the haft separated.

The shaft didn’t budge. Malachus remained still, though blood trickled faster from the wound.

“Bad luck but not the worst,” she informed her companions. “I think it’s in the cartilage.”

Seydom tensed. His task in here was about to become much more challenging. “Can you get it out?”

"I think so." Halani took up her knife. "Lamp higher, Mama."

Blood ran faster as Halani cut two incisions into the flesh surrounding the arrow shaft. Using the shaft itself as a guide, she slid the fingers of her free hand down the length and into the bleeding muscle swollen around the broadhead.

Her fingertips passed over the smooth horn face and the sharpened sides. "Ah, damn," she muttered.

Asil's lamplight wavered as she leaned in to see what made Halani curse. "In the bone?"

Halani gently withdrew her blood-coated fingers from the now gaping wound. "There's no bone in that spot, but that matters little. The broadhead's buried like I thought. I'll have to use the loop." She clutched the towel Asil passed her to wipe her hands and then the blade, setting both down to retrieve the length of silk from her supplies. Knotting it into a noose, she hooked the loop over a fingertip and wrapped the trailing length around her forearm to anchor it for leverage. Seydom had changed positions, settling himself behind their patient so that his knees rested just above Malachus's shoulders, ready to press down in case of a struggle. "Do you want me to do it?"

Halani shook her head. "You're stronger, but I've done this before. Just be ready in case he comes to and tries to kill us all from the pain."

Once more she dug through slashed muscle with her fingers until she located the broadhead's tang and slipped the silk loop over it, drawing the slipknot tight. Malachus jerked but didn't wake, even when Seydom pressed his shoulders down to hold him still.

This was the hard part. Halani pulled the winding length of silk more snugly around her arm and braced for a tug-of-war between her and the broadhead.

"Ready?" she asked. At Asil's and Seydom's nods, she placed her free hand on Malachus's chest and with the other wrenched back on the noosed tang. The broadhead came free with a sucking pop and a gout of bright blood. The oblivious wounded woke to the world with a bellow.

CHAPTER SIX

Malachus dreamed of his dead mother and sister. They had come to the monastery to visit him, waiting in one of the courtyards while a blizzard of pink blossoms from the sour cherry orchards surrounding the monastery swirled around them. His mother, a woman of stern visage and aloof demeanor, briefly returned his enthusiastic embrace before gently pushing him toward his older sibling.

Yain, beautiful as the dawn, lifted Malachus into her arms and spun him around, her laughter bright. "I've missed you, little brother!"

Confused by their visit but ecstatic they were here, Malachus hugged her close.

"Do you want to fly with us, Malachus?" His mother's voice deepened, turning throatier, bigger. Her body changed, dissipating first into a swirling mass of gray and crimson smoke. The smoke swelled, expanding out and up until it resembled a colossal storm cloud. Yain squeezed Malachus's hand. "One day we'll do the same, little brother."

The heavy smoke coalesced, solidifying into a familiar shape, one carved on the monastery walls and drawn on prayer flags, sketched in precious books and scrolls, even stamped on coins. Those were nothing compared to this, his mother's transformation from imposing human woman to majestic draga clad in armored scales shimmering in all the colors of earth's most precious gemstones. Leathery wings tucked tight to her sides had replaced her arms, two of the claws broken off at their tips.

Her great head, three times the size of an ox cart and crowned with a pair of spiral horns, swung toward him on a serpentine neck. Her nostrils flared to catch his and Yain's scents, the brief snort she gusted knocking them both back a few steps. Scaled lips pulled back to reveal teeth the length of spears and edged like sword blades. Her body filled the courtyard and beyond, past the confining walls that had somehow faded to reveal the muscular length of her tail and the backdrop of snowcapped mountains behind her.

Unafraid, Malachus clambered up the length of the leg she held out to him. For a moment he paused to stare at his hands where they rested against one of her glittering scales. A child's hands, smooth and small. Confused, he turned to Yain, who waited behind him, balanced precariously on one of the draga's claws. "I'm a child again," he said in a voice high and very young.

She grinned. "Of course you are, silly. It's the only way we've known you." She nudged him. "Hurry up. We don't have forever."

Though she'd spoken in a cheerful tone, her words raised a wrenching grief in Malachus. Another push from her sent him scampering across scales, using their almond-shaped ridges as handholds as he climbed up his mother's body. Once on her back, he scooted up the length of her neck until he found a spot behind her head where a ruff of scales acted as a windbreak. He buried his hands in the undercoat of scales, soft as fur, hidden beneath smaller, flexible pin scales.

Yain settled behind him, one arm wrapping around his middle to hold him close. She leaned forward, slapped a spot on their mother's neck, and called out, "We're ready!"

Malachus whooped his excitement and left his stomach behind

as the draga sprang off the ground in a powerful surge of muscle and the flap of enormous wings. The earth fell away beneath them, the newly budding treetops specks of green on the rugged slopes, the monastery indistinguishable from the hillside into which it was built. "Higher, Mother! Higher!" he shouted, only to have the wind snatch the words and fling them away. His mother heard and beat her wings harder and faster until she caught a swirl of warm air that slingshot her toward the clouds and the sun. Behind Malachus, Yain cheered and hugged him hard against her so he wouldn't slip as the draga banked to the right, shredding a wall of clouds to reach the blue of endless sky. The earth below was a puzzle of grays and greens as spring clawed its way toward summer.

Winter still held dominion in the higher elevations, and while Malachus shivered under the occasional blast of cold air swooping over him and Yain, the sun radiated a blistering heat upon them, as if his mother had flown so high, he could stretch out an arm and trace the streams of sunlight gilding her scales.

"It's so hot," he said as sweat dripped off his brow into his eyes. He dared not let go his hold to wipe it away for fear of falling off his perch, despite his sister's protective hold. His mother trumpeted a roar, its vibrations undulating down her entire length. She banked again in a broad swoop, her wings making a dull *thump* against the air with every flap as she leveled off to skim the roof of the clouds.

Even then, the sun still poured its heat onto his head, washing his body in waves until it felt as if his blood might boil and his skin blister. Yain's grip, at first reassuring, held him in a smothering vise, tightening so it soon became a struggle to breathe, and Malachus squirmed in her hold. Still she hung on, ignoring his struggles.

Draga roars filled his ears, resonating in his skull over and over until his eyes bulged. His stomach slammed into his throat when she suddenly dove, wings tucked tight, long neck stretched, as she plummeted toward the earth.

Terrified cries hung trapped in Malachus's throat along with his stomach as the ground rushed up to meet them. A flash teased his vision in one corner, and he glanced to the side in time to see another follow it, a bolt of lightning that arced off one of his mother's wing tips. This time her roar was triumphant, and every hair on Malachus's small body stood straight up.

"The lightning, little brother. It rides with us!" Yain whooped her joy, and the lightning answered, splitting the ether with silvery forks that buzzed the air around them as the draga sped even faster toward the earth.

Struck mute with terror, Malachus dug his hands into his mother's fur, begging her silently to please, please slow down, fly up. *I don't want to die.*

The draga roared, Yain laughed, and the lightning arced all around them. Malachus closed his eyes, certain they were about to smash headfirst into the mountainside from the exhilarating ride turned death spiral. A bright flash whitened the darkness behind his closed eyelids, and pain unlike anything he'd ever felt before tore through him. His eyes snapped open, and this time he didn't hold back his cry.

CHAPTER SEVEN

They'd prepared for a violent awakening, but not his strength. Malachus batted Seydom away as if he were a pesky gnat, smacking him so hard against the wagon's back wall, the vehicle tipped on its struts. Asil threw herself to one side, narrowly avoiding a kick to the belly.

Halani's own proximity and positioning kept her trapped against Malachus's flailing body. Before she could scramble away, he wrapped an arm around her middle in a vise grip and squeezed.

Air hurtled out of her nose and mouth on a wheeze, and she stared into a pair of deep brown eyes half mad with pain. If he squeezed any harder, he'd break her back. Asil launched herself at her daughter's captor, only to be sent tumbling down the wagon's length as easily as Seydom, who still slumped in a daze.

Halani cupped a bloody hand around her patient's chin and held up the dripping broadhead swinging on the length of silk so he could see. More blood poured from the gaping wound just under his collarbone, painting his entire side crimson.

"Help you," she managed to squeak. "No harm."

At least no harm intended. That turbulent gaze darted between her face and the broadhead. Confusion softened the ferocious scowl patterning his forehead "Halani?" he said in a hoarse voice. At her nod, he loosened his hold on her just enough that she could call out to her mother, who, undaunted by her earlier tumble, was prepared for a second attack on her daughter's captor.

"Peace, Mama. I'm fine. Stay where you are. I don't want you hurt."

"Are you sure, Hali?" Asil's voice warbled.

If Halani closed her eyes, she might think the question came from a frightened child. The ache in her chest had nothing to do with Malachus's crushing embrace. "I'm sure, Mama," she said, never breaking the stare she held with him.

"Halani of the Lightning," he croaked, his eyelids beginning to shutter over his eyes even as his arm relaxed to slide down her back. Still, he didn't release her.

Halani didn't dwell on his odd words. "You're here with me and Asil, Malachus, in our camp. Two men attacked you, put three arrows in you along with a dose of poison. Do you remember?" He blinked at her, uncomprehending. "They need to come out before they get infected. I got one." She gestured to the extracted broadhead. "I need to get the other two."

Twitch by twitch, he eased his grip on her. She let go of his face, leaving a red smear on his cheek and jawline. Halani tossed the broadhead to one side so she could ease him back onto the bedding. Behind him, Seydom shook off his daze and crawled back to his previous spot.

"He caught me by surprise. I'm sorry, Halani. I should have been better prepared."

She waved away his apology. "Don't worry yourself. He surprised us all. Now we know what to expect."

He was fast and strong, not only for a man badly wounded and reacting to severe pain, but for any man. Inhumanly quick reflexes and the grip of a vise.

She glanced at her mother, who'd crept closer, pale, wary. "I need your help again, Mama." Asil gave a solemn nod. "Go outside and tell anyone lurking nearby that all is well. That Malachus woke up while I was removing one of the arrows. They'll know what caused all the fuss."

Asil wore the look of a child whose best friend had stolen her favorite toy, then told her they weren't friends any longer. "I thought he was nice, Hali."

"He is, Mama. He's just out of his head from the pain and confused. He thought himself among enemies instead of friends. It's fine now. He knows he's safe with us."

Asil's expression brightened. "Do you want me to come back inside once I've told them?"

Halani adored her mother, and her stomach clenched at the memory of seeing the casual way Malachus had knocked Asil aside, almost sending her through the wagon door, as if she weighed no more than a thistle bloom.

"No," she said. "You can be my messenger in case I need to relay news."

"Whatever you wish, Hali." And this time Asil was all smiles as she scampered out of the wagon, struts bouncing as she skipped the steps to leap to the ground from the threshold edge.

Halani grabbed a wad of bandages and pressed it to her patient's bleeding wound. "You don't have to stay," she told Seydom. "But I'll need you to send someone else in your place to help me."

Seydom bristled, indignant at her suggestion though she hadn't meant to offend him. "I'll stay," he snapped, splitting his glare between her and their charge. "And this time he won't catch me by surprise."

The object of their discussion startled them both when he spoke in a tired, hoarse voice. "I promise to be still." He studied Halani through a slitted gaze. "And I thank you."

Halani paused in soaking up blood to study him in return. "Don't make promises you can't keep, and I haven't saved you yet."

A ghost of a smile flitted across his grim mouth. "But you're trying. That deserves my gratitude."

She replaced the saturated bandage with a towel, careful not to press too hard. There was still much more to do. Before the day was done, he'd be cursing instead of thanking her for visiting so much suffering on him.

"I'll remind you of that when you're shouting and threatening to hang me from the nearest tree branch the moment you're well enough to stand."

"But you'll know I won't mean it," he assured her.

She appreciated his outlook, though she didn't believe he'd maintain such acceptance once she started on the other arrows, and most especially when she cauterized the wounds.

His pale features pinched even tighter. "My horse." His hand skittered across the blankets. "My horse at the stables."

She remembered the sleepy-eyed mare who'd followed behind him when Halani had first crossed his path in the market. "Did you board her at Grecajin's stable yard?"

Malachus nodded, hands still moving restlessly as if searching for something. "I only paid for a day and night's board."

Half dead, poisoned, and in pain, he still worried for his mount. That stable yard was known for auctioning off a horse if its owner was so much as an hour late with boarding payment. "I'll send someone to retrieve her."

"I can pay."

"Oh, you will," she assured him with her sweetest smile. "We have your money purse." As his raspy laugh turned to a groan, she shushed him. "Don't laugh. You may be causing more bleeding inside, especially here." Her hand glided to the arrow shaft sticking out of his side. That one she'd face last, as it would be the most dangerous to remove and the one most likely to kill him.

"Mama!" she called toward the door. "Send Talen to me and then bring me a prayer stick."

At Talen's arrival, Halani handed her the money purse along with a description of the horse he called Batraza. "She's stabled at Grecajin's."

Talen tucked the purse into her bodice. "Pray he hasn't already sold her to the knackers," she said before leaving.

While she waited for her mother to return with the prayer stick, Halani checked the towel pressed against Malachus's shoulder, pleased to see the bleeding had slowed. The broadhead hadn't splintered when it penetrated. Even the sinew hafting the tang to the shaft hadn't disintegrated, saving her from excavating the wound even more, searching for bits of arrow shrapnel that would cause infection.

"What is this prayer stick?" he said, voice weary and slurred.

Before Halani could reply, Asil entered the wagon to hand her a short length of wood the thickness of her thumb and scraped smooth of its bark. "Will this do?"

Halani nodded and held the stick close to her patient's mouth. "Put this between your teeth and pray."

He opened his mouth for her to balance the stick between his teeth. "Don't be foolish and try to hold back your pain. No one expects your silence. If you have to scream, scream."

She had no wish to frighten him, but she wouldn't lie. This would be difficult and bloody and would hurt beyond belief. He nodded and closed his eyes, jaw flexing as he tested the stick's sturdiness against his bite.

Halani set to work on the arrow lodged in his hip. It wasn't as deep as the one under his collarbone and only lodged in the heavy muscle there. Malachus stayed still except for an occasional jerk or a grunt around the prayer stick.

She applied a folded towel to soak up the initial blood flow and called for Asil to replenish her supply. Seydom helped her mound blankets against his back to support him while he reclined on his side, and Halani examined the last arrow.

No bone or cartilage to contend with. But vital organs lay beneath that patch of flesh. Had the arrow sliced through any of those, he would have bled out by now. If she wasn't careful, he still might.

He was deathly pale, breathing harsh and uneven, but his expression was calm as Halani stared into his eyes with their ink-dark irises and dilated pupils. "You're not dead yet, which makes me think this arrow has somehow missed your entrails. If I remove it the way I did the others, I risk cutting into or tearing through some of your guts. The safest thing for me to do is push it through to the other side and cauterize the wound as soon as I do." She had no platitudes to offer to soften the reality of what he'd have to endure, nor any assurances he'd live through it.

They stared at each other for a few moments before he took the stick out of his mouth to say, "No wonder you call this bit of wood a prayer stick." He turned his head in such a way that he could see the shortened arrow shaft protruding from his side. "The waiting is worse than the doing. Get on with it."

The next quarter hour was a horror of blood and hot knives, burning flesh and guttural cries that became less and less human as Halani cauterized and cut, probed and poulticed, and bandaged her thrashing, tortured patient until he finally, mercifully, passed out. The prayer stick fell from his slack mouth, its surface riddled with the crescent shape of teeth marks.

Through it all, Seydom held him down, but just barely. When

it was over, he sat back on his haunches and breathed out a gusty sigh of relief. "Thank the gods that's done."

Halani, who had ended up sitting partway on Malachus, eased her weight back to observe her handiwork and swipe away a droplet of sweat hanging off the tip of her nose. If he lived, she'd be a month nursing him at least.

If the wound in Malachus's hip didn't end up infected, it would heal quickest, followed by the one under his collarbone. Halani worried most about the one in his side. There'd be no stitching for any of them right now. He was in a weakened state, up against grim odds. Halani didn't expect he'd live to see morning.

At the moment there was nothing else to do but go outside, brew a cauldron of willow-bark tea for the inevitable fever, strip the bedding from her and Asil's wagon to replace the ruined linens here, and breathe air that didn't smell of blood and sweat.

She wobbled to her feet, waiting for Seydom to join her. "Come on. He isn't going anywhere, and we both need a stretch."

"And a drink," he added, stepping carefully over their prone charge to follow Halani down the wagon steps.

The ground hummed beneath her tired feet, singing a soothing lullaby she felt more than heard as she joined Asil at their wagon. The tall rye not flattened by wagon wheels or feet arched toward her, whispering a welcome.

"Earth and earth," she murmured, a simple blessing Asil had taught her when she was a child. Meaningless on its surface, but her soul recognized the quiet laudation behind it.

Somewhere beneath the layers of soil and rock, past buried bones and the memory of tree roots, an ancient mother answered. *Forever the earth.*

A quick bath and a bowl of soup she downed without tasting rejuvenated her. Talen had returned with Malachus's mare, hobbling her in a spot just outside the corral where the caravan horses and mules were picketed.

"It's an odd thing," the cook's wife said as she eyed the mare with a speculative gaze. "The other horses don't like her, though she seemed uninterested in them."

"She isn't part of the herd." Halani sipped on her third cup of tea, grateful it wasn't the bitter willow bark she planned to pour down Malachus's throat by the bucketful.

"No, it's something more than that." Talen gestured to the other livestock pens. "Even the goats and sheep grew skittish as she passed."

Halani had seen something similar when the men had carried Malachus into camp, though at the time she'd been far more focused on getting him into the provender wagon without making his injuries worse. He possessed magic. She knew that for certain. She wondered if he was aware of it, this thing some called a gift and others named a curse, depending on which side of the Empire boundary lines you stood. Maybe the mare held some remnants of that sorcery as well, like a strong perfume that scented everything close to it. She thanked Talen for the help and returned to the provender wagon to succor her patient.

Kursak, who'd volunteered to stand watch, met her on the steps. "He's out of his head with fever. Hot enough to set fire to the blankets. It's like a bread oven in there, Halani. If I didn't know better, I'd think you were roasting the poor bastard on a spit."

"Fetch me cool water and towels, please. I expected a high fever." She didn't wait to see Kursak leave and was instantly buffeted by a wall of heat when she entered the wagon.

Malachus lay unmoving on the wagon floor, the new bedding Asil had brought twisted beneath him. He muttered in his delirium, sharp, angry words. His head turned from side to side, eyelashes fluttering against his cheeks as he battled some illusionary adversary.

Bright flags of color painted his wide-set cheekbones, and his skin burned hot beneath her touch. He was drier than parchment left in a desert sun, and if she didn't bring his fever down, he'd convulse.

Kursak returned with the water and cloths she requested, promising to keep Asil company while Halani stayed busy in the wagon. "I'll take her with me to get Hamod and the rest from Azarion's camp."

A frisson of panic shot through Halani. "Fetch the others but leave Uncle with the Savatar for now." At his puzzled look, she lifted her hand in a plea. "You heard that tirade he gave once he learned of Azarion's true identity. He'll want my head on a plate for bringing another stranger into our midst. I need time to come up with a good reason for why I did so." She sprinkled enough truth in the explanation to make it believable, though her impetus for keeping Hamod out of the camp had less to do with protecting herself and more with protecting Malachus.

Kursak was no fool, and he regarded her for a long moment. "As you wish," he finally said. "Asil and I won't mention your newest stray. A secret between us. She'll love the idea of holding something over her brother. And I doubt our fearless leader will need much coaxing to enjoy a little more of Azarion's fine hospitality." He waved away her thanks and left to fetch Asil.

Halani set the bowl down and grabbed an extra pillow to tuck behind Malachus's head so that water didn't run into his ears as she swabbed his face. He emerged from a doze just as she leaned in, pillow clutched in her hands. His gaze, bright with fever, shone in the wagon's dim lamplight, flitting from her face to the pillow and back again before narrowing. Something stared back at her from those dark eyes, something not at all human.

Halani stilled, instinct warning her that to move might put her in jeopardy. She kept her voice soft, assuring, even as her stomach somersaulted with an unnamed fear. "I've water to cool you down and this pillow to raise your head while I do so. You have a fever."

He blinked slowly, recognition replacing the feral suspicion in his fever-bright gaze. "Halani."

"Yes, I'm Halani." She still didn't move. "May I put the pillow behind you now?" When he nodded, she tucked the pillow under his shoulders and neck so that he was less reclined but still on his uninjured side.

His eyes closed with the first touch of the wet cloth to his cheek. Halani gently bathed his hot face, gliding the cloth over his forehead, nose, and cheeks, pausing a few times to saturate and wring the cloth before continuing on to his throat and the muscular slopes of his shoulders.

A faint smile played across his mouth, and his breathing deepened. "From torturer to nurse, you have many skills, Halani of the Lightning."

His voice was still raspy, and she offered him water from a flask she'd brought with her. At her urging, he sipped instead of gulped, turning his head away when he finished. She resumed bathing him, squeezing water from the cloth so that it trickled into his hair to wet his scalp.

His description of her made no sense, poetic though it was. "Why do you call me Halani of the Lightning?"

He didn't answer, and his body shivered as she ran the cloth down his arms and the exposed skin of his chest, careful not to touch the bandages. She twitched the covers away when he reached for them. "I know you're cold. The fever makes it so, but covering up will only make it worse. Give your body the chance to cool, and then I'll pull the blanket up."

His hand fell limply against his midriff where the edge of his bandages encircled his waist. "If you say so."

Halani continued her ministrations, wetting his hair by degrees to cool his scalp and pressing the cloth to the back of his neck. She thought him asleep until he gave her a start with a question.

"Where am I?"

"A provender wagon in a free trader's camp led by my uncle, Hamod the Imposing."

His eyes had been closed when he asked the question. One opened now to slant her a look. "A grandiose title. One he gave himself or given by others?"

She chuckled. The first time Hamod had introduced himself to someone as the Imposing within her earshot, Halani had cried with laughter. At twelve years old, she hadn't yet mastered the art of discretion. That slip had earned her a cuff to the side of the head and three weeks of laundry duty for the entire camp. Never again did she mock her uncle's self-christened appellation. "Himself," she said. "And he often lives up to the title."

"He sounds charming." Malachus shivered again. "My horse."

"Safe in the camp and tended by a boy who'd rather spend time with animals than people. He'll take good care of her. And Grecajin didn't put you completely in penury with his late fees. You still have *belshas*. I've put them with your clothes."

The tension eased in his shivering frame. "You have my deepest gratitude. I would have dealt with the loss of all my *belshas* much easier than losing Batraza. She and I have traveled far together."

Halani paused with her hand over the nearly dry water bowl. She had learned a little about this man since discovering him half dead not far from their camp—the strength in his body, the flow of his blood on her hands, the timbre of his magic in her soul. But she could only assume what might have landed him here under her care. "Why are people trying to kill you, Malachus?"

Silence greeted her. He'd succumbed to sleep, and Halani was pleased to note that while fever still raged through him, he was no longer as hot as the bread oven Kursak compared him to.

She left him then, switching places with Talen and taking the bowl with her. There was still more willow-bark tea to brew for the stubborn fever, more poultices to mix and bandages to prepare. She and Talen could take shifts watching over Malachus. Someone that badly injured required constant vigilance.

Marata visited her while she brewed another pot of tea and offered a plate piled high with food. "Thought I'd have to fight off those jackals tonight with a club just to save you a crust of bread."

Her stomach rumbled at the delectable smells wafting from the plate. She took it eagerly, inviting him to sit by her. "Outdid yourself tonight, eh?" she said before eagerly tucking into the supper. He preened at her praise.

They sat together without conversing until Halani had cleared most of her plate, and Marata watched the wagon door as if waiting for his wife to appear. "He still alive in there?"

Halani sopped up a pool of gravy with her hunk of bread. "So far." She popped the bread into her mouth, chewed, and swallowed before heaping additional praise on Marata's head. "I could eat a barrel of just your bread and gravy. Did you use some of the spices you bought at the market when we first got here?"

"Aye. The good stuff the Guild was hoarding until now. I can make a horse blanket taste good if I cooked it in some of those spices." He took over stirring the contents of the pot in front of them, testing the flavor with a quick sip. He shuddered. "Not enough spice in the world to make this swill taste less bitter."

"I don't need it to taste good. I just need it to work." She handed him her empty plate. "He's swallowed it down so far without complaint. Stay a little longer and you can walk back with Talen. I'll trade places with her."

"I'll bring extra supper for your mother when she comes back from the Savatar camp." He waved away her thanks, his expression dark. "You know Hamod will blister your ears for bringing another stranger into the camp. He'll say we don't need that kind of trouble again."

And he'd be a hypocrite for saying it. Halani kept the thought to herself. Considering how he'd insisted on obtaining the bone artifact despite her warnings, he was the last person to admonish her about not borrowing trouble. "Uncle Imposing wasn't with us at the time, and when he arrives I'll suggest he learn the value of a little kindness and compassion."

"You always were a softer spirit than your uncle," Marata said.

Halani snorted. "If you're implying that softness is a weakness or is the curse of women, I will drown you in this tea."

He laughed. "You know better. If I believed either of those things, I would never have survived marriage to Talen."

Talen's shrill "Halani, come quick! Malachus is on fire!" interrupted their conversation.

"What in the gods . . ." Marata said, hard on Halani's heels as she raced for the wagon. She leapt up the steps, shoved past Talen, now standing on the threshold, and stumbled to a halt at the scene before her. Malachus wasn't on fire, but tendrils of smoke rose from him and the bedding. His flesh didn't burn, not like the cauterization he'd endured under her care, but a charred smell still permeated the interior.

A powerful vibration purled under Halani's skin, the feeling familiar but much, much stronger than any she'd ever felt when barrow raiding with Hamod. Alarm bells sounded in her skull. She bent to touch Malachus, yanking her hand back with a yelp when her fingers met skin hotter than the surface of the cauldron in which she brewed his tea.

His eyes opened. No longer muddled from sleep or the effects of poison, his gaze once more hinted at something not quite human in its dark depths.

"Get out," he snarled in a voice made demonic by its sheer malice. Smoke poured from his lips and streamed out his flared nostrils. He jackknifed to a sitting position, unencumbered by his bandaged wounds. The edges of the bandages themselves were charred brown in some spots, and flaking away as black ash in others. Scorch marks striped the blankets he'd lain on.

Halani stumbled back and fell on her backside. She scrambled for distance, scuttling toward the threshold on hands and heels, not daring to look away from the terrifying sight before her.

"Get out!" he bellowed again, sweeping his arm toward her. She was out of range, but Halani still flinched, then screamed when an invisible force punched her backward through the wagon's doorway. The world tumbled for a moment before she struck the edge of one of the steps and rolled to a stop on the muddy ground.

Chaos erupted around her. Shouts of her name, calls for spears and bows, and one clear, unwavering command that sent panic surging so hard through her, she clawed her way up the two people trying to help her.

"Kill that fucking bastard!"

CHAPTER EIGHT

Malachus clutched the frame poles supporting the wagon's sides and drew himself up to his knees, then to his feet. Smoke swirled off him as the draga thrashed inside its human prison and fought to be let out. He'd awakened it when he tapped into its magic to overpower the poison coursing through his body and save himself from bleeding to death. Halani was wrong in assuming the arrow in his side hadn't pierced a vital organ. He'd been drowning in his own blood by the time she found him, saved only by the draga's power and its extraordinary ability to withstand such catastrophic damage. But that power came with a price, and what he was battled to break free from what he pretended to be.

Obligation propelled him toward the wagon's entrance, despite instinct screeching that outside another kind of death awaited him. These traders had tried to help him. He'd repaid their kindness with a perceived attack on their healer. He didn't need to burn down their wagon as well.

He careened to the edge, blinded by a red haze that descended over his vision. Halani's angry command acted as his guide to the wagon's doorway.

"Put your weapons down, gods damn it! I'm not hurt. Put them down!"

Malachus teetered on the topmost step, staring at a world dyed scarlet and populated by a battalion of angry fighters armed with weapons—all pointed at him.

Halani, splattered in mud, raced toward him. He held up a hand to ward her off. The small motion unbalanced him. He pitched out of the wagon just as the warning *thunk* of a fired cross-bow bolt sounded in his ear. He landed in the mud on his injured side, too weak to cry out when the fall sent spikes of agony through his wounds and made the draga inside him writhe even harder. He welcomed the earth's cool, wet embrace. It hummed beneath him, a sweet song that quieted the draga by slow degrees. Its song intensified when Halani's mud-caked shoes filled his vision as she crouched in front of him.

She didn't touch him, but her eyes held worry instead of fear as she stared at him. "What's happening to you?"

Malachus closed his eyes. "Cursed," he lied.

Not so much a curse but a blessing with thorns. A draga mother's way of protecting her offspring from the predation of humans until they were old enough and powerful enough to do so themselves. But right now, with his insides boiling like lava pools and the draga trying to explode from every pore of his body, it felt like a curse.

"Dear gods," she breathed in horrified tones. "Who hates you so?"

You do, he thought. *Every one of you standing here, ready to kill me now, and I still look like you.*

"I told you he was trouble, Halani. You shouldn't have stopped us."

"We're not murderers, Marata. If we killed every person who knocked one of us down, the Empire would be strewn with the bodies we left behind."

Malachus recognized Marata's voice. *Kill the bastard* still echoed inside his head. A man not inclined to give him the benefit of the doubt. The draga within coiled tightly, becoming more torpid with the earth's continuous hymn beguiling it to sleep. "Can you hear her?" he asked.

Halani drew a little closer, still not touching him. It didn't matter. She smelled of lavender, wet ground, and camp smoke. "Hear who?" Her voice had lost its earlier sharpness.

"The earth," he murmured, exhausted, hurting. "She's singing to me. To you."

Her withdrawal was instant, a cold-water splash against his spirit. Darkness closed in on him, swallowing the veil of sunlight penetrating his shuttered eyelids.

Quiet followed the darkness, with only the wordless tune of the ground beneath him still serenading him and the trader woman.

He awakened hours later, once more reclined on layers of blankets in the provender wagon. Still alive, still whole, and with no additional arrows sticking out of him. The blood in his body no longer simmered and bubbled in his veins, nor did smoke waft off his skin. He shivered under the fresh blankets piled atop him.

Plucking the covers aside, he raised himself on one elbow to inspect his bandages. New bindings swathed his torso and hip. Another wrapped around his shoulder and under his arm. Neatly tied, the bandages showed no bloodstains. Underneath them, his wounds ached but didn't burn as they had before. He smelled a mixture of astringent herbs and sweet honey, and beneath those scents, the iron tinge of blood and acrid stink of cauterized flesh.

Draga magic could heal the wounds at this point until they were nothing more than scars to add to his existing collection. Malachus dared not tease the beast inside him again. Fortune favored him. By all rights, he should be dead. Only a hymn of earth and the fierce defense of a woman with melancholy gray eyes had saved him. Best to embrace caution and the slow-healing days of his weaker human constitution. No magic, only time and the skill of a free trader healer.

With the single lamp hanging from its high hook as illumination, he had difficulty judging the hour. Malachus peered at the wagon's entrance. The door was open, allowing a cool draft to sweep in and keep the wagon's air from becoming stifling. Anemic bars of sunlight slanted across the floorboards and part of the door lintel. If he translated the light's movement correctly, twilight chased the sun. He'd been unconscious a full night and day at least, unaware of being moved back to the wagon, body bathed, wounds dressed, and bandages changed.

A low rumble in his stomach reminded him he hadn't eaten since the quick meal of Telkak's pies. He hoped someone might appear soon with something more substantial than tea.

Footsteps clattered up the treads. A wizened face framed by gray hair appeared in his line of sight—Halani's mother, Asil. She climbed into the wagon, carrying a cup with steam blowing off its contents' surface. "You're awake!" she proclaimed with such cheeriness, it made his awareness seem like a victory. "Hali thought you'd sleep right through to morning. Are you thirsty?" She held up the cup. "Hungry? Do you need to piss?"

Malachus blinked at her, stunned to silence under the bombardment of questions. "It's good to see you again, Madam Asil. And yes to all three questions."

His visitor edged closer to him, careful not to spill anything out of the cup. "Hali said you're to drink this." She sank to her knees, bringing the cup close enough to Malachus's nose that he got a good whiff of what it contained. He drew away, upper lip curling. Willow-bark tea, bitter, black, and foul.

"I'm no longer fevered," he protested when she thrust the cup at him.

She frowned before looking at the cup and then back at him. "She said it was for the fever, but if you don't have one . . ."

"I don't."

"Then you shouldn't have to drink it." Her disgust mirrored his. "It tastes horrible anyway."

Malachus decided he very much liked Asil. Her truths were simple and inarguable. He saw his opportunity to avoid the tea and get a breath of fresh air without being butchered by other free traders in the camp. "I do have to piss," he said.

Her frown instantly dissolved into a delighted smile. "I'll help you!"

His eyebrows shot up at her enthusiasm. Good gods, this wasn't what he intended. She acted like she planned to guide him through every step of the process. "I just need help out of the wagon, madam. That's all."

Asil squeezed one of her slim arms. "I'm just Asil, no madam business. I'm also strong. You can lean on me. Stay here. I'll be right back." She gained her feet, returned to the doorway, and tossed not only the cup's contents but the cup as well. She returned, a bright flare of excitement in her eyes, as if helping Malachus navigate the wagon's narrow confines and steps just to relieve himself was a grand adventure they planned to take together. "Now I have both hands free," she declared, holding them out to him so he could grasp her fingers and pull himself up.

"Just help me down the steps. I can take care of the rest." If any of the traders discovered Asil trying to "help" him with more than just a shoulder to lean on so he didn't fall, they'd kill him for sure and hang his carcass from the nearest tree. And Halani wouldn't stop them this time.

They made it outside without mishap. Garbed in bandages and a blanket knotted at his uninjured hip to preserve modesty,

Malachus imagined himself a ridiculous sight as he descended the steps, leaning as little as possible on Asil's small but steady frame.

Unlike the previous day, when he'd fallen out of the wagon, no crowds lingered nearby. He heard the activity of the camp, voices conversing or calling commands, the laughter of small children, and the bleats of livestock. The scent of food cooking wafted on the breeze to tease his nose and make his empty stomach growl. But no one saw him and Asil.

The cauterized wound in his side throbbed, as if Halani had not only burned him there but punched him for good measure before binding the wound. The wounds in his chest and hip didn't trouble him as much but still hurt enough to make him pant as he strained muscles weakened by the tears of a broadhead and the cut of a healer's knife. He could feel the damaged tissue repairing itself, one strand at a time. Still, credit went to Halani's skilled surgery and her sweet-smelling poultices for his improved condition.

"How's this?" Asil indicated a section of dry ground not so treacherous as the slippery sward in front of the wagon steps. Close enough to one of the wagon's wheels that he could hold on to the spoke for balance, it also provided a small bit of privacy with the addition of a natural screen of rye grass not yet trampled flat.

Malachus straightened away from Asil, exchanging her support for that of the wagon wheel. "I thank you, Asil." He prayed she'd allow him a solitary moment to appease nature's demands.

"I like to help people," she said. "Don't go anywhere when you're done. I'll be right back with Hali." She slipped away before Malachus could reply, a spry, agile woman with a sweet disposition and a strong back.

Left alone, he adjusted his stance to lean against the wheel so he could wrestle aside the blanket. He was in the middle of restoring his covering when the *squish* of footsteps in mud alerted him to someone's approach. He turned to greet his visitor, expecting Asil with her daughter.

Halani had arrived without Asil but not alone. A frown curved the corners of her mouth down as she stared at him. A woman stood next to her, taller than Halani, and leaner, with hair the color of a crow's wing. She wore her tresses loose over her narrow shoulders, the ends decorated in tiny silver beads. She didn't frown as Halani did, but there was a severity to her that the trader woman lacked. Halani's eyes were soft, somber. This woman's were dark and as hard as the banded iron striping the distant mountains.

He'd known gazes like hers before. Halani's as well. Halani wore the look of someone who'd witnessed, firsthand, life's worst cruelties. Her companion wore the look of someone who'd endured them.

"What are you doing?" Disapproval laced Halani's question, as if she'd caught him with his hand in the camp's money stores.

Malachus gestured to his blanket-wrapped body. "Lurking here for the chance to show off my naked, bandaged glory to any passersby. It seems you're the fortunate one today."

The woman with the hard eyes snorted, her amusement easing her stiff features enough to reveal hints of beauty. Halani's scowl dissolved. While she didn't laugh, her eyes narrowed, and she tightened her lips against a smile.

"I woke up with a bladder ready to burst and a belly trying to gnaw its way through my backbone," he explained. "Asil helped me here and left again to find you."

Halani's smile peeked out from the press of her mouth. "And are you still needing time alone with your bladder?"

He clutched the blanket closer, already fatigued by the short sojourn outside. "No, I'm finished."

She left her companion to skirt around a mud puddle and draw close to him where he stood on the dry patch of ground. "I'll help you back to the wagon, then." She glanced down at his feet, bare and muddy. "And clean you up before you go back inside. Did Asil bring you the tea I brewed?"

His nose wrinkled at the thought of swallowing the nasty brew. "I'm not feverish."

"You will be if you don't drink it."

"Even your mother agrees it's revolting." Maybe Asil's opinion would soften her stance.

"My mother's opinions regarding my drafts don't count at the moment." A sly expression crossed her features when his stomach rumbled long and loud. "Drink the tea, and I'll bring you something to eat, but not a scrap until you do."

"Don't argue with her; you'll lose." The black-haired woman winked at Halani before turning her gaze back to Malachus. "I was a patient of hers once. She won't budge, not in this."

The promise of food already had him ceding victory to his nurse, though he found her companion's remarks an interesting glimpse into Halani's personality.

Halani pushed her shoulder under his good arm. "Don't be afraid to put your weight on me. I'm stronger than I look."

"Your mother said something similar."

They took their time, aided by Halani's friend. Malachus tensed the moment she touched him, though she showed no reciprocal reaction to him as she helped guide him and Halani to the wagon steps, where he climbed to sit on the topmost tread.

Whoever she was, she carried the favor and power of a fire deity inside her. Malachus glanced down at his fingertips to see if they'd blistered from touching her. The pads were smooth, unblemished except for the usual calluses. She wasn't draga, then. Of that he was certain, but the sorcery of fire cascaded off her in an invisible stream, and not just the fire of hearth or camp. This was holy fire, the blood and spirit of a goddess gifted to a young human woman with a crone's gaze.

Asil, her counterpoint in both age and demeanor, returned, this time bearing a tray with a plate of food and a chalice filled with ale. Malachus nearly leapt off the step in a panic as the tray jostled in her grip when she caught sight of the fire witch.

"Gilene, you came to visit!"

"Have a care, Mama." Halani deftly rescued the tray. "I'll take that."

Gilene laughed and embraced the excited Asil. "Just for a short time."

Halani offered Malachus a sweetly evil smile as she set the tray just out of reach and handed him a newly filled cup of tepid willow-bark tea. "Drink and then eat."

He accepted the tea with a sigh, downing it in two gulps. He shuddered. The motion twinged the wound in his side. "Satisfied, mistress?"

She gently pulled his hand away from where he pressed it to his side. "Try not to shake so. And resist touching your bandages. You'll dirty them faster than needed." She took the empty cup, gaze sweeping over him. "I'm surprised you've been able to sit this long on the step. Does your hip not pain you?"

"Not as much as my neglected stomach." He gestured to the empty cup. "My end of the bargain is met."

"So it is," she said, her smile fully blooming. She brought the tray to him, perching on the lowest step with it in her lap and within easy reach for him. It wasn't much in the way of real food, just a bowl of broth, a large hunk of bread, and a piece of fruit, but his mouth watered in anticipation.

Halani addressed her friend as she handed Malachus a spoon, then the bowl. "Is Uncle behaving himself as your guest? If not, don't hesitate to tell us."

Gilene's amused chuff made Halani flinch a little. "Hamod is Hamod. I've left him with Azarion to tend. They're getting along well enough, if you don't count two arguments and a challenge to a fight to the death. I think Azarion enjoys his company."

This time Halani groaned. "It will be we who owe you a debt of gratitude. If you don't mind, we'll rescue you from him tomorrow."

Malachus silently ate his food. The women talked freely in front of him of mundane things, exchanging comments over a shared history in which he had no part. In the end, it didn't matter. These were not his folk, though he was indebted to them for their care of him. A debt he'd repay before he left to continue his hunt for the mother-bond. He'd forget all their names soon enough.

Untrue, a voice inside him argued.

Untrue indeed. He'd remember Halani of the Lightning and her jovial, peculiar mother, Asil.

Gilene hugged Asil again before giving Halani a quick nod and Malachus a measuring look, her gaze settling a little longer than polite on the places where the bandages didn't cover the scars left by the lightning. "We'll see you tomorrow, then. Stay to eat and have tea." Her expression saddened. "It will be long and long before we do so again, once we depart the Goban market."

Asil accompanied Gilene to the edge of camp, leaving Halani the task of filling a small bowl with water from a larger bucket placed outside the wagon and fetching towels. She set them down in place of the food tray and returned that tray to her lap.

Despite his earlier hunger, Malachus ate slowly, taking his time so he wouldn't sicken. He hadn't eaten this well in a long time.

"I'm impressed," Halani said. "I expected I'd have to warn you not to wolf it down."

"That would be a waste if I retched it." He finished the last spoonful of soup. "This is good. Did you make it?"

Halani gave a delicate snort. "Had I such a skill, I'd have monarchs worshipping at my feet. This is Marata's doing. He cooks for the camp most of the time."

"Ah, the big man with the hatchet."

"You remember?"

The memory of a man the size of an ox storming toward him ready to butcher him like a pig was emblazoned on his mind's eye. "Hard to forget." He peered closer at his empty bowl. "Tell me I didn't just dine on some other poor bastard who made your cook angry."

Her eyes widened before she burst out laughing. "Marata will happily cook most anything, but I think he draws a line at people."

He liked her laughter, admiring the way it rounded her cheeks and turned her pensive gaze blithe. "You should laugh more," he said. "Laughter suits you."

As quickly as her humor appeared, it disappeared behind a guarded look. A heavy silence fell between them, Malachus wondering why his remark had ended their fragile camaraderie.

Halani took his empty bowl and cup, stacked them onto the tray, and set it aside before grabbing one of the towels she'd brought earlier and dunking it into the water.

"Your feet are filthy," she proclaimed in a voice no longer lively. "You've already soiled a month's worth of clean bedding. I'll be in fear of my life if I let you lie down on the new blankets with mud caked up to your ankles."

He didn't argue, only watched the top of her head as she bent to wipe his feet clean. The darkness gathered around them, kept at bay by the flicker of small fires lit within the camp as families gathered near their wagons to eat or finish a final task for the day.

A larger fire crackled to life at the camp's center. Malachus caught glimpses of it beyond the inner circle of wagons, a merry conflagration that invited folk to gather and socialize around its light.

He curled his toes when she ran the wet towel along his arch. "Why are you doing this?"

She scrubbed at his shin. "I just told you. No muddy feet in the wagon or . . ."

"No. Not the foot bath, though I appreciate it." Malachus touched each of the spots where he'd been shot with arrows. "These. All of this. It's no easy thing to save someone from dying and nurse them back to health. I'm a stranger with no ties to you and yours."

And they were human. In his experience, humans didn't help each other without expecting repayment.

Her hand rested against his ankle, slender fingers encircling it like a shackle. She resumed her task. "Life has little enough worth under the Empire's rule. Maybe my worth lies in my ability to help someone else." She spared him a quick glance. "I don't want to become what the Empire would make of us. So this is more for me than for you. You just benefit from my rebellion."

Liar, he wanted to say but didn't. She could spin and weave her reasoning into a tapestry, but he'd never believe her. This woman possessed a compassionate streak as wide as a river. It made her admirable, beguiling. It also made her vulnerable to unscrupulous parasites who'd use that kindness to their advantage.

"You should be careful with your kindness," he warned.

"I'm always careful," she countered. "Though I'm not always kind."

Once more silence fell between them as he pondered her reply and she finished rinsing his feet, declaring him clean enough to enter the wagon.

"I want to check your wounds and repack the poultice," she said as she helped him inside. "Hopefully your wounds haven't poisoned since I last looked. That you don't have fever is a good sign."

Malachus might not have fever, but he was bone weary, and he suspected there was something more in the tea Halani brewed than just the vile-tasting willow bark.

She propped him up with blankets and pillows, promising to return with the poultice and extra bandages. The scents of honey and herbs teased his nose once more when she set the bowl down and carefully unwound the bandage swaddling his chest.

She silently cleaned away the remnants of the herbal pack and examined the wound, leaning in for a closer look. Her fingertips were cool on his skin as she pressed around the sliced edges where her knife had widened the wound so she could reach the broadhead.

Malachus tucked his chin to his chest to better see what had caused her sudden intense scrutiny. "You look as if you've discovered a jewel buried in there."

He enjoyed her touch, the way her hand glided lightly over the wound's perimeter. His thoughts strayed to wondering what it might be like to know the touch of Halani the lover instead of Halani the healer.

"I might be less surprised had I spotted a pearl or ruby nestled in there," she said. "You heal remarkably quick."

Draga magic had done its work, though the risk had been high and life-threatening. His lie of suffering a curse would stand him in good stead should he battle again for control of his body while he convalesced among the traders. Until he left, he'd pretend ignorance of his extraordinary abilities.

"Your surgery skills are impressive." The flicker of doubt in her eyes didn't fade at his compliment. "And your poultices strong." He remembered the earth's hymn resonating in his head when Halani had knelt beside him in the mud. "Maybe you harvested earth magic along with your herbs." A stillness descended on her like a prey animal waiting for a predator to pass. Her features shuttered, and for the remainder of her examination, she only spoke to order him to turn, lift, shift, and sit up as she changed bandages, cleaned his remaining two wounds, and repacked poultices.

It was probable she no longer wished to converse. The tea had taken hold of him in a grip that made his limbs heavy and his eyelids weightier than anvils. "What did you put in the brew?" he asked, his words slurred.

Halani helped him lie back and pulled the blankets up to his shoulders. "A touch of *kratom* to help you sleep through the pain."

He wanted to tell her not to drug him again. He was already vulnerable, and the *kratom*'s narcotic power muted the draw of his mother's artifact. The pull was still there but buried under a lethargy that sank him into the bedding like a stone.

"No more," he murmured, fighting to keep his eyelids up so he could meet her eyes. Mourning-dove gray, compassionate but resolute, and full of secrets.

She stroked his brow, pushing back strands of his hair from his forehead. "No more unless you say more. I will ask next time."

That she understood what he tried to convey in those two

words pleased him. He wanted to thank her but the drugged sleep overwhelmed him, and the world went dark again in the wagon.

He awakened once, groggy, thirsty, and with a mouth that felt stuffed full of wool rovings. Outside, low voices spoke near the wagon's open door. The draft swirling over him was chilly but welcome. The effort to open his eyes proved more than he wanted to expend. He was content to lie still and listen, his growing awareness of his surroundings and increasing clarity sharpening his hearing so that indistinct murmurs became precise words and individual voices.

Two men and a woman spoke in turns. Malachus recognized them, though he could only put a name to Halani's voice.

"I don't care for the idea of bringing a stranger, a cursed one by his own admittance, into our territories. What if he's an Empire spy gleaning whatever information and weakness he can find and reporting it back to Herself?"

Malachus was neither a spy for the Krael Empire nor a native son, but even he knew whom the man referred to when he mentioned "Herself." The empress was known throughout all the world. And judging by this speaker's tone, deeply loathed by some.

"Then he's one piss-poor spy considering the trouble he's landed himself in." Halani sounded tired. "Besides, what does the Spider or her spies care about a band of free traders? I don't expect you to welcome him, but I won't abandon him. He's healing incredibly fast. I, Asil, and possibly Seydom or one of the other men can stay here long enough to get him well enough and send him on his way. We can catch up with the rest of the caravan as it travels to Domora. Three people and one wagon can move a lot faster than an entire camp with all its livestock and supplies."

"Cutting his throat and tossing him into the sedge would do away with such annoyances."

Malachus admired the man's pragmatism, if not his bloodthirstiness. The draga inside him slowly uncoiled from its hard-won torpor, alert to a possible threat.

The second man's voice was far milder than the first, even a little amused. "I don't think Halani will appreciate one of us knifing her patient after she just worked so hard to save him."

The first man exhaled a long-suffering sigh. "He can stay for now. We'll keep a close eye on him. If he starts smoking and setting people's clothes on fire, I'll succeed where his attackers failed."

Don't count on it, friend, Malachus thought.

"He isn't joining our camp permanently and will be gone soon enough," Halani replied. "I'm grateful for your support, Kursak."

Malachus still didn't understand Halani's devotion to him, but he was glad for it. "As you say, he did Asil a kindness. That carries a lot of weight with me, though you're on your own with Hamod when he learns about our latest guest. You know what he'll say."

"I'm hoping the Savatars' hospitality will soften him some before he returns."

The more mild-mannered man spoke once more. "You have to admit, it's been a lot more peaceful in the camp without him here. Might do him—and us—some good if we sent him with the Savatar into the Stara Dragana for a season. And if you tell him I said that, I'll say you lied." Laughter followed his remark.

The Stara Dragana. In several of the old languages no longer spoken, it meant Womb of the Draga. One of several names by which the vast steppes were known. The birthplace of the first dragas, the burial grounds of many more. Malachus's mother and the monks had told him of the steppe, where the bones of ancestor dragas rested deep in the earth.

If he found his mother-bond, he might well delay his return

across the Raglun Sea to Winosia and visit the land of his ancestors, seek some tenuous connection to this foreign place crawling with humans who had done their best over the centuries to wipe his kind out. Malachus wondered what strange forces were at play that these same creatures succored him now.

Fate and fortune played an odd hand.

CHAPTER NINE

The outlawed magic market known as the Maesor bustled with commerce, all done in whispers and side-eye transactions accompanied by mysterious sign languages known only among a few. The business of sorcery fueled the market, along with the ever-present fear of being raided by the Empire's martial forces. Gharek picked his way along the narrow avenues in a world caught between worlds, where the price of admission to the Maesor was paid in blood, souls, money, or magical items.

The sky above him was not that of the world he lived in day to day. This firmament was an acetous orange without sun, moon, or stars. The strange illumination gave the illusion of daytime.

Cobblestone paths snaked through the marketplace in no discernible order, dead-ending at walls or disappearing into shadowed closes only the foolhardy might venture into on their journey. Each paver sported a carved sigil that either glowed or hissed under the press of a footstep. Gharek kept his hand on the pommel of the dagger sheathed at his belt as he navigated through the strangely quiet crowd. Stalls hemmed either side of the paths, displaying goods for sale that were never seen in the regular markets. Demon blood in sealed jars, tapestries in which the warp and weft trapped a soul condemned to serve whatever master owned the textile, scrying cards cut from cured human skin lavishly painted to catch the eye and disguise their macabre origin. There were countless other things to fascinate, to repulse, and to barter, all of them a guaranteed death sentence for anyone caught with even a single one in their possession.

He passed a table where a woman with a tattooed face offered love potions, virility elixirs, and poison powders capable of felling a battalion with the sharing of one full teapot. She raised a hand to motion him closer, then thought better of it at the dead-eyed stare he leveled at her. He'd done things for the empress that left a stain on his spirit forever, but something about the Maesor, beyond its sorcerous purpose, made his skin crawl and his soul shudder. Eager to conclude his business here and depart, he picked up the pace to his destination: a lavishly draped stall whose entrance was guarded by a blind man with milky eyes and a dog that watched Gharek's approach with ears swiveled forward and hackles raised in warning.

A low growl vibrated up from the dog's throat, and the guard tilted his head in Gharek's direction with a cloudy gaze. "I know who you are. What would the empress's cat's-paw be doing in the Maesor? Hoping to crucify or hang a few mages for Herself's entertainment?" Gharek didn't worry much when people recognized him. He wasn't an Empire spy. He didn't need to skulk in the shadows or pretend he was someone other than who he was. As the Spider's cat's-paw, having his reputation precede him worked in his favor. That this piece of human detritus knew him was of no importance.

"I'm here to see your master, Koopman."

"Give me your hand," the guard said. When Gharek hesitated, he chuckled, revealing teeth black with rot. "Give me your hand or you stay out here."

The cur's ears lay back flat, and its growls grew in volume when Gharek stepped forward. The animal only quieted when the old man tapped the top of its head and shushed it. Gharek's lip curled at the feel of the guard's moist grip, and he nearly jerked away, disgusted. His captor only held his hand more tightly, riding the rough pad of his thumb across Gharek's knuckles for good measure. "You serve a mistress more dangerous than all of us here combined. Only a desperate man walks willingly through a pit of serpents."

Gharek yanked his hand free to scrape it down his tunic. "Stop wasting my time. Is Koopman here or not?"

The guard waved him toward the entrance. "Of course. My master awaits." Gharek skirted the dog and ducked to enter the tent. He halted just inside the entrance, allowing his vision time to adjust to the gloomy interior.

Like the sky outside, the tent reflected a preternatural sense of place. Lamps hanging from cording tied to the tent's frame spilled pale green light across the fabric walls and a floor layered with mats and rugs. At the flicker of movement near his feet, Gharek glanced down to see a twist of shadow in the weave of one of the rugs. Liquid darkness slithered and trickled through the floor covering, moving independent of his own more rigid silhouette until it spilled like black oil over the rug's edge to disappear beneath it. Gharek barely resisted the urge to go up on his toes or leap onto the nearest bit of furniture.

"State your business, friend, so that I may know how we can benefit each other."

The voice came from one of the tent's corners. An ember flare from a pipe bowl joined its own small light to the green luminescence, and Gharek smelled the spicy scent of pipe smoke. A man dressed in expensive silk and finely woven wool slouched in an intricately carved chair. Smoke wreathed his head as he lipped the pipe's mouthpiece. Beads decorated his beard, a frippery at odds with his close-cropped hair and a face the gods had carved into shape with a blunt ax. Gharek's connection to the Maesor market had instructed him to find the tent with the blind guard and cur. The man who conducted business inside was well-known in the market, a purveyor of the rare, the perilous, and if those tapestries were anything to go by, the grotesque.

"He's known as Koopman," the connection had told him. "But no one calls him that direct. You don't either, not if you want to deal with him. He'll call you 'friend.' You call him the same. No one in the Maesor market uses their name anyway. Safer that way." Gharek was not a merchant, but he was well versed in the skills of prudence and diplomacy. He served Empress Dalvila and still lived to tell about it.

"I'm told you're the eye that sees in this market. Knows what comes in for sale, what's desired by certain buyers." He kept a wary eye on Koopman and one on the rug where the shadow reappeared, creeping slowly over the pile toward his feet.

"Flattery doesn't go far with me, friend," Koopman said with a snort. "Try pairing it up with something of monetary value. I might be interested then." Gharek retrieved a faceted ruby the size of a walnut from the pouch tucked into his tunic and tossed it to the other man. "Will this buy your interest?"

Koopman caught the gem and immediately held it up to one of the lit lamps hung on a hook near his head. He inspected it with a practiced eye before trading the pipestem for it and biting down. When it didn't crack under his teeth, he hid it away in a pocket of his tunic and returned to puffing on his pipe. "It might. A pretty bauble like that is worth a few moments."

Were he not in such need of this merchant's cooperation, Gharek would have rolled his eyes at Koopman's arrogance.

"Herself's spies have discovered that a living mother-bond has made it to these shores. Word is the offspring it belongs to is hunting it."

That earned Koopman's full attention. He straightened from his practiced slouch. "There are no live mother-bonds left."

Gharek moved away from the inky tendrils stretching across the rug toward his shoes like the legs of a spider. One grazed the top of his shoe, leaving behind a splinter of ice that soaked right through the leather and his stocking and into his skin. He skirted out of its reach.

"Maybe not in the Empire itself. This one's been imported from across the Raglun Sea."

"And you think it's living?"

Gharek shrugged. "I don't think anything. It's what I've been told. I've also been told to find it and bring it to Herself."

Koopman edged a little closer to Gharek. The eldritch shadow on the floor cowered away, fleeing across the rug to bleed once more under the fringe. "Trying to string up another version of Golnar? What makes you the special errand boy in this?" His voice had lost its touch of wry amusement, becoming menacing.

This was a dangerous man, but Gharek was his equal in that respect. He didn't flinch or cower, only raised his left hand to show the brand burned into his palm years ago. "I'm her cat's-paw."

The merchant's eyes widened a fraction before he backed away, his mercurial demeanor changing once more to that of genial interest.

"And the offspring that hunts it?"

Gharek shook his head. "Unknown. For now. But there's no doubt whoever it is has arrived on these shores as well. They can't ignore the mother-bond lure, nor do they want to."

"The bond is the bait. Herself wants the offpsring." Koopman's smile carried a touch of sly admiration. "There's a lot to be said of our empress, most of it . . . well, I'm sure you've heard a thing or two. But she's without a doubt ambitious and unafraid to pursue lofty goals. She wants a draga to replace Golnar."

Gharek didn't correct his assumption. Dalvila wanted things far more valuable than a replacement ceiling ornament. Koopman didn't need to know that. "Whoever has the mother-bond right now likely knows its sorcerous nature is valuable but too risky to sell in a regular marketplace. The price they'd want would draw undue attention. They'll bring it here."

"And you want me to let you know when that happens?" Koopman casually puffed a smoke ring into the air. "I can do that. For a price."

"Not just let me know. I want you to buy the mother-bond and hold it until I can retrieve it from you."

Koopman's guffaw was loud and disbelieving. "Do you have any idea what an artifact like that would go for in the Maesor? I'm a middleman, friend, not one of the Spider's cushy-born nobles with more wealth than brains who spend their coin by collecting valuable and illegal trinkets. For a fee, I'll pass along the information that the mother-bond has surfaced in the Maesor. You're out of your head if you think I'll penury myself to buy it."

A reasonable refusal, and Gharek had expected it. He fished a purse bulging with *belshas* from inside his tunic and held it up for Koopman to see. "This is for keeping watch and sending a message when the mother-bond shows up here. Send a proctor of your choice to the palace tomorrow. I'll be there waiting with an amount that should cover the cost of buying and holding it. Keep it an honest exchange," he warned. "If you think to steal from me, make sure you deem it worth your life, because I'll see to it the empress knows who stole from her."

Koopman paled, but his expression remained stoic. He eyed the pouch of *belshas*. "No palace. Bring the retainer to me here."

Gharek shrugged and offered a short bow. "Then our business is finished. I thank you for your time." He turned away, careful to avoid the hints of chilly shadow peeking out from the rug's fringe. He made it to the threshold before Koopman's frustrated exhalation sounded behind him.

"Wait." Koopman strode past him to block the exit. "Day after tomorrow, levy day, at dawn. Everyone will be hiding in their homes to avoid paying the publicans. The fewer people about, the better for me. I'll come myself."

Gharek didn't blame Koopman for not sending a factor. The size of the retainer precluded trusting anyone to actually return and hand it over to the merchant. "I'll be at the palace gates waiting."

With the first part of their bargaining finished and his fingertips virtually touching enough money to make him wealthier than many lower-ranking Kraelian nobles, Koopman displayed a far more jovial demeanor than when Gharek had first stepped into the tent. "Come. Stay a little longer and share a pipe. I've heard of Herself's cat's-paw but never thought I'd meet him in person." *Or wanted to.* The last sentiment hung in the air between them.

Declining the invitation, Gharek exited Koopman's tent. He ignored the blind guard's farewell and left the Maesor behind him. For the rest of the day, he suffered a vague sense of horror at the idea that he'd abandoned a tiny part of himself in the otherworldly market, a part the Maesor kept and fed upon, as if it were a living beast that took sustenance from those who traveled its paths and traded in its sanctuary.

CHAPTER TEN

"I should have followed through with my first thought and suffocated you when you were born." Hamod seethed with a quiet fury.

The words might have flayed Halani had she not heard them before. Instead, she faced her uncle, meeting his angry gaze with a stoic one of her own. "And you should have listened when I told you not to buy that damn draga bone from those two."

"It wouldn't matter if you hadn't decided to play nursemaid for some other mercenary looking to steal it back!" His rising volume drew curious looks from passersby, and Hamod lowered his voice again. "I need to make a few arrangements with Azarion before I leave here. By the time I get back, your 'friend' better be dead or gone, or preferably both."

They stood just outside one of the smaller *qaras* loaned to Hamod during his stay with the Savatar. He motioned for her to follow him inside, away from curious eyes. Before he could harangue her further, Halani cut him off.

"You can't go back. Not while you have the draga bone." His eyes narrowed, and she hurried to explain. "Even if Malachus is searching for it, he likely isn't the only one. Something that rare commands a high price. You know it. Otherwise, you wouldn't have bought it from those two mercenaries. They knew it too. They also knew they had to get as far away from it as they could. If you come back to camp, you're putting yourself and all of us at risk. I could poison Malachus right now or have the men drown him in one of the water barrels. It won't matter. Another hunter will take his place. For all we know, Malachus is a member of a guild of hunters or a family of them who'll want to know why one of their own met with a bad end. That bone brings misfortune to any who don't rightfully possess it." And if the next hunter was as resilient as Malachus, he'd be just as hard to dispatch.

"I rightfully possess it," Hamod snapped. "I bought and paid for it."

Spoken like a true free trader. Halani wanted to punch him for being so muleheaded. "You know what I mean. If you refuse to get rid of the bone, sell it in Domora. You bought it for a song. If you sell it for just double what you paid, you'll make a profit."

A calculating gleam brightened his eyes. "It's worth far more than that."

Halani growled. "Then sell the damn thing and enjoy the windfall!"

He could even sell it to Malachus. Or give it to him. The thought crossed her mind and quickly fled. If the draga bone did belong to him, it was the proper thing to do, but suggesting such a magnanimous gesture went beyond preposterous. Hamod would go from thinking her foolishly charitable to believing her crazed. And she doubted Malachus would respond well to the offer of selling back to him what was already his.

"Domora is the perfect place to resell it," Hamod said, his gaze no longer focused on Halani. "In the Maesor."

Halani blanched. This was not at all what she intended when she suggested the capital as the place to sell the draga bone. Once the summer capital, Domora was now the Empire's only capital, with a large percentage of wealthy citizens, among them the royal court. Draga bone commanded a fair price on the collector's market, enough to make it worth a treasure seeker's trouble to dig pits in out-of-the-way places in the hope of finding some. Hamod was right that the one he'd bought from the mercenaries was worth more. It was infused with magic. To try to sell it on the open market invited an execution, so he'd have to lie and simply tout it as a piece of precious bone dug up from an abandoned mine or plowed up in a farmer's field. Unfortunately in this case, Hamod's ability for intuitively knowing something's worth reared its ugly head, inciting his avarice.

"Are you mad?" This time it was she who had to lower her voice. "Even if you knew how to access the Maesor, do you understand the kind of risk you're taking? People who traffic there don't always come back from their excursions, and when they do, they aren't always the same." Rumors abounded of unfortunates who'd done business in the Maesor and returned very different from when they left, sometimes physically, sometimes mentally, sometimes both.

"Mind your tongue," he snarled. "I've had enough disrespect from you to last me a lifetime." Halani clenched her teeth in an effort to obey. Hamod's hot glare almost set her hair on fire. "Here's how this will work, and you'll abide by it, or I'll shackle you to the back of my wagon and make you walk all the way to Wellspring Holt, and that's after I draw and quarter the man you've lavished all your healing skills on so far."

At her twitching silence, he continued. "I'll take most of the caravan with me to Domora, including Asil." He bared his teeth in warning when a whine of protest escaped her lips. "She's safer with me than she is with you and that hunter, and it isn't as if I'm taking everyone with me when I visit the Maesor. You and a few others will stay behind for now, secure all the supplies and gifts Azarion has given us, and complete any outstanding business.

Take your time and don't be too enthusiastic with helping your patient heal fast. I'll use the opportunity to put distance between us and make a profit from the bone artifact. He's welcome to hunt for the thing in the Maesor all he wants after that, and good luck to him. Understand?" Halani nodded. "Good. When you go back, meet with Kursak to decide who goes with me and who stays. Whoever goes, send them and their wagons here. We'll depart from the Savatar camp when they arrive."

Halani wanted to weep. He didn't take Asil to keep her safe but to punish Halani. To be away from her mother, unable to watch over her . . . she'd age a decade from worry before they met up again in Domora.

Once he was assured of her acquiescence, Hamod's temper subsided but not his disapproval. A coldness settled over him as they finalized their plans. When Halani made to leave and return to the free trader camp, Hamod stopped her at the *qara* door. "Halani."

She turned, hiding her shiver. She and her uncle had always had a contentious relationship, but his reaction to her now was different, darker and unforgiving. In that moment, she realized not all good deeds were necessarily wise ones.

"This isn't a negotiation between us, nor a barter. Make no mistake, it isn't me bending to your will. Your suggestion for selling the draga bone in Domora is a good one and stands to profit all of us. You kept your counsel and didn't tell the others of the transaction between me and those traders, and for that I'm in your debt, but you rode the line of betrayal when you took in the hunter, knowing how I'd feel and the risk such an act exposed me to. Do something like it again, and I will exile you from the caravan. Permanently."

She left the Savatar camp after that, reeling from his threat and speechless with rage. Despite the circumstances in which she now found herself, Halani still didn't regret bringing Malachus to their camp. It was the right thing to do, though what was right wasn't always what was convenient. The philosophy didn't blunt the sharpness of Hamod's threat or the way it cut through her as no other insensitive remark from him ever had. He would force her to leave, separate her from Asil, who wouldn't understand why her daughter had abandoned her.

Kursak met her at the corral, took one look at her face, and pulled her into a brief embrace. "Didn't go well, did it?"

Halani blinked hard to keep back tears. "No," she said, voice unsteady. "Though it went much as you warned. We need to gather as soon as everyone is back from the market. Uncle has plans, and they include all of us."

Still smarting from Hamod's words, she sought out Asil at their wagon. The door was closed and the steps tucked away. During hot days like today, her mother liked to sit on a blanket outside the wagon and either sew or bead as she called out to or chatted with other caravan members. No blanket or Asil held court at the moment.

Halani had a good idea where her mother had gone and made her way to the provender wagon turned sickbed. She stopped at the tableau in front of her. A small crowd had gathered at the wagon, seated in a semicircle around a very pale Malachus, who reclined against a saddle draped in blankets. Shirtless, but with a cover draped across his lap for modesty, he was a scarred vision of ill health and healing wounds. Asil sat on one side of him, Talen on the other, both women alternately offering him food and drink or endlessly adjusting his covering as if the thing tried to creep away on its own. Three more women sat in front of him, two with their young children. All listened with avid expressions as he read from a book opened on his lap.

Five guilty expressions turned toward her when she cleared her throat to signal her approach. Malachus only smiled, gesturing for her to find a seat among his audience. "Welcome, mistress."

Talen, wearing a rueful look, explained. "I know he's still healing, Halani, but it was miserably hot in the wagon, so we helped him outside."

"And took excellent care of me," Malachus said in support of the decision. He held up a cup for her to see. "Sweet water, good conversation, and a cool breeze. I feel much better already."

"Say you aren't mad, Hali." Asil gazed at her wide-eyed. "Malachus said he didn't mind."

Halani sighed. "I'm not mad in the least, Mama. I would have done the same as Talen, and it's much too nice today to sit in a stuffy wagon, even if you're injured or sick."

"You really don't mind?" Talen said in a low voice so the others didn't hear.

"I really don't mind." Halani patted her arm. "I trusted you to know what to do while I was gone, and you did." She clapped her hands and addressed the group. "Off with you. You can all visit with Malachus later. I want to make sure you haven't exhausted him with so much socializing." She caught Talen's arm before the other woman walked away. "Help Kursak spread the word that I've called a meeting this evening just after dark. News from Hamod."

A frown wrinkled Talen's smooth brow. "Was he angry?"

"Furious, though we've settled things between us. It just means a few changes from our original plan for leaving Goban territory."

Once the others left and she was alone with Malachus, he lost the half smile he wore. She knelt in front of him, grateful for the book's distraction to avoid his searching gaze. She'd seen the tome among his belongings, nestled deep in one of the satchels Talen had brought when she retrieved Batraza from the stables. Her fingers itched to touch the pages filled with mysterious symbols. "You can read."

"I can. In six languages." The idea made her thoughts spin. "I assume you cannot?" There was no judgment in his voice, no disdain, just mild curiosity.

Halani shrugged. "No. None of us here can." Though it had always been a fervid wish of hers to learn. The chance to learn one language seemed improbable.

"You always have solemn eyes, Halani. Even more so now. Will you tell this stranger what troubles you or is this a burden to bear alone?"

Halani touched the bandage covering his chest, checking the binding to make sure it hadn't loosened. Her hand, browned by the sun, looked dark against his sickbed pallor. She raised her eyes to stare into his. So many secrets there. A grief as well, old and deep. He drew her to him with the power of a lodestone, had done so since she first crossed his path in the market. That fascination remained, and it had nothing to do with pity for his condition or her role as his nurse. "Alone," she said. "Though I appreciate the offer to listen."

"The offer stands should you change your mind. Not all wounds are of the flesh."

Her vision instantly blurred at his words, and she stood abruptly. "I'll be right back. I want to try a new poultice with some of the herbs I bought at market."

She fled, using the time to wrestle her tears into submission. Malachus was her patient, nothing more, and she refused to humiliate herself in front of him with angry sobs and regrets. She had value in this caravan. Loved the people who were part of it and was loved by them despite Hamod's willingness to cast her aside and bar her from ever seeing Asil should she defy his authority again. To tell Malachus some things, she'd have to tell him everything, so she chose to tell him nothing.

He hadn't moved from his spot, though her mother had returned to keep him company while Halani was gone. "What took so long, Hali?" She grinned at Malachus. "Now that Hali's here, do you need our help to stand and piss?"

Halani groaned and Malachus chuckled. "I'm fine, Asil, though if I need help, you'll be the first person I call for." He turned his attention to Halani. "Should I stand so you can reach the bandages?"

"You're fine as you are." She crouched down beside him, her bowl of poultice next to her, along with a towel to wipe her hands. She gestured for the book. "I'll have Asil return this. I don't think you want to get blood or poultice on the pages."

She worked in silence, carefully peeling away the bandages to inspect his wounds before applying the new poultice and rewrapping them. Asil kept up a steady stream of chatter, skipping from topic to topic without pause like a hummingbird on a cluster of blossoms.

"Whatever you just slathered on me, it smells foul but feels good," Malachus said.

"Stinks like a mule's arse," Asil volunteered. "But Hali always makes the best salves. You'll feel much better in no time, even if no one wants to sit by you."

Leave it to her flinchingly honest mother to lift her mood. Halani burst out laughing, which made Asil laugh as well, her face beaming at having pleased her daughter. In that moment Halani swore to herself she'd adhere to Hamod's edict, do whatever was necessary to avoid banishment and the loss of her mother, even if it meant deceiving a man to aid her uncle's larceny.

Unaware of her dark thoughts, Malachus joined in their amusement, holding a hand to his injured side to ease any twinges his laughter caused. "You're like no other I've ever met, Asil. And that's a good thing." His enigmatic gaze settled on Halani. "Like your daughter. Unique. Memorable."

Halani blushed at the unexpected compliment. She covered her embarrassment by sending her mother back to their wagon to return her supplies and bring a basket so she could gather laundry. Once Asil departed, she checked the knots she'd tied to keep Malachus's bandages in place. "Had I not dug the broadheads out of you myself, I'd say these wounds were older than they are."

"There is magic in your herbs," he said.

There was indeed, but not to this extent. "Hardly, and I'll thank you not to say that too loud. We can't stay here forever, and I don't fancy being burned on a pyre or hanged just because I harvested a potent patch of feverfew." He was a terrible distraction, scattering her thoughts with compliments. She stood abruptly and stepped away, putting some much-needed distance between them.

He frowned. "Are the people of the Empire such zealots about sorcery?"

Halani paused in straightening his blankets to give him a puzzled look. "You haven't been long in these lands, have you?"

"Less than a month, though I'm not ignorant of its edicts and laws. Sorcery is outlawed, punishable by death, but so is horse thieving and swiving a justiciar's wife, yet both of those happen regularly and are rarely penalized. Why would this be different?"

It was a legitimate question, one Halani wouldn't mind knowing the answer to herself. "Maybe because a horse thief and the lover of a justiciar's wife aren't considered threats to the Empire.

Sorcery is, at least to Empress Dalvila, who isn't known for her mercy. I don't possess magic, nor do I practice it," she lied through her teeth.

The long side-eye he bestowed on her made her stiffen. "Is that so?"

She refused to be baited into defending her claim, and changed the subject. "If you feel well enough this evening, you're welcome to join us at the communal fire for supper and a story." She tried not to get her hopes up that he might offer to read aloud again. He had a fine voice for it.

"An invitation I'd be a fool to refuse," he said. "Asil says you're a skilled storyteller."

"My mother likes to praise everything about me, which is lovely, but treat it for what it is—the love of a parent for a child."

One black eyebrow slid upward. "Your mother just said I smelled like the arse end of a mule, and no one will sit by me. Her honesty is, without question, lacking delicacy or partiality. If she says something, it's because she believes it. She says you tell the best stories. I believe her and wish to hear them for myself."

Halani stared at him. She had incurred her uncle's wrath for him, risked banishment, and questioned her own judgment in the decisions she'd made so far where he was concerned. His words reminded her why he fascinated her so. No one outside their caravan had ever viewed Asil the way Malachus did, and even then that view differed from theirs. Differed from hers. He was patient with Asil, kind, and most stunning of all, respectful. He recognized the child living within the woman's body and still treated her observations with the consideration reserved for an adult. He had called both mother and daughter unique. Despite her efforts to remain aloof, Halani began to think him extraordinary.

"I promise I'll sit by you if no one else does, no matter how horrid you smell," she said in her most solemn tones.

Malachus laughed. "Then I'll be sure to save you a place."

When Asil returned, Halani left him to attend to the many tasks she'd put off to visit Hamod in the Savatar encampment. When word got out that Malachus might join their group to share food and hear the nightly story, several people volunteered to keep him company, despite Asil's flat assertion that he smelled bad. Halani suspected she'd have to fight for a seat next to him.

The meeting she'd called prior to their evening meal promised a flurry of questions and protests, and it fulfilled that promise. Halani relayed Hamod's instructions for splitting the camp but kept his secret regarding the sale of the draga bone.

"I still don't understand the hurry," Kursak said. "Trading in the towns runs heavy the entire summer, and we're still in the beginning of it. It won't take that long to reach Domora from here. There's no need to split the camp while we finish our trading here, buy more carts for the new goods Azarion gave us." He gave a brief bow in the general direction of the Savatar camp, at which the others cheered. "There's decent wild pasture for the livestock, and the weather's been more or less agreeable."

"Malachus is too injured to make the trip with us," she said, bracing herself for the response to that statement.

"Why does that matter?" Marata frowned. "He's lucky we didn't just leave him in the field with the other two. What if we were in a hurry? Are we supposed to sit here and twiddle our thumbs until we can have the provender wagon back? Dump Malachus at a boardinghouse or brothel in the nearest town. He's a fat enough purse to cover any care they give him. Besides, I don't like the idea of someone cursed among us. What if it rubs off on one of us?"

His question elicited grumbles of agreement, though fewer than Halani expected. She'd prepared beforehand for this and been coached by Hamod on how to answer a question like Kursak's. "How many times have we all 'visited' a barrow, knowing there was probably a basket full of protection curses laid upon it? And now suddenly you're frightened of one?" The cook's face pinkened as a sheepish expression chased away his frown. "He's no danger to us, and except for that one moment, which was nothing more than a bit of smoke and a lot of unnecessary panic from all of us, he's been a model patient and guest."

There were more grumbles but no counterarguments put forth. Satisfied she'd cut the legs out from under Marata's protests, Halani turned to Kursak. "If we leave earlier than the other merchants, we won't have the same competition in selling our wares than if we left when everyone else did. Uncle will take half the caravan and travel ahead with those goods most desired and earn the biggest profit. The remaining half will follow with the supplies we plan to keep for ourselves."

"No one has a nose for making the best profit like Hamod," Marata said.

Kursak nodded. "Fair enough. We'll decide who goes with Hamod and who stays with me." He nodded toward the place where the provender wagon was parked. "I'm assuming since you're his nurse, you'll be traveling with me."

"Aye, though Mama will go with Uncle." Halani's throat closed up. She'd made sure Asil wasn't here to protest, tasking her with keeping Malachus company.

Surprised looks greeted her statement, and Kursak's scrutiny made her squirm inside. "Are you sure about that, Halani? She'll throw a fit and wonder why you're sending her away."

"I'll talk to her. No one say anything to her until I get a chance to speak with her about it." An unpleasant task requiring a delicacy Halani wasn't sure she possessed. She'd wait until tomorrow to approach Asil. With any luck and the blessings of the gods, her mother wouldn't pitch a tantrum and would be agreeable to leaving not only her daughter but her new favorite friend.

Later, when the cool breeze eased the day's heat and swept away the clouds of biting midges, Halani paid a visit to Malachus's mare. Batraza whickered a greeting, her ears swiveling forward when Halani held out her offering of a carrot. It hadn't taken long for the camp to realize that while the other horses refused to tolerate her presence in the corral with them, she didn't require staking or hobbling to keep from wandering. It was as if she sensed her master's presence nearby and chose to stay close.

She crunched contentedly on the carrot while Halani petted her neck and ruffled her mane.

"You've made a friend of her forever. Carrots are her favorite food."

Halani turned as Malachus approached, noting how he still favored his side and put most of his weight on his uninjured leg.

"I pilfered them from Marata's stores," she admitted, taking another carrot from her apron pocket to give to the mare. "Say nothing or I'll never hear the end of it."

Malachus chuckled, a melodious sound that sent a pleasurable tingle down Halani's arms. "And what would Marata say if he knew?"

Halani stroked Batraza's nose. "That we'll all starve now and be forced to eat your horse. And of course he'll blame it on me." She laughed when both Malachus and the mare snorted at the same time.

"If your camp is one carrot away from starvation, Batraza here would be in the stewpot." Malachus ran a hand down the mare's withers, gliding around Halani's hand. "Your cook has a flair for the dramatic."

Before Halani had taken on the role of their band's principal storyteller, Marata had been the one who entertained them after supper with tales fantastic, tragic, humorous, and glorious. Halani had learned them all from him, a legacy he'd passed on to her and encouraged over the years.

She'd been too busy looking after Malachus to treat the camp to her usual nightly storytelling, leaving the task to Marata. Tonight, if Malachus didn't need her, she'd resume that duty.

"Is all well with you and your folk?" He searched her face with a steady gaze. "You still wear a troubled look."

The plan to split the camp wasn't a secret. The impetus for doing so was, and Halani kept that between her and Hamod. "The Savatar *ataman* was very generous to us for bringing Gilene here." They were still sorting through the piles of gifts. "We have more goods now than wagons to transport them. A lot of what we bought in the Goban market will be resold within Empire borders. Selling for a profit is often a matter of timing. Half of the camp will leave tomorrow for the capital, Domora. The other half will stay here with the supplies we keep, buy a couple more wagons and mules, and meet the others later."

A stillness settled over him. "And you?" he said. "Do you leave first or stay with the second group?"

Butterfly wings fluttered in her belly. Halani ignored them, admonishing herself for even recognizing their presence. "You needn't be concerned. I'm staying to see you healed enough to continue wherever your journey takes you."

Somehow his ink-dark eyes managed to turn even blacker. "I'm glad you're staying. I enjoy your company, Halani of the Lightning, and hope to prolong it."

Butterfly wings turned to bird wings, flapping about her insides, beating against her rib cage. She'd never been one to flirt with or swoon over a man. The other women in the caravan always said she was too guarded, with a gaze that peeled back more layers than a would-be suitor cared to reveal.

This man didn't court her, but he didn't retreat under her scrutiny. He was reserved and enigmatic, a mystery that invited exploration and fascinated her a little more each day, even while she remained wary of him. She was certain he was somehow connected to the draga bone. Most of all, he made her mother laugh.

"Then you're in luck," she said. "You're stuck with me—and the pitchers of willow-bark tea I still expect you to drink."

She bit back a pleased smile when later he proclaimed himself fit enough to join their group for supper. Asil, giddy as a bride on her bonding day, danced in a circle in front of him, eliciting a chuckle from him and a promise that he'd sit by her through the meal and, if he still felt up to it, the storytelling.

Most welcomed his addition to their gathering with smiles and inquiries into his health. A few eyed him suspiciously, including Marata.

The cook leaned down as he filled the plates Halani held out to him from the large pan positioned over the coals. "He doesn't need to be here, Halani. He's an outsider."

"But not an outcast," she countered. "Would you have it known that Hamod's folk ignore the rules of hospitality and shun their guests?"

"I like him." Talen circled the fire, bearing a tray filled with cups of hot tea to pass out among the group. "He's polite to all of us who actually talk to him, and is pretty to look at." She winked at her scowling husband.

Supper that night was an even livelier affair than usual, spurred on by Asil's unabashed excitement over Malachus's presence and his repeated assurances that he intended to stay for the storytelling he'd heard so much about from her.

"What do you want to hear?" Halani asked the crowd ringing the communal fire. She sighed inwardly when a chorus of voices rose in one refrain. "The Sun Maiden!"

Of the hundreds of stories to be shared, that one was by far the most popular and the one she most disliked telling. Celebrating the heroism of a man who slew so majestic a creature as a draga simply for fame and fortune never sat well with her. She glanced at Malachus sitting at the perimeter of their circle, just at the edge of the firelight's reach. Asil sat next to him, face beaming with a child's delight.

Malachus, on the other hand, no longer wore a jovial look. His grim expression made her wonder what had caused the sudden change in mood.

Over the years, Halani had learned how to tell the story of the draga Golnar and the Empire hero Kansi Yuv so that it was her audience who did most of the telling, with strategic guidance from her. The free traders recited the major scenes of the tale: how the brave Kansi Yuv lured the greedy Golnar into a narrow ravine where a beautiful golden statue called the Sun Maiden waited. A draga's lust for treasure, especially gold, was its weakness, and Golnar couldn't resist the temptation to possess the bright statue.

"It was the monster's downfall," Halani proclaimed, lowering her voice to signal the story's impending climax. "For Kansi Yuv and his brave men waited with their ballistae and nets, and then . . ." She paused for effect, enough to coax the enraptured crowd to fill in the silence.

"Golnar crept into the ravine, ready to steal the Sun Maiden," Asil called out. Others nodded as if she spoke a sacred truth.

Halani spared her mother a smile before glancing at Malachus.

The guarded expression was gone, replaced by one of withering contempt. Her stomach somersaulted at the sight, and though she told a story familiar to many and loved by most, a wave of shame purled over her, leaving her in a cold sweat.

Despite her mortification, she finished the tale with help from the crowd, who eagerly described Golnar's attempt to steal the Sun Maiden, his death from one of the giant arrows fired from Kansi Yuv's ballista, the point slamming through the draga's natural scale armor and into the great heart. Revulsion joined the contempt stamped on Malachus's pale features at the recitation of Golnar's skinning and dismemberment.

Halani almost wept in relief when the story was done. Declining to tell another one, she turned the task over to Marata.

Malachus slowly gained his feet, waving off Asil's attempt to help. She captured his hand for a moment to give it a squeeze. He returned the gesture, then disappeared into the shadows beyond the firelight's reach. No one noticed when Halani skirted the circle in the opposite direction only to drift away and double back toward the path she guessed her quarry had taken.

She found him just outside camp, alone, face raised to the sky as he contemplated the gibbous moon gilding his silhouette in silver. The wild rye rustled against her skirts as she drew closer to him.

"Had your fill of telling stories of slaughter, Halani?" he asked without turning around. His voice was soft, flat.

"You didn't like the tale?" Her question was rhetorical. His expression had clearly conveyed his opinion.

"I hated it." The loathing in those words could have curdled milk.

Halani had told the story so many times over the years, she knew it by rote and could tell it in her sleep. Always, it had drawn praise from audiences, whether they were her own camp folk or the denizens of some town where they sometimes stopped to trade and earn extra coin by entertaining people in the town square or the public houses. This was the first time she'd ever faced such outright revulsion. The hot fever of embarrassment made her ears burn.

"I'm very sorry you didn't like the storytelling. I know you were expecting something better after listening to Mama's boasts."

Her prayers that he'd keep his back to her went unanswered when he pivoted. He didn't answer immediately, and with the moon's luminescence now backlighting him, his expression remained hidden in the shadows. "I didn't say I hated your storytelling, only the story you told."

Relieved but confused, Halani frowned. "Have you not heard the story of Golnar and Kansi Yuv before?"

"Oh, I know the story, just not as you told it," he said in a voice heavy with disdain. "The version familiar to me is very different from yours."

She took a step closer. "How so?" It was just a story, more fable than real. His reaction to it seemed out of proportion.

Though she still couldn't make out his features, she sensed his grim regard. "Beyond the fact that your version is a cauldron of lies stewed with a handful of half-truths?" His sharp tone dulled a fraction at her surprised inhalation. "Kansi Yuv." He virtually spat the name as if he'd bitten into something rotten. "The great hero was a liar, a butcher, and a coward whose name was bought with the blood of betrayal." He turned a little, presenting his profile just enough for her to view the strong arch of his nose and downward curve of his compressed lips. He stared at the ground for a moment before raising his head, and a glimmer of moonlight caught in his eyes, revealing a hatred fermented by time. "You've a true talent for weaving a riveting tale, Halani. Don't waste it on a man unworthy of the breath you spend in telling it."

CHAPTER ELEVEN

Moonlight was as kind to Halani as sunlight was, emphasizing the elegant lines of her face. An attractive woman made beautiful by the glimpses of her soul, which sometimes revealed itself in her eyes. A compassionate woman who had just entertained a crowd with a story so revolting it twisted his guts into knots.

He'd hoped she wouldn't follow him here, knowing she'd want an explanation for his reaction. He hadn't missed the stricken look in her eyes. For a moment, he wished desperately for a pipe and tobacco, so the mindless draw and exhalation of smoke could soothe the beast once more awakened inside him.

Halani had simply told a history she'd learned from generations before her. Its inaccuracy wasn't her fault. "Forgive me," he said. "You are undeserving of my anger."

"It's an ugly story when you take it apart. Is the version I told so different from the one you learned? Was Golnar the hero and Kansi Yuv the villain?"

She didn't ask outright why he'd reacted as if personally offended or even what spurred his admonishment that she not waste a breath on Kansi Yuv.

He hedged his answer. "Remember, this isn't my country. Our tales might be similar or not, some with the same characters but assigned other roles with different outcomes."

"And those that are altered distress you this much each time?"

A sharp bark of laughter escaped him. "No, just that one." He held up a finger to forestall her inevitable request. "I've no intention of telling you the tale I know. Not tonight anyway." He still seethed over the warped version that glorified a butcher like Kansi Yuv. Had the man not died long ago, Malachus would have welcomed the opportunity to gut him with his bare hands.

"Then maybe before you leave us." Halani crossed her arms, from either cold or self-consciousness. "I apologize for the story. It was never my intention to upset you."

Shot full of arrows and almost dying wasn't exactly a blessing, but Malachus thought it a twisted sort of luck. The mother-bond and the lightning might have led him to Halani, but it was the attack and her mercy that gave him the opportunity to learn more about her. As a draga in human guise, he found human women physically attractive and had indulged in brief relationships with a few. None had beguiled him the way this woman did.

He grasped one of her wrists to ease her arm straight before sliding his hand down to entwine his fingers with hers. She possessed small hands, capable of making him nearly bite through the prayer stick in agony and of soothing him to sleep with a caress across his brow. "You don't owe me an apology. My reaction is solely my darkness to shoulder. The only wrongdoing here belongs to history and its memory of someone long dead." He squeezed her fingers for emphasis before letting go.

Halani's gaze was soft, her eyes reflecting moonlight. "I'll leave you to your thoughts, then. Should you need anything during the night or suffer pain, don't hesitate to come to our wagon. Mama and I are both light sleepers. We'll hear a tap on the door. Good night."

She turned away, stopping when he called out to her. "Golnar was a female draga," he said. "Her flight into that ravine was one of rescue, not thievery. Kansi Yuv knew that."

Halani spun on her heel to face him once more, eyes wide, surprised. "Golnar was female?" Numerous questions filled her eyes, the slip and change in her perception of a tale where the actions of the hero suddenly came into question and became those of the villain.

"I promise to tell you soon."

He didn't tease on purpose and would have said more if the smoldering anger inside him didn't threaten to flare again and turn the draga restless. The last thing he needed was to lose control of that emotion while giving Halani the truth about Kansi Yuv and Golnar and end up immolating himself in front of her.

Her lithe form folded into the shadows cast by the wagons before disappearing into the darkness where the moon's light didn't reach. The creak of steps under footfalls and the soft click of a door closing told him she'd entered her wagon to join her mother.

He remained outside the camp as people drifted to their wagons to find their beds, and someone smothered the communal fire. Wolves howled in the distance, and the wind whispered secrets in a language only the grasses understood.

The moonlit landscape no longer appealed to him, and he made his way to the provender wagon to sleep a few hours.

The door of Halani and Asil's wagon bore intricate carvings created by a skilled hand. In the daylight, those carvings were awash in bright colors, muted now to shades of gray. Malachus paused to study them. They were runes, employed both as decoration and as wards.

Though he couldn't translate them, he recognized their function. Wards against evil, sickness, and nightmares. Others remained a mystery, as fascinating and enigmatic as the mother and daughter who slept behind the safety of their shield.

He walked past the wagon, gliding his hand over the rails and boards, the inset of the small window. Malachus sensed a charged stillness from inside, as if someone listened to him outside. He smiled and pressed the flat of his hand to the wagon's surface. "Sweet dreams, Halani of the Lightning," he said in a soft voice.

An equally hushed voice carried to him through the open window. "A fair moon above you, Malachus."

He spent the remainder of the night wide-awake in the provender wagon that had become his home while he convalesced. The mother-bond still called to him, though its draw remained murky. Despite the imperative to retrieve it, Malachus didn't find any joy in his impending departure.

He fell asleep close to dawn and woke to a camp swarming like a disturbed beehive. Leaning against the wagon's door frame, he watched as the ring in which the wagons were parked only hours earlier broke apart.

Several free traders led ox, horse, and mule teams to those wagons pulled away from the fractured circle. A few were already harnessed and in their traces. Those people not busy with the teams carried or rolled barrels and crates across the inner ring for loading into the wagons or strapping atop the roofs and flat hitches tucked under the doors with the steps. Malachus spotted Halani chasing a trio of sheep who'd escaped their pen. A sheepdog worked opposite her to herd the animals back to the enclosure.

Kursak stood amid the eddy and swirl of animals and humanity, barking instructions and giving orders with the ease of long practice.

It was orderly chaos, and Malachus chose to observe from his perch and stay out of the way.

Halani's gaze met his. She waved, shooed the last escapee sheep back into the pen, and jogged toward him, skirting the children, dogs, and squawking chickens in her path. She wore a bright smile in contrast to the tired crescents of shadows under her eyes. "How are you feeling this morning? Give me a moment to gather my things from my wagon, and I'll check your wounds."

He gestured to all the activity behind her. "Splitting the camp already?"

"Starting to." She darted away before he could stop her but returned soon enough, arms filled with a basket, bowl, and pitcher. She climbed the steps and joined him inside the wagon.

The day was still young and the sun not yet so harsh. The wagon's interior was cool and dim. Malachus stood this time as Halani peeled back his bandages for her regular inspection.

"Stand closer to the door," she said. "Morning light is better than lamplight for me to see how you look."

He did as she instructed, using one arm to brace himself against the wall as she unwound bandages and set them aside. Her cool hands drifted across his skin. A shiver shot down his spine, and he jerked a little when her fingertips glided along the edges of sore flesh at the wound on his hip, creating a ticklish pain that was almost erotic.

Behind him, Halani retreated before setting her hand on him once more, this time just above the wound. "I'm sorry. I didn't mean to hurt you."

"It didn't hurt," he replied in guttural tones.

She went still, a bird on a limb watching as a hunter passed beneath the tree. Where moments before the wagon offered peaceful solace, it now breathed with a growing tension. Malachus turned his head for a glimpse of his quiet companion. Her touch was an ember now, growing ever hotter as the blood tumbled fast through his veins directly to his groin. This wasn't earth magic that seduced him, but the sorcery of a compassionate woman who made him believe not all of humanity was beyond redemption. Too injured to do more than wish for a greater intimacy, Malachus succumbed to temptation and leaned into her. He expected Halani to move back, maintaining the slim distance between them. She didn't, and for a moment her breasts pressed against him while her other hand flattened along his ribs. Her breath whispered across his skin in short gusts. Silence hung thick in the air, time a motionless entity that waited for one of them to move or speak. Malachus dared not twitch a muscle for fear of ending the moment.

Halani lowered her hands and stepped away, severing the ephemeral connection between them. "Face me, please, so I can see the wound on your chest." Her voice was cool, her features stoic, when he turned and met her gaze. Her gray eyes were still soft, still warm, but oceans of secrets lay behind their misty color. Her glance flitted down, noted his erection, and flitted away. Pale pink stained her cheekbones, but her hands were steady as she inspected his chest wound.

She'd seen him naked several times, treating his nudity no differently than his clothed form. Malachus guessed that as a healer, Halani had seen more than her fair share of bare backsides and fronts as well in both men and women. It was not his lack of clothing that caused her to blush.

"Should I wear a blanket or tunic?"

Her wry look told him what she thought of the question and why he asked it. "Only if you're uncomfortable unclothed."

"I am not."

"Then you don't need a covering." She bent closer to his side, eyeing the arrow wound there with a worried frown. "You'll need another poultice pack and a new bandage. This one isn't looking as well as the others."

The tension between them eased, though Malachus wasn't

convinced that was a good thing. Halani seemed far more unaffected by his proximity than he was by hers. She instructed him to remain where he was while she mixed another salve, gathered the old bandages in a pile for laundering, and laid new ones out for wrapping. She talked while she worked, nothing in her tone to indicate how her breath had stuttered moments earlier.

"Ignore the commotion outside if you can," she told him before gently applying more of the numbing salve to his wounds. "Breaking camp, even just half of it, is always a loud affair."

"Am I the reason you're in the second group to leave, or is it just a bit of luck for me that you'll stay for other obligations?" he asked.

She rose, bowl in hand, and scooped out a small amount of the salve to place on his injury. "I'm staying to help man the camp while others take care of the market stall. It just so happens I can do the first and still play nurse to you." Her mouth turned down. "My mother will travel with the first group. She'll want to see you before she leaves."

That was odd. From what he'd seen, Halani and Asil were nearly inseparable, with Halani displaying a ferocious protectiveness toward her mother. He found it hard to believe she'd willingly let Asil out of her sight for long. "Why can't she stay with you?"

"You've never seen my mother guarding a goods table. She looks small and grandmotherly, but she has a hawk's eye when it comes to spotting cutpurses, and she's fast. I once saw her strip two thieves running in opposite directions after they pilfered off our table. She picked one of their pockets while she was at it. She's even earned a reputation in Wellspring Holt. The thieves there don't bother trying to steal from us if they see her watching our stall. The group leaving today will be trading in other markets.

The rest of us will pack up what's left behind. Mama's skills aren't needed here now."

A reasonable explanation, but Malachus heard the undercurrent she tried to hide in her casual tone. He stayed silent until she finished with his new bandages and helped him shoulder on a long tunic she'd borrowed from one of the free trader men. The garment had been sewn for a shorter man of greater girth, and it swallowed him in its folds while the hem brushed his knees instead of his calves. Halani stood before him, sliding the wooden buttons sewn down the tunic's front panel through loops to hold it closed.

Malachus rested a finger under her chin and tilted her face up to his. "You will miss your mother and worry until you see her again."

Her eyelids lowered, hiding the emotion in her gaze but not the tears that slid past her lashes to trickle down her cheeks. "Yes."

What must it be like to be loved this way? So devotedly that the person you parted with cried at your absence before you even left? He had known affection in his life, sincere if distant. This was something else, something he had no experience of. In that moment, he wished he did.

Malachus wiped her tears with his thumb, smearing a track of moisture over her cheekbone. She was lovely, even in her sorrow, and the urge to comfort her overwhelmed him. He bent and kissed her forehead, traveling from the space between her eyebrows to her left temple, where fine strands of her hair lay against her head. He retraced his path, lips brushing her right temple, lingering there before he kissed her damp cheek, then her nose and her other cheek. She tasted of salt and smelled of the herbs she'd mixed into the poultice layered under his bandages. He dared not kiss her mouth. If he did, he wouldn't stop. She didn't move, accepting his caresses with a faint sigh and the curl of her fingers in his tunic.

He straightened, not realizing until then that his hands had settled on her hips, stroking them through her clothing. "Don't fret, Halani. You'll see her again soon."

She opened her eyes and gave him a sheepish smile. "I'm far too old to be crying for my mother."

"Never let that trouble you. I cried oceans of tears for mine." Malachus prayed that whatever gods Halani and Asil worshipped, they'd be far more merciful to Asil than his mother's had been.

Halani regarded him with a measuring look. "You have a gift for knowing what to say and make it fit for that moment, though I have a hard time imagining you crying for your mother."

He gave a light snort. "I didn't say I did it as an adult." His lamentations didn't manifest as tears now but as rage. Buried deep and long-lasting.

She stepped away from his loose embrace, wiped her eyes, and bent to gather up her supplies and the old bandages. "Breakfast is catch-as-catch-can. One of us will bring you something to eat soon. Likely last night's leftover bread and some cheese. Marata and Talen are leaving with the first group, so he's dismantled his kitchen. Pray for all of us that it won't be Passarin who volunteers to take up Marata's duties. One pot of his stew can annihilate an enemy army."

Malachus wondered how many people of those remaining would weep copious tears as Marata waved goodbye to them from his wagon. Even when his stomach balked at anything heavier than a broth, he'd enjoyed the free trader cook's fare.

Unwilling to sit idly by while everyone else worked and sweated under the summer sun, he abandoned the stifling tunic and donned his own garb, which someone had laundered for him. The shirt didn't bother him; the trousers were another matter. He tied the drawstring in the waist so that they rested lower on his torso, beneath the bandages circling his middle. It didn't stop the material from chafing his injured hip, enough so that even the medicated padding didn't offer protection. Undaunted, Malachus used one of his smaller knives to split part of the seam where the garment rubbed the hardest. It looked odd but no worse than moving about camp swaddled in blankets or borrowed tunics too large for him.

Putting on shoes without help presented an even greater challenge. Slipping them onto his feet was nothing; bending over to strap them to his calves almost made him pass out from the pain. Perspiring and queasy, he finally left the wagon's confines, dressed, shod, and praying he didn't vomit.

Asil spotted him first and skipped to his side. "You're dressed! Who helped you?"

He imagined Halani saying the exact same thing but in a voice quite different from Asil's cheery one. She'd inevitably pin his ears back when she saw him. "I managed alone. I didn't want to miss seeing you before you left with the others."

Her bright grin dimmed, then faded altogether. "I wasn't going to leave without saying goodbye. You're my friend. Friends tell each other hello and goodbye."

There was something about Asil's simple wisdoms that went straight to the heart of every matter. It had been a privilege to meet this odd woman with the wizened face and childlike ways. He wouldn't see her again, but he'd remember her for all the days remaining to him.

"We're most definitely friends," he said. "And friends help each other. What can I do to help you for your trip?"

She chewed on her lower lip for a moment, considering his offer. "I've been too busy to pack any of my things from our wagon.

You can help me there." Her gaze traveled over him. "Unless you feel poorly. I don't want Halani mad at me if you aren't supposed to work."

"If she questions us, I'll tell her it was my idea, and I insisted on being given a task."

The wagon Asil shared with Halani was much more comfortable than the provender wagon he slept in. Two beds took up one end of the wagon, one on the floor, the other above it built on a platform, both layered in colorful blankets and bolsters that turned the top bed into a couch on which one could sit and entertain. Cupboards and locker seats built into the walls on the long sides of the wagon served as storage. Rugs covered the floor, their pile plush under his bare feet—something Asil insisted on before he entered the abode.

"Keeps things clean in here," she said. "Or we'd be beating carpets every day until our arms fell off."

Even the arched ceiling didn't escape decoration. Someone had painted a mural on the tongue-and-groove matchboards between the support frames, their detail highlighted by the sunlight spilling through the open clerestory windows set high into the walls of the wagon's long sides.

The interior reminded him of a berth on a ship, where every bit of space served a function.

Asil snatched a cushion from the upper bed and plopped it down on one of the locker seats. "You can sit here and help me fill my traveling chest."

Though Halani had been distressed at the upcoming separation from her mother, Asil seemed unbothered by it. She talked with hardly a pause between sentences as she and Malachus emptied one chest of possessions into another bigger one and added more Asil insisted she needed for the journey. Most of the items were clothes and grooming tools, hair scarves and her own personal apothecary chest of favorite herbals and elixirs.

A ragged doll sewn from scraps of fabric and bits of rope joined the items. Asil placed it carefully atop the pile, pausing to pet it with reverent hands. The doll had seen better days, its rag dress stained, the rope hair speckled with tiny bits of detritus. Malachus recognized a well-loved toy when he saw one. This doll had been played with so much, it threatened to fall apart.

Asil stared at the doll for a moment, features creased as if she wrestled with some grave, life-altering decision. She turned suddenly, presenting the poppet to Malachus. "Would you like to hold Dove?"

Her unexpected gesture surprised him. No one with eyes could mistake how much she treasured the doll, and he was hesitant to touch it, fearful that if he did so, the fragile thing would disintegrate in his hands. "I'm afraid I'll break her."

"It's all right if you do. I've had to sew her legs and arms back on several times, and her head twice." She thrust the doll at him. "Go ahead."

He took it gingerly. "Why did you name her Dove?"

"Because Hali has eyes like dove's wings. She made this doll for me when she was small and we played together. I made one for her, too. It looked like me. She made this one to look like her."

Truly terrified now that he'd do something to accidentally destroy the poppet, Malachus carefully handed it back to Asil, who gave the rope hair a quick kiss before setting it back in the chest. "It's a very fitting name," he said. "Halani does have eyes the color of a dove's wings." And skin like a silk ribbon. He shoved away the thought and the images it called to mind.

Asil closed the chest lid, securing the latch before perching atop it. "If I take the doll, it will be like having her with me until the real Hali meets us in Domora."

He had no reply worthy of such a sentiment. The bond between her and Halani was the stuff of childhood dreams, though in this relationship, the parent had assumed the role of the child and vice versa. It might not work for every mother and daughter, but for this pair it did, and Malachus found it a wondrous thing to behold.

"Does Halani still have the doll you made for her?"

She nodded and pointed to another chest tucked away in the corner. "She doesn't play with it anymore. She says it's too valuable now, though I don't think she'd get half a *belsha* for it if she tried to sell it."

Malachus sighed. Spoken like a true trader. "There's value in things all the *belshas* in the world can't buy. Your daughter's right. Your dolls are beyond price."

Asil shrugged. "She's too old to play with a poppet anyway. It's books now. I'd buy her one in Domora, but Hamod wouldn't like it. He'd say it's a waste of good coin."

Malachus frowned. While he had yet to meet the absentee wagon master, he'd overheard enough conversation about him to gain the impression that he was a difficult man at the best of times. Asil's comment only lowered his opinion. Books were like beloved poppets, their value immeasurable and never a waste of money. He wondered if Hamod would have changed his opinion had he seen the small crowd gathered around Malachus the day before as he read to them from one of the two books he had with him. The enthralled faces staring back at him held the same reverence he'd just witnessed in Asil's handling of her doll.

An idea took shape in his mind, a way he might repay Halani

for her care and something she could share with everyone else in the caravan once he was gone. "Halani said she can't read."

"She can't, but she likes books. Likes to hold them and turn the pages."

It made sense that none of the free traders were literate. The cost of a book limited the ability to read to those wealthy enough to afford one and a tutor to teach them. Malachus's extensive literacy was a rarity, one of many benefits he'd reaped as a foster with the Sovatin monks, who'd raised him in a society devoted to learning and whose god was education.

He remembered his first sight of Halani in the market, standing in front of the bookbinder's stall, a yearning gracing her features as she lingered under the merchant's narrow gaze to admire one of the books.

"Maybe you can read to her while you're here," Asil suggested.

Or teach her to read. If Halani was willing to learn, he could give her a few lessons before he was healed enough to continue his search for the mother-bond. A rudimentary education at best, but with that and maybe a book to help her, she'd find it useful in the future and remember him fondly when they parted ways.

The idea continually turned over in his mind as he helped Asil pack the rest of her essentials. While she refused to let him carry her chest for her, she did allow him to share the burden, and the two hefted it across the campground toward the wagon she pointed to as one she'd travel in for the journey to the Kraelian territories.

"What are you doing?"

They halted together at the question and turned in tandem to face Halani.

Arms akimbo, features set in grim disapproval, she eyed the chest suspended between them before turning a hard stare first on her wide-eyed mother and then on Malachus. She didn't wait for either of them to answer her before firing off another question. "And why are you wearing clothes?"

Malachus glanced at Asil, who returned it with one that told him he was on his own. He offered Halani a conciliatory smile. "I volunteered to help Asil. Doing so meant wearing something less awkward than a blanket or that tunic I borrowed." He showed her the cut he'd made in the trousers seam. "I made adjustments." Fortunately, he'd had Asil to help him with his shoes the second time.

"Asil!"

Kursak's shout startled the woman so that she jumped, yanking hard on the chest. The movement jerked Malachus's arm, which in turn tightened his chest muscles. He hissed as a shard of pain lanced his torso from collarbone to abdomen.

Halani leapt forward, her hand wrapping around his to help with the chest. "Mama, be careful!"

"Asil!" Kursak yelled a second time. "Bring the chest here."

Overwhelmed by orders shouted from two sides, Asil dropped her side of the chest and started to cry.

Abandoning Malachus, Halani enfolded her mother in an embrace. She raised a hand to Kursak, signaling him to stop. The wagon master leapt off the wagon's half-filled bed and joined them. He stood a little behind the two women. "Sorry, Asil," he said in a soft voice. "I didn't mean to upset you."

"It wasn't you, it was me," Halani replied. "Can you take her things from Malachus? I'll see to Mama and then him. I'm afraid he might have split one of his wounds."

"I'm well," Malachus told Kursak. "Just a twinge. I'm not so injured that I can't put a box of frocks and hair combs into a wagon by myself." There was a lot more in the chest than that, but he'd done the one thing he'd tried to avoid—made a nuisance of himself.

Kursak bent to take the chest. "No arguments. Hand it over. I learned a long time ago not to raise Halani's hackles if I can help it."

Freed of his burden, Malachus chose to leave mother and daughter alone, surreptitiously watching as Halani patted her mother's hair and dried her tears. She then kissed Asil's forehead, told her something that made Asil grin, and sent her to join Kursak, who was rearranging casks, pallets, and the problematic chest.

Malachus braced himself when Halani strode toward him. "You," she said, pointing a finger, "are trying to heal from life-threatening injuries. Stop undoing all my hard work."

He raised his hands in surrender. "Forgive me. Guilt got the best of me. Boredom as well. Is Asil better now?"

She gave him a knowing look from the corner of her eye. "Nice attempt at diverting me. Mama is fine, probably better than you. Now, back to the provender wagon with you so I can see what damage you've done."

After a steady stream of grumbling and admonishments, she pronounced him unharmed by his efforts. "If you wish to help," she said, "find a way to distract the children. They get underfoot in all the excitement. One of the mules almost stepped on Focana's toddler, and Seydom caught two of the boys trying to stow away in the grain wagon."

Malachus had no experience with children, unless one counted the childlike Asil. He hadn't a clue how one might go about distracting them. Then he recalled the expressions on a few of their faces as they sat with their mothers while he read.

He pointed to the single tree a short walk from the camp, its wide, leafy limbs providing ample shade. "Send them there. I'll meet them once I get a book from the wagon. I can't promise I can keep their attention long, but I'll try."

"You're going to read to them." She said it as if he'd just promised to teach them how to fly, wonder and yearning in her voice.

"Yes." Her reaction convinced him even more that offering to teach her how to read was his best idea. He chose not to mention it then, preferring to wait until things had settled in the camp and he had more time to speak with her.

Keeping small children focused on a single thing for longer than a breath proved more of a challenge than Malachus anticipated, but he managed the deed, employing some of the storytelling techniques he'd seen Halani and Marata use on the crowd. The children were as interested in the book itself as in what was in it, and Malachus held his breath more than a few times as grubby hands carefully turned the book upside down, flipped the pages, and traced the inked words inside. He breathed a sigh of relief when one of the free trader women came to rescue him.

She gathered the children with a practiced hand, unfazed as they dashed and danced around her like snowflakes in a strong wind. "The others are leaving now," she told them. "Come say goodbye." She nodded a silent thanks to Malachus for his help. "Halani said to fetch you as well, Malachus. Do you need my help to stand?"

He refused her offer and slowly gained his feet. This invalid treatment was growing tiresome. The children raced toward the cluster of wagons and people waiting on the camp's new perimeter. Malachus hesitated to approach the group. The free traders had offered him their unstinting hospitality and care, for which he was grateful. The fact that they'd taken him in instead of robbing him and leaving him for dead still amazed him. This was a farewell between members of an extended family, affectionate, teasing, worried, and familiar. He was a guest, a visitor, welcomed among them but not part of them.

Asil would have none of it. She shouldered her way through the crowd, Halani following close behind her, and ran toward him. "Malachus!"

Malachus planted his feet, bent his knees, and braced himself as Asil looked ready to launch herself at him. This was going to hurt.

"Careful, Mama! Wounded!" Halani cried out just in time.

Asil curbed her lunge toward him, pulling up short. She shuffled toward him instead, and he met her halfway, offering an embrace she enthusiastically claimed. He clenched his teeth against a groan when her arms squeezed his middle, and she nestled her face dangerously close to his chest injury.

When they parted, Asil's smile held a touch of sadness. "Will I see you again, Malachus?"

He lifted her work-roughened hand to his lips and kissed her knuckles. "You're a traveler like me. Such folk inevitably cross paths with each other. Be well, Asil. It has been my honor to know you."

She blushed, snapped forward to plant a damp kiss on his cheek, and scampered back toward the departing free traders. Halani turned to him, gratitude in her eyes.

"Thank you for not giving her false hope. Yours was a good answer."

"And as honest as I could make it without disappointing her." The likelihood of him meeting Asil again was slim. He touched Halani's arm. "Are you all right?"

"I will be." The forlorn look she wore gave way to a half smile. "You did better than you thought with distracting the children. I think they liked your book. Parents will sing your praises for days to come."

Again, that faint touch of envy in her voice. So far he'd read to a small crowd twice, and she'd missed both opportunities to hear. "I have yet to read to you," he said. "I can do so tonight if you aren't too tired. It's a good way to help daughters not dwell on their worry for their mothers."

Her half smile bloomed to a full one. "I think that's a wonderful idea."

They made plans to meet in front of her wagon after supper. "We'll all be too tired to listen to or tell a story tonight," she said. "My presence won't be missed at the main fire."

With no storytelling planned after the meal, the group dispersed to complete evening checks on the livestock, begin assigned guard duty, or find their beds. Malachus grabbed one of the lit lamps hanging outside the provender wagon and trekked toward Halani's wagon. Lit both inside and out by more lamps, it cast a welcoming glow in the darkness. She sat on a saddle pad before a small fire not far from her door, tending the flame. Malachus paused for a moment to admire the way light flickered across her features, emphasizing the width of her cheekbones, her fine jaw and slender nose. Golden highlights wove through her brown hair, tamed into a long braid that draped across her shoulder to coil in her lap. What did all that hair look like unbound?

She glanced up and he raised the book he held. "A different tome from the one I read earlier, so you'll be the first in the camp to hear me read from this one."

Halani clapped her hands, her expression delighted. She stood and gestured for him to hand her his lamp. "I'll take it and set it on the steps. Would you prefer a stool to sit on? It might be easier for you than getting up and down from the ground."

"I don't need the stool. A blanket on the ground is fine. I'm not enfeebled."

"True, but you're still healing. Believe me when I tell you no one will consider you enfeebled if you choose a stool or chair, so the offer stands should you change your mind."

He wouldn't and he didn't. Even were it not a point of pride, Malachus had no intention of giving up the opportunity to sit close to Halani as he read to her.

The second of the two books in his possession was a treatise on Winosia, its geography and resources, its kingdoms and politics. Material guaranteed to bore a child to tears, but he hoped would interest Halani. She listened to him without interruption, so focused on what he said that she visibly jumped when he closed the book.

"I think that's enough for this evening," he said. "We've nearly burned the lamps out and have probably outlasted whoever was assigned night's watch."

She gave a happy sigh. "I'd be lying if I said I didn't wish you could read several more hours. Your country sounds beautiful. Do you miss it?"

Malachus ran a reverent hand over the book's binding. "Sometimes." He watched her coax the guttering flame in the lamp next to her back to life. "But there are beautiful things here as well." She was one of them.

Satisfied with the renewed light, she gestured to the book. "What part of Winosia did you live in?"

"The land of long winter. A prefecture called Herkesh. The Sovatin monastery where I was fostered is there."

"Raised by monks, but you aren't one?"

He smothered a chuckle. He wasn't even truly human. "No. It isn't my calling. But I was happy there. The brotherhood fostered many children. Some became monks, some warriors; one or two even became kings." And one day, he'd embrace his own heritage and become a draga.

"And they taught you how to read and speak six languages." She eyed the book longingly.

"A valuable skill in the world, even if you can only read one." He offered her the tome. "Here, have a look. It isn't glass. You won't break it." Watching her hesitantly reach for the book reminded him of his own reluctance to take the poppet Asil had thrust at him earlier. Unlike the children he'd entertained that afternoon, Halani understood the value of such an item, not only the labor and material that went into making it, but the contents as well.

She curved her hands over the spine, stroking the cover with her thumbs in such a way that a jolt of heat flooded Malachus's limbs. "I've always wanted to learn to read."

His luck shone bright this evening. Halani had just given him the avenue he sought to make his offer. "I can teach you. The basics, of course, and you'd need to practice once I've left your caravan."

Her features went slack for a moment, whether from shock or disbelief, he couldn't tell. "From this book?" Her fingers tightened on it as if it might vanish while in her clasp.

"No," he said, pleased by her reaction. "It wouldn't do you much good learning to read a language neither spoken nor written in your country. I can teach you to read Sarvish. It's the alphabet used to read and write Common. I don't need a book to teach. A sharp stick and a patch of dirt will do for a lesson."

Her eyes rounded. "And I can teach others once you've gone." Her voice changed timbre, as if she spoke in prayer instead of everyday speech. "Do you realize the value of your gift?"

Malachus stared back at her, wondering why she was blind to her own worth. "Do you realize the value of yours? We wouldn't be having this conversation were it not for your care. Teaching a few letters is small repayment, I think."

She shook her head. "It isn't just letters. It's a door to a hidden world I know is there. I just can't open it yet." She returned the book to him, fingers lingering on the cover. "Can we start tomorrow?"

He grinned, pleased by her excitement. "The sooner, the better." He set the treatise in his lap, took the stick she'd been using earlier to stir the fire, and moved the coals around to stir up the flame. "May I ask you a question?" At her quick nod, he met her curious gaze. "Why aren't you married?" Her owlish blink at his inquiry tempted a grin, but he suppressed it, not wanting her to think he mocked her.

"Why do you ask such a thing?"

Because you're beautiful in every way. Sanctuary in the storm. A companion anyone would want at their side, be they draga or human. Instead he said, "Because most women your age are."

"Ah, a delicate way of saying I'm an old maid."

Malachus groaned inwardly. He'd expressed himself poorly and she'd misconstrued his words. "That isn't what I meant." He trod more carefully. "You're a woman of standing among your folk, with skills to spare and a kindness this world hasn't beaten out of you yet. That you're unmarried is surprising. That you don't have a line of suitors from here to the Goban market wanting to court you is remarkable."

Halani's cheeks reddened, her indignation giving way to an embarrassed pleasure at his straightforward praise. Her gaze dropped to the ground, and she fiddled restlessly with her skirt pleats. "You've a gift for honeyed speech," she said.

"It's honest speech, honeyed or otherwise." He waited until she lifted her gaze to him once more. "Why aren't you married?" he repeated. "Or even courted?"

One eyebrow rose. "I have been courted. Many times. Courtship doesn't always lead to marriage. I'm unmarried because I choose to be. I've yet to meet the man I want to bond with, and I refuse to settle for less."

His heart swelled at her answer, though there was no reason why it should. Halani was merely a bright candle along the dark road he traveled. He'd remember her fondly after he left, nothing more. Still, a nettle of disappointment stung him at the knowledge that there would never be more between them. "And what if you don't find that person to whom you want to bond?"

She shrugged. "My life will continue as it has," she said in a cool, uninflected voice. "I don't measure my days by when I may or may not find a husband. I will be happy in other things. Life is more than just a marriage. I am more than a woman waiting to become a man's wife."

In that moment, Malachus forgot to breathe. What would she say, he wondered, if he suddenly grasped her hands in his and begged her to journey with him once he was well enough to travel?

The thought—and the temptation—startled him. He was losing his senses to even entertain the idea. There were far too many reasons why it was not only impractical but also ludicrous.

"It is," he agreed. "And you are." He turned the subject yet again, still shaken by the wild notion of asking her to go with him on his quest to regain his mother-bond. "When does Kursak plan to move the remaining camp?"

A shadow passed through her eyes, and she stared at a point beyond his shoulder. "A week, maybe a little less. There's still a lot of inventory to account for and pack, three more wagons to buy, and the teams to pull them. By then you might be able to ride Batraza without too much discomfort, but I don't see you galloping merrily over the fields."

The image her words painted made him grin, though the way

she'd suddenly avoided his gaze as she spoke made him wonder. And while he knew his body better than she did, she was right in her estimate of how much he'd heal by the time the camp moved.

"And here I thought you eager to be rid of me," he teased.

"You just offered to teach me to read," she said, her smile wry. "Don't tempt me to shackle you to one of the wagons and keep you here until I can read all the languages you can." Halani rose from her place beside Malachus and dusted off her skirts before giving him a stern look. "I'm off to bed. We've an early day tomorrow and a lot of work."

He rose with her, sorry to see the evening end and already looking forward to the next one. He bid her good night with a bow, her gaze a warm stripe down his back as she watched him leave.

The provender wagon seemed a lonely place, and he lay on his bed, staring up at the plain ceiling before closing his eyes and opening his senses to the mother-bond.

No clear images appeared in his mind, and its beacon no longer felt as sharp or clear, as if hidden behind a miasma.

He refused to panic. Doing so accomplished nothing and did more harm than anything. If he stood any chance of recovering the bit of bone, he had to stay calm and clearheaded.

It might have been only moments that passed or hours as he sought to strengthen the connection between himself and the mother-bond. The miasma obscuring it refused to dissipate. This was purposeful sorcery. Whoever had the bone knew someone hunted it and worked to hide it.

CHAPTER TWELVE

Halani had saved a man's life and been given a world in return. Malachus's offer was a gift from the gods. She was a free trader woman destined to always travel on roads well-known and well-worn. They were as familiar to her as the lines on her palms and the ones creasing Asil's face. The rest of the world beyond the Empire had always been the stuff of dreams and imagination, until Malachus said he'd teach her to read. She'd remained awake the entire night, her heart thundering and thoughts spinning in anticipation of that first promised lesson. It was better than chewing her fingernails down to the quick worrying needlessly over Asil and missing her presence in their wagon.

Malachus's teaching exceeded every expectation, and she went to bed each night after that initial lesson dreaming of symbols drawn in ink and linked together so that sound became meaning and meaning became story.

Three days after Hamod took part of his band off for Domora, Halani was in the Goban market with Nathin's wife, Ruviti, to work the last day at their stall. The market's crowds had waned, though the streets remained busy. People browsed more than bought, biding their time and hedging their bets over which merchants would simply pack up and leave and which would discount their wares in order to capture that last sale. Halani prepared for a long day of coaxing people to their table. There would be no discounts. Hamod had never been one to follow that trend, and she let those who stopped to peruse their goods know that the price quoted today wouldn't change the closer they got to evening.

The smile she offered her latest visitor was wide and sincere. Gilene, looking every bit an *ataman*'s beloved consort, waved as she approached. Halani left her place behind the table she manned to hug her friend before leading her into the stall's shade.

Halani gave Gilene's hand an affectionate squeeze. "This is a nice surprise. I didn't expect to see you here." She'd wanted to meet with Gilene a final time before the Savatar broke camp but hadn't put much hope into it.

"I went to your camp first but they said you were at the stall." Gilene greeted Ruviti, accepting the cup of water offered her with a smile and thanks. "I didn't see Malachus, but I assume he's either dead or healing nicely if you're here and not hovering over him."

Halani grinned. "Not dead and feeling well enough to get bored and restless."

Gilene downed her water. "That was good. Better than wine. It's hot enough to melt leather out there today." She toasted Ruviti with her empty cup. "Did he say where he's going once he leaves your caravan?"

"West, I think, though he hasn't really said much about it." The thought of him leaving sent a rush of relief through her, followed by a hollow sadness she didn't like to examine too closely. "I'm glad you're here, but I don't think you came to see me to help sell our wares."

Faint sorrow passed over Gilene's face. "We're leaving today. One of the Savatar, a man older than the Gamirs, swears we have bad weather coming. He can feel it in his bones." Halani's eyebrows rose, and she leaned out of the shade cast by the stall's awning to peer at the bright, brutal sun in its cloudless sky. Gilene laughed. "That's what I think, too, but the Savatar take his word as truth, so Azarion wants to be within the borders of the Stara Dragana before it becomes too much of a misery to travel. I wanted to see you and say goodbye before we left."

"I'm glad you did. I have something for you." Halani left Gilene to delve into a crate pushed farther back in the stall. She returned carrying a small bag sewn of costly imported velvet tied closed with braided silk cord and offered it to Gilene. "It isn't much, but Asil and I thought you might like something we made together." She watched as Gilene carefully opened the bag, upending it. A small bundle bound in the same silk thread as the braided cord dropped into her palm. "A charm of protection, good fortune, and good health," Halani said. "A blessing of earth for fire, and a token of friendship."

At first glance, the charm looked like a twist of leaves and stems tied together by a length of plume grass. But for all its modest appearance, it fairly hummed with devotions and invocations of earth magic. At this short distance, Halani heard its song, a sweet tune to soothe the soul. She and Asil had spent several hours on it, chanting prayers as they harvested, dried, and tied the foliage together.

Gilene held it reverently. "I will treasure this." She pressed it to her cheek and closed her eyes. "I can hear it sing to me."

Halani grinned, delighted at the knowledge. Gilene was an *agacin*, a daughter of fire instead of earth, but she still heard Halani's magic in the charm. She and Asil had done it right.

Gilene withdrew something from an inner pocket sewn into her sleeveless tunic, allowing it to unravel on a length of glittering silver chain. "I have something for you as well." She handed it to

Halani, who spread it across her fingers so that it hung in a display over her hand. Nearby, Ruviti gasped.

Three charms attached to different spots on the chain spun and sparkled like raindrops on a spider's web. The chain was constructed of three smaller delicate chains, attached by links that created a scallop design when worn on the neck. Halani exhaled a slow breath of admiration, peering closely at the charms. Not just abstract designs but graceful renditions of silhouettes representing the profiles of a woman's face, a horse's head, and a draga's wing. "This is extraordinary," she said, glancing at Gilene. "Beautiful. I've never seen the like."

A pleased smile wreathed Gilene's thin features. "There's a story to it. The Savatar believe the goddess Agna fashioned three beings into existence. The draga was her first child and her most powerful. Shaped from fire, lightning, and stone, it commanded the skies and spoke the language of earth. The horse was her second child, fashioned from river waters and the long grasses. The Savatar sometimes call Agna the Great Mare. Woman was her third child, the youngest and least powerful, but most like Agna in aspect. She is Agna's avatar, the priestess who serves the will of the goddess. Apart, the three are incomplete, weak. United, they're unbreakable."

Chills raced down Halani's arms. "The explanation is as amazing as the piece itself." She placed it carefully over her head, locking the charms together until they made a medallion of swirling shapes. She posed for Gilene. "What do you think?"

"I think it looks wonderful on you."

"So do I," Ruviti said. "Wait until Talen sees it. She'll be drooling over it and harassing Marata to find something like it for her."

Every fine piece of jewelry that found its way into the caravan always found its way out again to a trade table. The jewelry Halani and the other free traders wore was limited to colorful gimcrack beads and bits of carved bone. Halani would have to battle Hamod to keep him from trying to sell Gilene's gift for a tidy sum.

"Like your charm, it's worn as protection against evil and illness." Gilene hugged her. "I hope you'll think of me when you wear it."

Halani returned the embrace, blinking back tears. "I'll think of you even when I don't. If the Goban market is here again next season, I'll talk Hamod into coming back. I hope you and Azarion can return too."

When they parted, Gilene sniffled. "So do I. Farewell, friend, and safe journey back into the Empire."

She hugged Ruviti as well before slipping into the stream of market customers. Halani watched her until she disappeared from sight.

They made their last sale just as Nathin arrived with a small crew to dismantle the stall. Halani stayed long enough to help Ruviti wrap and pack up the items that hadn't sold, then got out of the men's way as they took down frame poles and stacked pallets. She and Ruviti walked back to the caravan together, Halani tired but eager for the coming evening and her reading lesson.

Kursak met her as she headed toward her wagon. "Gilene find you?"

She touched the spot just below her throat where the charm rested hidden under her shirt. "Yes. She said one of the Savatar is predicting bad weather on the way, so they're breaking camp now to beat the rain."

He stared up at the sky with the same expression she likely wore when Gilene told her the story. "Is that so?" His snort of disbelief made her chuckle. "I think we'll wait a little longer. Is the stall emptied?"

"Nathin and the others are breaking it down now. They should be back before nightfall." She preened a little. "We even managed to sell a few things as we were trying to pack them away." Every sale was a welcomed godsend, one more *belsha* to add to the communal treasure they depended on to see them through the hard winter months, when trade was practically nonexistent.

Kursak clapped his hands. "May the gods bless last-chance buyers." He noted the way Halani scanned the encampment. "If you're looking for Malachus, he's with his mare." He laughed at her blush and whistled a tune as he walked away.

She didn't immediately seek Malachus, continuing to her wagon, where she washed her face, straightened her clothes, and brushed and rebraided her hair. The small mirror hanging from a hook on one of the wagon's frame supports reflected a face with high, round cheekbones, a smooth brow, and a pale mouth. The sparkle in her eyes was new. As Malachus, and others, had pointed out on different occasions, hers was a somber gaze. Gray as a burial shroud, though Asil had once said her eyes were the color of dove's wings. Halani liked that comparison a lot more.

Why do you care how you look? a sly voice inside her asked.

"Oh, shut it," Halani muttered, giving her skirt one last shake to loosen any wrinkles, and left the wagon.

As Kursak said, she found Malachus with Batraza. If she faced her mirror now, she had no doubt her smooth brow was gone. "What are you doing?"

He paused, one hand on the pommel, the other on the cantle of the saddle someone had placed on Batraza's back and cinched. He turned his head slowly, a sheepish expression settling over his features. "You're back. Sooner than I expected."

"Obviously," she replied, infusing all of her disapproval in that one word. "Who saddled Batraza?"

He flinched. "I did." His frustrated exhalation ruffled Batraza's mane. "Halani, I hurt in places I didn't think were supposed to feel pain, but I'm no longer an invalid. I need to move, need to make my muscles remember what they're supposed to do. I came to these shores for a purpose, and I've put it off far too long. Besides, Batraza needs exercise."

She crossed her arms. "And you're the only who can exercise her?"

This time he turned fully to face her. "I want to exercise her." He offered her a small bow. "Shall we negotiate? If I can get in this saddle without help, you can ride pillion to make sure I don't fall off, and we'll have an extra-long lesson tonight."

He'd obviously been among free traders long enough to adopt one of their less desirable traits—negotiating everything. Halani nibbled at her lower lip for a moment, considering. "That seems fair, but only a short, *slow* ride, and you must tell me the version of 'The Sun Maiden' you learned." He might adopt the ways of bargaining, but he was a beginner. She was a master.

"Done." Having gained her agreement, he returned his attention to the saddle, testing its hold on Batraza's back. The mare whuffled at him when he attempted to mount and failed.

"Do you need help?" Halani called to him.

"No." Malachus didn't look at her, and his short reply carried a breathless quality. He tried again and failed again.

"Are you sure?

"Yes."

He achieved success on the third try, with a vault into the saddle that belied the labor of the previous two attempts and the pallor of his features. He settled into place and offered Halani a victorious smile. He held out a hand to her. "Ready?"

She refused to use his arm as leverage to mount behind him. It didn't matter that it was his uninjured side. As he said, he hurt in places he didn't think felt pain. She refused to make it worse. Instead, she had him ride Batraza to the nearest wagon, where she used the steps to put her level with Batraza's back before climbing up behind Malachus. She rested her hands on his waist, worried she'd somehow press on the healing wound in his side or even the one on his hip. "Slow," she reminded him.

"Yes, mistress," he said in a wry voice.

The good-natured mare readily responded to her rider's silent commands, ambling away from the camp to cut a path through the rye grass toward nowhere in particular. Halani swayed with the horse's rolling gait, resisting the temptation to constantly ask Malachus how he felt, and simply enjoyed the view, the quiet, and the companionship.

Malachus sat easy in the saddle. He'd told her that both he and the mare had journeyed far and long together, and Halani wondered where they had gone and what they had seen in their travels.

Her thoughts drifted until one stilled and refused to flutter away with the rest. "Animals avoid you and Batraza, though neither of you have shown them any hostility. Is that part of your curse? Was Batraza cursed with you?"

The flutter of tensing muscle teased her palm where it lay against his skin. Malachus turned his head a little so she could hear his reply. "I never thought of it, but it makes sense."

His answer only inflamed her curiosity. Free traders were a taciturn folk, a characteristic required in their vocation. Halani clamped her jaw shut to keep from spilling all the questions she wanted to ask Malachus about his curse.

"Go ahead and ask," he said. "If you don't, you'll burst apart." His amusement made her blush but didn't deter her.

"Why are you cursed? Did you anger a god? Defile a temple? Take a sorcerer's wife to your bed?"

He laughed outright. "While those are all epic reasons for cursing someone, the answers are no, no, and no. I can see why you're the caravan's principal storyteller. My curse isn't one wrought from malice but from desperation. Its details aren't ones I can share, but the one who cast it didn't mean for it to become a curse."

"Do you know how to break it?"

"Yes, but it takes a special item to do it, and that's something I don't yet have."

The dread blossoming inside her threatened to choke Halani, not to mention the guilt fighting for space in her chest. Was this special item the draga bone Hamod had taken with him to Domora to sell? Her stomach twisted itself into knots. Her actions in warning her uncle to leave and get rid of the draga bone had been spurred by the certainty that the bone was valuable, coveted, and bad luck—three things that never boded well for whoever possessed it. Malachus had killed the two men who'd sold the bone to Hamod. If this was the item he hunted, she had no doubt he'd kill Hamod as well if he had to, to take it back. And who could blame him? A curse that threatened to immolate you without warning wasn't the same as one that made your feet smell or your hair fall out. Had she condemned a man to an undeserved death in a misguided bid to protect her greedy uncle? Halani closed her eyes and stiffened her spine against a shudder.

"You've gone quiet back there." Malachus clicked to Batraza, turning her so the setting sun was behind them. "No more questions?"

Thoughts reeling in a whirlwind of guilt, Halani struggled to gather them together so she could give him an answer that didn't alert him to her distress. She had one question in her arsenal sure to distract him. "Why aren't you married?"

His amused snort eased her panic. "Who says I'm not?" His question ignited it again.

Her hands fell away from his sides. "Well, you haven't said, so I'm asking." She thanked the gods for the calm tone of her voice. Why had she assumed he was unmarried? Just because he was a wanderer didn't mean there wasn't a wife waiting for him somewhere in far-off Winosia. The idea made her queasy.

He allayed her fears when he said, "I'm not married. What woman would want a cursed husband?"

Halani wondered if this was what it might be like if you climbed to the top of a mountain and celebrated your victory, only to be pushed off the precipice. And then do it all over again. "One willing to help you break the curse."

"True," he said. "Though I think I desire one who can cook like Marata or better."

She chuckled, forgetting her worries for a moment. "I want a wife like that myself."

They shared laughter, then more silence as they rode across a pasture of shorter grasses toward the haunted Pumon Ridges in the distance. After their last conversation and the racing thoughts it inspired, Halani was reluctant to remind him of her bargain but too curious to shunt it aside. "Will you tell me your Sun Maiden story now?"

He sighed, any hint of amusement gone from his voice. "It isn't the gladdening one you tell, Halani."

"I'd still like to hear it, if you feel up to telling me."

"I said I would, and I'll keep my end of the bargain."

They rode farther away from the caravan, once more in silence, as Malachus gathered his thoughts. Halani found herself stroking his sides with her fingers and stopped, mortified.

"Kansi Yuv," he finally said, adopting the storyteller's cadence, "was more ambitious than heroic. A common soldier who rose through the ranks until he gained the emperor's attention and admiration for his feats in battle as well as his strategies for conquering his enemies. He won a lot of wars for his sovereign, but he wanted more. Wanted to rise to greater heights and bring his family the status and elevation reserved for the aristocracy.

"He met a woman named Yain who fell in love with him and made her his concubine. She lived with him for a decade, content, until he discovered something about her that changed everything."

Instantly ensnared by the telling, Halani leaned into him so she could hear better. "What did he discover?"

Malachus had grown stiffer in the saddle. "Yain wasn't human but a draga female who'd taken on the guise of a woman. And she was Golnar's daughter."

Halani's eyes rounded. "Golnar had children?"

"She did. I used to wonder why other stories always depicted her as a male draga. The texts about dragas stored in the monastery's library described female dragas as bigger than the males, more aggressive, more formidable, and Golnar the fiercest of all. Maybe making her male in the tales made Kansi Yuv more heroic."

All the stories Halani told to entertain paying crowds and her fellow free traders featured a hero facing off against a male villain. There was never a heroine or a female villain. She remembered Gilene's backstory of the charm she now wore. A Savatar goddess had created the first three beings to populate the earth: draga, horse, and woman. Had the first two been female as well? The progenitors of their kind, deserving of stories never shared?

She sensed this version of "The Sun Maiden" bore no similarity to the one she told, a tragedy instead of a triumph. "What did Kansi Yuv do when he found out?"

"Wielded his knowledge as a weapon." Contempt dripped off Malachus's words. "The gift of a draga would immortalize Kansi Yuv and make it so he'd have everything he desired, just short of the emperor's throne itself. He just had to find a way to trap Golnar."

By now, he was rigid as a stone pillar. Even his body felt cold to her touch, despite the sun's heat bearing down on them. Sensing her rider's souring mood, Batraza tossed her head, snorting a protest.

Halani reached to squeeze his muscular arm. "You don't have to tell me the rest, Malachus."

It was just a story, an old history recited around campfires and passed down from one generation to the next. Its principal participants were long dead. Even Golnar's skeleton no longer existed, destroyed in the conflagration of god-fire that swept the old capital. Yet Halani knew she hadn't misheard the fury in Malachus's voice, or the grief, as if the events that played out in the Sun Maiden story held a very personal sorrow for him.

A rough palm covered her hand. "It needs to be shared, especially since it's the true one and not that glorified pile of horseshit everyone on this side of the Raglun Sea believes." He spat the words from between his teeth. She had only a glimpse of his profile, but it was enough to reveal the flare of his nostril and tight downturn of his mouth. Was this the expression the sell-swords saw just before they died? For the first time since she'd met him, Halani suffered a frisson of fear, not for him, but of him.

If he sensed her faint withdrawal, he didn't comment, only returned to his telling of the story of the Sun Maiden. "Kansi Yuv didn't commission a gold statue of a woman to be made. He turned a living woman into one." Halani gasped, horrified. "He betrayed Yain, had her bound, bespelled into docility, and painted from head to foot in gold paint like a treasure, believing the draga couldn't resist entering the ravine, despite knowing it was a trap. He was right; she couldn't. Golnar died trying to rescue her daughter. Yain watched, helpless, as her lover and his men shot arrows into her mother, then butchered her in front of her."

"Dear gods." Halani barely managed to force the words past her tight throat. "Not a hero at all; a monster." Sickened, she dreaded Malachus's answer to her next questions. "What happened to Yain? Did she turn into a draga herself? Escape Kansi Yuv?"

Where before his words nearly vibrated with rage, they now sounded dull, flat. "He gave Yain to the emperor as an additional gift, a coveted pet. But she escaped Kansi Yuv and the fate he planned for her. She died in a fire of her own making before he could deliver her to the palace." A gravid silence swelled between them before Malachus said, "And that is the true story of the Sun Maiden. Of beautiful, unfortunate Yain, who loved a man who betrayed her and murdered her mother in front of her."

Malachus's back was a blurry wall. Halani wiped away her tears with the heel of one hand to clear her vision. She sniffled several times and cleared her throat twice before she attempted to speak. "I know now why I've never liked the Sun Maiden story. I always thought it was because the draga were forever gone from these lands, hunted out of existence, with Golnar one of the last to die. The truth is worse. So much worse. Thank you for telling me, Malachus. I'm sorry it pained you to do so."

He brought Batraza to a gradual halt, looping the reins so they rested on her neck. With his hands free, he captured Halani's where they lay against his sides and raised them until they rested across his breastbone. His heart beat steady under her palms. "I'm glad I told you," he said in a low voice, its vibration adding to the percussion of his heartbeat. "Telling it to another is like lancing a boil and draining the poison. Even if no else hears this version of 'The Sun Maiden,' another person in these lands now knows it."

Halani leaned her head against his back, enjoying the feel of his hair against her forehead. "It's no wonder the woman sitting on the Kraelian throne is so corrupt. So bloodthirsty."

"What do you mean?"

"Empress Dalvila is a descendant of Kansi Yuv's line. Rumor has it that when the Savatar goddess destroyed Kraelag, Dalvila raged in her sickbed for days, not because the fire killed the entire population behind Kraelag's walls but because it destroyed Golnar's bones as well."

He slumped in her embrace, as if the invisible strings holding him tall and straight in the saddle broke. Alarmed he might pitch from the saddle, Halani wrapped her arms hard around him, no longer so cautious about his wounds. A fall from Batraza would hurt a lot worse.

He didn't fall, and his voice held both disgust and satisfaction. "It seems blood will out, even across centuries. Good for the Savatar goddess. After so long, she set Golnar completely free of her murderers."

The drone of insects and the swooping flight of bats on the hunt reminded Halani that twilight bore down on them, and they'd wandered a fair distance from the caravan. "We've ridden longer than I thought. How are you feeling?" She pressed a hand to his forehead. "No fever. That's good."

Malachus chuckled. "Ever the nurse. I'll be stiff later. I can feel all the warning twinges now. I won't be galloping toward the horizon anytime soon, but Batraza and I can manage a fast walk."

They made it back to the encampment in time for supper. Halani declined the request for a story, telling the others she had a reading lesson.

"How dull," one boy, just shy of his first beard and with a voice that resembled a goose's honk, muttered to his mother. "I'd much rather tell a story."

His mother, seeing an opportunity, gave his shoulder a nudge and pointed to the spot where Halani usually stood to tell her tales. "Would you, now? Well, here's your chance. Get up there and tell us a story!"

A hue and cry of encouragement along with whistles and the shouted chant of "Tell us a story! Tell us a story!" burst from the crowd. Halani took that moment to abandon her audience for her wagon. Malachus followed after her, and the two set up their usual reading spot on the ground in front of the door, with the light of multiple lamps around them.

While Malachus cleared a patch of ground down to the dirt and retrieved a slender stick to use as a makeshift quill, Halani brought her small brazier outside and started a fire to brew a pot of tea. When it was done, she poured a cup for him, sprinkling a pinch of *kartom* powder in it. He took it, giving the contents a cautious sniff.

"It's just a wild rose and strawberry tea," she said. "There's a little *kartom* in it. You won't be sleepy like before and not so sore in the morning. Are you sure you feel up to a lesson?"

He set the tea aside to cool. "Of course. I'd insist upon it if you tried to back out of our bargain."

Thrilled that he wanted to teach despite the earlier physical and emotional exertion, she threw herself into the lesson, reciting back to him the letters she painstakingly drew in the dirt with her stick.

He smoothed the dirt flat at one point. "Now draw the letters you've learned tonight from memory and speak the sounds they make."

The writing part of it she embraced, marking quick flourishes in the dry dirt, celebrating inwardly at each approving nod he gave. The verbal part was harder, more embarrassing. Halani sounded out the letters, peering at Malachus's face and mouth as he enunciated slowly, exaggerating the movement of his lips, tongue, and teeth. She copied his actions, feeling as if something pulled and twisted her cheeks into weird shapes.

"I'm sure I look foolish," she said after one practice with a letter combination that sounded fine when spoken at natural speed and bizarre when enunciated slowly.

"You don't look foolish at all," he assured her, lamp flame reflected in his dark eyes.

A fall of heat cascaded down her back that had nothing to do with the lamps, the brazier, or even the summer evening, and everything to do with his gaze.

He showed mercy after that, allowing her to practice more of her writing. Halani bent to draw one of the letters, only to have her braid suddenly escape its pins. It uncoiled in a long rope, falling on her sketched letter to smear its shape. She set the stick down. "Hold on," she told Malachus, reaching up to find the pins still in her hair. "Let me pin this back up, and I'll redraw it." She halted when he caught her wrist, an arrested look in his eyes.

"Wait. Would you unbraid it? I've wondered what it looks like loose."

A simple request, without the flowery adornment of compliments to the color of her hair or its length, and yet Halani found herself eager to grant it. "As you wish."

She sat down cross-legged on one of the blankets, skirts flowing over her knees, the thick plait coiled in her lap, and parted the tight weave. She started at the tip, working upward until she reached her nape, where she separated the curls with her fingers until they cascaded over her shoulders to cover her lap and spill onto the blanket. One springy curl fell in front of her eyes, and she blew it out of the way before capturing it to tuck behind her ear. "Now you can see why I keep it braided," she said, suddenly self-conscious under his heavy-lidded stare. "Sometimes I think it's a creature all its own, getting into everything, tangling around everything, including itself."

Malachus remained silent for what seemed like centuries. Unsure what to do or say, Halani waited, wondering what thoughts swirled behind that impenetrable gaze. "My gods," he said in reverential tones. "It is your glory, isn't it."

Thank the gods she was sitting or his comment would have made her fall. "It's just hair."

As if ensorcelled, he slid closer, arms outstretched until he buried both hands in her hair, lifting the curling locks to let them spiral around his arms and fingers before falling away. "Just hair," he breathed.

He was close enough to her now that she could return the gesture. His hair, as thick as hers but straight as an evergreen bough and as dark as his eyes, fanned across the back of her hand. "Yours is nicer, easier to tame. My uncle says if I left mine unbound, I could trap a wild horse with it."

"Or a draga."

She smiled at the odd notion. "That would be impressive. I'd be famous."

He continued admiring her hair with both his eyes and his hands, separating one curl from the rest to straighten, then let it go so that it bounced back into its natural coil. "Asil's hair only has waves."

"We think the curls come from my father, though we'll never know."

He turned his full attention to what she was saying. "You never knew him?"

Asil's history, shrouded in shame and secrecy, was something Hamod forbade anyone in the caravan to discuss. It was the one thing Halani had never argued with him about for fear of upsetting her mother. Yet here she sat, tempted to tell Malachus at least some part of her story. Not all. Not the details, just the surface facts that gave Halani a past, no matter how dark or brutal. Hamod wasn't here, and there was no one around her and Malachus at the moment to eavesdrop on their conversation. Besides, what shame there was, it didn't belong to Asil or to her.

She tamed her hair into one long skein, then split it into three smaller ones before plaiting it again. She spoke as she braided. "No. My mother was abducted by slavers before my uncle formed his own caravan. The wagon master he and my mother traveled with didn't care that she'd been taken. You've seen her behavior. Strange, childlike. Uncle says a head wound when she was still on lead strings made her that way. He took care of her after their parents died from disease. Since no one in that caravan was interested in rescuing her, he set off by himself, found her in the Ryndamiss slave markets a few months later, and escaped with her. Neither of them knew she was pregnant with me by then."

Silence had weight. Sometimes it was a light thing, gossamer as a spider's web and just as enduring. Other times, it raised the hair on one's nape and made the heart beat a trebled rhythm. And sometimes it became a thing alive. For Halani, it was this living silence that hovered between them after her revelation. Her breath hung in her nose and mouth as all expression bled away from his face, only to rush back with a shock wave that seemed to age him ten years.

Halani looked away, unable to face what she knew she'd see in his eyes. Revulsion maybe, but worst of all, pity. A fingertip nudged her chin up, and she stared into dark eyes lacking any pity or disgust. Instead, they shone with an admiration that made her gasp softly at the sight.

"I think your mother is probably one of the most remarkable women I've ever known."

It was Halani's turn to crumple like a puppet with the strings cut. She smiled, caught between the urge to cry and the urge to laugh. She settled for widening her smile to a grin. "Thank you, Malachus. I think she is too."

Caught in a mutual spell of desire and shared sorrows, they leaned toward one another. His lips brushed hers, soft as a down feather. Another brush, a little harder, a little more open so that his breath teased the sensitive skin on the underside of her upper lip. A third pass, and this kiss bore no resemblance to the first two. Scorching hot and openmouthed, pulling a soft groan from the bottom of Halani's chest as Malachus's tongue filled her mouth to sweep its contours before retreating to do the same to her lips. She mimicked his actions, making him moan as well.

She was on her back and he lying half on top of her when the sound of voices drawing closer brought her back to her senses. Malachus retreated to his place on the blanket before standing with a lithe grace she envied. While his knees looked none the worse for it, her own had all the rigidity of water after that soul-searing kiss. Malachus reached down and helped her up. His eyes blazed in the semidarkness, and his chest rose and fell with staccato breaths. They stared at each other for long moments. She was tempted, oh so tempted, to invite him inside her wagon and finish what they'd started the day she brought him wounded and unconscious into the free trader camp.

It would be so easy. And later, when he left, it would be so crushing.

She stepped back from the temptation he represented and all the heartache that came with giving in to it. "We're done with the market and will start packing in earnest tomorrow, so the day will start even earlier than usual." She didn't dare offer to check his wounds. "I'll leave you to find your bed."

Taking one of the lamps, she left the rest to him to snuff and put away, along with the blankets they shared. He said nothing as she passed close by him to climb the wagon steps, though he brushed her skirts with his hand. Halani paused, one foot on the last stair tread, one on the wagon's threshold. Her lamp highlighted the hunger in his expression. She suspected she wore the same look. "You know, you're welcome to stay longer and travel south with us until you're fully healed."

"Ah, fair woman," he said on a sigh. "Were my journey and task of a different sort, I might ask you to go with me."

Her sigh matched his. "Were my obligations of no importance, I might say yes."

"I won't forget you once we part, Halani of the Lightning." He caught her free hand and pressed a kiss to her palm before letting go.

Halani crossed her threshold and closed the door behind her, staring at the comforting home she'd always known and seeing the cage it had just become.

CHAPTER THIRTEEN

Were he not in danger of literally going up in flames, Malachus would have tried to coax Halani to his bed in the provender wagon or wooed her for an invitation into hers. He kept an eye on her until she disappeared inside the wagon, then turned his attention to his hands. Smoke streamed in tendrils from his fingertips and wafted from the confines of his sleeves.

Relieved that the voices that interrupted their captivating kiss hadn't drawn closer, he strode away from the camp, avoiding the corrals and livestock pens. Every prey animal in range would sense a predator approaching and raise an alarm. The draga within him was awake, restless, wrenched out of its enforced torpor by Malachus's desire for a woman he had no right to pursue and every reason to crave.

He halted his solitary trek in the middle of the open field he and Halani had ridden across earlier, and stared up at the few bright stars winking back at him through a vaporous veil of clouds. Here, with the darkness thick around him and the silence of night closing in, he could sink into his own thoughts, douse the internal fire roused by a free trader healer, and remember the main reason he was in this unfamiliar land in the first place.

The mother-bond's pull on him never ceased; it only waxed or waned with either distance or the manipulation of sorcery. Ship captains might envy such a consistent instrument of navigation.

Now his senses veered not west, but southeast, into the lands of the Kraelian Empire instead of the steppes that belonged to the Savatars and other horse nomads like them. He was tempted to call down the lightning once more, let it blast through his body in a javelin of white fire, leaving images and convulsing muscles in its wake. The last time he'd done so, the lightning had shown him Halani. Lightning divination was often mysterious and abstruse, open to numerous interpretations, but it was never wrong. Halani didn't posses the mother-bond, but she was tied to it in some way.

His birthright still eluded him, as it had since looters stole it from the Sovatin necropolis long ago. Then the search had been a matter of pride. Now it had become one of survival. He had matured to an age that demanded a first transformation from the guise of a man to the full form of a draga. He hadn't lied when he told Halani he was cursed. His mother's magic, meant to protect him, placed a heavy burden on him as well.

A small flame burst across the fingertips of his right hand and marched merrily toward his wrist. Startled by the swift change from smoke to fire, Malachus smothered the flames with his other hand. The draga inside snarled its frustration, and he worked feverishly to calm it, turning his thoughts to mundane things.

He recalled an earlier conversation with Seydom, who had done him a favor and promised to keep it secret from Halani.

The free trader had taken the *belshas* Malachus had given him and returned to the caravan from the Goban market bearing a thick square of cloth. He joined Malachus in the provender wagon and placed the package, along with change, into Malachus's hands. "I bought the largest one I could with the *belshas* you gave me. The bookseller was happier than a wolf with a fat sheep, and tossed in an extra quill." His own jovial expression sobered. "Is this a courtship gift for Halani?"

Malachus unwrapped the cloth, pleased beyond words with Seydom's choice. "No. Repayment for her care. She saved my life, and that's a debt I'll never be able to repay, but with this I can thank her." This was the book he'd seen her admiring, her hands caressing the leather binding with a lover's worship.

"Maybe you should have given her something else."

Yanked from his own admiration of the journal and visions of Halani's expression when he gave it to her, Malachus glanced at Seydom, frowning. "Why do you say that?"

The other man's shrug belied the disquiet in his eyes. "Because a man who'll give Halani a book understands what moves Halani. She's fond of you; it's obvious to all of us. Too fond, I'm thinking, and that gift will only make her more so."

Seydom's words sent a rush of euphoria surging through Malachus, guilt hard on its heels. The blood shouldn't rush hot through his veins at learning of Halani's affection for him, one overt enough that others had noticed. And worried. "It's for her to share with others in the camp," he told Seydom.

Partially pacified, the free trader handed him the quills and a bottle of ink. "As long as she knows that, it won't be so bad when you part company with us."

His words plagued Malachus's thoughts, even as he sought to force the draga into its torpor once more. He had grown as attached to Halani as Seydom claimed she was to him. His desire for her beat through every part of him. He wanted only to please her, but the one thing he couldn't do—and she'd even asked in her own oblique way—was to stay with the free traders. He didn't wish to hurt her when he bid her farewell. What was better? Push her away now and pretend he had no feelings for her beyond that of a grateful convalescent? The notion made him recoil. He hadn't always been truthful with her, but in this she deserved his honesty and not some false manipulation of her emotions.

A damp wind smelling of rain turned his thoughts yet again, this time to the environment around him. The moon sank low toward the west, waxing gibbous as it phased toward full in the coming days. More clouds shrouded the sky, and even the brightest stars were no longer visible. They'd get rain tomorrow.

He returned to the caravan camp with its undercurrent of constant noise from livestock and sleeping humans. He gave Halani's dark wagon a quick glance but didn't stop. If he did, he'd find himself perched at her doorstep begging to come inside. He continued to his own temporary abode. Compared to some of the places he'd slept for a night, these were luxurious accommodations. He left his shoes by the doorway, disrobed, gave his wounds a cursory inspection, and stretched out on his bed. He fell asleep with the sweet memory of Halani's taste on his lips and in his mouth.

He awakened to rain pounding on the roof and opened the door to a camp turned into a mud puddle. People raced back and forth working to get items under dry canopies and checking on the livestock that stood in the downpour in either silent misery or bleating protest. Flocks of chickens sheltered under some of the wagons, the sheepdogs not put to work keeping them company.

Malachus dressed and pulled on his boots. Instantly soaked in the deluge, he slogged toward Batraza, who gave him a gimlet stare as if blaming him for the bad weather. Other than being as wet as he, she was fine and gave him a petulant snort when he left to help others in the camp. He spotted Halani in the distance, whistling to the dogs as they herded the sheep into one of the grassier pastures fenced off for feeding purposes.

They worked through the day in the rain. Some of the women split the task of feeding everyone lunch between them, brewing tea and boiling broth on individual braziers inside the wagons. By midafternoon, there was nothing left to do but wait out the downpour and try to dry out.

Malachus, sodden and muddy, stood under a leaky tarp, sharing a pipe with an equally sodden and muddied Kursak.

"Never again will I doubt some rickety old Savatar's predictions about the weather," the wagon master groused as he glared at the rain.

Malachus wondered what rickety old Savatar Kursak had spoken with recently but didn't ask. He'd intended to speak with the wagon master that morning, but with the sky trying to drown everyone in a single rainstorm, they'd all been too busy until now. "If you'll have me, I'd like to stay a few more days and travel south with you. I can pay you for my continued use of the provender wagon as well as the food I eat, and hunt to contribute to the camp larder."

Kursak blew a stream of smoke past the pipestem clamped between his teeth before passing the pipe to Malachus. "I thought you planned to travel west."

"I do, but I'm not looking forward to a solitary ride through days of a downpour without any shelter. And I can use more time with teaching Halani to read." *And bask in her company. And wrap my hands in her hair. And kiss her until neither of us can remember what it is to breathe separate from each other.*

"Have you said anything to her about staying longer?"

Malachus shook his head. "No. I wanted to speak with you first. You're the wagon master." He tucked the pipestem in the corner of his mouth, letting the pipe smoke swirl across his tongue as he breathed.

An amused chuff greeted his statement. Kursak accepted the

pipe back. "Don't let that title fool you. Halani has almost as much say over what happens in this caravan as Hamod. I know you're teaching her to read so she can teach the rest of us who want to learn. Bring in supper from a few hunts, pay a little rent, and I'll consider it a fair exchange."

Kursak's easy agreement surprised him. Malachus had expected more reluctance and been prepared to present an even better offer.

When he told Halani his change of plans, her wide smile rounded her cheeks so hard, she squinted.

"I'm glad you decided to stay longer. I'd have worried for you traveling alone in this weather."

Later that evening, with the rain still falling and people huddled in their wagons to have their suppers, she invited him to hers. "Have supper with me."

"Do you have enough to share?" He'd happily watch her eat as his stomach growled in protest just for the chance to spend time alone with her.

She waved away his concerns. "There's plenty. Maybe we can read afterward?"

He dashed from his wagon to hers, wedging himself into the shallow overhang of the arched weatherboard above her door. Halani handed him a large towel to dry off and tucked his muddy boots and one of his satchels into a corner close to the door where she stored her own mud-caked footwear. Barefoot and mostly dry, he joined her in the main part of the wagon, where the carpets underfoot were warm and the spicy scent of hot tea and hot food cooking on her brazier filled his nostrils. There were palaces in wealthy kingdoms that would never feel so grand or welcoming as this small free trader wagon.

"Leave the door open, please," she said. "So the smoke has a way out and it doesn't get too warm in here."

Malachus did as she requested, pausing to stare into the rain-washed night and listen to the roll of thunder. "I think it's coming down even harder now." He joined her where she sat on the floor tending the brazier and her pots.

She poured tea, adding a dollop of honey to each of the cups before passing one cup to him. "Hopefully it won't last long and we don't get any lightning strikes. The last big storm we had, we lost two ewes to a bolt."

"The roads will be hard to roll a wagon over if it gets too muddy." Free trader wagons were homes on wheels, built high off the ground and heavier than the standard transport. Malachus blew on his tea to cool it before he drank. "Has Kursak said anything about waiting until the rains move through?"

Halani sipped from her teacup before setting it aside to serve up plates of boiled grains topped with bits of mutton and gravy. Malachus's mouth watered. She might not have Marata's skill, but what she served him made his stomach snarl in anticipation, and both he and Halani laughed at the sound.

She handed him a spoon. "Enjoy." She answered his question while she served her own plate. "The main road back to the Empire territories is decent for travel even in a hard rain, but this much over several days will turn it muddy. With enough travelers on it, it'll become a quagmire in no time. Kursak will want to avoid that and be one of the first groups to leave."

While they shared supper and tea and discussed topics involving the camp and the weather, an awkwardness grew between them. Malachus knew the source from which it stemmed. The memory of the kiss hovered like a ghost in the confines of her wagon, burning hotter than the brazier. She'd invited him into her home, but for a meal, not a swiving. As much as he might wish for a repeat of the kiss they had shared, he wouldn't assume anything. She'd asked him to supper. He was here for nothing more.

Except to give a gift.

He rose and padded to the spot where he'd laid the damp satchel next to his boots. His riding satchels were oil-tanned and easily sloughed off the rain. Inside, the book was dry, as were the quills and ink bottle. He presented them to her, first the ink and quills and then the wrapped book. "For you, so you may continue practicing and teaching others when I leave."

Halani rose to her knees, cupping the ink bottle so she could hold it up to a lamp and peer at the purplish liquid inside as if it were a magical elixir. She then ran the quill over her knuckles and pressed her finger against the sharpened tip. Finally, she unwrapped the book, her gasp loud when she folded the last bit of cloth aside to reveal the journal she'd coveted at the bookseller's stall. Her gaze flickered back and forth between him and the journal as if she couldn't quite believe either was real. "Why?" she asked, the one word swelled with a hundred questions.

Because it pleases you, he wanted to say. Instead, he said, "To help with your lessons. On days like these, when you can't draw your letters in the dirt, you can still practice them. And I'll teach you how to make more ink if you don't already know. If you can brew an elixir, you can make ink. It's easy."

Eyes shining with delight, Halani hugged the book to her breasts. "Thank you, Malachus." She knee-walked to him and set the book aside to embrace him.

He gathered her close, nestling his face into her pinned hair, wishing it was loose so he could wrap the thick mass of ringlets around him. "It's a small thing," he whispered near her ear. "Certainly compared to what you've done for me."

She leaned away from him with a frown. "Not a small thing at all. The value isn't in the leather or the parchment but in the sentiment behind the gift. You haven't known me long, and yet I think you know me best."

Her words echoed Seydom's prophetic ones, trapping Malachus between elation and regret. He teetered on the edge of temptation, almost succumbing to the allure of Halani's mouth as she settled into his arms and once more turned her face up to his. The memory of fire dancing over his hand and the draga awakening was the only thing that stopped him.

He cupped her face in his hands, offering a truth he hoped wouldn't offend her and might serve as an explanation for his refusal of her advances. "There's a danger to both of us here, Halani, some of it for reasons over which I have no control. Were it otherwise, I'd kiss you again, and I wouldn't stop with just your mouth." He shuddered, pushing away the evocative images his own words created in his mind. "I think it's time I bid you good night."

Halani stared at him without speaking for the longest time, and Malachus thought he might barter his soul to her if she revealed just one of the thoughts hiding behind those rain-cloud eyes of hers. She turned her head a fraction to nestle her cheek hard into his palm, never breaking her stare. "I trust you," she said, and with those words nearly shattered every restraint he'd clamped onto his lust.

He closed his eyes for a moment and prayed for fortitude. He rose and helped her stand as well. "I enjoyed supper. I'd extend the same invitation but I'm not much of a cook, nor do I have a brazier." *And soon I will lose my reason if I don't leave.*

"You're welcome to eat supper with me each night," she said. "We can read afterward if you wish."

"I'd like that."

Before he left, he allowed himself the pleasure of kissing her hand. "Tomorrow, then," he said. "We'll read after supper." Maybe then he'd have better control of his desires.

"Thank you again for the book." She cradled the journal in her arms as if it were a beloved infant. "It's a gift beyond price."

Back in his dreary wagon, with the dismal flicker of a single lamp to light the interior, Malachus recalled her farewell. "One day, Halani," he told the silence, "a very fortunate man will say the same about you." Whoever that man was, Malachus would loathe him to the end of his days.

The following day was even more miserable. Kursak ordered the wagons hitched and ready. The temporary corrals and pens were taken down, the sheep herded into a tight group by darting dogs. Oxen lowed in their traces and were joined by the mules, who brayed their objections to the weather.

Malachus tied Batraza to the back of the last wagon and joined the free traders who walked beside the slow-trundling vehicles. As Halani had feared, the rain hadn't slowed and the trade road had become a mud pit. Several times, a driver whistled for aid, and a team of six or more put their backs and shoulders into lifting a back wheel out of the sucking mud.

By the time they made it to a stretch of firmer ground, exhaustion had claimed most of them. Malachus stared down at himself, slathered in mud so thick, even the pouring rain didn't wash all of it off. His wounds ached, especially the one in his side. No doubt Halani would demand a look at them later and probably snarl at him for not being more careful.

He stood next to Kursak and Seydom, who leaned against one of the wagon's sides to rest. "Maybe we should check the road farther up to see what's waiting for us."

Kursak grunted, too tired to even turn his head. "Good idea. Find a rider."

Happy to be on horseback instead of sprayed with mud from a stuck wagon wheel, Malachus volunteered. "I can ride ahead and let you know."

He didn't bother with a saddle or bridle and rode Batraza bareback parallel to the caravan line, using his knees and heels to guide her. He nodded to Halani, seated on the driver's perch of her wagon next to the caravan's farrier.

A horse and rider moved a lot faster on the slippery road than a heavy wagon, and Malachus reconnoitered the conditions ahead of them in quick time, returning to Kursak with grim news.

"Worse than we imagined," he said. "Mud is deeper and looser farther ahead. It's a guarantee you'll sink these wagons the instant you roll the first wheel forward. Those travelers who managed to get past it before it turned into a slurry are stuck another half league out and blocking what part of the road isn't washed away, and floodwaters are covering the road."

Some of the men had gathered around them. Kursak curled one hand into a fist and punched it into his other palm. "Fuck!" He took several deep breaths before addressing Malachus once more. "Send a message down the line. We stop where we stand and see what the morning brings."

Nathin spoke up. "We'll block the road completely."

"I don't give a godsdamn," the wagon master snapped. "Whoever tries to get past us will just end up like the ones ahead of us—stuck and in danger of drowning."

At Kursak's orders, the caravan halted, and nervous free traders stayed up to keep an eye on their wagons in case they started to sink. Malachus remained outside with them, discussing what to do in case that happened or floodwaters overwhelmed them.

Halani met up with him just as he went to check on Batraza. The rain had lightened to a heavy drizzle, plastering Halani's clothes to her small frame. The hint of a curve at her waist and hips teased him, and she held a wrapped bundle in careful hands. It was the finest sight Malachus had seen all day.

"No reading or supper tonight," he told her. "We're all on guard duty." Though guarding wagons from mud was a first for him. "What are you doing out here, Halani?"

She slowly unwrapped her bundle and presented him with a cup from which tendrils of steam wafted. "Broth," she announced. "Hot."

Had he not been on his knees in the mud several times already, Malachus would have knelt in front of her and worshipped. He took the cup, breathing in the scent of herbs and salt. "You are a goddess," he proclaimed.

"If I was, I'd stop the rain." She produced a small hunk of bread from the magic bundle. "Here. This is for the broth."

He thanked her for both, then admonished her. "You shouldn't be out here, Halani."

"Unlike this road, I'm not going to melt."

Her statement encapsulated every fear every free trader trapped on the road had.

Malachus finished the food in short order, shaking the cup to capture the last drop. "I think that was the best I've ever had."

Halani laughed. "As you've had to swallow a vat of willow-bark tea recently, I'm not at all surprised you'd say that."

He considered telling her to return to her wagon and get dry, then thought better of it. She was an adult woman who made her own decisions. And while they couldn't read in this mess, it didn't mean they couldn't have a lesson.

"What is the letter that looks like half a pheasant's tail?"

At his quizzing, her eyes rounded with delight, and she eagerly followed his lead as the rain cascaded down on them.

She stayed with him through the night, refusing to leave even when he teased her over her numerous yawns. Their sleepy levity faded as the gray light of another wet day revealed land that was now a lake.

Kursak called a gathering of the caravan. "The road's falling apart as I speak, and we're turning into an island. I'm open to ideas for how we can get out of this with the caravan intact."

One of the free trader women spoke, saying aloud what everyone already knew. "Even if the rain stopped tomorrow, the rest of the road won't be fit to travel for several days."

"What about the old fen road?" Nathin's gaze swept the crowd. "We'd have to double back about a league, turn west, then south. It would put us back on the main road not far from Domora. We'd have about a day's travel east to get there, but the entire trip would take less time than waiting for this road to dry."

Unfamiliar with the landscape, Malachus thought Nathin's suggestion a good one. Others did not.

"Through Hedock's Fen?" Seydom scowled. "Are you jesting? If the rains are washing out roads here, that fen is a shallow sea by now."

"But not the road itself. When the old emperor ordered it built, his engineers knew the fen would flood from just a spat of rain, so they elevated it high enough to stop it from going underwater when the fen did." He looked to Kursak. "It's more a causeway than a road."

Kursak frowned, hesitating. "I don't know."

Malachus gaped at him. "Why not? If it's elevated, we can get across."

"Because crossing the fen isn't the problem. The fen road ends not far from Icsom's Retreat. It's bandit country there. Most free traders avoid it and stick to the safer, more traveled roads."

"There are enough of us to defend ourselves if we're attacked." Nathin nodded at each man standing in the group, including Malachus. "All of us know our way around an ax or a bow."

Kursak still hesitated. "Some of those raiders travel in bands as big as twenty."

"We're more than that."

"We are, only if you count the women and children."

They were getting nowhere with the two men volleying back and forth. Against his better judgment, Malachus had already questioned Kursak's hesitation in taking the fen road, and once again he ignored the voice that told him he wasn't a free trader or an elder of this group. "However you decide, you should know that if we get another day of rain, the floodwaters will reach us here. The travelers at risk now are probably already retreating. We can block the way of those behind us, but we're also blocking the ones in front. If they can't get out of the way because of us, and they can't go around us, they'll go through us. If you're avoiding the fen road because you fear confrontation and fighting, you'll end up facing it against people trying not to drown instead of those wanting to steal. A desperate man in fear of his life makes a more formidable opponent than a greedy one."

A heavy silence descended on the group until Kursak broke it. "I want to see the upper road myself. When I get back, you'll have my decision. Be ready to move in case I choose the fen road." He left to find a mount, and the group dispersed for their wagons and any tasks they needed to complete in anticipation of moving.

Halani laid a hand on Malachus's arm. "I'm glad you said what you did."

He basked in her approval. "I'm not one of you, but it seemed wrong not to say something."

"Until you leave, you are one of us. Kursak is a reasonable

man. You made a reasonable argument. I'll be surprised if we aren't on our way toward the fen road by midday."

She was right. Pale and even grimmer than before, Kursak returned to the caravan, snapping out orders before he'd even dismounted from his horse. "We'll leave the road and cut across the spots where the land rolls higher." He eyed Halani. "We'll need you for this."

Need her for what? Malachus had no time to ask her nor Halani the time to explain. They began the laborious process of turning the wagons in the opposite direction so that they faced perpendicular to the stretch of half-drowned rye grass.

Halani strode to the front of the caravan line, a poplar staff in one hand, eyes half closed as she stared into the distance. Kursak came to stand beside Malachus for a moment as he watched Halani.

"The Empire punishes those who deal in sorcery. It's a death sentence for them." The wagon master's eyes were grave, filled with both threat and warning. "If you have any affection for the woman who pulled you back from death's threshold, you'll say nothing to anyone outside this caravan about what you see." He walked away then to join Halani, leaving a perplexed Malachus to mull over his words. He understood soon enough why Kursak said what he did.

She denied any knowledge of earth magic or the skill to use it, had warned him of the dangers of even alluding to some power she might have, fearful of the Empire's eyes and ears. Yet now she called forth the hymn of earth, her entire being centered on its song, to guide her and the slow-moving caravan over treacherous ground to reach their destination.

Except for the creak of wagon wheels and the occasional bleat from a ewe, they moved in silence, mindful of Halani's concentration as she led them across waterlogged pastures. They had to stop twice, once to heave a wagon that had veered off the narrow path out of the mud, another time to partially unload and reload the heaviest wagon so it, too, wouldn't sink.

The journey took an eternity, and night rushed toward them as Kursak's triumphant whoop burst into the silence. "The fen road!" he shouted, pointing to a narrow causeway just ahead of them.

A cheer rose from the caravan, and Kursak snatched a wilting Halani into his arms to twirl her around. Several of the other men did the same, including Nathin and Seydom, until Halani raised her hands in surrender and begged not to be twirled again. She stared at Malachus with glassy eyes as he approached her.

He stroked her cool cheek with two fingers, noting the violet shadows under her eyes, the paleness of her mouth. "Well done, daughter of earth," he said softly.

"It was, wasn't it," she replied with a sweet smile before blood spurted from her nose. Her eyes rolled back and her legs crumpled beneath her. She collapsed in his arms.

CHAPTER FOURTEEN

The distant chime of the courtyard's gate bell sounded in the solarium. Gharek stiffened. A visitor at this late hour didn't bode well. He watched his daughter where she sat across from him on the floor. She ignored the chime to study the cards laid out between them in a neat square, their faces beautifully illustrated and used to hide the winning numbers on their undersides. Her small features pinched with concentration.

"You have to pick sometime, Estred," he told her. "It's not going to flip over by itself."

Estred chewed on her lower lip. "I don't want to pick the wrong one."

"It won't matter. You've won the three games you needed to win the wager between us. I've already agreed you can stay up longer this evening."

Not to be hurried by her impatient father, she stared at the cards as if to will them into giving up their secrets to her. "If I win this one, then maybe I can stay up tomorrow too?"

Gharek arched an eyebrow. At seven years old, his daughter was a consummate negotiator. What a diplomat she'd make once she was an adult. The thought nearly crushed him. No matter her natural talent and intelligence, Estred would never go beyond the walls of this city, maybe not even the walls of this courtyard. Not if he failed in the task handed to him by the empress.

"Out of the question," he replied. "You can win the next dozen games, and you'll still go to bed at the usual time tomorrow. You're lucky I weakened tonight, especially when I suspect you might have cheated at the last play."

She bristled. "I won that game fair and honest, Papa!"

He held up both hands, prepared to apologize, but stopped at the light footsteps entering the solarium.

Estred's nurse, Siora, stood in the doorway. When he met her eye, she inclined her head toward the hallway.

He turned back to Estred. "My apologies. I only tease. I know you don't cheat. Keep studying your cards. I want to have a word with Siora in private. When we're done, I'll return, and we can finish the game."

She tapped her small, bare feet on the floor in an excited dance and grinned at her nurse, who was standing behind him. "Can I have a bowl of honey pudding since I'm staying up late tonight, Siora?"

The woman pretended to consider the question as if the world's existence hinged on her answer. "I'll think about it. Let me talk to your father first; then I'll give you my answer."

Siora possessed a voice that always soothed his daughter, yet Gharek found it uncanny for no reason he could explain. Her gaze, as well, made him uncomfortable every time it landed on him. And yet he trusted her with his daughter's care. With a single act of profound courage, she'd proven her devotion to Estred and earned a place in his household, no matter how uneasy she made him.

She followed him down the hall, finally stopping near the courtyard entrance. Siora gestured toward the gate leading from the courtyard to the street. "There's an Unknown outside with a message for you."

Gharek's breath caught. He hadn't expected this, not so soon. He'd heard nothing from Koopman since giving him the fee for information. Not a word, and he was prepared to extract the monies given to retain the wily merchant's services from Koopman by force if he didn't earn them. Not that a fat purse of *belshas* would help Gharek when he approached the empress to explain he'd failed in the task she'd given him. He'd simply use the money to get Estred safely out of the Empire and away from Dalvila's vengeful clutches before she had him vivisected in front of her terrified court.

"Did he say anything?" He flinched at the idiocy of his question.

Siora's inscrutable expression never changed. "No, master. All Unknowns are mute."

He scowled. This beggar woman made servant never failed to make him stumble in a way no one else did. "Keep Estred occupied. I don't need her sneaking into the courtyard to hear. She's too curious for her own good."

"Be careful, master. An Unknown never comes bearing good news."

Gharek stared at her, caught off guard. Was that a note of concern he heard? He shook his head. He was more tired than he thought if he imagined such things from the enigmatic Siora.

He left her in the hall for the courtyard. A lush oasis within the teeming city, the space provided Gharek and his small family and staff a sanctuary surrounded on three sides by the house itself and closed off by a stone wall on the fourth, with a stout door and gate that led to the street and was barred and bolted from the inside.

The sultry air hung redolent with the scent of night-blooming flowers. In the daylight, the garden gave privacy and a place for

Estred to play and study, away from the cruel taunts and prying eyes of people who saw only her deformity instead of her character.

At the moment, the courtyard wore a layered cloak of shadows, turning it into an eerie place, made vaguely sinister by his awareness of the messenger waiting patiently for him in the narrow space between door and gate.

Gharek eyed his visitor, who offered no greeting or salute. Whatever expression the Unknown wore lay hidden behind a blank white mask whose only embellishments were cutouts for the eyes, nose, and mouth.

Unknowns belonged to a mysterious guild whose members were gleaned from the poorest of the poor within Kraelian society. Offered the chance to escape starvation, prostitution, and a myriad of other miseries, juveniles older than nine clamored to join the cryptic guild of messengers.

Such beneficence came at a high price. The Guild required that their recruits cut all familial ties, shun all friendships, and pledge their loyalty only to the Guild. They surrendered their identities and their names, as well as their tongues. Like eunuch guards castrated for their service in a royal concubines' prison, Unknowns had their tongues cut out upon entering service. A mute messenger couldn't be tortured into revealing the information they conveyed between parties.

Once healed and trained, they took up their new role, mute, masked, and nameless to anyone outside the Guild. Their unique attributions made them valuable to the Empire's aristocracy and nobility as well as the empress's vast network of spies.

The one who stood before Gharek now passed him a sealed letter and stepped back to give him privacy to read. No emblem marked the seal. Gharek didn't need it to know who sent it. The faintest hint of sorcery hummed against his fingers as he ran them over the wax depression before breaking it open.

Under the flickering light of a hanging lamp, he scanned the contents, heart speeding up with each sentence he read. To anyone else, the letter was a dull, nonsensical soliloquy. Gharek, however, read the real message beneath the mundane one. The mother-bond had surfaced in the Maesor market. Koopman requested Gharek's appearance at his stall as soon as possible.

"Is anyone waiting for you to return with an answer?" At the messenger's nod, Gharek removed one of the rings bearing his family seal from his finger and gave it to the Unknown. He didn't have the time to draft a response, and while the ring would verify his receipt of the message and confirmation of his impending arrival, its value was minimal. He could afford to lose it to Koopman, who'd no doubt forget to return it to him.

The Unknown tucked the ring away, then silently waited until Gharek unbarred and opened the gate. Once on the street, the messenger swiftly joined the darkness, disappearing from sight.

Gharek returned to the solarium, finding it empty and dark. A light and voices drew him to the kitchen, where he discovered Siora sitting at the preparation table with Estred, sharing a bowl of honey pudding. Limber and supple as a ribbon, the little girl gripped the handle of her spoon between her toes and tucked spoonfuls of pudding into her mouth with her foot. She giggled at something her nurse said.

Siora's gaze fell on him. She set her spoon down and pushed the bowl closer to Estred. "Finish up and don't forget to put the bowl and spoons in the dry sink. I'll turn your bed down for you."

Once more they met, this time in a different hallway. "I have an errand to attend that can't wait."

Unlike his other servants, Siora didn't always accept his statements with a silent nod or quiet acquiescence. She didn't argue with him but never failed to make a point that left him with the certainty he'd just been lectured, no matter how gently done.

"These are hours that make any journey through the city, no matter how urgent, perilous to the traveler. Footpads rule the streets right now."

"I'm capable of defending myself, and the Unknown made it here without injury."

Siora looked through him as if he were a window to a scene only she could see. "Even the stupidest thief knows not to touch an Unknown unless they want their entrails knitted across the city gates, and you go where even an Unknown refuses to travel."

All the hairs on Gharek's nape rose. What did this strange woman see? He didn't have time to interrogate her. Koopman knew no one else could match what Gharek was willing to pay for the mother-bond, but he didn't trust the man to hold it for him indefinitely. He couldn't afford to let it slip through his fingers.

"Tell Estred I'll see her in the morning."

"Of course. She'll wonder why you aren't here to bid her good night. What do you want me to tell her?"

"Whatever you think will pacify her. I won't be long."

The streets of Domora were mostly deserted at this hour. Unlike destroyed Kraelag, Domora was a more genteel city on the surface. Murderers and thieves, slatterns and slavers, still patrolled the avenues and alleyways as they did in the old capital, but were far more subtle about it.

Siora's warning that he'd battle packs of footpads never materialized, though figures observed his passing from dark alcoves. It was true he wasn't an Unknown, but he was the empress's cat's-paw, with a reputation that made the city's wolves think twice about attacking him.

Koopman's letter contained directions to a brothel set back from the main avenue. A grand affair, it served a wealthy clientele, complete with guards at the door to keep undesirables away.

A guard allowed Gharek through once he uttered the password Koopman had included in his missive. Inside, a young woman, as silent as an Unknown, led him through the brothel to a set of stairs. He followed her up the carpeted treads, their steps soundless, until they reached a landing from which three corridors branched off in different directions.

His guide pointed to the shortest, most dimly lit of the three and finally spoke. "Enter the last door on your right." She left him there, her task complete. Had her perfume not still teased his nose after her departure, he might have thought her a figment of his imagination.

While the hallway's distance looked short from his place on the landing, he had the uncanny sensation he walked ten times its length, maybe more, before he stood in front of the door the prostitute had instructed him to open. A chill buffeted his face as if he stood within the swirl of a winter wind. The door lever under his hand burned with cold.

No gateway to the Maesor market was ever the same or appeared in the same place. The sorcerers who created the gates possessed varied skills. Whoever created this one wielded a talent for manipulating temperature.

Gharek shivered in his summer garb, depressed the handle, and pushed the door open. The busy street traffic of the Maesor greeted him, ebbing and flowing around him like a silent river over stone. A few people glanced his way before returning their attention to their tasks.

Though he had entered and departed through the ensorcelled

gates before, Gharek's senses reeled, and he paused to gain his bearings. Behind him, the door had disappeared, and he stood in front of a stall selling the shrunken heads of various creatures, including humans.

The Maesor's glowing amber sky remained unchanged, and the chill surrounding the gate gave way to balmy temperatures with no wind blasting through the streets. The market's location, a place between places, a time between times, protected it from the elements of the real world and the laws of the Empire, which made the Maesor and its denizens rogue.

More familiar now with the spiderweb network of thoroughfares and avenues that made up the sprawling market, he found Koopman's stall in little time. The blind guard and his ratty mongrel were as he remembered, still tasked with vetting all comers to the rug merchant's place of business. The dog growled when Gharek passed through the entrance, but its master remained quiet, milky gaze following Gharek into the stall.

Koopman welcomed him inside with an avaricious smile and invitation to stay for tea. Gharek eased past a stack of the vile, soul-infested rugs the merchant stocked, accidentally brushing the edge of one. He leapt away when something cold and moist slithered against his shoulder.

"Careful with that one, friend," Koopman said. "I've the soul of a pimp woven into that carpet. A man out of Kevesin Province just bought it for a handsome sum as a gift for his future mother-in-law."

Gharek eyed the ripple of motion oozing between warp and weft. Apparently Koopman's customer wasn't fond of his bride's mother.

"I received your letter. Do you have the mother-bond?" He

wasn't interested in niceties nor did he wish to stay in the market any longer than necessary. His heartbeat drummed double time at the thought of the mother-bond close at hand.

Koopman crooked a finger, eyes shining in the stall's gloom with a feline luminosity. "Follow me." They moved toward the back of the stall, and like the brothel's hall, the space seemed to go far beyond what one saw of the stall from the street. He stopped in front of an ornate cabinet and produced a key from a pouch belted at his waist.

Anticipation tested Gharek's patience as the merchant blew on the key's tip with a gentle breath and muttered an incantation. He then fitted the key to the cabinet's lock. The locking mechanism hissed as he turned the key one way, then growled when he twisted it in the opposite direction. A snick and click followed before he opened the doors to reveal a succession of small drawers stacked one atop the other, each outfitted with its own lock. A second key, with a spell of its own attached to it, unlocked one of the drawers.

He reached inside and pulled out a nondescript dagger, its blade encrusted with dried blood, and presented it to Gharek with a flourish.

Gharek stared at it, then Koopman, then the knife again, puzzled by the man's strange humor. "What is this?"

"Blood from the man who came to the market with the mother-bond."

For a moment, Gharek wondered if he was supposed to laugh at what was a terrible joke; then he noticed Koopman's expression, excited but lacking any dark humor that came with a prank played. "Where is the mother-bond?"

Koopman's features froze and his grip tightened on the dagger's hilt. Gharek tensed, waiting for a sudden lunge or fast swipe with the knife. He hadn't come here to fight the merchant, but so far none of his expectations were manifesting as he'd hoped.

The rug merchant relaxed his grip, and his face eased into its usual jowls and creases. He didn't let go of the knife and warily eyed Gharek. "You paid me to keep an eye out for the motherbond. I did, and the man who has it arrived in the Maesor this evening just as you thought he would."

"Did you see him yourself?" Gharek worked to control his disappointment so he could think clearly. He had assumed too much when he read Koopman's note. A mistake he'd never make again.

The other man nodded. "He came here, said he'd heard I might be the man to talk with about brokering the sale of a rare artifact. He was a free trader just arrived from the new market in Goban territory."

Koopman's last revelation blunted Gharek's frustration. Dalvila's spies had said the bone had disappeared in or near that market. "Did he try to sell it to you?"

Koopman sighed. "It's what I was aiming for. He was jumpier than a ground spider. When I asked to see what he had, he told me he didn't have it with him, that he'd only bring it if he were guaranteed a sale, sight unseen. I told him that wasn't how I or anyone else in the Maesor did business but that I was still interested in setting up negotiations between him and a buyer. I demanded a blood accord from him." He pointed to the bloodied dagger. "I used a different blade to draw my blood."

This trip hadn't been a complete waste, and Gharek no longer despaired at the thought of a future meeting announcing his failure to the empress. Not yet at least. "Do you think he'll return?"

"Who can say?" Koopman lifted one shoulder. "As I said, he was more skittish than a virgin before her first bedding."

Gharek glanced around him, at the rugs and tapestries with their repulsive occupants woven into the threads. "I couldn't imagine why."

"Me either, but I got his blood for a reason." The merchant crooked a finger for Gharek to follow him farther back into the stall to another small room, empty of goods and furniture except for a loom on which was stretched a colorful swatch of woven wool. "This bit of rag is useful for my line of work," he said. "We can put it to good use right now."

Wary of any of the tapestries or carpets in Koopman's stall, Gharek reluctantly edged closer, seeing nothing out of the ordinary about the square of cloth. "What makes it so special?"

Koopman puffed up like a proud parent bragging on a favorite child. "It's a trap shadow, smuggled out of the haunted city during my father's youth. It traded hands a few times before I got it. It can decipher memory and images from blood."

Gharek recoiled. That it came from cursed Midrigar was bad enough. That it was a trap shadow made it beyond grotesque. Infused with a soul condemned to slavery and bound eternally to the fabric, a trap shadow had the ability to harvest impressions and bits of memories from things and people living and once living. If the mage who owned one were caught and executed for their sorcery, the spell enslaving the soul was broken. Owning a trap shadow carried many risks. The soul, sentient, often hostile or half mad from its long enslavement, looked for any opportunity to betray its master. Koopman obviously enjoyed a life of peril combined with lucrative payoff if he held on to a trap shadow out of Midrigar. The gods only knew what manner of entity slithered through the cloth.

"And it can harvest images from the free trader's blood?"

Koopman nodded. He pressed the flat of the blade against the fabric's surface.

Gharek inhaled sharply as the pattern of colors shifted, rearranging themselves as if rethreaded by the hand of an invisible weaver. They snaked around the blade, drawing the blood off the steel into the fabric's threads. A draft of cold air, smelling of decay, wafted up from the swatch. He covered his nose against the stench.

Koopman grinned at his reaction. "This trap shadow has never much liked me."

"I can see that," Gharek said in his driest tone.

The merchant's grin widened, revealing a row of yellow teeth filed to points. He waited until the threads loosened from the knife to reweave themselves back into their original position before lifting it and setting it aside. Gharek noted that the blade gleamed dully in the lamplight, not a single drop of blood on it. Koopman then plucked at one of the warp threads knotted tight to the loom's frame. Like an out-of-tune harp string, the warp thread made a discordant sound. "Show us what the blood holds."

Threads wriggled on the loom, shrinking and contracting like a knot of convulsive worms. Gharek's skin crawled at the sight. Colors set in random designs wove themselves with purpose, becoming discernible faces. The threads switched quickly, not allowing much time to view them, until Koopman snapped, "Slow down."

The fabric did as he commanded with ill grace, rattling the loom on which it was stretched before pausing on one visage, that of an older man with gray hair and eyes to match.

"That's the free trader who came to visit," Koopman said.

The threads shifted and wove again, this time to show the lined face of an old woman bearing a slight resemblance to the free trader. Gharek stared at her for a moment, arrested by her expression. "Who is that?

Koopman shook his head. "Who knows? The trader came alone to the Maesor."

The trap shadow wove and rewove again, showing numerous faces. When it wove one of the last, Gharek gasped. "Stop."

The trap shadow didn't stop, unraveling yet again to construct a new visage. This time it was Koopman who yelled, "Stop." The threads froze. Koopman smiled. "I can see why you wanted it to stop. I'd climb on top of her in a heartbeat."

Gharek ignored the vulgar comment. The somber face of a pretty woman stared back at him with a guarded expression. She bore a strong resemblance to the free trader and a weaker one to the old woman. He had no solid evidence to prove the importance of the two women in his bid to obtain the mother-bond, but he never second-guessed his instincts, and right now they were screeching inside his skull that if he found either of them, he'd get his hands on the mother-bond.

"How often can your trap shadow reweave the faces from the free trader's blood?"

Koopman instructed the fabric square to be still, and it settled once more into an innocent-looking weave of bright colors. "Three or four, though the faces lose their detail with each weaving until they fade altogether."

Gharek's thoughts raced. "Hire a good artist who knows how to keep his mouth shut and have him sketch three faces from your trap shadow's weave: the free trader, the old woman, and the pretty one who looks like them both. I want the portraits delivered to me as soon as they're finished. I can put the Spider's spies to work then."

The skin-crawling sensation that had plagued Gharek from the moment he'd stepped foot inside Koopman's stall had only intensified as he watched the trap shadow do its work. He was eager to leave and planned to scour the first layer of skin off his body as soon as he returned home.

Time in the Maesor market passed differently than it did in the normal world. The hour he'd spent with Koopman translated to half the night in the normal world, and he walked home through empty streets.

He barred the gate and locked the heavy courtyard door behind him, releasing a tired breath as he stepped into the courtyard. The house was dark, but he found his way unerringly to his daughter's room. Watery moonlight built shadows more than it cast light, but he spotted Estred asleep in her bed, sharing the space with Siora, who spooned against her.

The scene reminded him of why he willingly embraced the role of cat's-paw to the empress, despite the risks. Every trial, every danger, every sacrifice, was worth the chance to give Estred the life she was meant to have and not the one cruel gods had bequeathed to her from birth. From Dalvila's malice to the enslaved evil of trap shadows, even to the capture, killing, and butchering of a near-mythical creature, Gharek had no intention of turning away from any of it. If necessary, he'd burn down the world for his daughter, even if all of history and its survivors cursed his name through eternity.

CHAPTER FIFTEEN

Halani woke to the sound of falling rain and the sight of Malachus's handsome face looming over her, drawn with worry.

He stroked her cheek. "Welcome back, earth's daughter." The strain in his voice contrasted with the relief in his dark eyes. "You gave us all quite a scare."

She blinked and pressed her palm to her forehead where a headache throbbed hard enough to make her ears ring. "The fen road."

"We're on it, thanks to you."

She burrowed past the hazy layer of pain to memories of the earth's ever-changing pitch as she dowsed a path over soggy ground, seeking out those places where the wagons wouldn't sink. Triumphant cheering had erupted behind her when she and they sighted the narrow stretch of elevated road built long ago through Hedock's Fen.

"I remember," she said. The road and more: Kursak spinning her around, his sun-cured face smiling and triumphant, several of the other men doing the same, until she was breathless. Then Malachus, more reserved but with a gaze brimming with admiration and something else that made her knees go weak.

Well done, earth's daughter. Exhausted by the dowsing, Halani still grinned at his praise. She had answered him, though she didn't recall what she had said. A hot tickling in her nose preceded a river of wetness suddenly gushing over her top lip, and the world around her shrank to a pinpoint of light in the middle of a rushing darkness, until it too faded away. She'd known nothing else until now.

Comforting warmth pressed against her back as Malachus's arms cradled her in a careful embrace. She lay draped across his lap while he perched on the top tread of her wagon steps, protected from the wet by the weatherboard overhanging her door.

"Was I bleeding?" She touched the shallow dip between her nose and lip. No wetness or crusted blood there now.

Malachus nodded, the pinched look he wore emphasizing the sharpness of his nose. "Yes. I cleaned you up while you slept. How do you feel?"

"Like someone's joyfully beating a gong inside my skull."

Footsteps splashing through puddles alerted her to a visitor. Kursak climbed the first stair tread, wearing an expression similar to Malachus's. "You're awake." He turned his head to bellow over his shoulder, "She's awake!" before giving her a mock glare. "Gods, Halani, stop trying to scare a decade off my life. I need those years. Good thing Asil wasn't here, or she'd have my balls on a spit for asking you to dowse that much ground at once." He reached for her hand and gave it a squeeze. "You'll forgive me?"

"Stop being wooden-headed," she admonished him. "There's nothing to forgive. I had a nosebleed and now a headache. Nothing a little butterbur can't fix." That, and she'd awakened in the arms of a man who set fire to her blood with a kiss. A sweet reward for a task completed.

By the time she'd finished her sentence, most of the other free traders had gathered to thank Halani and praise her efforts. There were offers to bring food and drink and take over her chores while she rested and regained her strength.

"How do you feel?" Kursak echoed Malachus's earlier question.

"I won't be dancing around a campfire, but I'm fine otherwise. Malachus's lap is comfortable, but I should get up." She tried to sit, only to have Malachus press her gently back down.

"No need to flail around. Take your time. You've funneled a lot of magic through your body. It doesn't just disappear once you stop using it."

She didn't protest, happy to spend a little more time in his arms. His last comment made her pause. "How do you know that?"

"Know what?"

The hymn of earth was a constant around him, and she'd grown used to its soft lullaby in her mind every time he was near. She had no doubt he was an earth witch like her, though she'd never seen him wield sorcery of any kind. "That magic doesn't just fade away once you stop using it."

He slanted her one of his enigmatic looks. "I'm well-read. Six languages, remember?"

Kursak snorted. "You can teach her those later. Give her to the women and help check the wagons for any damage to the wheels or struts." He wagged a finger at Halani. "Get dried off and in your wagon to rest. I'll have someone bring you something to eat."

"But . . ." She was exhausted, but she wanted to see the fen road and the fen itself.

"No arguments. Who knows if we'll need you to dowse again soon. You need sleep and food to regain your strength. We have to start rolling again." The wagon master motioned for two of the free trader women to join him. "Can you see to her?" At their nods, he gave Malachus a sharp gesture and strode away.

"Such an overbearing man," Halani muttered.

Malachus chuckled and eased her into a sitting position before guiding her to the women waiting to help her down the steps. "Another reason why he makes a competent wagon master."

Before he went to join Kursak and the others, Malachus caught her braid, pulling it gently over her shoulder to caress its length before letting go. "I'll echo Kursak. I've lost a century off my life span today. Rest. You need it more than you realize."

"A century? Not a decade? You're a long-lived man, Malachus," she teased. His knowing half smile made her wonder. He bowed to her and the other women before leaving to help the men.

After much cajoling and threatening from her helpers to cooperate and not sneak out of her wagon, Halani, dried and clad in a thin shift, crawled into her bed and huddled under the covers. She fell into a deep sleep, no longer bothered by her headache or the residual ring of earth music throbbing in her ears.

She didn't rouse until the following morning, pulled from a deep sleep by the lurch and sway of her wagon and the sounds of the caravan on the move. The pocket door built in the front of the wagon allowed access to the driver's perch when slid aside. She discovered Nathin seated there, puffing away on his favorite pipe and coaxing the mule pulling the wagon to stop falling asleep in its traces. To her delight, the rain had finally stopped, and splinters of anemic sunlight sliced through the low-hanging clouds.

Nathin glanced over his shoulder. "Want me to whistle back to Ruviti to bring you breakfast?"

Appalled at the idea of having someone act as a servant or nursemaid to her when the most she suffered from was a lingering headache, Halani quickly refused and closed the pocket door. She dressed, pinned up her bedraggled braid, and silently blessed whoever had cleaned the mud off her shoes from the previous day's trek. She propped the back door open using a hook latch and stood at the threshold, holding on to the door frame for balance.

The free trader driving the wagon behind hers waved to her. Halani edged farther out on the threshold for a better look at the expanse of fen on either side of the road. Water and clumps of half-submerged sedge grass for as far as the eye could see. Herons stalked the watery landscape for frogs and fish, their long legs creeping through the water.

"If you lean any farther, you're going to fall off the ledge, Halani." Malachus rode up alongside her wagon, mounted on the caravan's slowest draft horse, ironically named Falcon.

She stared at the big, sleepy-eyed horse, then at his rider. "Where's Batraza?"

"Enjoying the leisurely pace at the back of the line and the grooming I just gave her. We're on a narrow road, and I didn't want to unsettle the teams by riding her alongside them." He guided Falcon a little closer to her wagon. "Care to join me?"

An offer she'd be mad to refuse. "I'd love to. Pull him to the side, and I'll jump down."

Malachus frowned. "I'll ride to the front and tell Nathin to stop."

"No need. This wagon is moving slower than those herons out in the water, and I've done this plenty of times." She proved her boast by leaping off the slow-rolling wagon to the ground. A few quick steps brought her to Malachus's side.

His frown had worsened to a scowl as he stared down at her from his high perch atop Falcon. "Risky," he said.

"Only if I lie down in the road and wait for Tursom's team to walk over me." She grasped the arm he offered, then paused. "Speaking of risky."

"I've been shoving wagons out of the mud for the past two

days, Halani. If I haven't torn or split anything yet, I doubt it will happen helping you onto this horse."

He was right. Using his forearm for leverage and the saddle cantle for balance, she hoisted herself onto Falcon to sit behind Malachus. At her "I'm set," he coaxed the animal back into its plodding gait.

"Who was the wit that named this unhurried creature Falcon?"

Halani sneaked a caress of Malachus's hair, admiring the way the weak sunlight gilded some of the strands. "Seydom's son. Falcon's dam is the long-legged mare pulling Kursak's wagon. When she foaled, Brecka was certain her colt would be fast as a courser, though I'm not sure why he ever thought so. Anyway, hope sometimes wins over sense, and he named him Falcon."

After so much rain, the humid air felt thick enough to wear, and newly hatched midges gorged themselves on people and animals alike. Halani ignored both except for the occasional swat to her arms or Falcon's tail slapping her leg as he too brushed away the pesky flies. These were minor annoyances, especially when compared to the pleasure of sharing this time with Malachus. His sojourn with the free traders was almost done. She'd not beg him to stay, though she dreaded the day he'd tell her farewell. For now, she'd simply bask in the feel of an emerging sun on her shoulders and enjoy the way his slim torso flexed under her hands with the horse's gait.

Malachus reined the languid Falcon around one of the wider wagons to capture a spot where the line widened to give them a better sense of privacy as they talked. "How far until we reach the end of the fen road?"

A part of Halani wished the road might never end. "I'm not sure. At this speed, with stops overnight, we might be a sennight on it." Knowing Kursak, he'd push their pace a lot faster tomorrow. They'd all had a day and night to rest, and the fen road, while high and mostly dry, cut through a dreary landscape unsuitable for travelers.

She stared at the endless expanse of submerged fen before addressing a question that had nagged her since Malachus first rode up on Falcon. "How is it this horse tolerates you when the others don't?"

Her heartbeat thumped a little faster when Malachus laced his fingers through hers and tugged her hand forward until it rested against his ribs instead of his side. "This animal is so tranquil, you could put a starving wolf on his back, and he wouldn't care. I noticed it when I tied Batraza near him one evening. He ignored her."

They fell into a comfortable silence after that, with the sounds of the caravan swirling around them as they rolled slowly down the narrow fen road. Halani prayed Kursak's worries about traveling through bandit country didn't come to fruition and that the rains and flooding had kept such hornets at home. She said as much to Malachus.

"You're in a worried mood today," he said. "Calm your thoughts and enjoy these hours. The sun is out, the sheep are dry, and according to Nathin, you free traders are capable of defending yourselves. I can help as well should it come to that."

She didn't doubt it. From the look of things when she and the others discovered him in the grass with the dead mercenaries, he'd dispatched them with ease and efficiency, even with three arrows lodged in him and poison running through his blood. She'd never seen him fight but suspected he made a formidable opponent.

Despite his good advice and her delight in his companionship, she still worried, and over something that had plagued her since they'd first brought him to their caravan. "Malachus?"

"Hmm?"

"If you tell anyone what you saw me do yesterday, it will be a death sentence." Halani didn't truly believe that once he left their caravan, he'd chat about their trip to the fen road to strangers in a pub, but he was an outlander in an unfamiliar country, and while he might take offense at her constant reminder of the Empire's punitive measures against witches and sorcery, she felt it necessary to reiterate the dangers.

His thumb slid along her knuckles in a back-and-forth caress. "Kursak said the same before you even started. Allay your fears. Should anyone ever learn of your abilities, it won't be from me. Besides, I knew you wielded earth magic, despite your denials. It's infused in your salves and your elixirs, and the earth sings differently under your tread. The only surprise was just how much sorcery you can wield. Earth doesn't share her power easily, even with those born blessed with her favor." A hot shiver bolted through her when he lifted her hand and followed the path of his thumb with his lips. "Why would I put you at risk? This is a hard world, made better for you being part of it."

She was already afraid she'd lost half her heart to this man, and his words threatened to take the other half as well. "I don't understand how you don't have a swarm of hummingbirds and butterflies constantly circling you. I swear, nectar drifts off your tongue." She traced the faint ridges of ribs under his skin, making him twitch from the ticklish sensation. "How many women have you seduced with such sweet words?"

He snorted. "None that I'm aware of. I was terrible at courtship. The brotherhood taught their fosterlings how to read, write, fight, and survive in the wilderness. The ways of courting, though, I learned them on my own through trial and error. A *lot* of error."

"Truly? I find that difficult to believe. You're well-spoken, intelligent, with a strong frame and handsome face." Thoughtful and humorous, too, possessed of confidence but lacking in arrogance. Those were the things that truly endeared him to her. That he was pleasing to the eye didn't hurt, but Halani had never been in danger of falling for a pretty face.

"Speaking of nectar on the tongue," he said. "Trust me, if I'm ever in the position to counsel a boy just reaching his first beard, I have a wealth of information to share on what not to do when trying to charm or court a woman."

"Oh, come now, it couldn't have been that bad. And we all fail at courting at least once."

"But I failed spectacularly and often."

The storyteller inside her perked up, sniffing out a good tale in his words. "I want to hear this."

He groaned as if in agony. "You would dine on my humiliation?"

"While I have my doubts it's as bad as you say, I promise not to gloat over your supposed botch-ups."

He soon had her laughing helplessly and cringing in sympathetic embarrassment. "I warned you," he said after one awful recounting of his attempt at wooing a nobleman's sister.

Halani wiped away tears of mirth, her sides aching. "I'm sorry. I know I shouldn't laugh. It sounds awful, but you tell it in such a way . . ."

"I'm pleased to make you laugh."

He was doing much more than making her laugh, though she'd never say that to him—or herself—out loud.

They circumnavigated the caravan line, ending up back at her wagon just as one of the women hailed her from another wagon for help in passing out lunch to the drivers. Unconcerned by the interested looks she and Malachus received from the others, Halani offered him a wide smile as she dismounted from the half-snoozing Falcon. "Thank you for inviting me to join you in racing the wind on this fleet-footed steed," she teased.

Malachus leaned out of the saddle, close enough that if she stood on tiptoe, she could kiss his smiling mouth. "Now that you know of my courtship debacles, my dignity is in your hands and at your mercy, Halani of the Lightning."

There it was again, a moniker he'd attached to her name that only made sense to him. "Will you ever tell me why you call me that?"

He winked. "Maybe."

"If you do, I promise your dignity will remain intact."

"Ah, spoken like a true free trader. A bargain is struck. I promise to tell you before I leave."

The reminder that he'd soon leave them made her smile falter. His did the same. "No dark thoughts, Halani," he said softly before straightening once more. "I'll see you later tonight for supper and a reading lesson."

Halani lived for the reading lessons. For her, they were true magic—making sense of previously fathomless symbols, connecting them in ways that created a fountain of knowledge to fill her mind and made her thirstier every time she drank from it. She practiced on her own each chance she got, though her favorite time to do so was in Malachus's company. He was a demanding teacher and the worst sort of distraction. More than once she'd lost her concentration in learning her letters or the rules of how they were put together while listening to the way he read in that low, accented voice.

Supper on the fen road wasn't the communal one enjoyed while they stayed on the outskirts of the Goban market. With the wagons in a line instead of a circle, it was easier to stay near one's own wagon and tend to household tasks. Both Halani and Malachus had joined one of the free trader families for supper. A meal for a story or, in this instance, something from one of Malachus's books.

Halani was happy to cede him the stage and listened, as enthralled as the others, as he read accounts of Winosia's history, the rise and fall of its kingdoms, its deities and religions.

"The monks who fostered you, who did they worship?" Their host for the evening, Kadena, puffed on the pipe he'd lit. "And why aren't you a monk too?"

Malachus traced the edge of his book with a finger, his expression far away as if he recalled the years spent in the Sovatin monastery, learning from the monks who passed on their storehouses of knowledge to him. "I considered it, but I'm a wanderer." Several heads nodded. Wandering was in the blood of every free trader. "I lived with the brotherhood for a long time but was restless, ready to fly away by the time I was old enough."

That nomadic nature had brought him here, where he'd crossed paths with Halani, and for that she was thankful. Even were he not on a quest to break his mysterious curse, that same nature would send him away from her. She pushed aside the melancholy thought and concentrated on what he was saying.

"The brotherhood worship the sky god, Pernu, and his wives, Ninsurgha of earth and Suela of rivers. But they are devoted most to Pernu, the father of draga, of men, and of horses."

Halani touched the medallion Gilene had gifted her. It lay cool against her bare skin, hidden beneath her shift. "The Savatar have a similar story," she said. "Though it's their fire goddess, Agna, who created all three, and it was woman she created first instead of man."

"I want to hear how Pernu made a draga!" One of Kadena's large brood of children waved the toy he clutched at Malachus as if to spur him on with the suggestion. "Something besides Kansi Yuv and old Golnar." Several more children added their support of the idea.

Malachus pretended to consider, cajoled by the pleading and whining from his audience until he gave a long-suffering sigh and said, "All right. I'll do it, though not tonight, and I can't promise I'll tell as good a story as Halani does."

"We don't mind!" one child said, bouncing up and down in her older sister's lap.

With supper finished, Halani and Malachus bid their hosts good night. The provender wagon occupied a spot farther back in the train than Halani's did. When he offered to walk her to her wagon, she readily accepted.

They strolled toward their destination with the slowness of Falcon's relaxed gait. Lamps hung on hooks attached to the wagons' exterior boarding cast pools of light across the fen road, lighting their way. At her wagon, Halani reached into the neckline of her shift to pull out her medallion. She unclasped the chain and offered the necklace to Malachus. "Take a look at this. A gift from Gilene before she left. It was she who told me the story of Agna and her children." She showed him how to disconnect the medallion's three pieces, then repeated the Savatars' creation myth.

Malachus inspected the silver abstracts representing draga, woman, and horse. "This is finely wrought work. I didn't know the horse people of the steppes were also silversmiths." He held up the draga design for more study. "Agna's first child and her most powerful? While the draga wasn't Pernu's first, she was his greatest and most beloved."

Halani focused on one word in his statement. "She?"

"Pernu's draga was a female named Vuri Silyn, the first of her kind." He interlocked the three symbols together once more. Instead of handing the necklace back to Halani, he reached around her to attach the clasp, fingers drifting slowly across her nape so that she shivered. The medallion rested against her breastbone again, still warm from his touch. Malachus cupped her face, hard hands cradling her jaw. "The medallion is unique, beautiful. Much like the woman who wears it."

"Nectar on the tongue," she whispered, eyes drifting shut as he lowered his head.

"As I'm about to discover." He kissed her—a leisurely exploration of her mouth that invited her to do the same to his. Halani wrapped her arms around his back, mapping the ridges of muscle there as well as the indentation that marked the length of his spine. The vibrations of his low groan tickled the inside of her mouth as she slid her tongue across his to taste him.

The hands that had cupped her jaw moved to her hips, fingers kneading her flesh while drawing her ever closer into the shallow cove his body made as he bent into her. Heat rolled off him, a fever of desire. When they paused to draw breath, Malachus continued kissing her, only this time it was to feather a path across Halani's cheek and over the bridge of her nose. He halted and pulled away just enough to gaze into her eyes. "I shouldn't have done that. I know better than to succumb for reasons beyond count, but mostly because I think when I leave this caravan, I will be incomplete."

His words acted as a cold-water splash on Halani's ardor. Her invitation for him to join her in her wagon hung in her throat. She, who had guarded her heart for so many years, had surrendered it to a cursed outlander on a quest. Would she give away her soul as well if she took him to her bed? The thought both horrified her and sent the blood surging hot through her veins. For her own sake, she put physical distance between them and returned his half smile, certain hers wavered. "Not so," she said. "You'll take memories of your time here with you." *And me,* she thought. *You'll take part of me.*

"Halani," he said, her name an invocation on his lips.

She backed up her stair treads to the threshold, never breaking the gaze they shared. Her heart clattered against her ribs. "Good night."

It was a coward's retreat, yet leaning against her closed door in the wagon's darkness, she felt no shame. Better to run than to fall.

The following day left no time for melancholy reflection or even awkward conversation. The sun's glory didn't last, and the sky clouded again, promising another deluge and the danger of lightning. Kursak eyed the gravid clouds and cursed.

"Gods damn it!" he said, virtually snarling the words. "Are we going to have to sacrifice a sheep to get this to stop?"

"I doubt some poor ewe's blood is going to make a bit of difference on whether or not the rain stays." Halani, standing next to the wagon master, dragged her hands over her face and sighed. "I'm very much done with being soggy."

Kursak slapped Seydom on the back, his face grim. "We've loitered enough. Ride the line and tell everyone to pick up the pace. We travel all day with short rests and then through the night."

As if it heard his words and laughed at his plans, the sky opened, and the rain fell in windswept sheets. Halani drove her wagon, calling out encouragement to her mule even as the thunder boomed above them and lightning illuminated the roiling clouds. The hard rainfall raised such a noise on the fen, she had to shout to be heard. She almost didn't hear the command to halt that traveled down the caravan line, startled when her seat rocked to one side and Malachus climbed up to join her.

"Stop your wagon, Halani. Problem at the rear."

As if sensing Malachus's presence, her mule's ears lay back, and it pranced in its traces. Halani tightened the reins, bringing the vehicle to a gradual halt. The wagon in front of her went a few wheel rotations more before doing the same. "What's going on?"

"Broken front axle on one of the supply wagons."

She groaned. "This couldn't be worse timing for a wagon repair or on a worse wagon. Has word gotten to Kursak?"

Malachus wiped rain from his face. "He saw the break when it happened. They're unharnessing the team now. I'm headed back to help with unloading while your wheelwright sees what can be done to fix it. Be ready to overnight here. No one's going anywhere until we get the axle fixed."

She was about to reply when he grabbed her hand and planted a hard kiss in her palm before leaping off the seat to jog back the way he came. Her hand tingled where he kissed it, and despite the rotten news and equally rotten weather, Halani smiled.

Malachus had joined those chosen to lift the wagon onto the jacks, his back to one of the long sides, knees bent as he waited for the command to lift. His shirt lay plastered against his skin, and at some point he'd tamed his hair into a queue at the back of his neck. It reminded Halani of a horse's tail, thick and straight.

"That's a fine bit of male persuasion there," Ruviti said, joining Halani where she watched the men work. "You're lucky to have that in your bed for the trip."

In circumstances less worrisome, Halani might have laughed. This time she only replied in a distracted voice, "He doesn't share my bed."

Ruviti nudged her arm. "Come on, girl, we're not much help

here. Let's join the other women to prepare food. They'll all be ready to eat the wagon by the time we're ready to serve it."

Halani resisted. "I don't think I should leave. I brought supplies in case someone gets hurt."

The other woman didn't give up so easily. "Gods forbid someone does, but if so, you'll be here fast enough to help. Right now you're a distraction." She nodded toward Malachus, who watched them from his place by the wagon. He briefly looked away to reply to something the free trader next to him said. "He may not be in your bed, but it's obvious you're in his thoughts, and right now isn't a good time for that."

Heat flooded Halani's cheeks from a mixture of guilt over the notion she might be a hindrance instead of a help and delight in the idea that Malachus's thoughts were as wound around her as hers were around him. "You're right," she told Ruviti. "Let's go."

By the time the food was ready, Halani's stomach was growling its own demands for sustenance. She and three others, along with a bevy of older children, volunteered to bring the men the food in carts covered in oilskins.

Malachus's fingers were cold when he took the bowl of stew she offered him. He inhaled the steam rising from its surface, closing his eyes as he did so. "I'm hungry enough to eat the bowl itself." He opened his eyes once more and smiled. In the day's dreary half-light, his irises were as dark as his pupils.

As much as she would have liked to spend time talking with him while he ate, she couldn't stay, and she left him with a generous portion to devour while she delivered more to the men surrounding the wagon. By dawn the wagon was fixed and reloaded.

Kursak called a quick gathering of sleepy, drooping people, his own face gray with fatigue. "I know I said we'd keep moving, but that wagon axle took us by surprise. Most of us need rest. Without it, we'll get careless and make mistakes. Those of you who managed to get a little sleep last night will have to see to things today. The rain's still coming down, but the road isn't flooding. This is as good a place as any to stay another day and night. We'll head out in the morning and take it slow. "

The group dispersed, and Halani made her way to Malachus where he waited on the other side of their temporary circle. His eyelids sat at half-mast as he gazed at her. "We've worked you hard since you've been with us. Not much sympathy for a convalescent. Are you sorry you traveled this far with the caravan?" A flutter of anxiety winged its way up from her belly to tickle her rib cage.

He offered her a sleepy smile. "No. I'm only sorry I won't be able to travel farther." He reached past her to grasp her braid and pulled it over her shoulder. "Before I go, I hope you'll let me see your hair loose one more time."

Halani blinked away the suspicious ache in her eyes. She shouldn't cry. It changed nothing. "Leave your clothes on the lamp hook outside the wagon. I'll come for them to wash and not disturb you." She turned away before he could see the telltale redness in her eyes.

The rain continued another two days before stopping. Twice Malachus had ridden next to her for a short time, once on Falcon, once on the more lively Batraza, until Halani's mule bucked in its traces to protest the mare's nearness.

"Kursak thinks we're near the end of the fen road," she told him. "Soon we'll reach the place where it meets up with the main road leading to Domora." He could leave at any time. There was nothing keeping him here any longer, neither her nor the rain.

The weather had provided her uncle a decent span of time to reach Domora and sell the draga bone. She assuaged the guilt of her deception by telling herself that Malachus had mentioned nothing regarding a search for a bone, that his run-in with the mercenaries was truly a coincidence, and that the curse he hoped to break was more of an annoyance than a life-or-death dilemma. If she told herself these things enough times, she might almost believe them.

"Then we need to have a reading lesson tonight, even if Kursak doesn't want to stop." Malachus frowned. "We haven't had a moment to sit together for one since the rain started again."

"I'll make sure he stops."

Malachus chuckled. "Say it like that, and I'd be worried about telling you no if I were Kursak."

"Kursak doesn't fear me in the least." He was ten years older than she and much like an older brother who tolerated his younger, irritating sister.

"But he does respect you. I think if you asked him to swim across the fen for you, he'd do it."

"Thank the gods for his sake, then, that I'm not so frivolous." She winked at Malachus. "I have many faults, which I'm sure he'd be happy to share with you."

His chuckle became a laugh, and he executed a deep bow from the saddle before riding toward the front of the line to report to Kursak updates on the rest of the caravan. Halani could only guess he must have said something else to the wagon master regarding their travel, for he ordered a halt for the night and a call for a supper gathering to celebrate the fact that the end of the fen road was close. Even if more rain came, they were out of flood danger. The land had risen higher, the road now well above the waters.

Halani had just turned her mule over to Nathin to lead back to the herd when Kursak approached her, Seydom beside him.

"Let's take a walk. I want to show you something."

Curious, she followed him and Seydom to a spot where she

had a clear view of the southern horizon and the vague shadow of a tree line that marked the end of the fen. By fast horse, they could reach that marker in half a day.

Kursak pointed to a landmark east of the road, rising from the fen itself like the back of a water-born beast breaching the shallow waves. "Am I seeing what I think I'm seeing?"

She squinted, wondering the same thing Kursak did. "Who'd put a barrow in the middle of a fen?"

"Someone who hoped its location would prevent others from cracking it open." Kursak pivoted in a slow circle, taking in their surroundings. "At least we know for sure we're headed toward higher ground. The barrow isn't half submerged."

Dread welled up inside Halani. She knew what he was about to suggest.

"Do we want to pay it a visit?" Seydom peered at the barrow as hard as she and Kursak had. "To get to it, we'll have to get wet. Again."

These men were her friends, her family, and she loved them dearly, but they suffered the same bewitchment her uncle did: the irresistible temptation and thrill of barrow raiding. And it always involved her. "It isn't worth our time," she said, praying they'd agree and leave the grave be.

Kursak's eyes were narrowed, and Halani could almost hear the plans whirling inside his head. "Maybe. Maybe not. We're not far from it. It's close enough to reach on foot, and while the ground might not hold a horse or a wagon, it should hold a person without sinking them. We can just take a quick look."

"And if we find something?" Halani flinched at her use of "we," knowing her slip of the tongue had just revealed her willingness to help despite her misgivings.

"When have the dead ever minded when we did?"

"That barrow wight in Carridosh two years ago sure minded." Seydom responded to Kursak's glare with a perplexed expression. "What? It's true. The thing almost caught Halani and nearly took your arm off."

Halani hadn't forgotten that incident. She still woke from the occasional nightmare about it with a scream trapped in her throat.

"What about Malachus?"

She silently thanked Seydom for asking the question hovering on her lips.

One of Kursak's eyebrows rose. "What about him?"

"If he sees us and says something to folks in Icsom's Retreat or especially Domora, it could go badly for us. Most people are as quick to hang a barrow raider as they are a horse thief."

"I don't think he'll say a word, even if he disapproves." Kursak's knowing look made Halani's face heat. "Halani?"

She frowned. "Just a look around. That's all I'm agreeing to. You know I don't like this, and I don't fancy fighting off an angry wight."

"Fair enough. The three of us plus Tursom. I'll get him when we're ready. Seydom, you fetch Halani. We may not even need lamps for the trek if the sky continues to clear. The moon will give us plenty of light." A wary glitter shone in his eyes. "I think it best to keep it just between us. The more who know what we plan, the greater the chance someone will slip and mention something to Malachus."

"But you said—" Seydom began, only to have Kursak cut him off.

"I know what I said, and I stand by it. Besides, if he planned some malice, he has more than enough to see us all hanged and Halani burned since he saw her dowsing a trail for us. I just think he doesn't need to know everything we do."

"Because it's wrong and unsavory?" Halani stared at the two men. "Repulsive and detestable?"

"Save your righteous indignation for another time, Halani." Kursak's brow knitted. "You know as well as I and Seydom that barrow raiding has saved us more than a few times from a lean winter and empty bellies."

"This is summer, and we have wagons stuffed to the roofs with supplies."

"No one's making you go. Feel free to stay in the caravan and pretend we didn't have this conversation."

She blew out a defeated breath. There was no possible way she'd let them go to the barrow without her. It was her earth magic that helped them avoid wights, and only once had it failed her, or rather, she failed it. "I'll be waiting in my wagon. Just tap one side twice. I'll come out."

The thought of their evening raid on the barrow troubled her enough that even Malachus's lessons didn't hold her concentration the way they usually did. The two sat on a blanket on the perimeter of a makeshift circle built around a cluster of braziers. Kursak had agreed to a communal supper but not the fire.

"Not enough room," he said. "And I don't care if we have leagues of water around us. One stray spark leaping from wagon to wagon, and we'll be burned out and homeless in less time than it takes to piss."

Happy to stay put for the evening and socialize, no one argued, and they made do with blankets and the braziers. Halani had offered her help with the cooking but was sent on her way with instructions to pay attention to Malachus's lessons so she could learn something and pass it on. At the moment, she was failing.

"You're far away tonight." He eyed the square of brazier ash they were using as her practice board for writing her letters. "That's the third letter you've drawn backward."

She set her stick down. "Forgive me. I've been lost in thought all day. It's made me a poor student."

Malachus scraped the faulty letter away with his foot. "Then we'll take it up another time. It won't do either of us any good if you can't focus." He settled into place once more. "Do you want to share what's troubling you?"

Oh, gods no, she thought. And see the disgust crawl across his face when she did? The idea made her shudder. Instead, she grasped onto something that plagued her as much as the barrow raiding. "Once we're off the fen road and turn to Domora, what will you do? Ride to the west as you originally planned?"

His features hardened, reminding her of that moment when he awoke from a restless sleep to discover her holding a pillow as if preparing to suffocate him. The expression had given her pause then. It gave her pause now. "Maybe. I think I'm fairly close to what I seek. I just need to determine which direction I turn."

His cryptic reply didn't answer her question, and she suspected his words had been carefully chosen for just that purpose. She didn't pursue it, though her curious nature tempted her to do so. Instead, she changed the subject. "Will you read from your book tonight or tell the story of Pernu and his draga?"

Malachus leaned back on his elbows, the perfect picture of relaxed contentment. "The second, and I wish to borrow the story Gilene told you, if you don't mind."

"I don't mind at all. Stories are meant to be shared, not hoarded. If Gilene's adds to yours, that can only be a good thing." She'd looked forward to his telling of the creation story the brotherhood believed and raised Malachus to believe. One more small thing he'd leave behind when he rode away to resume his journey. One more thing for her to treasure.

The growing crowd around the braziers and the call to supper ended their more private conversation, and soon they were surrounded by chatty, jovial free traders happy to share food, ale, wine, sympathetic rants regarding the weather, and praise for those who helped fix the supply wagon.

Night fell dark but clear on their gathering, and there was much admiration of the heavens and the unobscured stars. The moon hung bright above them, and plenty of teasing and banter regarding the superstition that such a moon blessed women with fertility and men with virility passed back and forth among the group.

"You can sleep outside tonight," a scowling Yeris informed a terrified-looking Kadena as they both stared at the moon and then at their large brood surrounding them.

It wasn't long before numerous calls for a story erupted from the crowd, with one young clear voice rising above them all. "Tell us about Pernu and Vuri Silyn!" One of Kadena's children, the one who'd expressed his boredom with the story of Kansi Yuv and "old Golnar," met Malachus's eye. "You said you'd tell that one."

"So I did." Malachus glanced at Halani as if asking for permission. She nodded enthusiastically, as eager as Kadena's boy to hear the tale.

Malachus stood up and asked for the loan of a pipe and tobacco. Halani didn't realize just how many pipes the free traders possessed until Malachus made the request. He carefully prepared the pipe Kursak passed him, all the while stoking the audience's anticipation until it grew into a palpable thing. Halani grinned. He might not claim to be much of a storyteller, but he had a natural instinct for how to work the crowd into a white-knuckled eagerness to hear what he had to say.

"This is a short story," he said between smoke puffs. "And begins with the goddess the Savatar call Agna." Every person leaned forward, instantly ensnared. "What do you call the lands of the Savatar?"

"The Stara Dragana," the crowd replied.

It was the name everyone within Empire territory used except the Nunari, and their term for the steppe matched that of the Savatar: the Sky Below. While Halani had only glimpsed the edge of the steppe from one or two of the trade roads the caravan traveled, she found the term fitting.

"The Stara Dragana," Malachus repeated. "It sounds very similar to 'draga,' doesn't it?" Several people nodded. "That's because it means Womb of the Draga. The Savatar believe the draga was created by their fire goddess, Agna, her first and most powerful child. In my country, we believe the first draga was created by the sky god, Pernu. Her name was Vuri Silyn. She was the first draga but not Pernu's first child, though she was his most powerful. Pernu had created Man and Horse first. Their mothers were Ninsurgha, goddess of earth, and Suela, goddess of rivers. Pernu grew jealous of his wives because while Man and Horse had affection for their father, they loved Earth and River more and often ignored Pernu."

He paused then to sip on the pipe while his audience digested his words. Nathin spoke into the waiting silence. "My da barely knew I was alive, and didn't much care one way or the other. Man and Horse were lucky to have a father like Pernu."

Malachus tipped his head toward Nathin. "Pernu certainly thought so. His resentment over his children's neglect and disregard grew until it became a rage. He wrecked the skies, sending rain heavier than anything we've seen these last few days to drown the land and destroy the crops." The crowd gasped in tandem, and it wasn't just the children who wore wide-eyed expressions. "The rivers burst their banks, tore trees out of the ground, and swelled the oceans." He raised his arms as if beseeching the sky. "Lightning scorched and burned anything that didn't lie beneath the water. The animals made by Ninsurgha and Suela to live alongside Man and Horse died beneath the sky's fury until Man and Horse begged him for mercy for the world. Their pleas fell on deaf ears, so they turned to their mothers to implore Pernu to calm his anger."

Pernu sounded like a spoiled toddler, in Halani's opinion.

"Ninsurgha," Malachus said, "Pernu's first and most beloved wife, bargained with him." That garnered several approving whistles from the audience. "If he calmed the clouds and stopped the rain, she would give him another child, one who would love only him. He agreed, and together they created the draga Vuri Silyn, favored child of the lightning god, Pernu. She was greater than Man or Horse in size, more powerful, with the wings to embrace her father's sky and the heritage of fire. Ninsurgha loved her as much as Pernu did and gifted Vuri Silyn with many powers of earth, but she abided by her bargain with Pernu and gave the draga to her father to raise. In return, the rains paused, the rivers no longer raged, and Man and Horse once more governed that over which Ninsurgha and Suela held dominion.

"The sky, though, it belonged to Vuri Silyn and her descendants, their inheritance from Pernu until the last draga falls and returns to Ninsurgha's arms in death. For lightning has always and will always love the draga."

Malachus bowed to enthusiastic applause with several in the audience bellowing, "Another! Another!" He shook his head and stepped back to the circle's edge. "I'm done," he said. "I don't have the treasure trove of stories in my head that Halani does. I'd need another day to remember one or two more."

"Your turn, then, Halani," Seydom called out.

Like Malachus, she refused. "I don't think so. I'd much rather sit here and bask in the story of Vuri Silyn." And the residual bewitchment of Malachus's voice as he spun words with a sorcerer's skill.

Another child waved his arm to catch Malachus's attention. "So does that mean Golnar was Vuri Silyn's grandchild?"

Malachus nodded. "More of a grandchild of a grandchild of a grandchild, but yes."

The boy, a couple of years away from a cracking voice, frowned. "Maybe Kansi Yuv shouldn't have killed Golnar, then."

Beside Halani, Malachus went rigid, though his expression didn't change. She stared at the boy, impressed by the insight in one so young.

Malachus remained unmoving and seemingly unmoved by the boy's remark, and Halani decided it best to deflect the crowd's attention from him. "Have Nathin tell everyone how he convinced Ruviti to marry him."

A few groans followed her suggestion, including Nathin's. "We've heard that story a few times," one free trader groused.

"And it's funny every time." Kursak, sitting on one side of Nathin, shoved him with his shoulder. "Go ahead, Nathin, tell your version of it so I can watch Ruviti stab you with that brazier fork she's holding."

The crowd laughed and turned their attention to teasing and coaxing Nathin to once again share his proposal story. Halani's deflection had worked.

Malachus emptied his spent pipe and gave it back to Kursak.

He returned to Halani and held his hand out to her, saying nothing, though his gaze asked many things of her. She entwined her fingers with his, and they left the camp. No one commented and no one followed, though more than a few speculative gazes tracked their progress into the wagons' shadows.

As soon as they were out of the crowd's sight and hearing, Halani pressed Malachus's hand between hers and grinned. "You can't leave us. Ever. You have to stay and be the second storyteller. With tales like that, we will enthrall whole cities and be showered in *belshas* by worshipping crowds."

She barely had the words out before he pulled her into his arms and kissed her. Hard. This wasn't the gentle exploration of the previous time that grew by degrees into a simmering cauldron. It was fiery, desperate, thought destroying and soul capturing.

As quickly as he initiated the kiss, Malachus ended it to stare into her eyes. He cupped the back of her head with one hand, while the other lay flat against her back, holding her so close to him, their shadows melded into one misshapen silhouette, and his heat enveloped her in a cocoon. "What story can I tell that will bewitch you into coming with me when I leave?"

CHAPTER SIXTEEN

His question sent her heart crashing to the ground and tears flooding into her eyes. How she wished her answer might be different. "There isn't one. As much as I might wish otherwise, my place is here. It will always be here for as long as . . ."

"As long as Asil lives," he finished. His body, strung tight as an archer's bow, relaxed, the intensity of his expression becoming melancholy. He sighed, a mournful sound, and kissed her forehead.

Halani gripped his tunic. "You say you have to leave. Can you not come back?" *Please come back.*

His hand stroked her hair. "I don't know, Halani. If I didn't, it wouldn't be because I didn't want to." More than moonlight shone in his dark, dark eyes.

She stared back. "If I asked you to wake with me in the morning, would you?"

It was a dangerous question with all manner of answers. The risks were numerous, the joy anticipated, the heartache guaranteed. He would leave, and she would tell him goodbye without asking to go with him or begging him to stay. She didn't believe they'd cross paths again, and if a night in his arms resulted in a child, that child would never know its father, just as Halani never knew hers. The difference was that this man would care.

Malachus brushed his thumb over her cheekbone. "Do you truly think we'd sleep to wake?"

"No, I don't." She hoped they wouldn't. Time was too short and too precious for sleep.

They kissed again before he said, "Are you sure?"

She took his hand and led him down the wagon line to where the provender wagon he used was parked. "I'd invite you to my wagon, but it isn't uncommon for people to knock on my door in the middle of the night for some draft to soothe a troubled stomach or an aching head." A truth cloaking a lie. She shoved away the guilt.

He opened the door, ushering her inside the wagon's dim interior. A brief blaze of light made her squint before the flame inside the lamp he'd lit settled.

Time. There was very little left, and Halani chose not to waste it on regrets or inane chatter. She stepped into Malachus's welcoming arms and took her turn at kissing him.

She started at his hairline. His forehead was smooth under her lips, cool to the touch. His breath whispered along her chin, and the flutter of his eyelashes tickled her jaw. She moved to his temples, then down to his closed eyes. The fragile skin of his eyelids twitched as she gently grazed them before kissing a line across one cheekbone, over the bony bridge of his nose to the other cheekbone. His cheeks, clean-shaven, unlike those of the other men in the caravan, were smooth against her palms.

He remained perfectly still during her exploration, except for the rise and fall of his chest, which quickened as his breathing shortened.

Halani bypassed his mouth, smiling when he uttered a faint protest. The protest changed to a low sigh when she pressed a kiss to his neck, following the strong line there that flowed into his collarbone. He tilted his head back to give her better access, and she rewarded his cooperation with a small swipe of her tongue in the hollow of his throat. This time a soft groan escaped him, and his hands, idle at her waist, flexed, pressing into her flesh.

Her own hands were busy. She stroked his cheeks once more before tracing the broad width of his shoulders, then his muscular arms, which tightened under her touch. She had seen him in every state of dress and undress, knew the scarred beauty of the body that lay currently hidden under tunic, shirt, and trousers. He smelled of brazier smoke and sweet tobacco.

His hair spilled dark and heavy over his shoulders, and she gathered it in one hand only to let it go in a cascade through her fingers. His locks lent an aspect to his features that only enhanced his appearance. When she first met him, she'd thought him more memorable than striking, with a face too angled and harsh for ideal male beauty like Azarion's.

She no longer thought that way. There was beauty in severity, in unforgiving lines and hollows. She fell asleep at night with his image painted across the inside of her eyelids and found him breathtaking.

"Such sweet torture," he said softly, eyes still closed.

Halani loved that he gave her these moments to learn his body without interruption, discover this kingdom of slopes and valleys. But she explored not to tease but to learn. "Do you want me to stop?"

"No."

The one word might have been a plea or a command. Either way, Halani was glad he hadn't said yes. She found the hems of his tunic and shirt, lifted them, and slid her hands beneath the fabric to rest them against his midriff. Muscles tensed, tightening even more as she nuzzled aside the tunic's neckline to reach his collarbone and kiss a path along its prominent line just above his nearly healed wound. A thin trail of soft hair bisected his torso. She stroked it briefly before spreading her fingers on either side to explore the sculpted muscle over his ribs, careful to avoid the place where the second arrow had punctured his body.

Malachus tilted his head back on a gasp when she mapped a route to his groin and the swollen erection hidden behind his trousers' placket. She cupped him, her own heavy heartbeat a drumming of hot blood and desire to take this man into her body as deeply as she'd taken him into her soul.

A startled squeak escaped her when he suddenly forced her head up from his chest and brought his mouth down on hers. His passive stillness was over.

They kissed until they could no longer breathe, Halani's tongue chasing his and his hers as she stroked the interior shape of his mouth and savored his taste. He swept the outline of her lips with the tip of his tongue and nibbled the lower one with his teeth. His breathing turned even more labored with every stroke of her hand on the rigid length of his shaft.

She followed his lead when he coaxed her closer to the bed. He grabbed the lamp, hanging it on the hook nearer to the ceiling so that the light spilled warm across them both. "My turn," he said.

Halani stood still, shivering at intervals from the pleasurable darts his touch sent across her body as he undressed her. At every patch of skin revealed, he paused to worship there with either the brush of his lips or the stroke of his fingers or the flick of his tongue. By the time she stood nude, she was clutching him for support and murmuring his name in prayer.

"I thought you pretty when I first saw you," he breathed into her ear, drawing her against him so that the rough fabric of his tunic brushed her breasts, lightly abrading her sensitive nipples. "But I was wrong. 'Pretty' doesn't do you justice."

Such seductive words. Halani pressed herself as close as she could to him, hands busy with unlacing the numerous ties that held his garments closed or up. "It's still hard to believe you once had trouble wooing women," she said.

He stroked her back, drawing an invisible line along the length of her spine with his forefinger. She jerked at the ticklish sensation. "You inspire me to give my best effort." And oh was he succeeding.

"I want to see you as well," she said, folding back the unlaced collar of his tunic.

"You already have. Several times." Malachus ignored her insistent tugging on his shirt in favor of stroking her from hips to shoulders and sucking gently on the valley of flesh where her neck met her shoulder.

"That isn't the same, and you know it." She rucked the tunic upward, and he laughed, finally giving in to her silent command by shrugging it and the shirt beneath it off. His trousers followed just as quickly, until they both stood, clad only in lamplight and each other's admiring gazes.

"I don't think you've ever been pretty," Halani said. "But you're certainly beautiful."

He caught her up in a tight embrace. "And you accuse me of possessing a honeyed tongue."

"Oh, you do," she insisted, holding him just as close as he lowered her to his bed. "You've kissed me. You taste like honey."

She earned one of those kisses for her compliment, one only interrupted when he rolled them both so that he lay on his back and she sat atop him, mounted to ride.

"You'll tell me if I hurt you?"

His hands settled on her buttocks, cupping her, and he blew softly on one of her curls that had escaped her braid and bounced across his nose. "Any pain I'm feeling at the moment, Halani, has nothing to do with arrow wounds." Amused, and breathless with the sensations tumbling through her limbs, she braced her hands on his chest to lift a fraction higher, shifting the position of her pelvis. He groaned at the movement, pushing up against her. Hard, aroused, seeking entrance into her body.

Pink color graced his cheekbones, and his dark eyes reflected the lamp's flickering light in their depths. "If I immolate us both before this over, Halani, it won't be because of my curse."

A subtle shift in his position rubbed a spot between her legs just the right way, and he enhanced the sensation it elicited in her by paying slavish attention to her breasts with his mouth and tongue. Halani gasped, arching into him. If this continued, it might well be she who set them both on fire, and she wasn't even cursed.

Her hands slipped from his chest to the floor to steady herself. A lift, a tilt, a slow slide down that forced a guttural sound from him, and she seated him within her.

Had she the ability to breathe, she might have moaned with him. Instead, she stayed silent, eyes closed, reveling in the feel of him heavy and thick inside her. He filled every space so fully that she spread her thighs even wider to better accommodate him.

They moved together in a careful choreography, each learning the feel of the other, the scent of mutual arousal, the way their skin felt under each other's hands, how it tasted on the tongue and the lips, the way their limbs fitted together.

Soon, the measured dance turned frenetic, far more primal, and Halani gripped the sides of Malachus's narrow hips with her knees to hold on as he bucked beneath her, fingers pressing hard against her backside as he thrust harder, deeper. His mouth worked a tandem magic, and it wasn't long before Halani gasped out his name, arching her back as the climax he coaxed from her consumed every thought and sensation.

Malachus soon joined her, sitting up to envelop her in an embrace that threatened to bruise her ribs. He buried his face in her neck to mask his moans. Sweat slicked his back and shoulders, every muscle quivering as he shuddered in the throes of orgasm.

They held each other, wordless but unquiet as her numerous gasps matched his and her heartbeat thundered in her chest and her skull. She kissed his damp face, tasting salt. A low purr vibrated in his throat, the sound clinging to his mouth when he captured hers in another drugging kiss that left her faint and with the blood singing through her veins.

They'd managed to twist the bedcovers around them. Malachus flung them off before rolling to his side, taking Halani with him so that they faced each other, legs and arms tangled together.

Content to rest in his arms and calm her racing heart, Halani spent several moments twining a lock of his hair around her finger, letting it slide away only to recapture it in her grasp. Malachus's indulgent half smile told her he didn't mind.

He spent the quiet, postcoital moments mapping her contours in a leisurely fashion. "I wondered if I'd ever have the privilege of seeing you unclothed. The gods know you've seen my bare arse more times than I can count. It's about time you played fair in that." He winked.

Halani bit him gently on the top of his shoulder, prompting a gasp from him along with the renewed stirring of his arousal. She stared at him, wide-eyed. "Already?"

Malachus snorted and cupped one of her breasts, fingertips brushing her nipple. She pressed into his palm, craving his touch, even now when she still thrummed from the fading vestiges of release. "If you could see yourself now as I see you, you'd only be surprised that I wasn't already fully engorged and begging to stay inside you."

Blunt and to the point, his words were no less beguiling for their lack of flowery sentiment. She kissed the tip of his long nose. "How do you always know what to say to me and make me believe every word of it?"

"Because I mean every word of it."

The gods would never be so kind as to allow this man to remain with her forever, but they'd granted an unforeseen boon by placing him in her life for now, for these moments. She'd find joy in that and be grateful for what was given instead of bitter for what was not.

She hugged him harder, drawing closer until there was no space between their bodies. "You are a gift, Malachus," she whispered.

"And you're a blessing, Halani of the Lightning."

They made love again, a slow coupling as intense as the first one and just as breath stealing. Afterward, her thighs slick with Malachus's seed and her body languorous and heavy from his attentions, she lay with her back to his chest, spooned against him. Outside, the camp had grown quiet, and the scent of brazier smoke no longer permeated the air as it had earlier. Except for those assigned to night's watch to guard the livestock, the rest of the free traders had sought their beds for the night, some to sleep, a few to wait until the moon was old and the night was older. Slowly, slowly, Malachus's body pressed heavier against her, his breathing slowing as he slipped from a light doze into deeper sleep. Next to him, Halani stared at the wall, wide-awake, counting each breath and trying not to weep.

She waited another half hour, pretending to sleep as well, before gently easing out of his hold to gather her clothes and creep out of the wagon. She dressed outside while the camp slumbered under the haloed moon, and if any watched her dress, they chose to enjoy the view without commenting or making their presence known. Halani shrugged away the concern. A body was a body, and hers was just one slight variation of every other woman's body in the caravan, and not something no one else had ever seen before. She didn't have the luxury of indulging in false or useless modesty.

Once in her wagon, she took a hurried sponge bath from her washbasin, rebraided her hair, and waited for Seydom to fetch her, wishing with all her soul she was back in the provender wagon in Malachus's embrace instead of waiting to slog through mud and water for the chance to rob the dead.

The expected taps on her wagon wall came just as she doused her lamp. Outside, Seydom waited by her steps, a faceless silhouette cloaked in shadow. "Kursak wasn't sure you'd be in your wagon, or alone in it at least."

Halani frowned. If that wasn't fishing for information, she wasn't sure what was. "As you can see, I'm in the wagon. Alone." She folded up the steps and hooked them under her threshold. "Do you have a lamp? We'll need one to see into the barrow." At his nod, she strode past him. "Let's get on with it, then."

Kursak and Tursom were already at the front of the caravan. "Where's Malachus?" he asked Halani.

"I assume in the provender wagon, asleep." At least he was when she had reluctantly left him.

The wagon master eyed her for a moment but didn't question her further. "We're all here. Let's go.

They left their shoes on the road, the men rolling up their trouser legs while Halani tied her skirt between her legs so the fabric made a makeshift pair of trousers. She grimaced at the slimy mud oozing between her toes as they waded toward the barrow.

"We'll probably be covered in leeches once we get out," Tursom said, the disgust in his voice making Halani grin.

"If we are, save the ones you pluck off you," she said. "All the ones I had are dead. I need to resupply." Founder in their horses and oxen was an ever-present risk, and Halani always tried to keep leeches on hand in case the farrier needed them to apply to a lame animal's coronet.

The mound was an old one, its entrance collapsed and sunken, one side raised higher than the other so that it took on a lopsided appearance. Not only constructed in a poorly chosen location but also poorly constructed, period. Barrows were laborious to build, reserved for wealthy families who could afford the labor and material to erect one and pay for a rogue necromancer to raise a wight as its guardian. Whoever had this barrow built had ambitions of wealth and status but not the means to ensure a well-made tomb or a coveted location for it. Then again, a barrow in the middle of a fen discouraged all but the most determined grave robber from visiting.

Tursom held up the single lamp they'd brought for a better view. "We slogged through that soup for this?"

Seydom was even less impressed. He took the lamp from Tursom, venturing close to the barrow's half-collapsed entrance for a look inside. "We'll be lucky if there's a broken spoon or a rotten shoe in there. So much for putting a barrow out in a fen. Looks like other raiders got here first. A long time ago."

Kursak and Halani ignored them, she to concentrate on the varying pitches and tone of soggy earth supporting the barrow, he to watch her. "Anything?" he said.

"Not so far." The hymn here was blunted, as if earth sang to her through a thick layer of drying cloths. Suddenly, the sweet chime of a single bell rose from the murk, and she froze. "Wait."

The men fell silent as she listened, eyes closed, to the rising peal of one bell, then two, then several. Drawn by the sound, she stepped over a small hill of stone rubble held together by rooted sedge, using the partially fallen lintel to aid her balance. The ethereal music chimed in her mind, its vibrations pulsing up her arm to flood her body with an unmistakable resonance and familiarity.

As impossible as it seemed, this barrow held gold inside its collapsing interior. Gold or silver. Whichever it was, the precious metal beckoned with the shivering sound of bells.

"What?" Kursak demanded. "What do you hear?"

"Gold or silver." She shushed him. "I need to listen." Excitement surged through her. Gold. Definitely gold. She closed her eyes, concentrating on the alluring sound, searching for its source, her palm gliding across the barrow's lichen-covered surface as she shuffled around the perimeter.

Nothing else mattered, not the midges swarming around her head or the way she sank ankle-deep, then calf-deep, into muddy water. Even the heavy drag of her tied skirt didn't trouble her nor the strain in her leg muscles as she trudged through mud. Only the chimes mattered, their music so bright and beautiful that when she opened her eyes once more, all she saw was a wash of gold light filling her vision.

"Halani, watch your step, you're drifting from the mound back to the water." Kursak's warning was a distant birdcall, easy to ignore.

The chimes grew louder, still beautiful beyond description, just like the golden light hazing her vision. Hip-deep in the water now, she felt something brush her legs, like the hesitant, curious touch of a new lover. The sharp blade of a whistle sliced through the chime's ballad and split the curtain of golden light shrouding her vision.

Halani blinked, disoriented by the view in front of her. She no longer faced the mound. Instead she'd turned away from it, toward the fen's watery expanse. Behind her, Kursak called her name. In front of her, to her horror, Malachus slogged toward her, his expression a combination of fury and fear. It was he who'd split the air with his whistle and ended whatever sorcery had beguiled her.

Kursak called her name again. Halani turned so she could answer him, when something cuffed her leg in a bony clasp. She tried to jerk away, and the cuff tightened into an unyielding grip that yanked her off her feet. She fell as whatever monstrosity had hold of her tried to drag her farther into the water.

Mud embedded under her nails and oozed between her fingers as she clawed for purchase and struggled to kick free of the thing pulling on her. She screamed when the feel of bony talons crawled up her calf, sinking into her skin for a better grip on her leg.

Her companions fell to their knees around her, clutching her to pull her free from the fen creature's relentless grip. All three slid toward the water as Halani sank deeper.

"Malachus!" Kursak bellowed. "Hurry!"

Halani echoed his cry in her head, over and over, a chant to keep mindless terror at bay as whatever had hold of her dragged her farther into the water.

Splashing sounded behind her, followed by the lap of a shallow wave that purled over her back and shoulders. This time a pair of hands, blessedly human, brushed hard against her legs. Suddenly, whatever held her in its unyielding grip let go. With no more resistance, the three men holding her upper body pitched backward, pulling her out of the water as they fell.

Behind her, Malachus slogged onto the firmer shore and hauled her to her feet. Halani found herself staring into the hard face of a stranger. His hands patted her down before bunching her wet skirt in his hand so he could inspect her legs.

"Luckily just scratches, but you'll have bruises tomorrow," he said in a voice cold enough to freeze a river. He met her wide-eyed stare with a distant one of his own. "Are you hurt?" She shook her head, throat closed far too tight to speak. "Good. Let's get you back to the road."

He turned his attentions to the others, who'd gained their feet and stood behind Halani in a protective half circle. "Had I known you planned to spend the evening doing a little grave robbing, I would have warned you about the risks of navigating fens like this one. There are things more feral than snakes and frogs lurking among the sedge."

"What caught Halani?" Kursak eyed the water, and Halani followed his gaze. Her skin crawled at the sensation that something malevolent and hungry watched their group from the veil of sedge grass and black water.

Malachus shrugged. "I don't know what lives in your wilds here, but in my country, we have fen hags. Ambush predators who possess a touch of water magic." His gaze slid to Halani. "Yours is earth sorcery, but all magic comes from the same source. It must have sensed you the moment you dipped your toe in the water and started a hunt."

"Well, that fen hag is still out there, so are we trapped here?" Kursak had unsheathed the dagger he always carried, ready to hack away at anything that might break the water's surface.

Pinned by Malachus's chilly scrutiny, Halani could only stare back and wish she'd never, ever agreed to investigate this barrow. Malachus's voice was no warmer than his stare. "No. We can wade back as a group. Stay close together. Hags always go for a single individual. If this one tries a second time, it will go for Halani again."

"I'll carry her back," Seydom volunteered.

"I will." The veiled threat in Malachus's voice deterred any argument.

A knowing expression settled over Kursak's features before a scowl took its place. "Halani said she heard gold or silver when she walked the barrow's perimeter."

Malachus spoke to her directly once more. "Disguises make an ambush predator effective. So do traps, which I'd wager is exactly what this barrow is. One kind of magic can manipulate another. Earth and fire, water and air, but especially earth and water. The hag knew how to manipulate yours."

Mortified, Halani closed her eyes for a moment and wished herself anywhere but here.

"You mean there's no gold or silver in there?" Seydom stared at the barrow, aghast.

"Probably not, but you can always check for yourself." Malachus bent and lifted a silent Halani in his arms. "I'm not staying while you do. Neither is Halani."

No one stayed behind to search. The free traders struggled to keep up with Malachus as he waded toward the road and the small crowd waiting for them, their lamps firefly beacons of safety amid the perilous fen. Halani gasped when Malachus suddenly stumbled. She choked back an alarmed cry and clutched his shoulders.

Malachus's dark chuckle lacked any humor or warmth. "You'll

not find me easy prey, hag," he said, addressing a fleet black shadow that sped away just under the water's surface.

They continued their journey in a silence thicker than the mud at the bottom of the fen and twice as cold. Malachus held her close but not in the way of the lover she'd embraced earlier. Had that been only a couple of hours earlier? It felt like a lifetime.

Grave robbing wasn't outlawed in the Empire, but it was frowned upon by most, and those who did it tended not to speak about such nefarious actions. While Hamod never suffered a moment's hesitation in desecrating a grave for the purpose of enriching himself and his caravan, it had never set easy with Halani. She'd participated in the activity since she was a child and Hamod discovered her talent for "hearing" the sounds of precious metals hidden deep in buried caches and stored away among the skeletons and decaying corpses of a rich family's barrow. He'd exploited that talent, using everything from threats to indebtedness to gain her cooperation.

But Hamod wasn't here, and she should have followed her first instinct and refused to accompany the others to this barrow. She'd almost died because of her poor judgment, and while she'd half expected Malachus's disapproval if he found out what she'd done, she hadn't anticipated this quiet, seething loathing that poured off of him now.

"This was free trader business. I didn't think you needed to know," she said in a soft voice.

"Believe me, I wish I didn't."

Some inner voice warned her to stop, to say nothing else as his arms tensed even more around her. She dared a glance at his face, so grim and hard, it might have been chiseled from stone. "Once we reach the road, will you let me explain?"

He stared straight ahead. "No. I've no interest in what you have to say." When he finally deigned to look at her, her heart withered inside her chest. So much contempt. "Thieves of the living are like ticks on a dog. Parasitic, repulsive, unavoidably common. Thieves of the dead, though . . . that is a special kind of serpent, and one just slithered out of my bed."

CHAPTER SEVENTEEN

The moment his feet hit the road, Malachus set Halani down and walked away from her. His shoes squished with each step, and he was waterlogged from the waist down. If he was lucky, he didn't have a leech or two attached to him. And it could always be worse. A fen hag attached to him was infinitely worse.

Halani. Beautiful, compassionate Halani, who desecrated the dead for the chance of obtaining a necklace or a *belsha,* no better than those who'd looted the Sovatin necropolis and stole his mother-bond. "Gods," he said under his breath, sick to his soul at the discovery.

He entered the provender wagon, closed the door behind him, kicked off his shoes, and stripped naked. Inside, the wagon was a tomb itself, so dark Malachus could barely make out the shape of his hand when he held it in front of him. He sat down on the wooden floor, avoiding the bed within arm's reach. The rumpled covers still held the musky scent of lovemaking in their folds, evoking memories that should have brought pleasure but instead sent a spike of pain through his chest worse than any poisoned broadhead.

The dark whelped other memories as well, ones older but equally painful. Images of the monastery and a journey he'd taken as a child with some of the brotherhood and a bevy of other fosterlings to the Necropolis of Zersha, where the monks from the beginning of the brotherhood's existence were interred when they died. It had been a pilgrimage to pay respects to those who kept alive the faith in Pernu and offered sanctuary to Vuri Silyn's off-spring.

They had journeyed there, excited, eager, ready to pay their respects, only to discover destruction and chaos. The monks with the fosters had fallen to their knees, rent their clothes, and cried out their grief at the sight of the ransacked necropolis, its tombs destroyed, bones strewn like garbage across the loggia and down the hillside, carvings and reliefs on the walls defaced or obliterated completely by hammer and chisel. With the exception of a few, the treasures there were of modest value and didn't justify the devastation the thieves had visited on the necropolis.

Of the things the robbers had made off with, one was priceless—Malachus's mother-bond. Those who'd first stolen it were long dead before he was old enough to leave the monastery and exact his revenge, and he'd spent a lot of time and a lot of fruitless effort—not to mention spilled blood and an attempted murder—since then trying to retrieve it.

A faint protest struggled to break from his consuming fury. *That isn't Halani.*

But the rage prevailed. *It is Halani. A thief who steals from the dead because the dead can't protest, can't fight back. Not only a greedy thief, but a craven one.*

Never before had he doubted the accuracy of his judgment. Until recently, with the exception of the monks who'd raised him, he'd at first found humans generally detestable. They tended toward pettiness and cruelty, their short lives defined by a ferocious need to rise in the world by whatever means necessary and motivated by an avarice that defied and superseded any greed ever assigned to the most rapacious draga.

The monks, and his own experiences in the world outside the monastery, had taught him not all humanity was that way. The free traders' care of him and generosity toward him had confirmed it. Or so he'd thought. They were no better than the worst of their kind. Venal and deceptive, and Halani with her somber gray eyes the worst of them all.

Had she made love to him because she wanted it as much as he did, or had it simply been a means by which to distract him? Reason told him the second possibility made no sense on multiple levels, and he discarded the notion. But why she'd chosen tonight to be with him didn't make much sense either, especially when they'd been on the verge of falling into bed together before this.

He raked his hands through his hair, ignoring the heat rising in the closed wagon, from both the temperatures of a summer night and his anger, which had once more awakened the draga. Halani's departure from his bed had been a furtive one. The care she took in trying not to wake him had been motivated not by thoughtfulness but by fear. He could smell it on her as she peeled back the blankets and eased out of his arms, her steps a slow, mindful tread. She'd gathered her clothes in her arms, opening the door just enough to squeeze through before gently shutting it behind her. A woman willing to stand naked outside in the dark to put her clothes back on wasn't one worried about waking a sleeping lover but one terrified of doing so.

As soon as she walked away from the wagon and he no longer heard her footsteps, Malachus rose, dressed, and followed her. Except for the ubiquitous sound of slumbering animals, the camp was quiet. He spotted a movement near the livestock, likely whoever was assigned watch for the evening, and kept to the shadows. The faint glow of a single lamp flickered in the clerestory windows of her wagon, and Malachus listened to the splash of water and shuffle of feet.

Was she bathing the memory of his touch off her body? The thought saddened him. His melancholy evaporated when Seydom suddenly appeared, knocked on the side of the wagon, and waited at the steps until Halani appeared at the door and joined him, dressed in the same clothes she'd worn earlier, a grim look on her moonlit features.

Malachus had followed the two, unnoticed, to the front of the caravan, where Kursak and Tursom waited. Puzzled by their clandestine gathering, he stayed out of sight, watching as they waded into the fen. Shock seized him the instant he guessed their destination and their intention. The fury that followed nearly blinded him. Grave robbers. They were grave robbers.

The memory of the destroyed necropolis with its scattered skeletons and grief-stricken monks burst across his mind's eye. The men responsible for the desecration were grave robbers as well. Tombs stripped of things not worth half a *belsha*, and his mother-bond, his mother's gift to him, his very heritage, trading hands across cities, countries, even lifetimes, as thieves stole from each other for the chance at filling their money pouches from the sale of things that didn't belong to them.

Neither shock nor rage had kept him on the road when the fen hag yanked Halani into the water. The emotions had served only to fuel his strength and speed while he cut a swath through the water toward her and the panicked trio struggling to hold on to her as the fen hag pulled her relentlessly deeper into the fen. He hadn't feared for himself or hesitated in plunging his hands into the waves, where a cadaverous shape clawed at Halani's leg.

Draga power surged through his muscles as he broke the hag's grip by snapping off its bony fingers like dried twigs. The thing convulsed, raking its other hand against his leg as it thrashed away from him. He barely resisted the urge to crush Halani to him as he carried her back to the road, torn by his revulsion for her actions and his terror at witnessing her almost drown.

She'd displayed no surprise at his anger, just a sorrowing acceptance, which made his rage burn even hotter. He couldn't set her down and walk away fast enough.

The night crawled on broken legs toward the dawn as Malachus packed his possessions into his satchels and wrenched the draga within him back into submission. He was done here, forgetting his original purpose while under the enchantment of an earth witch who corrupted her sorcerous gift in the worst way. Lightning had shown him her image for reasons other than possession of the mother-bond. She'd saved his life and he'd now done the same for her. His debt was paid in full. He no longer owed her anything, and she had taken more than enough from him already.

A few of the free traders nodded good morning to him or called a greeting as he strode toward the back of the caravan to retrieve Batraza. He ignored them all. Batraza was the only one whose greeting he responded to, and he set to brushing her down before tossing pad and saddle over her back.

"Leaving us?"

Malachus didn't bother turning around. He'd wondered when Kursak might turn up. "I should have left days ago."

"Have you told Halani goodbye?"

Malachus's bark of laughter sounded harsh to his own ears. "You can tell her for me."

Kursak was suddenly beside him, his eyes sparking with an anger to match Malachus's. "You killed two men while half dead from arrow wounds to defend yourself and faced down a fen hag to save her. I never took you for a coward." He allowed a lengthy pause to hover between them. "Until now."

Malachus ignored the insult and obvious challenge. He had nothing to prove to a grave robber.

When he didn't respond, Kursak exhaled a frustrated breath. "Halani has never approved of the barrow raiding."

"Good for Halani."

Kursak yanked on his arm. "Is it really the barrow raiding or the fact that she sneaked out of your bed to do it?"

The thin cord keeping his anger in check snapped. Malachus seized Kursak by the throat with one hand, jerking him forward until they were nose to nose. "Touch me again, and I'll break you in two." He shoved the wide-eyed wagon master away hard enough to make him fall. "I don't owe you an explanation for a godsdamn thing."

He had to admire Kursak's persistence, reckless though it was. The man scrambled to his feet, red-faced but determined as he approached once more.

"Maybe not, but you owe her one. She headed for your wagon this morning to thank you for saving her from the hag. I stopped her. Figured this would be the kind of reception she'd get from you. I'm here to thank you as well and to ask you to at least bid her farewell. Think about it. She's taking her turn minding the sheep."

Having had his say, he marched off, leaving Malachus to stare unseeing into the middle distance. The mare's short whuffle snapped him out of the mire of his thoughts. He finished bridling and saddling her, tied his satchels and weapons to the saddle rings, and led her to where the livestock milled on the road.

He found Halani standing amid a cluster of sheep, serenaded by their bleats and surrounded by clouds of flies. He didn't come any closer, so as not to panic the flock. When she saw him, her face paled and her mouth thinned, but she waded her way toward him, whistling for the dogs to keep to their tasks. Dressed in different clothes and no longer muddy, she made his gut clench. A thief more beautiful than the moon.

Her gaze, even more solemn now than when he'd first met her, passed over him and Batraza. "You're leaving. Did Kursak send you?"

Malachus nodded. "He has a persistent manner."

"One of his many good traits." A shadow drifted over her face. "I came to see you earlier. To thank you for saving me."

"He told me. He was wise to stop you."

She tilted her head to one side. "Why? Would you have shouted at me? Struck me? Called me names in front of the others?" A faint warble entered her voice. "What was it you said? 'A special kind of serpent.'"

He'd meant to draw blood with that insult. It seemed he'd succeeded. He felt no triumph at the thought. "Why do you thieve from the dead?" If there was one thing he had to know before he left the free traders, it was this.

Her face cleared of all expression, settling into an inscrutable mask that restoked his anger. "Because they won't care if something comes up missing."

His hand clenched Batraza's reins. "And that makes it right?"

Halani eyed his hand before meeting his gaze once more. "No, but it makes it easy."

The draga inside him thrashed, restless. "It doesn't matter if that barrow had been stuffed to the roof with gold. You and the others had no right to it."

She snorted. "Of course we didn't have a right to it. It wouldn't be called 'raiding' if we did." Her tone gentled. "I know you disapprove, that it disgusts you, and I wish you'd never found out. Why do you think I sneaked away? I hoped you'd sleep through the night and waken never knowing what we'd done. None of us expected a fen hag." A flash of horror passed through her eyes. Malachus toyed with the idea of breaking Kursak's nose for his recklessness in putting Halani's life in danger.

"I was already awake and watching you four wade toward the barrow," he said. "You aren't who I assumed you to be. None of you are."

Her eyes narrowed. "What did you think we were? Paragons of virtue saving wayward outlanders who manage to get themselves shot full of arrows by mercenaries? And now you feel made a fool of by all of us because of those assumptions." The blade of her mockery cut deep. "We're free traders, Malachus, not bandits, and most of the time not even barrow raiders. But sometimes we take from the dead to help the living. Necklaces decorating skeletons, *belshas* hidden under burial shrouds. What good are they to those who've died? We take what we find and resell it on the markets, use the money to buy supplies, food, thread and needle, iron for wagon hardware. Things those of us still living use to survive."

He blinked, stunned by her ability not only to justify their thievery but to turn it into something noble. "And you must think me the perfect dupe. How much horseshit are you hoping to shove down my throat before I've had enough and walk away? Is there no limit to humanity's greed and its power over their every action?"

"Spoken like a man who's never known the joy of starvation," she snapped. "I'm not defending, only explaining. It is wrong. No one here will argue that with you, especially me. Condemn us if you will, but know why we do it, not why *you think* we do it."

He dropped Batraza's reins, closing the gap between him and Halani. She tensed but didn't back away. Malachus slid a finger under the length of silver chain visible above her shift's collar and tugged upward, revealing the medallion she kept concealed there. "When you die, will you ask your loved ones to bury you with this?" Tears filled her eyes. He dropped the chain and stepped back.

They stared at each other for long moments. Halani's throat muscles visibly contracted, and her jaw flexed. Her tears gradually dried, leaving behind only the gray he'd always associate with a dove's wings or the morning mist. "If you'll follow me back to my wagon, I'll return the book and ink you gave me. The quill too." Her voice was firm, without any noticeable emotion.

"Keep it," he said. "It's yours. You've earned it." He groaned softly and closed his eyes. That didn't come out at all as he intended. He was certain he heard Halani's back snap. He opened his eyes to see her staring at him, white as the chalk cliffs that hugged the shore of faraway Berenwren.

"I'm not a whore, Malachus."

He scraped a hand down his face. "Gods, Halani, that isn't what I meant when I said it."

Halani shrugged, no longer as pale but as distant from him as the moon. "It doesn't matter if you did. There's no shame in earning your keep, even if you do it on your back." She glanced at Batraza, then back at him. "May the gods favor you both on the rest of your journey and throughout your lives. Goodbye."

Malachus watched her turn and walk back to the sheep. His hands literally cramped with the need to snatch her back, toss her on the back of Batraza, and gallop away from the people she loved, who loved her yet still risked her life—and theirs—to thieve.

He climbed into the saddle and guided Batraza toward the front of the caravan. He resisted the urge to turn back for a last look at Halani, then gave in. She stood at the front of the flock, the dogs racing behind and beside her as they kept the sheep in a tight formation. Wearing a dress in varying shades of red, she resembled a bright poppy amid a washed-out field of gray grass. She raised a hand in farewell. Malachus did not. He couldn't.

He discovered a crowd gathered at the front of the caravan, staring down the road. A rider galloped hard toward them. As they drew closer and details became clearer, cries went up among the crowd. Several of the free traders jogged forward to meet them, calling out a name and waving in greeting.

Malachus recognized Clamik, who'd left with the first half of the caravan led by Halani's uncle.

Clamik's horse snorted a protest and pranced in place as the free traders surrounded them. Malachus noted Kursak, slower to approach and wearing an expression of unease.

The newly arrived free trader half-heartedly returned the enthusiastic greetings, his attention solely on Kursak. "Thank the gods I guessed right and took this route. I was afraid you'd decided to go a different way once the rains flooded out the Serpent Road."

Kursak didn't bother with the niceties. "You didn't run that horse into the ground because you missed us. What's going on?"

Clamik searched the crowd. "Where's Halani?"

"With the sheep," Malachus replied before Kursak could. "I'll get her and bring her back." *One last glimpse of her*, he told himself. *Just one and not for long.* Besides, whatever news Clamik brought with him, it wasn't good, especially if he asked for Halani before he said anything else.

Halani's shocked expression at his return might have been comical were it not for her red, puffy eyes and splotched cheeks. Despite his still-simmering anger, he ached to take her in his arms and soothe away her anguish. Instead, he waited for her to reach him before offering her his hand. "Clamik has ridden here with a message. He's asking for you."

Fear flared in her eyes. She grasped his hand and swung up

behind him. Malachus turned Batraza and set her on a fast trot back to where the crowd had grown. He waited for her to dismount, then followed her.

Kursak stared at him. "You're staying?"

"No, just staying long enough to hear this, unless you say otherwise."

The wagon master shrugged. "Suit yourself." He turned his attention back to Clamik. "Halani's here. What news from Hamod?"

Clamik wiped a sleeve across his sweating brow. "We'd made it to Domora. Trade was brisk. Kraelag might be an ash heap and the Nunari running raids on the Empire territories west of the Veil, but the summer capital and the surrounding towns are busy and thriving. Resupplying the army and clearing off every merchant ship that sails into the sea harbor or river ports."

"That's good news for us, then," one of the free traders said.

Clamik nodded. "We've made a decent profit from what we bought in the Goban and sold in Domora so far."

"Get on with it, man," Kursak snapped. "That isn't why you're here."

The free trader tapped his hands down in a gesture for patience. "Hamod was keen to find a wealthy buyer for what he kept calling a prize of all prizes, a treasure of monarchs, but he had to sell it on the Maesor."

Malachus stiffened. It wasn't unusual for trader bands to sell priceless objects as well as mundane ones, even in the far lands across the sea, but something about this unfolding story set his instincts on edge. Halani's frozen expression and the despairing look in her eyes when she met his gaze only intensified them. "What is the Maesor?" he said.

Kursak answered. "Rogue marketplace where sorcerous items

are bought and sold. It exists outside of this world and time, supposedly safe from the imperial justiciars and their witch-hunters. It's almost impossible to get into the Maesor. If Hamod managed to worm his way in, I don't know how he did it."

"And did he find this buyer?" Halani bit out the words.

Clamik shook his head. "We don't know. He left with the promise of returning by evening. He never did, and we haven't seen him since. We've searched all over Domora for him." Gasps and distressed cries greeted his words. His features turned even more haggard as he looked directly at Halani. "The news is worse. Asil's missing too."

"What?" For all its quiet tone, Halani's single-word question dropped into the sudden silence like a thunderclap. "What do you mean Mama is missing?" Still quiet, she bit each word out between her teeth, advancing on Clamik like a she-wolf on a cornered ewe.

He backed away from her, sending a pleading glance to Kursak for help. "We discovered her gone the day after Hamod disappeared. We think she followed him somewhere."

The Halani Malachus once thought he knew continued to surprise him. She abandoned the seething quiet in favor of full-blown panic and launched herself at Clamik. "You lost my mother in Domora?!" Both Malachus and Kursak caught her before she reached him.

"Gods damn it, Halani, calm down!" the wagon master bellowed.

Malachus wrapped his arms around her from behind to hold her. "Halani, stop. Stop."

Gradually his command penetrated the cloud of panic that seized her, and she slumped in his arms. He tipped her head back to rest on his shoulder, and the tears she cried now weren't for him. They were for Asil.

"My gods, Malachus, Mama is lost in Domora. It could only be worse if she was lost in Kraelag."

He loosened his embrace enough to turn her around to face him. Behind her, the free traders watched them with expressions of pity and worry. Somehow fate had woven another tether to keep him bound to these people, regardless of his intent to turn his back on them. "I can find Asil for you, but I need your help to do it."

She dug her fingers into his arms as if he threatened to drop her off a precipice. "Anything. What do you want me to do?"

He recalled the look in her eyes when Clamik told the others of Hamod's purpose in Domora. He knew what her answer would be to his question, and that knowledge opened a frozen hollow inside him. "Do you know what your uncle wanted to sell in the Maesor?"

The despair in her gaze only confirmed what he suspected. She'd deceived him from the very start. "Part of a large claw with engravings on it that glow. Those two men you killed? Uncle bought—not stole—it from them, against my advice. The thing is practically pulsing with sorcery. It's what you were hunting in the Goban market, wasn't it?"

"Yes, and you knew it." He reeled at this latest revelation, numbed by it instead of furious. That would come later, when he was alone and could indulge in a blistering rant that only Batraza heard.

Halani sighed. "I suspected, though I wasn't sure until now." She hugged herself. "Knowing what you do now, why would you help me?"

"Because Asil, out of all of you, is worth the effort, and I have a better chance at finding her than you do running off to Domora in a blind panic and with no plan." He stepped around her to reach Kursak. "Keep your folk back here, no matter what you see. You'll also need to keep more than one person near your flock and herds."

Kursak's perplexed scowl almost made him smile. "Why?"

Malachus gazed at the sky, noting the patches of blue sharing space with clusters of white and gray clouds. Storms made it easier, but he didn't always need one to call down lightning. "You'll see soon enough," he told the wagon master.

He left Batraza with them. Of all the animals traveling with the caravan, she would be the one least likely to panic at what he was about to do. The last bit of the fen road unfurled ahead of him, and he stopped far enough away from the caravan that his actions wouldn't affect them but close enough that they had a clear view.

The last time he'd called down lightning, it had been less of a summons and more of just waiting in a strategic spot for the right moment. This time required tapping into the magic his draga heritage hoarded for the day he'd embrace it fully. Doing it created the inevitable result of stirring up the draga within him. Already made restless by his anger, it twisted inside him.

The first lightning hadn't misled him. Malachus had simply assigned it the wrong interpretation. It had shown him Halani because while she didn't have the mother-bond in her possession, she knew who did. Saving his life had only been a fortunate coincidence for him. Falling in love with her, his greatest failure so far. Her betrayal of his trust cut his legs out from under him, and he staggered inside from the awful pain of it.

He stood, facing in the direction of the dilapidated barrow, closed his eyes, and called up both draga magic and prayer, silently imploring the favor of Pernu and the blessing of lightning. For a long time the sky didn't answer, and the sun beat down on his head with a merciless heat. Suddenly, his senses caught fire, and the fine hairs on his body rose at the warning sizzle in the air. A bright flash was his second and final warning before Pernu's deadly blessing struck Malachus full force, a javelin of agony that punched through his back and out his midriff. He jittered in its grip, and his eyes rolled back in his skull. Far away, he heard a woman's voice scream his name.

Images, bright and clear, flashed past his mind's eye. An older man with gray eyes and features like Halani, hiding like a rat in the shadows. Asil, sitting on a bench in a walled garden, her vacant stare broken only by the occasional blink of her eyelids. A child with no arms joined her and offered her a doll, while another woman kept watch nearby. The images flew even faster, became more confusing, showing his mother-bond in the garden with Asil and also in the hands of a beautiful woman with the abyssal gaze of the damned.

The lightning bolt died with one more crackling flash, unshackling Malachus from its lethal hold. Darkness swept in where vivid pictures had filled his inner vision. He stumbled, his muscles jerking involuntarily from the lightning's residual effects. Once again he smelled the char of burnt clothing and looked down at himself. A *belsha*-size burn hole marked a spot in his shirt just above his navel. Strands of his hair floated straight out in front of his face, crackling with the remnants of lightning's power.

Pernu's blessing had lasted for less time than it took to exhale, and left him with enough information that he could use to find Asil, though far less than he wanted to make it an easier task. He embraced the shiver that started at his feet to envelop his entire body, then shook it off and strode back to where the free traders waited with Batraza.

They all gaped at him, eyes glazed with shock, mouths hanging open. When he stepped closer, they retreated. Only Halani didn't move, and in her face he saw wonder, awe, and a terrible sympathy.

He bent to whisper in her ear, telling her in a small way that he was more than the man she saw, and also less. "Lightning," he said, "has always loved the draga."

CHAPTER EIGHTEEN

Gharek counted his breaths at the same time he counted the steps that led from the summer palace's ground floor to the prison below it.

Unlike the upper chambers, built to allow both sunlight and moonlight to stream in at the best angles and highlight the architecture's soaring grace, the underground was a dark, dank, despairing place. Here, torchlight battled with shadow thick as lamp oil. The smell of human suffering and excrement mixed with the acrid stench of smoking pitch. Viscous pools whose contents were best avoided puddled on the treads, making the descent into the gloomy labyrinth slow and treacherous.

His hand clenched around the artifact hidden in his robe's pocket as if it were a talisman against evil or a charm of luck. In a way, it was the second, representing a chance to elevate his family name and change the fate of his daughter's future.

He followed the palace servant who led him down another flight of slippery stairs toward the sounds of something in the throes of agony. They turned a corner, coming abruptly to a dead end, where a cell lit by a trio of torches had been hollowed out of a stone wall. A lattice of rust-coated bars sealed off the cell from the rest of the corridor but provided observers a view of anything happening in the cell. Gharek stared for a moment at the horror before him and swiftly turned his gaze to the figure perched in an ornate chair in languid repose.

Empress Dalvila's deliberate scrutiny always made him think of a snake, and he the rabbit caught in its power. This time was no different. "Where is the draga you promised me, Gharek?" She sounded bored, as if her torturer's work on what was left of his victim was no longer entertaining.

"Soon to be reunited with its mother-bond, Your Greatness. And we have the mother-bond." He removed the bone from his pocket, presenting it to the empress with a low bow.

It wasn't quite the same as when he first took possession of it, but she wouldn't know that.

She plucked it from his grasp, turning it one way and then another while she studied it from every angle. Her growing frown raised a cold sweat on Gharek's brow. "Not at all what I expected. Rather disappointing." One shapely eyebrow arched. "Was this a very small draga?"

Disappointing Dalvila was just as deadly as offending her. "No, Your Greatness. If the drawings of dragas kept in the archives are correct, this is a small piece of a wing-tip bone. Likely the end of a claw."

Her own clawlike fingernail stroked the bone's edge as if to test its sharpness. "And what did you do with the free trader who had it?"

"Dispatched him, Your Greatness. He was of no use to us." The lie fell off his lips as naturally as his exhalations.

Dalvila's empty blue gaze returned to the wreckage of the person slumped in a bloodied heap at its torturer's feet. Gharek couldn't tell if the poor creature was a man or a woman, only that death, in its final mercy, couldn't come soon enough for them. "My dear cat's-paw, you are, as always, an efficient man."

A gurgling rose from what remained of the prisoner in the cell.

The torturer looked to Dalvila, who rolled her eyes. "Finish him. I'm tired of the noise."

The man nodded and, with one efficient swipe of the bloodied knife he held, cut his victim's throat.

Released from his agony, the dead man pitched sideways to the cell floor. A part of Gharek, the part where cold-blooded reason had long ago supplanted sympathy, wondered how the unfortunate prisoner still had any blood left to bleed out.

He looked to the empress, cruelly beautiful on her makeshift throne, and thought that here, in the prison's subterranean gloom, she seemed far more at home than in the soaring, sunlit receiving chamber where she held court among her scheming nobles.

She rose and tucked the draga bone into her bodice. The amputation of her arm had no effect on the feline grace of her movements. She motioned for him to follow her up the stairs to the palace's first floor, a pair of guards closing ranks behind them.

Once they emerged on the ground floor and stood in the middle of one of the palace's many gilded corridors, Dalvila halted. "I'm about to send my armies into Nunari lands and take back what we lost during Kraelag's siege. I plan to join our generals once we're victorious and show those lice-ridden savages why they should have never cast their lot with the Savatar and turned on the Empire." Her vocal register had lowered to a guttural seethe, and once more Gharek noted that any life glittering in her eyes came from the promise of violence. "I intend to do it with a body made whole again and a draga's newly flensed skeleton in tow." A flow of servants, slaves, and soldiers eddied around them at a safe distance. Dalvila's beautiful face grew only more so as the summer sun spilled through the high windows and cast her in sublime luminescence. Gharek had never beheld such a cruel visage. "You have until the end of summer, Gharek, to bring me that draga."

Gharek heard the implied threat. If he wasn't careful, he'd end up like the human wreckage they'd just left in the cell below them. "I believe it will be sooner than that, Your Greatness."

She regarded him for a long, terrifying moment. "And how is your child? The daughter born without arms. She must be hideous to behold."

Horrified, he lost the ability to speak for a moment. Dalvila didn't care one whit for anyone but herself. This was a prelude to a warning. Some measure of his horror must have revealed itself in his face, because her chilly smile widened.

Hers was a question layered in traps. Revealing any affection for someone would give her even more power over him. Manufacture false contempt for Estred's physical shortcomings, and Dalvila would see it as mockery of her own disfigurement. She wouldn't hesitate to punish him—and Estred—for the insult.

"Some have expressed their discomfort when they see her, Your Greatness," he said. "As her father, the lack doesn't bother me. She's a child with a child's interest. Nothing more. Nothing less."

A flicker of admiration for his noncommittal answer passed over Dalvila's features, and Gharek exhaled the breath he held. "And your aid to me can only help her later."

"Yes, Your Greatness." Serving this vile woman was simply a means to an end. They both knew it.

Her lethal smile became a smirk, and she ran a slender finger down his arm. It took colossal effort for him not to recoil. "I approve," she said in a purring voice. "There are those who'd find such a child unique. A delicacy. You would do well to find the draga as soon as possible and bring it to me." She patted her bodice where the mother-bond nestled. "I'll keep this safe until then. Don't make me regret my patience, Gharek."

Her gown's long hem, made filthy from the muck of the prison floors, hissed across the polished marble beneath her feet as she walked away. Gharek, bent low in a bow, swallowed back a hatred that nearly made him forget all reason and plant a knife in Dalvila's back. Reason won over hatred. He'd be dead before he took the first step, shot full of arrows or stabbed by the watching guards who lined the corridor. And it would be Estred who paid the price for his treason. His guts twisted into knots at the thought. Her punishment would make what happened to the man in the cells below look like child's play.

The last time a courtier had forgotten his place and displeased the empress, she'd had him decapitated and his head mounted on a puppeteer's stick. For the next week, she used the grotesque apparatus to address the court, maneuvering the hidden wires and hinges embedded in the head's mouth and jaw so that it moved up and down by means of a lever she controlled with her hand. For Dalvila, it had been a source of great fun and entertainment. For a court numbed by years of witnessing her excesses and cruelties, it had been a horrifying reminder that their empress possessed a thirst for the sadistic that defied measure. Gharek had no intention of becoming a rotting mouthpiece perched on a stick.

He returned home, shaken but resolved not only to complete his assigned task but to do so in a way that would change his daughter's life.

The courtyard hosted two occupants enjoying the sun and the flowers when he arrived. Or at least the servant set to watch the old woman sitting on a nearby bench was enjoying them. The crone didn't notice. She didn't notice anything, didn't say anything, just sat silent wherever someone placed her and stared unseeing at whatever was in front of her. Gharek glanced at the housemaid. "Has she said anything?" He'd asked this same question several times over the past three days.

The maid gave him the same answer as all the others. "No, master. Not a word."

He crouched in front of the old woman, staring into blank eyes whose gaze saw through him. "Where's Estred?" he asked the maid.

"With the beggar, master."

Gharek's mouth lifted at one corner. His staff still hadn't accepted Estred's nurse into their fold, wondering why their employer would bring a lice-ridden beggar woman off Domora's streets to care for his daughter. He owed them no explanation. "Fetch Siora," he said. "And stay to keep Estred company until I send her back."

The maid bowed and left to do his bidding. Alone in the courtyard with the old woman, Gharek reached into his tunic, pulling out the real mother-bond. Made of polished ivory, sharpened along one edge, and engraved in glowing sigils, it pulsed in his hand. It wasn't quite the same as when he had found it on this woman's person, made fractionally smaller by the splinters he'd shaved off its curve to have infused into the bone of a bear. The Maesor market wasn't the only place that dealt in black market magical items; it was just the biggest. Gharek had no doubt Dalvila had turned the artifact he'd given her over to her sages, those men who practiced sorcery in the empress's service and were therefore exempt from the punishments leveled against the general populace for practicing the same. Exempt at least until a morning when Dalvila awoke and arbitrarily decided it was a fine day to immolate a sage as part of her breakfast amusements. While they lived, they'd serve her not in the capacity of counselors like the sorcerers of the old courts, but as the equivalents of hounds or poison eaters. He'd wager they were inspecting the copycat bone he'd turned over to Dalvila, casting all sorts of spells on it to verify its nature. Gharek was thorough, with the financial means to enlist and reward a skilled counterfeiter. It was a shame he could only use the man's services once, but the risk of future extortion was too great. He'd pocketed the fake and left the dead counterfeiter in the alley where they'd met.

He waved the true mother-bond in front of the crone's face. "Will you not speak, grandmother, and tell me who this belongs to?"

She said nothing, moved not at all except for the involuntary blink of her eyes.

Gharek studied her, his thoughts whirling. He'd crossed paths with this woman by happy accident, spotting her flitting through the narrow alleys that mapped a warren of mazes throughout Domora. Gharek had first doubted his own eyes. No one had that kind of luck, but that day he did. Despite what he'd told Koopman, he'd enlisted his own watchers to keep an eye out for the three people Koopman's macabre trap shadow had revealed in its weave. So far they'd not found the older man or the young woman who looked like him. But Gharek had found the crone.

Capturing her had been easy, holding her as she tried to shred the skin off his face and arms far more difficult. He'd cuffed her into unconscious submission, tied her hands with his tunic sash, and carried her back to his house. While he was loath to bring any of his business home, it was the place where he wielded the greatest control. He'd put her in one of the storage pantries off the outdoor kitchen at first and kept watch until she wakened.

He used the time to search her person, looking for clues as to her identity and her relationship to the mother-bond he sought. His breath had wheezed out his nostrils when he discovered the very prize he was searching for tucked away in a hidden pocket sewn into the folds of her skirt, and in that moment Gharek changed course from cat's-paw to traitor of the crown. At least it would be so in Dalvila's eyes, should she ever discover his deception. Not all had moved in his favor. The crone had gained consciousness but not awareness, as if her abduction had so terrorized her, she'd retreated from the reality of the world. He was certain his strike had not caused this twilight existence, nor did he believe she pretended this state. It would be far too hard to keep up over an extended period without slipping, and she hadn't slipped once. Hadn't spoken, hadn't moved, and only responded to basic commands. But she'd carried a living mother-bond in her dress pocket, and somewhere behind that blank stare, she held the knowledge of whom it belonged to. Telling him wasn't a necessity. He had the one thing guaranteed to bring a draga to his front door. That in itself was both a boon and a risk. Gharek played a dangerous game, one he couldn't afford to lose.

"You summoned me, master?"

He glanced up, surprised to find Siora standing there. He wasn't accustomed to people sneaking up on him, purposefully or otherwise, yet the quiet Siora had appeared before him on soundless feet, studying him with a gaze that never failed to raise the hairs on his nape. Had she not once saved his wayward daughter from a stoning in the streets, he wouldn't have brought her here. Were it not for Estred's abiding affection for her, she wouldn't have stayed.

Gharek nodded toward the crone. "Has our guest said anything to you or Estred while I've been gone?" For all that he found Siora eerie, he also found her honest. He didn't trust his longtime servants not to lie to him, but for reasons he couldn't explain—call it instinct—he trusted Siora to tell him the truth.

"Not a word," she said. "Though her lips moved as if she tried to speak. I did my best to coax her to talk, but to no avail. She walks the Dream Road, I think."

Gharek agreed. Some who suffered through prolonged tortures escaped their agony within the sanctuary of their own minds. People called it walking the Dream Road. While he hadn't tortured this woman other than to subject her to his cook's meals, which weren't actually that bad, his abduction must have triggered a long-forgotten horror to resurface. She had retreated to the Dream Road and was still there.

"Keep trying," he said. He knew in his gut that if anyone had a chance of waking the crone from her state and coaxing her to talk, it was Siora. The eerie drawn to the oddity maybe. Whatever it was, Gharek needed it to work. If the crone wouldn't or couldn't talk, she was still bait to draw in the free trader man in hiding or the young woman who was obviously related to him. In turn, they'd share with Gharek, willingly or otherwise, what they knew of the draga that hunted the mother-bond.

If he could get to the draga before the empress did, he could bargain for some of his valuable blood. Not much. Just a swallow. Nothing like the empress, who planned to bathe in it in the hope of regaining the arm she had lost and retaining her youthful beauty. Gharek wanted just enough to give Estred the arms she'd been born without and the life she was robbed of because of her disfigurement.

He dismissed Siora and sat down on the bench beside the still crone. Her hands, weathered by the sun and gnarled from hard work, rested in her lap like fallen birds. Gharek lifted one and placed the mother-bond in her palm. Instantly, her fingers curled around it and her body twitched. He surged to his feet when a single word escaped her lips in a hoarse whisper.

"Malachus."

CHAPTER NINETEEN

Are you certain you want to travel with him to Domora, Halani? He's revealed himself as a sorcerer. That makes his company as dangerous to keep in the Empire as yours."

Halani paused in stuffing her one satchel with basic supplies: clothes, shoes, a comb, and a small apothecary box. She left the book, ink, and quill Malachus had given her in the wagon. There'd be no reading lessons on this trip.

She gave Kursak a smile meant to reassure him. "I'm sure. Except for his anger over our barrow raiding, he's the same man he was before the lightning strike. I trust him. He's had a soft spot for Mama since they first met. He might not have much use for me any longer, but he'll walk through fire to help her."

The wagon master placed a hand on her arm. Regret turned down the corners of his mouth. "I owe you an apology, one long overdue. One your uncle owes you as well." He paused, as if searching for the right words. "We take your skills for granted because you've shared them with us all your life. I couldn't give two shits if Malachus has his prick in a knot over us raiding that barrow, but he's right about one thing. You don't shove your loved ones into dangerous situations just for the sake of a trinket or a coin. If any of us barrow raid in the future, we won't be telling you about it, so you won't feel obligated. Besides, after this last confrontation with a fen hag, it's lost its luster for me."

Halani hugged him. "I chose to go, though I'm glad you'll exclude me in the future. I hope you abandon it too, but Uncle won't be so easy to convince."

Kursak squeezed her until her ribs creaked. "You don't worry about Hamod. With Asil missing, he has a lot to answer for and shaky ground to stand on. I'll handle him when the time comes."

There had been many times over the years when Halani wished with all her heart that Kursak was their principal wagon master instead of Hamod. This was one of those times. "Tell Kadena and Yeris they're welcome to use my wagon while I'm gone."

"They'll appreciate that. Last time I was in their wagon, I thought I'd stumbled into a rabbit warren."

Malachus waited for her with Batraza near the caravan, his austere features revealing nothing of his thoughts. "Ready?"

She nodded and handed him her satchel to secure to the saddle. Halani bid her farewells and promised to deliver messages of well-wishes to Asil when she and Malachus found her. No one said "if." To even consider that outcome pressed the weight of an overloaded wagon on Halani's chest, making it hard to breathe but oh so easy to weep.

Malachus mounted first then offered his arm so she could swing onto Batraza's back. Malachus coaxed the mare from a fast walk to a gallop, and they left the caravan behind.

They reached the end of the road by late afternoon in stony silence, except for the beat of Batraza's hooves as she kept a steady trot. Halani recognized the crossroads as one the caravan had traveled before when they traded farther south and east in Domora.

"We'll walk for a while," Malachus told Halani. "Batraza can cool down, and I can give her water. I hear a stream nearby." He pointed to a stand of trees just off the path.

Halani used the opportunity to answer nature's call, stretch her legs, and wash her hands and face in the cool stream that ran where Malachus indicated. She sat on its banks, trying to clear her mind of worry and fear for Asil. She had to stay clearheaded so she could plan the best and fastest way to find her mother. Hamod's welfare troubled her only briefly. He wasn't her first concern. Asil was everything.

She watched Malachus lead Batraza and stand beside the mare as she drank. He avoided Halani's gaze. She could apologize to him until she was blue in the face. It would still be a waste of breath.

He spoke only after Batraza finished drinking and only with a single word. "Ready?"

Halani rose to follow him, and soon they were on the road once more, riding for the nearby village of Icsom's Retreat.

It was her turn to speak as they approached the village's outskirts. The sky had taken on the lavender hue of twilight, and in the west the sun blazed a fiery line across the horizon. "Icsom's Retreat isn't much more than a way station for drovers, despite its nearness to Domora. There's an inn with rooms to let, though I've heard for the luxury of a roof over your head, you'll sleep on sheets of questionable cleanliness and battle legions of fleas. But you can get a hot meal. There's also a stable, but it won't be much good to us with Batraza."

Malachus's reply was flat. "The stream runs not far from the village. There are cleaner, less vermin-ridden places on the forest floor to sleep if you don't mind going without the roof. We can leave for Domora once dawn breaks."

"I don't mind." She bit back a sigh of relief. She'd take a night sleeping under the stars any day over a skin-crawling stay in a filthy inn.

He found a pleasant spot in the shadow of a willow tree not far from the stream's edge. Halani scoured the surrounding area for sticks and branches to use as firewood while Malachus untied the satchels and unsaddled Batraza. He removed her bridle, leaving on the harness and lead rope before sending her off to graze on the thick grass growing under the trees. He and Halani worked in tandem in utter silence, sharing and switching tasks when necessary with the smooth transition of a couple with long practice in such work. She found it an odd thing and a natural one too. If they worked this well together while in the midst of hostilities, she could only imagine how well they might do together were they friends again, or lovers. The last made her close her eyes, and she forced down the sharp regret for what was lost.

Their supper consisted of road rations warmed over the fire—simple, filling, forgettable. Halani passed Malachus a cup of tea she'd brewed. The scent of mint and verbena drifted on the air, and he gave the cup an appreciative sniff and her a short "Thank you," before focusing his attention on the cup's contents.

After a full day of it, the tension frayed her nerves and tested her patience. Halani wasn't naturally a chatty person, and she appreciated a comfortable quiet the same way she appreciated a good cup of tea. And while her current cup of tea was good, this quiet was anything but comfortable. "At some point, Malachus, we'll have to talk to each other so we can plan how we'll find my mother in Domora."

"I already have a plan." He drained his tea and set the cup aside. "The lightning showed me Asil sitting in a walled garden. It's a good starting point for searching the city."

Her eyebrows rose. "That's very little to go by. Just how many walled gardens are in Domora?"

"Not as many as you might think. Those kinds of courtyards are luxuries reserved for the wealthy, especially in a city where space is precious and therefore costly. This rules out all the public spaces and most of the living quarters in any city. I doubt Domora is any different. The garden I saw her in was manicured but of modest size, so that excludes the grand estates of the Empire's more powerful nobility and the palace itself. Homes with gardens like these won't line the royal avenue but be nearby."

Halani paused with her teacup partway to her lips, astonished. "How often have you hunted for lost people?"

The possibility of a smile brushed his mouth before fading. "Often enough to know how to start a productive search."

His explanation eased some of her anxiousness. "That's good to know. And the girl without arms? I'd never wish that hardship on a child, but will it help your search? Surely people would remember her if you asked them?"

Malachus nodded. "They would, and if she belonged to a family with connections, they'd waste no time in telling the family that a stranger was asking about such a child. Whoever has Asil would be quick to move her elsewhere."

Halani rested her forehead on her knees and stared at her lap. "Why would they take Mama in the first place? She's a child herself in all but body." She turned her head to look at him and saw softness in his dark gaze. It disappeared in an instant.

"I don't know. I can only guess that someone in Domora knows what a live mother-bond is as well as its value. If they've discovered the connection between Asil and your uncle, they'll use her as bait to try and flush him out and take the mother-bond." He met her gaze, his a measuring one. "I know you want to find your mother right away. I do too, but if Hamod has the mother-bond, I can find him faster, and he may know or have an idea where she is."

If her uncle was here right now, Halani would wrap her fingers around his throat and squeeze. He'd taken Asil with him as a way of punishing Halani for her rebellion and then lost her in Domora. "If we find him, why don't we just use him as bait to flush out those holding Mama?"

Malachus's eyebrows climbed toward his hairline. "I'd have no issue with that at all. It's a good idea, though I'm surprised by your suggestion."

"He and I have never gotten along very well. I'm the product of his sister's abduction and rape. He's told me more than once he almost smothered me when I was born and would have done so had Mama not begged him for mercy."

"Gods, Halani, what kind of bastard says that to a child? Especially one who's a member of his family?" Malachus's eyes, black and cool as polished onyx until now, shot angry sparks.

She shoved around the coals in their fire with the stick she held. "A man burdened by the guilt of not saving his beloved sister in time or preventing her capture by slavers in the first place. My existence reminds him of her torture and his failure."

More silence settled between them for a few moments until Malachus spoke again, and this time his voice wasn't so flat or distant. "You look very much like your uncle. Enough so that people could mistake you for his daughter. Does he know this?"

Her chuckle sounded humorless to her ears. "It's one reason I'm still alive, I think. Whoever my father was, I took nothing from him in appearance. In that the gods were kind. But despite our conflicts and the fact that I could cheerfully blacken both of his eyes at the moment, I owe Hamod a great deal. I was raised among people who loved me despite my origins and gave my mother a safe haven in which to heal and reclaim the innocence she'd lost. Not all things work out for the better, but sometimes they work out for the acceptable, and for that I'm grateful."

Malachus didn't reply and after a time rose from his place beside her. "I'll be right back. Batraza's wandered farther afield than I like." He disappeared into the blackness where the trees grew thick and the mare had traveled during her grazing.

He returned with Batraza in tow and stopped in his tracks. "You've taken your hair down," he said, stating the obvious in a voice gone raspy.

Halani stared at him, comb in one hand, a skein of her hair in the other, and butterflies beating themselves against her rib cage. "I always comb it out before I plait it for bed."

The mare nickered a greeting at Halani before pulling on her lead rope. Malachus let it go, and she ambled to a patch of grass she hadn't yet nibbled down.

Malachus returned to his spot by the fire. Firelight danced across his body, creating shadows that cavorted over his shoulders and chest, flickering across his face. Halani found him breathtaking.

Bitter anger purled off him to beat against her in a steady, chilling tide. His closed expression didn't invite overtures from her, and the hard downturn of his mouth warned he'd either ignore anything she said or verbally strip off a piece of her flesh if she tried.

She resumed her grooming, using the comb she'd brought to battle the knots in her curls. She hummed under her breath as she worked the long length, and soon she felt his stare on her, forbidding, heavy, intense. He watched her with half-closed eyes, his face a study in conflicting emotions—yearning mixed with fury.

Ringlets sprang back from the comb's stretch, defying her efforts to tame them until she finally gathered the mass together and swiftly plaited it. Desperate to break the roiling silence between them, she held up the comb to Malachus. "I can comb and braid yours for you if you'd like. I have an extra hair tie."

His dark gaze went from her face to the comb and back before he gave a wordless nod. The air in her lungs thinned, and her heartbeat drummed a little harder. He hadn't bitten her head off or refused her offer. She motioned for him to turn his back to her and scooted closer until she knelt behind him, her knees pressed to his hips as she captured his hair in her hand. She indulged in her admiration of his mane by sliding her fingers along the strands before running the comb through its length.

"You have beautiful hair. I wish mine was so easy to manage." He surprised her when he lifted her braid from where it had fallen across his shoulder when she'd leaned forward to capture some of his locks that eluded her grasp. "As I said before, this is your glory. Maybe I should call you Halani of the Curls instead of Halani of the Lightning."

Was that a teasing note she heard in his voice? They had been friends and then lovers, both relationships now wrecked by what he saw as her perfidy and betrayal. Anger still burned through him, and until now, she despaired of ever seeing a real smile from him or hearing a civil word. Did she yearn for something so badly she imagined it?

"Are you finally going to tell me why you call me that?"

He didn't let go of her hair, curving the braid's end into a loop before releasing it, only to repeat the action. "Because I first saw your face in the lightning. Not the bolt I called down on the fen road but another before I came to the Goban market. It showed me a winsome woman with gray eyes who was somehow connected to the draga bone I sought. And it was so."

She combed his hair back from his face, weaving it into a tight, simple braid similar to hers, and tied the end with her remaining hair tie. "Done," she proclaimed, mulling over his words, both strange and poetic.

He released her braid and turned to face her. The restrained hairstyle gave his already harsh face an even colder quality, emphasizing the hollows of his cheeks and long nose. "Am I handsome?" He asked the question with a lofty solemnity that belied the glimmer in his eyes.

Breathtaking, she thought but said instead, "To make the maidens swoon. I'm very good at braids."

"You haven't swooned yet."

She arched an eyebrow. "I'm not a maiden, as you've discovered."

"Then next time I'll request you braid my hair in such a way that you will swoon." A shadow passed over his face as soon as the words left his lips, and the brief spark of humor died. Halani mourned its loss and mourned even more his obvious withdrawal from her, both physically and emotionally.

To lessen the awkwardness between them, she rummaged through their supplies, retrieved a blanket, and wrapped herself in it. She lay on her back and stared at the stars, denying to herself that she listened to his breathing and counted every inhalation and exhalation.

"Comfortable?"

Halani glanced at him. He'd brought a pipe with him and was busy filling the bowl with aromatic leaf. "Yes, thank you." She stared at him a moment longer. Light worshipped him; sunlight, candlelight, campfire light. Even lightning blessed him with a bludgeoning touch. The free traders, seeing him survive such a strike and come away with nothing more than a burn hole in his shirt, were suitably awed by the stunt, certain they beheld the power of a weather mage at hand. Halani disagreed, though she kept it to herself.

Lightning has always loved the draga. His words echoed in her mind. He searched for a mother-bond to lift a curse, and his grief and anger over the corruption of the Sun Maiden story had seemed strangely personal. He healed at an extraordinary rate. The fact that he hadn't died outright from his wounds was cause for wonder. And he smoked. Literally. Plumes of it wisping off his skin and hair as if a fire burned unseen inside him. She stared at him, no longer seeing just a dark-haired man with a harsh visage but the shadow of a creature much bigger, much older, infinitely more powerful than a normal man.

"You're staring, Halani." Malachus lowered his pipe. "If you want to share the pipe, just say so."

She grimaced, relieved that he had misread her intense scrutiny. "I've never developed a taste for it. You're welcome to it." She closed her eyes, seeking sleep even as her tired mind chased thoughts like starlings: Asil's abduction, Hamod's disappearance, Malachus's secrets as well as his fury.

Sleep remained elusive, and the prickly feel of being watched made her open her eyes to find Malachus watching her. "What's wrong?"

"Everything is wrong," he snapped. "It's partially why we're here," he said. "But that isn't why I'm staring." He looked away to stir the fading embers in the fire pit she'd made earlier. "I was just remembering a temple I once visited during my travels, before I sailed to these shores," he said in softer tones. "A temple to a goddess of spring. The entrance doors were carved with the reliefs of twin priestesses with flowers in their hair and ivy encircling their arms and bodies. The statue of the goddess herself was an impressive thing. A deity who looked as if she'd beat you with a tree if you annoyed her."

Obviously worshippers in Winosia took their nature deities very seriously.

"The twins, though, were beautiful to behold," he said with a supplicant's awe. "A balm to the spirit, a pleasure to the eye." His gaze returned to her, black and starless. "You remind me of them."

Held in thrall by that look and afraid she might ruin the moment, Halani didn't dare blink. "Spring is my favorite season," she said softly.

"I doubt that comes as a surprise to anyone." His tense shoulders relaxed, and while he didn't smile, she heard the ghost of a teasing note in his voice. "Maybe I should call you Halani of the Spring."

Halani wrinkled her nose. "That doesn't sound nearly as grand as Halani of the Lightning."

"True," he said, "but it's spring, not lightning, that has always given men hope."

CHAPTER TWENTY

Unlike Halani, Malachus remained awake. Troubled men rarely found sleep, and he was a troubled man. Or draga.

He had spent the last century and a half journeying through the lands of men, learning ways and beliefs outside those he'd been raised with among the brotherhood. His naivete when he first ventured from the monastery's sanctuary so long ago had faded quickly enough, and while experience and maturity had brought him wisdom, humanity still flummoxed him at every turn. This time a woman in a trader caravan had managed to twist him into knots more tangled than the rigging on a shipwreck.

Condemn us if you will, but know why we do it, not why you think we do it.

Her earlier words echoed in his mind like a chant, no matter how much he tried to ignore them. It was easy to condemn and judge when the reasons for a crime seemed not only clear-cut but petty. Halani's response to his accusations and fury had caught him off guard. She hadn't justified the grave robbing. Nor had she denied it. She had simply explained why they did it and left it to him to accept or excoriate. His fury drove him to choose the second. Now, when possessed of cooler emotions, he was torn.

He'd never approve of their raiding. He'd seen the destruction grave robbers left behind once they gutted a gravesite, had watched as gentle monks fell to their knees in anguish or held the scattered bones of skeletons to their chests and wept at the violation of their holy dead. Those thieves had stolen goods, dignity, and Malachus's birthright. Even now, the mother-bond remained elusive, an ever-present pull in his soul but still just beyond his reach. He'd been too young at the time to take his revenge. By the time he was old enough, those thieves were dead.

Even were he not plagued by the memory of the necropolis's looting, he'd still find the practice repugnant. And dangerous. He wanted to beat Kursak bloody for taking Halani with him on this latest raid. The horror of seeing her yanked off her feet and dragged into the water burned a nightmarish image in his mind, one he'd never forget.

No doubt she believed her sins doubled when she told him her uncle had the mother-bond. Her confession had rammed a fist into his gut even when he'd anticipated what she would say. She had taken his heart and given him her body, then turned and planted a knife in him. His cooler reason only now began to prevail. Despite their intimacy, her first loyalty wasn't to him but to her family, and he hadn't been forthright with her about his quest, playing coy with the curse explanation. Could he truly condemn her for her deception?

But he would never rob a grave.

Spoken like a man who's never known the joy of starvation.

He had not, but her grim statement made it plain she had. Had such a horror turned an otherwise generous people into something more feral, less reverent? Made those who survived starvation determined not to suffer it again, no matter what it took?

Those questions kept him awake the remainder of the night, and as the stars faded with morning's approach, so did his anger. In the end, even if Malachus considered himself righteous in his condemnation (and that was no longer so), his disapproval was his to bear, not Halani's, not the other free traders'. He wasn't one of them and wouldn't face their hardships.

She gave him a wary look when he woke her at dawn with the offering of a cup of hot tea and a half smile. "Everything all right?" she asked. "Did I miss something while I slept?"

"Only my soul-searching," he replied.

He didn't have to urge her to hurry her morning ablutions. The worried lines creasing her brow told him they couldn't get to Domora fast enough to suit her and calm her fears for Asil.

They were on the road in short order, and this time Malachus rode pillion while Halani held the reins. She sat stiffly in front of him at first, guarded and quiet. His hands rested lightly across her midriff, though he longed to nudge her back against him and hold her close. Not yet. Not until they cleared away the lingering hostilities and hurt.

"You were right," he said. "I denounced in haste and judged without knowledge. And I purposefully insulted you. I don't expect you to forgive it, but you should know I'm sorry and wish I could take it back."

Her faint gasp and the jerk of her body told him he'd shocked her. Halani drew on the reins, and Batraza halted. Halani stared straight ahead. Her voice was soft, though the grip she held on the reins had turned her knuckles white.

"I don't understand. What's brought about such a change of heart?"

He tapped Batraza's sides with his heels to get her moving again. "A night of sleepless self-reflection and some of what you said when we argued." He touched her chin, coaxing her to turn her head so he could see part of her face and the expression she wore. "I've never known starvation, but you have. How old were you?"

"Eight," she said with a sigh. "We lost a third of our number during the Great Blight. I never forgot it. None of us did." She studied him. "Knowing that shouldn't change how you feel about barrow raiding."

"Nothing's changed my mind. I still think it's a detestable act deserving of harsh punishment. But I no longer believe all those who do it are strictly motivated by greed."

"Most are," she said. "I wish I could tell you differently, that only a few rob graves because of an appetite for possessions and riches, but I'd be lying. And I'd be lying if I told you I hadn't felt a rush of pleasure at hearing the chime of gold or silver under dirt and grass as I walked a barrow's perimeter." She placed one of her hands over his where it rested against her. "I've stolen from the dead, Malachus, but I swear I've never desecrated the bodies, never destroyed their resting places, never rejoiced in lifting bones and folding back shrouds. My uncle always feared that doing so would call up a revenant to take revenge. For me, it was guilt. I'd already invaded a sacred place. To ransack it seemed a worse sort of offense."

Malachus hadn't intended to tell her about the necropolis and its destruction, fearing she might interpret the revelation as an attempt to justify his earlier censure. At her last words, he changed his mind. "It is the worst offense," he said. "The one the living remember most clearly."

When he finished telling the tale, she leaned back against him of her own accord. "No wonder you were so angry when you discovered what we were up to. I'm sorry. So very sorry. For that. For keeping silent about my uncle having the mother-bond, for making your task of retrieving it so much harder. I wish I'd done things differently."

This time it was he who stopped Batraza. His arms tightened around Halani. He leaned forward, even as she turned more fully toward him, and cupped her cheek. The kiss they shared sent multiple bolts of lightning through Malachus's body, only these weren't of Pernu's making, but Halani's. She moaned into his mouth, her grip on his wrist tightening as he deepened the kiss. Batraza's impatient snort and the shift of her stance broke them apart.

"We will forgive and learn from each other," Malachus said against her temple, relishing the feel of her soft hair against his lips. "We'll be in Domora before nightfall. With any luck, we'll find the rest of your caravan shortly after. I don't know where we'll sleep or if we'll even have beds, but if we do, will you share mine once more?"

"Yes," she said with a fervency that was almost a prayer.

Domora was a sprawling place of soaring edifices made of polished granite that gleamed in the sun. Malachus was reminded of the quiet garden ponds tended by the monks with whom he'd lived, their surfaces covered by water lilies whose delicate blossoms bloomed under early morning light in shades of gold and pink, ivory and pale yellow. Domora's greatest structures, including the palace at its center, possessed those same soft hues. They contrasted with the more ramshackle buildings that spread out from the center to the city walls, becoming dingier and more rundown the farther they stood from the palace.

"Kraelag was much bigger and the Empire's main seat of power, but Domora has always been the more refined," Halani told him. "The most profitable trade for the finest goods is here in Domora."

They made their way slowly along the main avenue, caught amid the traffic of carts and citizens going about their everyday tasks. Numerous troop units wearing the insignia and uniforms of the Kraelian army moved among them, some directing the flow of traffic, others monitoring its mood and breaking up impromptu brawls that spilled from some of the streetside public houses into the throng.

Malachus noted the number of soldiers. A large representation, even among a crowd this size. "Domora is a hive of activity," he said. His nostrils flared at the faint whiff of brine. "And the harbor isn't far away. I can smell salt water and fish."

Halani half turned to look at him. "You have a discerning nose. All I smell are ripe people and hot grease."

He steered Batraza away from one cluster of soldiers who watched him with too much interest. "Domora is a city whose current purpose is to prepare for war."

"Not surprising. The empress is probably spoiling for revenge against the Savatar or set on taking back the territories she lost in both the west and the east."

If the Spider of Empire was only a fraction like the rumors and gossip portrayed her, she'd punish the Savatar and her rebellious vassals with utmost brutality. There would be no quarter given, no mercy granted.

The closer they got to the armory, the more troops they saw, among them throngs of army followers, including cooks and tailors, armorers and farriers, and a large contingent of prostitutes. The din of voices—human and animal alike—rose to a roar. "I won't lie, Halani. We may have a difficult time finding Asil or Hamod in such a crowded city."

She twisted in the saddle to better see him. "But if he has the draga bone still, won't you be able to at least find him that way?"

"It will make it easier. If it's still in his possession."

Worry clouded her gaze. "Can you sense the artifact easier now?"

If she only knew. "It's here in Domora. I've no doubt of it, and somewhere in the direction of the palace. As soon as we find the caravan and get Batraza settled, I'll leave you with your folk so they can help you look in one part of the city while I search in another. The mother-bond's draw is powerful here. If your uncle has it, I should find him soon enough. You can start searching for your mother. Your people will know best where she might have been taken. Remember, the garden I saw her in is modest but manicured, a wealthy man's house but maybe not a nobleman."

Halani suddenly pointed to a spot beyond the edge of a cluster of buildings. "There. I can see the top of my uncle's wagon."

Malachus guided Batraza toward the place Halani indicated. A small group of free traders gathered at the edge of the encampment, curious as to who rode toward them. People emerged from the wagons or left small cook fires to join their growing number as Malachus and Halani entered the camp. They were greeted with great fanfare, and Batraza snorted a protest at the commotion. Malachus halted in front of the group, dismounted, and helped Halani out of the saddle.

She was quickly enfolded in a welcoming embrace. Malachus watched from his place beside Batraza, fascinated by the overt display of affection. Humans were so very odd in their ways. Reserved and exuberant by turn, kind and cruel, loving and hateful. As unpredictable as weather and often as harsh. Seeing Halani and her kin like this lightened his spirit. He admired some of their ways and heartily disapproved of others, but none could find fault with their devotion to each other. This was a tight-knit group.

Saradeen, a tall free trader with a sun-lined face and red hair, was the first to speak to Malachus. "You're looking a lot better than when I last saw you, friend." The two men shook hands.

"I've come to help Halani find Asil. And Hamod. Clamik told us they'd both disappeared from the camp within a day of each other. Have any of you heard or seen anything from either of them?"

Saradeen's features turned gloomy. "Nothing. Not even a scrap of rumor. We've scoured the city as best we can. Bribed servants who work in the palace, to no avail. It's as if Hamod has fallen off the edge of the world, and Asil with him." His eyes were grave. "I'm sorry, Halani. I'd hoped to have better news."

Halani twisted her fingers together, knuckles whitening. "Not even the middens or the gallows?"

The free trader shook his head. "In that, I'm pleased to tell you no."

Malachus pressed his hand to her back when her shoulders slumped, and addressed Saradeen. "We've traveled hard to get here quickly. Had we arrived earlier, I'd suggest a city search, though I know you said you've already gone that route once. But it's late, the shops are closing, people are less willing to talk when they're eager to go home. Morning would be better." Halani looked to argue, and Malachus continued before she could. "We're both tired, need some food and a bed. We'll serve Asil and Hamod better if we're alert and well rested when we start our hunt."

His words inspired a deluge of offers to make meals, bring blankets and pillows, and vacate wagons for Halani and Malachus to use. Halani accepted the offers of tea and food but declined the others. "We'll use Uncle's wagon. I assume it's standing empty?" At several nods, she turned to Malachus. "He isn't here to protest."

With Batraza taken care of for the night and a quick meal at the main campfire, the two made their way to one of the more ornate wagons in the caravan circle. Malachus paused just inside the door, carrying his and Halani's satchels slung over his shoulders, and stared in awe at what her lamplight revealed.

The wagon he'd used as his temporary shelter was a spartan affair, a provender wagon cleared of enough content to give him space for a bed and a little room to move around. Halani's wagon was a home on wheels. Of similar size to the supply wagon, it was far more welcoming, with furnishings and decorations that invited one to stay and visit. Hamod's wagon was a different affair altogether.

Overdone, overstuffed, and overwhelming, it reflected something of the man Halani called uncle. A man who fancied himself not just the wagon master of a free trader caravan but the monarch of a small rolling kingdom. A man who called himself Hamod the Imposing with all seriousness. A man who robbed graves not for survival but purely for profit.

"I think I'd prefer to sleep under the sky," he said.

Halani's surprise at his declaration faded, a knowing gleam entering her eyes. She nodded. "The weather is decent enough, and it's cooler out there than in here. Opening the windows won't do much to lessen the heat."

He took the lamp she passed him. "Will you join me?"

She bent to gather up extra blankets and pillows from the sumptuously made bed and smiled at him. "Of course. Where else would I wish to be?"

Her words sent a rush of desire through him, almost as powerful as what had swamped him when he returned to their camp and discovered her combing out her hair.

They made up a bed close to the wagon, away from the path of foot traffic. The noise of the city swirled outside the camp, even as it gradually fell asleep. The joy of having Halani in his arms once more almost drowned out the tug of the mother-bond on Malachus's soul. He refused to waste the ever-diminishing time he had with her dwelling on it. She welcomed him into her arms and into her body once more as the stars wheeled above them, and he worshipped her with his hands, his mouth, and his heart.

Afterward, they lay entwined, their voices low as they spoke of inconsequential things and Malachus played with Halani's loosened hair. She stared into his eyes, puzzlement creasing her forehead. "What?" he asked.

"Lightning has always loved the draga," she said, echoing his earlier statement. He paused in coiling one of her ringlets around his fingers. "The others saw you call down lightning and thought you a weather mage, but you aren't, are you?" She didn't wait for an answer. Her hand pressed to his jaw. "This is the face of a man who's lived three decades, give or take a couple of years." The same small hand passed down his neck to flatten against his chest. "Inside, though, beneath what's human flesh and bone, lies something else. Something much older, more long-lived than a mere man." Malachus caught his breath when a terrible sympathy settled over her features, and her eyes grew glossy as she stared at him. "'The Sun Maiden' is more than a story for you, isn't it? Who were Golnar and Yain?"

He didn't look away, didn't deny the truth of her speculations. He no longer wished to hide it from her. "Golnar was my mother and Yain my sister." No matter how many times he said their names aloud, the pain it brought never blunted, never weakened.

Halani wrapped her arms and legs more tightly around him, as if she tried to offer sanctuary by melding him to her. "We are awful, brutish creatures," she whispered.

Malachus stroked her bare back, returning the comfort she offered him. "Not all of you," he said, planting a kiss into her hair. "Not you. Never you."

He held her as she wept the tears he no longer did and grieved for the mother and sibling whose images as both women and draga remained as sharp in his mind now as they had centuries earlier.

"You're not cursed are you?" Halani asked, returning to their bed after retrieving a cloth to wipe her face and blow her nose.

Malachus gathered her close. "No. The curse is my birthright, the mother-bond the means by which I can claim it before it consumes me. The guise of humanity can hide and hold a draga for only so long before I have to change and embrace what I truly am."

"No wonder the livestock always grew skittish when you came close. They sensed the draga."

"Yes."

"But they do it to Batraza, too, and she doesn't fear you. Is she a draga in disguise as well?"

Malachus grinned. "No, but she's painted by draga magic, under a spell that binds her life to mine for as long as I breathe. If I were to die today, so would she. She's not much younger than I am."

Halani's mouth fell open. "You have what? A two-hundred-year-old mare?" The idea shocked her even more than having him verify for her his own origins.

He laughed. "Something like that."

"It explains why she's so tranquil. She's had a long time to settle into her bones."

They grew quiet once more, and Malachus thought Halani might have fallen asleep, until a small giggle drafted across his neck where she'd nuzzled her face. "What's so funny?"

Another giggle. "Never, in all my life, did I ever imagine I'd meet a draga, much less swive one."

He shifted so he could stare down at her smiling face. "And what have you discovered?"

That smile took on a come-hither quality. "That dragas make wonderful lovers."

They made love again, and this time their intimacy contained the strengthening bond of a shared secret, of unconditional trust, and for Malachus, the inarguable fact that he'd fallen deeply in love with a woman he'd soon leave behind.

She fell asleep in his arms afterward, and he lay there, savoring the feel of her body, heavy with sleep, against him. He wished they could stay that way all night, but it wasn't to be.

He'd suggested they begin their search for Asil in the morning, but that had been for Halani's benefit. He was stronger than she was, not plagued by the same exhaustion she suffered from the worry over her mother's fate. He'd use the small hours to reconnoiter the city as an extra measure.

Slowly, carefully, he gathered Halani into his arms and stood, blankets and her hair cascading over his arms. She didn't wake when he climbed the steps to Hamod's wagon and shouldered the door open. She only muttered in her sleep when he laid her across the luxurious bed and straightened the covers over her. He dared not kiss her. If he did, he wouldn't leave.

Outside, he silently dressed, armed himself with his two favorite daggers, and left the free trader camp for a nighttime exploration of Domora, guided by the powerful pull of his mother-bond.

The city stretched out before him in an orderly grid of streets that radiated from a central point: the graceful summer palace perched on the highest point of the slope upon which the city's many structures were built. His mother-bond lay in that direction. While he had no illusions regarding his chances of entering the palace through means not nefarious, it was as good a place as any to start.

The mother-bond's draw had taken on a strangeness. Instead of a clear, singular beacon flashing an internal light from within the palace, it pulsed with a broader wave, as if it sat not in one particular spot but across an area. Still close to the palace, and even within it, but acting more like a halo of light than a splinter of it. Malachus growled, frustrated with this newest complication. He prayed he didn't face the same difficulty with finding Asil in tomorrow's search.

His nocturnal exploration took him straight through the heart of the city and onto the wide royal avenue where trees lined either side of the broad street. Deserted in the small hours, the street welcomed him as its lone visitor, an assumption Malachus abandoned when something or someone moved among the trees, following him.

Two shadows, from what he could tell. Quiet, practiced at lurking and likely at ambush. Unfortunately for them, they'd chosen a difficult target. He picked a spot in the street with room to move that didn't trap him in a narrow place or a dead end and halted to confront the pair who'd scurried from the shadows of buildings and shrubbery as they tracked him. "You might as well stop hiding," he called out. "Try to rob me, and I'll leave you in pieces in the street." He wasn't in the mood for games, nor had he the time for them.

One of the shades emerged from behind a wall of hedges, solidifying into a man with squinty, rattish features.

He moved like a rat too, with the same scavenging scuttle.

"I got something you might want to know," he said, lisping the words through the gap where his front teeth should have been. "It's about the woman you brought with you to the city today."

While his instinct for trouble had served him well, alarm exploded inside Malachus at the footpad's statement. He extracted a coin from the bag tucked into his tunic and flipped it silently to the man.

The footpad caught it deftly, inspected it, and promptly disappeared it among the dirt and fleas of ragged clothing. "I need a little more," he said. "This is good information."

"That's all you'll get and be grateful for it." Malachus tilted his head, listening to the furtive movements behind him. "For all I know, you're about to feed me a dung cart full of lies, and I can always just beat the information out of you. And back your friend off before you both regret it." He rested a hand on the hilt of the knife he carried.

The footpad's eyes widened. He gave a quick nod, and the creeping steps behind Malachus halted. "Your woman. Half of Domora has been looking for her."

Fury fueled by panic roared through Malachus. He clenched his jaw, fighting to keep down his rising fear as well as the draga's innate aggression. "Why is that?" His voice revealed nothing of his inner turmoil or the urge to sprint back to the free trader camp and ensure Halani's safety.

The footpad shrugged, the sly gleam in his eye signaling he wasn't completely fooled by Malachus's apathy. "Don't know other than the empress's cat's-paw has his lackeys scouring the city with drawings of a man and two women. All three look alike, and the younger woman is the one you rode into Domora with today. Word's gone out that anyone who spots one of these three and reports back to him, they'll get a reward."

Malachus recognized the term "cat's-paw," a disparaging description for a henchman. "Did he say why he's looking for them?"

"No, and ain't no one who knows him that stupid to ask."

"The name of this cat's-paw?"

The footpad shrugged. "Gharek. A gutter rat who rose through the ranks and fancies himself gentry now." His upper lip lifted in a curl of contempt. "Dangerous but known for paying well if you give him what he wants."

Dangerous and hunting for Halani and her mother, using drawings of their likenesses. Where the hell had he gotten those? Malachus barely resisted the urge to have done with the niceties and simply beat the information out of the footpad. "If he's so generous and the reward significant, why aren't you on his doorstep telling him instead of talking to me?"

"Because there's probably a crowd already lining up at the Dead Hound Pub waiting to tell him and get the reward."

"And you'd make more money by selling me a warning." From a strictly mercenary perspective, it was a smart move and did nothing to lessen Malachus's revulsion for this scavenger. "Where does the cat's-paw live?"

His new informant cocked his head to one side, studying Malachus, his rodent face becoming even more rattish. "You're new to Domora, aren't you?"

"Don't make the mistake of thinking that makes me an easy mark."

The footpad shrugged. "Don't know. And if I did, I wouldn't go there. I heard the last time someone paid Gharek a visit at his house uninvited, he returned the man's entrails to his wife in a bag."

A very dangerous cat's-paw indeed, and unhesitating when it came to killing. Malachus tossed the man another *belsha*. "And no one's seen the other two he's looking for?"

"Not that I've heard." The man's sly mien intensified. "If I do, I can tell you before I tell the cat's-paw."

"For a price, of course." Good thing Malachus still had a decent bit of coin in his possession. He suspected he'd be beggared by the time this was over.

The rat's face creased into a rotting smile. "Of course. And if you plan to stay in that free trader camp, I can find you. Then again, so can the cat's-paw. Might want to consider stashing your woman somewhere else. No business with Gharek is ever good business."

Malachus flipped another coin to him. "To show my continued interest. If you do spot the man or the old woman from the drawings, see me. I'll match the cat's-paw's reward. Tell anyone else, and I'll sell your guts for garters."

The footpad pocketed the coin, bowed, and scurried away with his companion. Malachus watched them for a moment before abandoning his nighttime exploration and hurrying back to the free trader camp, plagued by a growing fear that he'd meet a terrified Saradeen waiting to tell him that Halani had gone missing just like her mother and her uncle, a prisoner of a vicious cat's-paw with plans of his own.

He'd been tempted to follow the pair, but they'd expect it and likely take him on a false chase through Domora that had him running in circles, or worse, lead him into a dead-end path where he'd be trapped and have to fight his way out. Besides, the urge to race back to the free trader camp won out. Even the wrench of the mother-bond on his senses succumbed to the need to assure himself that Halani was still in the camp, still safe.

His heart pounded in his chest the entire way back, and not just from the sprint to get there. The camp was just waking, a few people out seeing to morning chores. When they saw him, they waved or called out a greeting, reassuring him that those in the camp paid attention to who entered.

Emerging light through the clerestory windows in Hamod's wagon illuminated the interior enough to reveal Halani still asleep, reclined on her side, her back to the door. Her hair tumbled to the floor in a waterfall of curls. Malachus thought his heartbeat might slow down once he ascertained she was here and unharmed, but he was wrong. It only drummed harder in his chest for another reason.

Were circumstances different, he'd strip naked, crawl into bed, take her in his arms, and make love to her once more. He burned for her, body and soul, a fire unlike the draga's imperative to be free but no less consuming.

"Halani." He ran a fingertip down her spine. She arched away, muttering a protest at the ticklish touch before rolling onto her back.

She stared at him through slitted eyes. "You're dressed." Her eyes opened wider, gradually losing their sleepy squint. She blinked in confusion at her surroundings. "We're in Uncle's wagon."

"Yes to both," he said. "I carried you in here before I left." He didn't have the luxury of joining her in bed, but it didn't stop him from gathering her into his arms and kissing her, consumed by a combination of desire and relief: the first because she was Halani, the second because she'd come to no harm while sleeping alone and unguarded in her uncle's wagon.

She was the one to end the kiss. Her fingers were cool on his face as she traced the bridge of his nose. Her eyes rounded. "You've been out searching Domora, haven't you? Did you find my mother?" Her fingers dug into his shoulders, hope chasing fear across her face.

He wished he had such good news. "Not yet. Get dressed. We need to talk to Saradeen and the others. After you fell asleep, I left to scout a small part of the city along the royal avenue." He smiled at her frown. "I was careful, Halani, and I've been in cities more perilous than Domora."

"I can't help it," she said, rising from the bed and giving Malachus a lovely view of her body before slipping on her shift. "I keep seeing you in the grass looking like a pin-poppet with all those arrows sticking out of you."

Her words filled him with warmth. And longing. What a fine thing it would be to claim this woman as his and declare himself hers. It wasn't to be, but he'd hold the idea close during the years to come when he dreamed of her face and the grace of her in his arms.

Once she was dressed, they left the wagon and she led him to Saradeen's wagon. Most of the camp was awake and outside, packing up their wares to take to the market square, where Hamod had secured a space to hawk goods to buyers.

Malachus recounted his jaunt through the city and his unexpected meeting with the two footpads. "I don't believe he was lying when he said there'd be a line waiting at that pub of people who saw Halani. They'll be wanting the reward money, even if it's only enough to purchase a tankard of ale. This lookout was either a little smarter, a little greedier, or a little more reckless in approaching me with the information he had."

"Double his take and maybe more by telling two interested parties." Anger darkened Halani's eyes. "Do you think this Gharek is the one who has my mother?"

"There's a good chance, and he just hasn't said anything to anyone about it yet." Malachus prayed such was the case. Another person holding Asil captive with the hopes of extorting the cat's-paw would make things even more complicated.

"It burns my guts that someone's been spying on us the whole time we've been in Domora." Saradeen downed the rest of his tea as if it were hard spirits and reached for the teapot on the brazier grate.

"Maybe not the whole time but probably since Hamod went to ground." Malachus gestured to the camp as a whole. "Your setup here discourages visitors from trying to creep about unnoticed, but all this cat's-paw needs to do is place a watch or two at the city gates and outside the camp to see who comes and goes. My guess is lookouts at the gate reported our arrival. Any outside the camp now are just keeping an eye on Halani and will report back if she goes anywhere."

"Did the footpads say anything else to you about Mama?" Halani's voice was calm, but she couldn't hide the fear in her eyes.

Malachus hugged her against his side. "Nothing other than no one had yet spotted her or Hamod. I'd have kept searching through the night, but after what the one told me, I wanted to come back here, check on you, and let you all know what you're dealing with in Domora, and it isn't just finding Hamod and Asil. We aren't the only ones looking for them. This Gharek is also searching for you."

She shuddered. "I don't like being hunted."

He damn well didn't like it either. He addressed Saradeen. "I'd hoped we could split into two search parties today. I'd go alone on one route, Halani and a few of you on another, as we searched for Asil. That's no longer a reasonable plan." Nor was a methodical, unobtrusive search through the city's upscale neighborhoods. Malachus decided a more direct approach was needed. He had a pub to visit and a proctor to chat with this morning.

"You want me to stay here." Halani wore a resigned expression now. "You can't search for Mama if you're too busy keeping me from getting captured as well."

A thoughtful, practical woman, his Halani. Malachus kissed her forehead. "I know you want to find your mother, and sitting here waiting for news will test your patience, but you're right. Staying in the camp with the others so they can keep watch is the better plan. If you were taken like Asil . . ." He paused, the idea of that very real possibility making the draga inside him bristle. "I'd level Domora to find you."

"Far too much effort for one woman," she said, leaning harder into his side. "Just find my mother and bring her back so we can leave this accursed place."

Malachus noted she said nothing of Hamod. He turned to Saradeen. "I need to borrow a crossbow and a couple of quarrels."

He left the camp armed with his own weapons and the borrowed crossbow with bolts. His lips still tingled from Halani's hard kiss. "Good fortune, Malachus. Be careful," she said.

Finding the Dead Hound Pub was easy enough. An establishment located in Domora's poorer quarters, it catered to patrons for whom a *belsha* or two meant one could eat something better than a baked onion or weevil-infested bread for supper. A few citizens had pointed him in the pub's direction, with one offering advice.

"If you're going for a reward from the cat's-paw's proctor, you best walk fast. There's already a line going out the door waiting to see him." Considering why they were lined up, Malachus wasn't cheered.

Even with dawn no more than two hours behind them, the inn was a bustling place, and the man who'd described the turnout for a monetary reward hadn't exaggerated. The line did indeed extend out the door and into the stable yard. Those who'd only come to buy an ale or time with a serving wench had to shoulder their way across the threshold. He needed to get inside long enough to familiarize himself with the interior and discover where the proctor had set up his money table. He'd have a hard time of it without being noticed. Loading a crossbow in front of a crowd was guaranteed to draw attention.

The narrow sliver of alleyway between the pub and the opposite building provided a means for him to access its kitchen. He barely avoided a dousing from a chamber pot emptied out of one of the adjacent structure's second-story windows and hop-skipped over reeking puddles of human and animal waste that traveled in rivulets toward the main street. The smell, mixed with that of food frying in hot tallow, turned his stomach.

A blast of hot air struck him when he reached the threshold of the pub's kitchen. Someone had propped the door open in an attempt to cool the room. A fire roared in an open hearth positioned in the middle of the floor. It was crowded with spits of roasting meat and cauldrons suspended from tripods, their contents boiling or frying and tended by a bevy of scullions and undercooks.

He searched for the head cook, spotting her near one of the big prep tables, spatchcocking chicken carcasses. She noticed him at the same time. Her eyebrows, and the meat cleaver she held, rose threateningly.

"Who are you and what are you doing in here?" At her question, work in the kitchen stopped and all gazes landed on Malachus, none of them friendly.

This wasn't the more polished staff of a nobleman's household. They were laborers in a rough pub in one of Domora's more lawless neighborhoods. They'd know a thing or two about fighting, and at the moment, they all looked more than ready to deal with this unexpected intruder.

Malachus wasn't here to brawl with scullery maids and cooks. He fished out a handful of half *belshas* and laid them on the table closest to him. "No trouble," he said. "You can't get through the front door to order an ale or woo a maid. I just want to see if it's worth my time to fight the crowd to the barkeep."

Greed, he'd discovered early on, was the most predictable of all human failings. As much as he despised the trait, he wasn't above using it to his own ends, and once again it worked in his favor. The cook scooped up the money and dropped it in her apron pocket before giving him both a nod and a blind eye. Her staff, no longer interested in Malachus, turned their focus on their mistress. He wondered if there'd be a brawl in the kitchen after all.

He made his way to the pass-through between the kitchen and the common room, keeping out of sight but with a view to the room's layout and especially the location of his quarry. Like most alehouses of its type, this one was dark and smoky and smelled of sweat and sour ale. Benches and stools filled the space, with a patron perched on every one, even at this early hour. Ale wenches wove through the crowd, bearing pitchers and tankards. Through a break in the crush of people, Malachus spied his mark.

The cat's-paw's proctor, a portly man dressed in shabby finery, sat in a back corner, the table in front of him a barrier against the other occupants. A pair of brutish guards stood on either side of him. He picked a small pouch from a heap of identical pouches in front of him and handed it to the man standing across from him. Behind him, the line of people snaked out the door.

Any notion of slinking about trying to obtain the cat's-paw's whereabouts through subterfuge flew out the window the moment he and Halani had passed through Domora's gates. Now he'd have to depend on the elements of shock, speed, and brutality to get what he wanted.

With his prey in sight and the lay of the land noted, he stepped back from the entrance and shrugged the crossbow off his back. The kitchen staff watched him curiously but didn't interfere. Only after he slid his foot into the crossbow's stirrup, drew the string back behind the locknut, and slipped a bolt into the rail did anyone react, and only then with a disbelieving gasp.

Malachus charged into the common room, shoving patrons aside and knocking over stools. The proctor's two guards didn't have a chance to react before he aimed the crossbow at the guard closest to him and shot. The bolt slammed into the man's boot and through his foot, pinning him to the wooden floor. His eyes bulged before he let out an unearthly howl of pain that sent half the pub's crowd stampeding for the door and the other half flattening themselves against the walls to get out of the way.

Malachus didn't stop, using that split second of his opponents' stupefaction to shove the table hard against the proctor with one hand, trapping him in his corner. The mound of money purses fell to the floor. He flipped the crossbow around with his other hand, swinging the stock like a mace. It caught the second guard in the head, felling him.

The cowering proctor slid off his chair and crawled under the table in a futile attempt to escape. Malachus waited for him to emerge before yanking him to his feet by the back of his robes. Malachus kicked the foot of the guard pinned to the floor by the crossbow bolt, making the man set up a new round of howls. Pain like that would keep him from concentrating on anything else but trying to get the bolt out of his foot.

Malachus hauled the proctor closer to the kitchen, pausing long enough to survey the stunned crowd. He nodded toward the table. "You all might want to see to those pouches on the floor before the second guard comes to." He dragged the proctor with him, leaving behind a common room that erupted into greater chaos as those still inside surged toward the *belshas* he'd left behind.

The proctor alternated between pleas and threats as he stumbled through the kitchen, tethered to his captor by the unyielding grip Malachus kept on his tunic. "Why are you doing this? Let me go, and I'll pay you what you ask. My patron is wealthy and considers me his friend. He'll avenge me if I come to any harm, and he's greatly feared in Domora."

They paused by the table where the head cook had been working. She and her staff were gone, either fleeing the pub or joining the pandemonium in the common room. Malachus changed his grip on the proctor, grabbing the man's thick wrist. "As the cat's-paw is your dear friend, you can tell me where he lives."

The man twitched, his eyes shifting toward the open door that led to the alley. "I have no idea."

Liar, Malachus thought. The shifting gaze told him what he needed to know. He didn't bother with cajoling the man to spill his secret. He set the crossbow on the table, tightened his hold on the proctor's wrist, and yanked it down until he'd forced his hand flat on the table next to the chicken carcasses. The cook hadn't bothered putting away her meat cleaver. Malachus snatched it up and brought it down with a solid whack, chopping off the tip of the proctor's little finger to the first joint.

The man screamed as blood spurted from the wound. Malachus held up the severed tip, showed it to his screeching captive, then tossed it into the open hearth. He seized the proctor's face, squeezing his jowls until his mouth closed and his cries became muffled.

"Had I time, I'd work my way up your arm until you told me what I wanted to know." Malachus kept his voice low, pinning the proctor in place with a hard stare as imprisoning as the hand on his wrist. "But I don't have the time, so I'll skip to the important parts. I'm going to ask you the same question. If you don't give me the answer I want, I'm going to carve out your right eye and then your left, and if going blind to protect your friend is acceptable to you, I'll go low and cut off your balls and then your prick." While he spoke, the proctor's face turned a ghastly shade of gray. "Now, tell me, where is the house of the cat's-paw who calls himself Gharek?"

The proctor's loyalty and friendship to the cat's-paw died a quick death in the fires of fear, pain, and survival instinct. Malachus released his face, and the words tumbled from his lips faster than river rapids: where Gharek lived, the knock to use to alert a servant of an approved visitor, and how long it would take him to reach the man's residence on foot.

Malachus shoved the proctor away and retrieved the crossbow. "You've signed your death warrant by giving me such information. I suggest you see to your wound, pack your necessities, and leave Domora. If I find you've lied to me, you'll have two of us hunting you with the sole purpose of taking your head."

The proctor whimpered, clutching his bleeding hand to his chest and backing away from Malachus as far as he could get and still not fall into the hearth.

Heart racing with the first triumph after a series of setbacks, Malachus bolted from the pub's kitchens and into the alley, his destination a deadly opponent's home, and with any luck, the place where he'd find Asil and bring her back to Halani.

CHAPTER TWENTY-ONE

Halani gripped the bat with both hands and swung as hard as she could at her target. The impact sent jitters through her hands and up her arms when the bat connected with the hapless carpet. A cloud of dust burst from the weave, and the carpet rocked back on its line. She hit it again, this time imagining the textile was the face of the man who hunted her.

If a grave robber sat on the lower rungs of the social hierarchy, a thug for hire like a cat's-paw was the stool on which the grave robber stood to climb higher. *Thwack.* Gharek was the reason she was trapped here, unable to help look for her mother, stuck with nothing to do but take out her frustrations on the rugs in need of a cleaning. *Thwack.* He was probably the one who'd taken Asil for his own nefarious purposes. *Thwack, thwack, thwack.*

She stopped to rest and shake the kinks out of her shoulders and wipe the perspiration sheening her forehead. The task did nothing to distract her from worrying about Asil or Malachus. He'd left with a crossbow, obviously with a plan in mind but no time to share it with her, only a promise to return.

Rejuvenated by the quick rest, she took up the bat again and set to beating on the second carpet, imagining it was the cat's-paw.

"Halani, stop for a moment." Jorgan, Saradeen's son-in-law and the caravan's wheelwright, stood out of hitting distance, warily eyeing her and the bat she held. "I left a hollow auger with Hamod when we traveled to Domora. I forgot about it until now. I checked the side chests on the wagon, and it wasn't in there. Did you see it when you were inside?"

"No, but I'll go with you and we can look together." Glad for the respite, she accompanied Jorgan to Hamod's wagon. Her uncle wasn't there to tell them where the auger was, and at the moment she didn't care if they invaded his privacy by opening boxes and drawers to find it while he was gone. Anger over his greed and faulty guardianship of Asil still simmered in her gut.

As they neared the wagon, she put a hand on Jorgan's arm to stop him. "I closed and locked the door when I left," she told him in a low voice, staring at the door, which had been cracked open to reveal a sliver of the dark interior.

Jorgan unsheathed the knife at his belt. "Maybe you didn't slide the bolt enough and the wind pushed it open."

"What wind?" It was a typical summer day in the city—hot, stifling, and dead still. The sound of the latch bar sliding into place echoed in her mind. She'd latched the door. Someone had entered the wagon after she left. And might still be there.

From the corner of her eye, she caught sight of two more of the free trader men and waved them over, finger to her lips, indicating that they should stay quiet. When she whispered she thought someone was in the wagon, they did as Jorgan had and took out weapons, prepared to confront an uninvited guest. After Malachus shared the news of the cat's-paw's machinations, everyone was on edge.

Jorgan motioned for them to step farther away from the wagon. "Deric, stay here with Halani. Brecka and I will pass on either side of the wagon, see if we can hear anything inside." He turned to Halani. "Did you leave any of the windows open?"

"No. I didn't want dust getting in."

"Good," Jorgan said. "It'll be easier for us to walk along the wagon without being heard if we step lightly."

They put their plan into action. While Jorgan and Brecka reconnoitered the wagon's perimeter, more free traders, curious as to what they were doing, joined Halani and Deric. It wasn't long before they resembled a small army, with several brandishing everything from knives and crossbows to washing bats and iron skillets.

The tension in the group ratcheted higher when Jorgan paused in his inspection, forehead creased in concentration as he listened. His expression darkened. He pointed at the wagon, nodded to confirm he'd heard someone inside, then pointed to himself and then the door, indicating he was going in. Several of the men formed a ring around the wagon, blocking off escape routes.

Jorgan abandoned his efforts at staying quiet as he strode to the door. "Halani," he shouted, as if she stood across the camp instead of a stone's throw away from him. "If the auger isn't just lying out where I can see it, you'll need to give me the key so I can check the chests." When his words failed to flush out the intruder, he jerked the door fully open and vaulted inside the wagon.

For a moment nothing moved. Suddenly the wagon rocked on its struts. A series of muffled thuds followed, accompanied by grunts and a pained groan. The crowd collectively jumped when a body flew out the door to land in the dirt with a thump. Jorgan stood in the doorway, sporting a newly split lip and a red patch under one eye that promised to bruise by evening.

"Caught him going through Malachus's satchels," he said.

He didn't get a chance to say anything else before the free traders descended on the thief like wolves. A gasp sounded from the pack, followed by more until the crowd withdrew, leaving their victim to stumble to his feet.

Halani gawked as hard as the rest, hardly believing her eyes. "Uncle?"

Hamod stood before them, bedraggled and bruised. He blinked at those he lived with and led as if they were strangers. Hostile, vicious strangers intent on tearing him apart.

"Gods' bollocks," Jorgan snapped as he leapt from his perch in the wagon's doorway. "Why didn't you say something?"

The leader of their caravan had always presented a formidable figure, a man possessing both confidence and cunning, and a demeanor that warned he could back up a claim or a command with physical force. He was sly, manipulative, and unquestionably devoted to the survival of their caravan, even if it sometimes meant the sacrifice of one member for the good of the group.

Halani had grown up admiring and sometimes fearing her uncle. He was her elder, the caravan leader, and her mother's beloved brother. Halani didn't much like Hamod, but she respected him. The shambling creature standing before them now, looking like he'd been dragged through a back-alley sewage canal and smelling almost as bad, bore no resemblance to the daunting wagon master.

Her shock didn't last. The fear and anger seething inside her since Clamik had told her of Asil's disappearance erupted, and a red haze descended over Halani's vision. She cannoned into Hamod so hard they both went down. Knees digging into his chest, she held him pinned under her, whacking him once across the side of his head with her hand. "Where is my mother, you bastard?" she roared directly into his face. She hit him again, this time on the other side of his head, while he cowered beneath her, shielding his face with his hands.

She didn't struggle when several people grasped her shoulders and arms to pull her off Hamod. Two of the free traders helped him stand once more, keeping a cautious eye on Halani, who glared at him through her tears. "I should never have let her go with you," she spat. "You were supposed to protect her."

Silent until that moment, Hamod glared back at her from bloodshot eyes. "If you hadn't brought the outlander into our camp, she could have stayed."

Halani gasped, noting the puzzled looks exchanged among the others. "Don't you dare place that blame on me. I told you—begged you—not to buy that draga bone."

"Enough!" Saradeen planted himself between the two combatants. "Whatever arguments you have between you, they'll have to wait." He turned to Hamod. "What happened to you? We scoured Domora several times. Not even a hint as to where you might be. You said you planned to find a way into the Maesor to sell this bone Halani doesn't like, and then you disappeared. Asil was gone the next day. Most of us thought you were dead." He sent Halani an apologetic look. "We don't think the same about Asil." His face hardened again when he returned his attention to Hamod. "What happened?" he repeated.

Haggard and filthy, wearing clothes that looked like he'd stolen them off a beggar, Hamod closed his eyes for a moment before speaking. "I've been hiding in different places throughout the city. Coming back here wasn't safe. For any of us." He crossed his arms and shivered. "I made it into the Maesor. Blood tithe in exchange for entrance."

A shadow passed through his eyes, making Halani wonder what such an exchange entailed and whose blood was traded for the privilege of entering the Maesor to trade. A splinter of sympathy for her uncle pierced the armor of her fury.

He continued with his explanation. "I met a man called Koopman, who seemed very willing to do business with me and broker the sale of the draga bone." He frowned at Halani. "I told you I would sell it."

She snorted. "It wasn't yours to buy or sell."

"Did you make the sale?" Saradeen's gaze reflected the doubt in his voice. By the look of him, Hamod didn't have a half *belsha* to his name.

Her uncle shook his head. "No." He spread his hands in a gesture that begged for patience and understanding. The Maesor is an . . . unclean place. You go in fully human, but I don't think you come out that way." The same shade of horror once more flitted through his eyes. "And the longer you stay there, the less human you become."

It seemed the Maesor lived up to its reputation as a perilous place to trade, and that danger didn't just come from the risk of getting caught by the Empire's witch-hunters.

"What made you abandon the sale?" Halani asked. It would have to be an extraordinary event to make Hamod walk away from something potentially so lucrative.

"I didn't at first. Once I was in the Maesor, I met with Koopman." He shuddered. "He trades in rugs and tapestries. Nothing you'd want to put in a wagon. There are enslaved souls woven into them."

Murmurs of "Now, there's evil in the making" and "Who would be mad enough to weave a soul into a rug?" echoed through the crowd.

Hamod plucked at his filthy clothing and scratched his head. Halani wondered if they'd have to purchase bags of onions for a future lice treatment. "Koopman also trades in information and, as I mentioned earlier, acts as a broker for more costly items sold to the wealthy in the city. I was in his tent waiting for him to return with what he said were promissory documents when I overheard a couple of people speaking on the other side of the tent wall. It seems word had gone out that someone might be trying to sell a draga bone on the Maesor, and when it happened, Gharek of Cabast was to be told."

"The cat's-paw," Halani said. This Gharek was involved in all manner of schemes and plots.

Hamod stared at her, surprised. "So they call him. The empress's henchman and feared even by the likes of Koopman."

"And he's hunting for you, Mama, and me. Easy to understand why he wants you, but why me and Mama?"

He ran a hand down his face as if trying to scrub away mistakes and bad decisions. "Once I found out someone was already looking for the draga bone, I knew the sale had gone sour before it even happened. I wouldn't see a single *belsha* from the transaction or even survive the deal. I sneaked out of the Maesor before Koopman realized I was gone. I found your mother waiting for me once I returned." He winced. "She'd followed me and I never knew it. I'd only been in the Maesor for an hour at most, but a full day had passed here while I was gone."

"Why did she follow you?" Why did Asil do anything? Even Halani, who knew her mother best, was sometimes mystified by the reasons Asil gave for her actions. So was Hamod.

He shrugged. "Who knows? I probably should have asked her, but I was desperate to get us both out of there and her away from me in case someone in the Maesor came after me. I sent her back to the camp with a message I wouldn't return until later." Despite his ordeal, the song of avarice hadn't yet ceased to sing to him. "That draga bone is much more valuable than we realized," he said in yearning tones.

If you only knew, Halani thought.

"Asil never mentioned she saw you." Saradeen shook his head.

"All she told us was that she got bored in the camp and went to explore, and she only said that after she returned to camp while we were all in a panic trying to find her. To keep a better eye on her, we took her with us to the market, hoping that keeping her busy might encourage her to stay put. That's where she disappeared."

Halani's stomach knotted. Her sweet, childlike mother was probably frightened out of her wits. "Who else besides the cat's-paw would want her? He's figured out she means something to you. You have the draga bone. He'll use her as bait to lure you out." It explained why Gharek was looking for Halani as well, though she still didn't know how he'd discovered what she looked like.

Hamod's face had paled while she spoke, and he stared at the ground, mumbling something. Her eyes narrowed. Hamod had never acted this way before. Even when he lied to your face, his gaze remained direct and unwavering. "Speak up, Uncle. We didn't hear you."

"I don't have the draga bone. Asil pickpocketed me before I sent her back to the camp. I didn't realize it until hours later when I was trying to hide from both Koopman's and Gharek's scouts."

Were their situation not so dire, Halani would have laughed at Hamod's revelation and his humiliation at being pickpocketed by his own sister. Now all she wanted to do was scream. And bludgeon her uncle with her carpet bat.

"Too bad Malachus isn't with us to hear this," Saradeen said. "It would have helped him in his search for Asil."

Halani's frustration lessened a tiny bit. At the moment, Malachus was on a search for two things he believed to be in separate places. If Asil still had the mother-bond, he could find her through the shared connection he had with the artifact. An awful thought immediately took hold. If, however, the person who took Asil only needed her as a way to get the mother-bond, her usefulness ended the moment they discovered it on her person. Halani's heart seized. "I think you've killed my mother," she told Hamod in a flat voice.

The last bit of blood drained from his features. He backed away as if to ward off a blow. "No," he said. "No."

She might have struck him again if one of the free traders acting as camp guard hadn't sent up an alarm whistle, warning everyone they had unexpected visitors.

"Get him back in his wagon, quick!" Saradeen instructed both Deric and Jorgan, who each grabbed one of Hamod's arms and hustled him out of sight. "You should hide, too," Saradeen told Halani.

"If I get in that wagon with Uncle, only one of us will walk out alive," she replied. She gestured to the woman closest to her. "Loan me your head scarf. I can use that to hide my hair and part of my face."

A trio of guards approached, escorting their visitor between them, crossbows angled in such a way that if he so much as sneezed the wrong way, he'd end up bristling with arrows.

"What strange bit of business is this?" Saradeen muttered beside Halani.

Masked and silent and draped in a shapeless garment, the visitor made directly for Halani despite her attempt at obscurity. They held out a folded piece of parchment to her.

"Don't shoot," she ordered those with loaded crossbows. The gods forbid any of their more hot-blooded traders let loose an arrow. Their unexpected guest was a messenger, and not just any messenger. They were an Unknown. Kill one of them, and Hamod's caravan would never be able to set up in Domora or its satellite towns again, and that was if they actually made it out of Domora alive.

She plucked the missive from their hand, turning it this way and that, staring at the unfamiliar wax seal holding it closed. The seal made an audible crack when she broke it to open the letter. She shouldn't have bothered. Malachus's lessons had opened up a new world of possibilities for her, and he was a good teacher, but in no way did her rudimentary reading skills hold up against cryptic script that was nothing more than ink scratches. She sighed and handed it back to the Unknown. "Tell whoever sent this to try again. You can't talk and none of us here can read."

The Unknown took the letter, gave a quick nod, and strolled out of the camp, unconcerned that a dozen crossbows were trained on their back.

"What do you think that was all about?" Saradeen asked.

"With any luck, it's either from the cat's-paw or whoever has Mama. If I were to guess, they want to bargain." Which meant they hadn't yet discovered that Asil had the mother-bond. It seemed too good to believe. Too convenient.

She spent the time waiting for the new messenger to arrive by interrogating Hamod where he hid in the wagon. More than once she had to walk away to rein in her temper. This time, the guard's whistle brought most of the camp running. The new messenger wasn't an Unknown, and he lacked his predecessor's uncanny ability to single out the message's recipient. His gaze touched on each person, settling a little longer on those holding weapons at the ready. "I seek a woman who looks like Hamod the free trader."

Halani stepped forward. "That would be me. I'm Halani. You'll have to read the note to us."

He nodded. "So I was told." He held the parchment by its top and bottom edges and cleared his throat before reading. "I hope this message finds you well. I am Gharek of Cabast and have news of interest to you regarding a woman with a child's spirit." All the air left Halani's lungs. The messenger didn't notice and continued reading.

"I invite you to meet me on the Galdoka Bridge this afternoon. A safe place for us both, in view of many. If you agree, my messenger will escort you there."

The cat's-paw had Asil. It was her worst fear and best hope combined in a single moment. Halani remembered to breathe and recalled Malachus's cautionary advice. Stay hidden; stay safe. She didn't have to think twice. The time for caution was over. "I'm ready," she said. "Take me to the bridge."

CHAPTER TWENTY-TWO

When she arrives, the two of us will have a short chat. If she accepts my offer, she'll come with me. If she doesn't, take her to the palace with a message for the empress that the woman is of use as additional bait. She'll know to what I'm referring." Gharek handed a folded missive with his seal to the spokesman of the small group he'd brought to the Galdoka Bridge with him. "If you end up taking her to the palace, she goes unmolested. I don't want to hear of so much as a scratch. She's only valuable if she isn't broken."

The group's leader tucked the missive away. "You expecting a struggle from her?"

Gharek shrugged. "I have no idea what to expect. This will be the first time we meet."

He had the original portrait made of her with him. While he refused to admit to it, he'd looked at the woman's visage, with its blend of gentleness and resolve, more often than necessary. The artist he'd employed to draw the likenesses of those people revealed by the trap shadow had a gift for capturing more in his subjects' features than just their bone structure and surface expression. There was something arresting about the younger woman's face, something that made Gharek wonder how she moved, how she sounded when she spoke. He would soon find out.

The bridge he waited on was an ornate affair, spanning a wide man-made canal that served as both irrigation and a watery avenue on which pleasure boats slowly glided. It was a popular place and crowded. Gharek had chosen it for this meeting for that reason. The men he'd hired blended in well enough not to draw attention, and the woman would be far more willing to meet him in a public place where the illusion of safety worked to his benefit.

He spotted the second messenger and his companion. The woman was of average height, with a round face and defined jaw. Days in the sun had burnished her skin a light bronze, highlighting her high cheekbones and leaving streaks of blonde in the brown hair she wore in a long, loose braid. Gharek recognized the likeness between her and the free trader.

When she finally saw him, her generous mouth thinned. The messenger bowed and introduced the woman. "As you've requested my lord, I bring you Hamod the trader's relative. This is Halani."

Halani. A soft name for a soft woman. Gharek offered her a hand in greeting. "Your portrait doesn't do you justice, Halani. Your eyes are even more memorable. I'm Gharek of Cabast."

Considering the circumstances that prompted this meeting, he hadn't expected a friendly response, and he didn't get it. Halani ignored his outstretched hand and raked him with her flinty gaze.

"Where's my mother, and how do I get her back?"

Gharek's eyebrows arched. Blunt and to the point. After the complex manipulations he'd navigated in his dealings with Dalvila, where every word had layered meaning and the wrong expression displayed could get you castrated or worse, he found it refreshing to negotiate with someone with no inclination to engage in such antics.

"I wondered how she was related to you, though you bear a stronger resemblance to the trader. Your father?"

Her eyes narrowed. "Does it matter? Chatting about who I look like isn't why I'm here. What do you want in exchange for my mother?"

This would be far easier than Gharek had hoped. One never knew what relationship a parent had with a child. He'd have let both of his parents rot in their captivity. "Information," he said. "That's all. Help me, and I'll take you to your mother. You can both be on your way after that."

Killing the old woman was more trouble than leaving her alive. She still stared off into space, only now she did so inside the confines of an abandoned forge not far from the palace. Gharek had used her blood in the same way Koopman had used Hamod's—fed it to Koopman's trap shadow to see what images it might weave from her memories. Dread mixed with no small amount of anticipation surged through him at the images the trap shadow wove—of Halani again, this time tending a man suffering from arrow wounds and liberally decorated in scars that resembled a tree's leafy branches. The man didn't interest him at first. Halani was obviously the healer in her caravan tending to a free trader who'd likely crossed the wrong people. Nothing interesting until the trap shadow wove a scene in which the man's entire body was wreathed in smoke, and he hurled Halani out of the wagon without ever touching her. Gharek trusted his instincts, and they were screeching in his head that within the dark workings of the trap shadow's weave, he stared at the draga disguised as a man. The moment he returned from the Maesor, he moved the crone out of his house and to the forge, guarded by two men who understood the value of their discretion.

Halani chose a blunt approach in her dealings, but Gharek adopted a more subtle one. Led in the right direction, people always revealed a secret or two. "Several people saw you enter the city with Malachus and ride to Hamod's camp. What is he hoping to do once he recovers the mother-bond?"

The briefest flicker danced behind the mist of her eyes, and Gharek bit back a triumphant smile. He'd guessed right. His silent, unresponsive guest hadn't made a peep until he placed the mother-bond in her palm, and then she'd only said one word, a man's name. He'd taken her blood then to feed the trap shadow and learn more. The images of the man in the weave and the name the crone spoke had no overt connection between them. Gharek had played a hunch, and it had just paid off.

Halani gave up her secrets in tiny increments. "Why do you think I'd know any of Malachus's business? I healed him when he was injured. He offered to help me find my mother as payment for my help. That's all."

Malachus. The name the crone whispered. "Is that so? And do you usually bed the men you heal under the light of the stars?" When the watcher he'd assigned to the free trader camp reported back to him with those details, Gharek had admonished him for wasting time when he should have kept an eye out for Hamod trying to sneak back to the camp. It seemed that bit of voyeurism now had a use.

Halani blushed to the roots of her hair, and the flare in her eyes was one of embarrassed affront. "Did the spies you planted around our camp have nothing better to look out for?"

He shrugged. "I asked the same thing at the time. Let's try again, shall we? And the longer you delay in telling me what I need to know, the longer you have to wait to see your precious mother."

Before he could repeat his question regarding Malachus's search, frantic movement in the corner of his vision made him turn. His steward raced toward him, face white, eyes wide as he plowed through the meandering crowd. Gharek gestured minutely to the men who accompanied him on the bridge. They positioned themselves in spots that cut off any escape. Halani had no chance of bolting away, though he doubted she would. She wanted her mother back.

His steward almost ran over him, stopping at the last moment to gasp out a panicked "Master, news!"

Gharek raised a finger to the frowning Halani. "One moment." He grasped the steward's arm and wrenched him a short distance away. "What is it? And keep your voice down."

The man struggled to catch his breath for a moment. "You must come home. A visitor, unexpected, awaits you. He says his name is Malachus, and he's come for the old woman."

Gharek's heart seized in his chest. He gripped the steward's arm so hard, the man yelped. "Estred," he bit out. "Where is Estred?"

The servant audibly swallowed. "She's still there. Except for me and her, he's locked the rest of the staff in the buttery and is waiting for you. He let me go to bring you the message."

Gharek abruptly pivoted, strode to where Halani waited, and gripped her by the base of her braid, yanking her into his arms. Her shocked gasp changed to a pained one, and tears sprang to her eyes. "What trickery is this?" He used his other hand to grasp her chin and glared into her wide eyes. "How did you and your lover know I'd be here?"

She garbled something at him, made incoherent by his hold on her jaw. He loosened it enough for her to speak but didn't let go. All around them, people eddied and flowed, sparing only quick glances for the tableau in front of them. If the free trader woman thought she'd find help from that quarter, she was mistaken.

"I don't know what you're talking about. You were the one to reach out to me. You said meet at the bridge. I'm here at the bridge."

The pulse under her jaw raced. Confusion, pain, and terror clouded her features, but not guile. Gharek could scent a lie better than a hound could a spoor. Halani wasn't lying. She had no idea what game was up at his home.

He gestured for the hired guard closest to him. When the man drew near, Gharek shoved Halani into his arms. "Take her," he said. "And make sure the empress gets my message." He ignored Halani's outraged cries and sprinted across the bridge for home.

His steward called after him, but Gharek didn't halt. In those moments when he ran through Domora, he wished he could fly. His thoughts raced as fast as his feet, fueled by terror and horror—terror because he had a draga in his house with his daughter, horror because all his plans for luring the draga to him before it reached the empress had come to fruition but in a way he never intended.

The street on which he lived was a quiet one, set away from the main boulevards with their bustling crowds and noise. Here the buildings' facades were meticulously kept and the streets swept clean of detritus. A genteel neighborhood populated by those who lacked the pedigree of the heritage nobility but who possessed the money, ambition, and snobbery to emulate them.

Gharek's house was plainer than his neighbors'. Whitewashed stucco without adornment, its only bit of visual interest, the heavy iron-and-wood door built to withstand the abuses of a battering ram. Gharek halted in front of it, breathing hard from his run. His heart slammed against his breastbone at the sight of the door cracked open, as if it mocked all his efforts at keeping Estred safe from the cruelties of the world outside.

He touched the outline of the mother-bond hidden behind the layers of clothing he wore. It pulsed softly against his chest with a life of its own, a pulse that accelerated much like his own the closer he got to his destination, until he felt as if he had two hearts pounding under his ribs. The mother-bond sensed its master's nearness. No doubt such a connection worked both ways, and the draga simply waited for Gharek to make an appearance.

Sneaking in served no purpose. He had a few choices at hand, all of them bad: get rid of the mother-bond by tossing it in an alley or midden pit in the hopes the draga would go after it like a dog, hold on to it and use it to bargain with the draga for a bit of its blood as he originally intended, or just hand it over and beg the creature to spare his daughter.

He eased the door open, stepped into the courtyard, and closed the door behind him with a soft click. The courtyard bloomed with all the lush shades of summer, flowers of every variety spilling over the pathways and down the high walls.

No one was about, neither Estred nor a single servant who might have escaped imprisonment in the buttery, but he heard voices through the open door between the foyer and the courtyard, one childish and full of excited delight, the other deeper, adult, obviously male. Gharek's terror gave way to cold calculation. He unsheathed the dagger he always carried. Who knew what use it might be against a draga, but he'd paint the parlor walls with its blood if the creature so much as put a scratch on Estred.

He eased into the foyer and crept down the hall on silent feet. His stomach somersaulted at the sight greeting his eyes. His daughter stood in front of a dark-haired man of similar height to Gharek and a build that suggested strength and whipcord speed, but still just a man. One currently wreathed in tendrils of smoke that drifted off him like meandering revenants and made Estred laugh in delight.

The intruder's indulgent smile suddenly hardened, and his dark-eyed stare shifted to Gharek hovering in the doorway. That stare held within it something not human. A slender hand settled on Estred's narrow shoulder, interrupting her chatter. He spoke softly, in tones that might soothe an anxious child to sleep but made Gharek's hackles rise. The man turned Estred to face the door. "Your father's here, Estred. Just as I promised. Tell him hello."

CHAPTER TWENTY-THREE

Were he not wide-awake, entertaining a child without arms while he waited for her father to appear, Malachus might have thought he dreamed once more of riding on Golnar's back, a child himself, flying too close to a sun that threatened to burn him to ash. The blood bubbled in his veins like the fiery rivers that sometimes spilled down the faraway Sameris Mountains. Smoke plumed off his body, and inside him the draga snarled and writhed, sensing its freedom in the mother-bond's nearness.

Estred jumped up and down in front of him but stayed where she was instead of rushing to her father. "Papa, you came back! I was afraid for you."

The little girl's concern revealed more to Malachus than he was sure the cat's-paw wanted him to know. To his credit, the man standing in the doorway retained a stoic expression, though he couldn't hide the horror—or the fury—in his eyes at seeing his daughter with Malachus.

He gestured with one hand to Estred while keeping his other hand just behind his back out of sight. Malachus had no doubt he held a weapon. "I always come back for you, Estred. Now, come to me."

Malachus prepared to tighten his hold on Estred in case she chose to follow Gharek's command. He had no intention of harming the girl, but he didn't need her father knowing that at the moment. If he let Estred go to him, Malachus would have to kill him in front of her. Fortunately, she did as he'd instructed her earlier, shaking her head and remaining in place, much to Gharek's consternation.

"I can't," she said. "Malachus says you could get hurt if I do."

For a moment, the stoic mask cracked, a promise of murder flickering in Gharek's eyes as he met Malachus's. "What bewitchment have you put her under, draga?"

He laid down the gauntlet with that address. Malachus didn't accept the challenge. "None. I've simply told her the truth. Staying by me guarantees *your* survival." He didn't say what they both understood. To turn over Estred to Gharek meant Malachus was no longer interested in negotiating for Asil's whereabouts or the mother-bond. He'd simply kill Gharek, take the artifact, and figure out on his own where Asil was. This was mercy, albeit a dangerous mercy, and Malachus still wasn't sure if Gharek deserved it. Fortunate for him that Estred had proven herself a child for which her parent was worth not killing.

Gharek didn't see it the same way. He tried again, crouching down to crook his fingers in a come-hither gesture. His voice was soft, coaxing. "He's telling you a lie, Estred. I'm your father, and I love you. I won't lie to you. Nothing will happen to me if you come here."

The little girl didn't budge, though the look she gave Malachus now held a touch of doubt. He patted her shoulder. "Children are uncannily good at knowing when an adult is lying to them and when they're telling the truth. I'm neither bewitching nor lying to Estred."

Gharek rose from his crouch. "But you're still using a small child as a pawn."

"Just as you're using an old woman with the mind of a child as one," Malachus snapped. A dull thump sounded within the deeper recesses of the house. "Your staff is enjoying a brief sojourn in your buttery," he said.

"Siora is in there too." Estred grinned. "She said not to worry. That I was safe with Malachus, and you'd be home soon."

The murderous glint in Gharek's eyes was no longer reserved for his current adversary. "Is that what she said? Thank you, love. I'll remember that."

Malachus wondered if the child's nurse had any idea of her employer's nature. He wore two faces, one that of a protective father, the other that of a cold-blooded extortionist. No doubt he'd also embraced the role of assassin a time or two.

"What do you want?" Gharek bit out the question. His disdainful gaze swept Malachus and the smoke wafting off him. "Or should I say 'what do you *need*?'"

His patience diminishing at the same rate his own desperation grew, Malachus narrowed his eyes at the continued pretense. The time between him sending the terrified steward to fetch his master and Gharek's arrival on his doorstep hadn't been long. The cat's-paw had come running the instant he received the news of his uninvited guest. "Don't be tiresome. We both know what I've come for. The only thing you get to decide is what you're willing to sacrifice to keep them from me." He glanced down briefly at Estred.

The draga inside him convulsed, beating like a tide against his senses, raging to be free, sensing the mother-bond's nearness and its call, bright and clear as a bell's peal. Gharek had the mother-bond somewhere on him. For Estred's sake, Malachus played her father's game. He wouldn't for much longer; he couldn't.

Gharek's eyes had narrowed to slits. "It's said draga blood is magic. That it imparts great healing powers, even restoring limbs. It also gives one who drinks the blood the gift of long life."

Malachus swallowed a groan. Gods, were humans truly that ignorant regarding draga-kind? That stupid to believe such nonsense? Had he not witnessed the flare of desperate hope in the other man's eyes as he described such magical properties or seen Estred's disfigurement, he might have scoffed at such ridiculous notions. "And you believe this drivel?"

The cat's-paw's casual shrug didn't fool him. "It doesn't matter what I believe. The empress does, though, and she's had me and a bevy of spies looking for you and anyone associated with you."

Oh, it did matter to this man, with his innocent daughter watching her father as if the stars rose and set at his command. "And yet as unimportant as you say your beliefs are, you're the one in possession of the mother-bond, not the empress. And you're holding a woman I call friend as your hostage. Not the actions of someone only operating in the service of the empress's interest. What do you want from me? Or do I even need to ask?"

Gharek was quiet for a moment, as if choosing his words carefully. "The empress will butcher you when she gets her hands on you. Help Estred, and she'll never know you're here."

Gharek was Malachus's enemy. Still, a faint sympathy touched him at the other man's fruitless hope in something no more real or true than a mirage cast by the summer's heat, and he wished with all his soul he could grant his request and make Estred whole. It was not to be.

He exhaled a long sigh. "Whoever ascribed such powers to draga-kind was wrong. Humans have slaughtered us based on fables, greed, and the fear of dying." He paused before saying more, watching as the spark of hope in Gharek's eyes guttered. "It is the nature of draga to live long and heal quickly, nothing else. One can't share it or give it to another. Drinking their blood or bathing in it would have no more effect than spreading human blood on a dog. One is longer-lived than the other; it doesn't mean a man can impart the gifts given to him as a man onto his favorite hound."

"You're lying. You refuse to help Estred." Gharek's voice held a flat note, as if he didn't believe his own accusation but wielded it anyway in a vain attempt to hold on to that dead hope.

"I am not." Malachus smiled down at the little girl, who returned the smile with a hesitant one of her own. She might not understand the layers of conversation exchanged between her father and his visitor, but she sensed the tension in the room. "If I could help her, I would, but I can't. Even if draga blood worked the way humans assume, I'd have to be draga. Drawing blood from me in this form would do nothing." He swept a hand in front of him to encompass the room. "Neither you, nor Estred, nor this house would survive my transformation."

He didn't exaggerate. His skin burned hot, smoke wreathing off him in ghostly plumes, and the draga inside threatening to commit suicide by transforming without the aid of the mother-bond's magic. Malachus held on to his control by his fingernails while the sweat poured down his back and his heart felt like it might burst.

A draga's transformation was both epic and violent. He'd witnessed it twice while he fostered at the monastery, and each time was so horrified by the event he'd consulted the sympathetic monks as to how he might reject his heritage and remain human. If he changed now, even with the mother-bond's help, he'd destroy this house and everyone inside it.

Defeat slouched Gharek's shoulders, and his head drooped. Estred took a step toward her father. "Papa?" Tears thickened her voice.

Had he not learned of Gharek's vocation as the empress's cat's-paw, Malachus might have dropped his guard at the sight of the other man's crestfallen demeanor. The foreknowledge served him well. Gharek's head snapped up, his eyes hard as marble and just as cold. He pressed his free hand to his chest as if his heart pained him. "Then this is of no use to me," he said. A sleight-of-hand movement and he turned his palm to reveal the thing Malachus had hunted for a lifetime across numerous kingdoms and two continents—his mother-bond, Golnar's most lasting gift to him, given at his birth as both his heritage and his protection. The only physical part of his mother left in this world.

The sound erupting from his throat bore nothing human in it as a surge of longing mixed with a draga's impatient fury slammed into him at the sight. For a moment, Gharek's eyes rounded, terror darkening his irises as he glanced down at his prize and then at Estred, who'd wrenched herself from Malachus's touch to press herself against the wall.

Gharek pivoted, raised his arm, and pitched the mother-bond toward the opposite end of the corridor. He didn't pause to see how far it sailed, spinning around again, dagger drawn, to lunge for Malachus. Sunlight winked off the blade as he slashed, aiming for his midriff.

Malachus leapt back, barely avoiding a gutting but still catching the blade across the top of his leg. "To me!" he shouted, using the language of the draga.

As if sentient and powered by its own force, the mother-bond rebounded off the floor where it lay and shot back toward him. It clipped Gharek on the top of his shoulder as it whipped past, landing in Malachus's palm with an audible smack. Startled by the hit, the cat's-paw checked his second lunge.

Unfazed by the wound Gharek had carved into his leg, and rocked by a tide of power that smashed through him when he finally held the mother-bond, Malachus snagged his adversary's wrist, twisting his arm over his own forearm until the other man went up on his toes. He hooked the mother-bond's sharp curve under Gharek's throat. A harder bend on his elbow and the cat's-paw dropped his bloodied blade.

Threatened by the mother-bond's sharp edge, he still struggled in Malachus's grip. "Run, Estred!" he bellowed to his screaming daughter. "Run!" The little girl fled down the hall, disappearing from view. The moment she was out of sight, Gharek laughed. "Now what, draga?"

Fire roared through Malachus's veins, backdrafting into his muscles until they twitched under his skin, and his vision clouded in a red haze. Gharek's bitter amusement sounded far away, though they were almost locked in each other's arms. The mother-bond seared his palm, throbbing with a magic both potent and familiar—the last vestiges of his mother Golnar's spirit captured in bone and bequeathed to her son. It was power and heritage, birthright and salvation.

And it was incomplete.

"What did you do to the mother-bond?" He practically snarled the words, fighting down the draga's imminent rise. Something about it was wrong, missing. He pressed it harder to Gharek's throat, the feel of warm blood trickling over his fingers.

Gharek laughed again, unafraid. "I diced in two games and lost in both. I'd planned to lure you and take a small portion of your blood for Estred, unlike the empress, who plans to harvest every last drop. I gave her a replica of the bone with enough splinters of the real thing embedded in it to fool her sorcerers."

His heritage, desecrated by human hands. Draga bone was dense, hard to break, but not impervious to damage or, in this case, the whittle of a human's knife or chisel.

Desperate rage swamped him. If he didn't need to know Asil's whereabouts, he would have cut Gharek's throat in that moment. He needed *all* of the mother-bond to transform. Never, in any of the scenarios he imagined regarding the difficulties in retrieving his birthright, had he considered that someone might break the claw tip apart. The hope that he'd manage to transform and avoid the empress burned to ash. He had the mother-bond but was now worse off for it. "Where's Asil?"

Gharek swallowed, the movement pressing the bone's edge deeper into his skin. More blood trickled over Malachus's fingers. "Is that her name? Halani never said."

Malachus had never mentioned Halani's name, yet Gharek knew it and alluded to a conversation between them. The cat's-paw had somehow gotten his hands on her. The hot rage turned icy. He was done with games and with mercy, even for the innocent Estred's sake. Like him and so many others, she'd learn to live without her parent.

"I'll take you to her," a voice said from the doorway. Siora, Estred's nurse, stood there. Somehow, she and the others had escaped their imprisonment in the buttery.

Malachus wasn't concerned about them. He'd have no trouble dispatching a group of servants if necessary. "Where are the others?"

"Gone. Fled to their houses." Her strange, faraway gaze landed on Gharek for a moment. "I sent Estred with the cook."

Her devotion to her charge didn't win any favors from Estred's father. "Help this bastard," he said between clenched teeth, "and I will hunt you across the Empire for your betrayal. There will be no place you can hide from me."

He gasped out a curse when Malachus curved his bent arm a little more. "You're assuming you'll survive today," he told Gharek. "And if you do, you'd best look to yourself and your daughter's survival. The empress will hunt *you* across her empire once she discovers your deception." He looked back at Siora, uncowed by Gharek's threat. "Why would you help me?" He was a stranger to her, a threat to her charge, and for a short time, the person who'd imprisoned her and others. She had no reason to help him.

"Because he's wrong in what he's done," she said. "And because you've spoken for those whose voices most refuse to hear." She didn't explain that last odd statement. Her serene gaze shifted from Gharek to him. "I'll take you to the old woman if you let him live. He's all that stands between Estred and a rock-throwing mob offended by her appearance."

Just as she had no obvious reason to help him, Malachus had none to trust her, yet that didn't matter. He needed whatever help was offered, even at the risk of entrapment or betrayal.

Gharek made no sound when Malachus cuffed him hard on the side of the head. He slumped in Malachus's grip.

"Put him in the wine cellar," Siora instructed, as Malachus tucked away the mother-bond inside his tunic and hoisted the unconscious man over his shoulder. "His steward has a key to every room in the house except that one." Malachus halted next to her, waiting as she rifled through Gharek's clothing before triumphantly producing a key. "I'll hold on to it for now and return it later."

"If you want to live, you can't come back here," Malachus told her as he followed her down the hall toward a narrow flight of stairs leading to the floor belowground. "You've exiled yourself by helping me."

Siora shrugged, pushing open the cellar door to let Malachus and his burden through. "I'm used to homelessness." She pocketed the key and set to work helping him bind Gharek with strips of the sleeves they cut away from his tunic. Malachus used the last strip to gag him before wedging his body into the narrow space between two wine casks in the corner farthest from the door. No doubt one of his staff would find him soon enough.

He and Siora left the house, closing the courtyard door and its gate behind them before strolling away together as if they were simply visitors returning to their own home. Malachus concentrated on diminishing the smoke twisting around him until it completely disappeared. The draga inside him continued to thrash.

"You've stopped bleeding," Siora said. She gestured to his leg where Gharek had slashed him.

Malachus glanced down at the injury. The cut no longer stung, and as his companion noted, it no longer bled. The motherbond had worked its magic, inciting the draga but also strengthening his healing abilities tenfold. Beneath the skim of dried blood staining his leg, the wound itself had healed. Siora's observation held an unspoken question. He sighed. "Were you out of the buttery while I talked to Gharek?"

She nodded. "For the last part. Blood on a dog and all that." A tiny frown knitted the space between her eyebrows. "It's difficult not to wish otherwise, especially for Estred, and especially in the face of such obvious magic."

"It's only magic for the draga to whom it belongs," he said.

"I wish you could help her."

He closed his eyes for a moment. If dragas possessed all the abilities humans assumed they did, they'd be gods. "So do I," he said.

Siora gestured toward a street that curved away from the line of houses. "This way," she said. "Hurry."

She was a petite woman, neither long-legged nor powerful, but she sped through the crowded city with Malachus in tow, instinctively finding those ever-changing spaces in a sea of people that seemed to open up before them and close instantly once they passed. Malachus was ready to shoulder aside any who got in their way but found he needn't bother. In no time, he and Siora had raced halfway across the city, into its murkier depths where the streets became closes, the buildings more ramshackle, and the people far less well-heeled.

They halted at the entrance to an alley garlanded by lines of laundry hung to dry. Dreary hovels, leaning against multistoried dwellings in danger of collapsing at the first hard sneeze, lined either side of the close, and Malachus glimpsed between the flutter of hanging linen the high brick wall where the close ended.

Siora pointed to one of the hovels with its roof partially caved in. "There. That's the forge where he's hiding her." She made to walk that way, stopping at Malachus's grip on her arm.

"You owe me no loyalty," he told her. "But know that if you've led me into a trap, the cat's-paw will never have a chance to hunt you." He was fresh out of forbearance. If Siora attempted to stitch him, she wouldn't live to regret it.

She had large round eyes, nearly as dark as his own, and farseeing. Just like with Gharek's threat, her serene expression didn't change, and Malachus didn't sense any fear in her. "No trap. There will be one or two guards keeping watch. They're hired men with no allegiance to him other than what his money has paid for."

Which meant they wouldn't risk their lives to keep their captive from being taken. Malachus hoped his assumption proved true. It would make it that much easier and quicker to retrieve Asil and return her to Halani. To improve his odds at triumphing in a confrontation, he nocked the last bolt he had into the crossbow he carried. With any luck, he wouldn't have to fire it.

Another frown disturbed the placid set of her features. "I haven't been wholly honest about your Asil." Malachus froze, and his hand flexed on the crossbow. Siora glanced at the crossbow, and for the first time fear flickered across her face. "Gharek didn't hurt her. I know that for sure, but her captivity must have brought about memories of terrible things. She's walked the Dream Road the entire time he's held her."

"What is the Dream Road?" When she described it, he nodded. "I've heard it called by similar names. Those who suffer escape their suffering one way or another." He scowled. "Are you certain Gharek didn't abuse her?"

She nodded. "Gharek uses cruelty for a purpose, not entertainment. Torturing Asil didn't serve a purpose, though he did take a smear of her blood while she walked the Dream Road."

In that moment, Malachus almost lost control of the draga. "What?" He growled the word.

Siora stepped back. "A shallow cut on her forearm, just enough to wet his blade. He took it to Koopman in the Maesor to feed to his vile trap shadow. It's how he learned of you."

"Why didn't you tell me this earlier?"

Her long stare burrowed into his soul. "Would you have let the cat's-paw live if I did?"

"No." He wouldn't have left him in one piece, much less let him live.

"I thought not. My first loyalty isn't to Gharek, to you, or to Asil. It's to Estred, and she needs her father to live. Nobility is an indulgence for those with only themselves to consider. It's a harder thing to embrace when others are at stake. You held Estred to help Asil; I protected Gharek to help Estred. He was wrong to abduct Asil. I'm righting that wrong by helping you. I won't make Estred pay for her father's sins by letting you kill him."

Malachus studied the small woman in front of him, remembering Halani's pinched features as she weathered his scorn and condemnation over his discovery of her grave robbing.

I'm not defending, only explaining. It is wrong . . . Condemn us if you will, but know why we do it, not why you think we do it.

The fury inside him died, allowing him to calm the draga enough to keep from combusting on the spot. Halani and Siora were of like minds and philosophies. Philosophies he was just coming to understand, even if he didn't always agree with them.

"Take me to the forge," he said.

Siora remained true to her word. No trap or ambush awaited him and only one guard kept watch over Asil. It seemed almost too easy to dispatch him. Malachus left Siora to stand watch over his unconscious form while he searched for Asil in the abandoned smithy.

He found her next to what was left of the actual forge, tied to a support beam by a length of rope with one end knotted around her thin wrists. She didn't react when he approached, her slow-blinking gaze even more distant than Siora's, looking upon another world only she saw. Her features were slack, her breathing steady but slow, as if she slept with her eyes open. And she was filthy.

Had Malachus dragged Gharek with him to the forge, he would have broken both his arms and his legs as punishment for Asil's condition. Never before had he seen Asil other than neat and tidy. This was not the same woman. Caked in dirt, her hair a matted rat's nest and her clothing reduced to rags, she reeked. He thanked the gods Halani wasn't here to see her mother's appalling condition.

Malachus crouched in front of her so she could look him in the face. Even this close, her eyes didn't quite meet his. She sat not far from the beam to which she was tied, her bony hands resting on her knees. He dared not touch her, afraid that doing so would send her deeper into whatever sanctuary she'd found in her mind. "Asil, it's me, Malachus. Do you remember me?"

No reaction, and her distant stare remained unwavering. A roach crawled down her arm, and Malachus flicked it away. He tried again, this time speaking to her as if they met together for a quick chat.

"Halani is here in Domora. She wanted to come with me to find you, but I told her I'd bring you to her. She'll be very happy to see you. She loves you and has worried about you." He eyed the knot binding her wrists together. "I'm going to untie you. You'll feel some tugging on your hands."

Still she said nothing, but her lips moved with the soundless utterance of words. Was it the mention of her daughter's name that had brought out this response? A small triumph, but one that gave him hope Asil might yet abandon the Dream Road and return to this world.

She remained placid while he worked the knot loose and when he rose to cut the rope from the beam. He tossed it aside before returning to her. "Can you hear me, Asil? I want you to stand and walk with me. I'll help you. If you can't, then I'll carry you." He recalled Halani's grim story of Asil's capture. "The choice is yours. I'll do whichever you wish, but we have to leave here so you can go home to Halani."

He'd barely finished the sentence when she suddenly stood, neither stumbling nor weaving as he'd expected, considering her physical state. Her arms hung limp at her sides, and her eyes stared beyond him, but she didn't shy away. To his amazement, she reached out and grabbed his hand, dirty fingers entwining with his.

Humbled by her trust, Malachus gently squeezed her hand. "Good choice," he said. She walked beside him with sure steps as he guided her through the forge's gloomy interior to where Siora still stood next to the unconscious guard.

The woman's eyes widened for a moment, and her face thinned with a shocked sadness. "I didn't realize. She wasn't like this when he took her from the house." Siora moved closer to peer at Asil, subjecting her to that same dissecting stare she'd turned on Malachus. "Come back, Asil," she said in a soft voice. "All is well. Those who love you are eager to see you again." When Asil only looked through her, Siora bent her head for a moment before turning to Malachus, her expression mournful. "If I had known . . ."

"It doesn't matter now." Malachus eased his hand out of Asil's grip, set the crossbow aside, and dumped the guard into the long-dry slack tub once used to quench hot metal. When he returned, Siora stood at the threshold, keeping watch on the street and an eye on Asil.

"Asil," he said, keeping his voice soft. "The fastest way for me to take you back to the camp is to carry you. I'll need to pick you up, and I need you to put your arms around my neck and hold on." He shouldered on the crossbow while waiting for a nod or reply. When Asil offered neither, he bent to lift her in his arms.

She weighed less than a feather, and while she hadn't answered him, she'd heard and understood, clasping her hands behind his neck. Her breath warmed the space where his shoulder met his chest as she leaned her head into him. Malachus held her a little tighter. *Ah, Halani,* he thought. *This wasn't how I'd hoped to bring her back to you.*

When he paused beside Siora, she tucked Asil's skirts more tightly around her legs, smoothing down the ragged edges of her hem. "When you leave from here, take the second road to your right and head south. The distance will seem longer, but the streets that way are less crowded, there are rarely any soldiers patrolling, and you'll reach the camp faster. If anyone gets too curious, tell them she's leprous. No one will stop you for long if you say that."

"Where will you go?" He dared not offer her sanctuary with the free traders despite her invaluable help in finding Asil. With Gharek now her enemy, she was too much of a danger to any who might offer succor.

There was about her a sense of otherness, as if she walked a line separating this world from another and was far more interested in the second. She shrugged. "Somewhere away from Domora. Gharek doesn't concern me. The empress will learn of his deception, if she hasn't already. He'll be too busy avoiding her to pursue me." She studied him with her disconcerting gaze. "Before you go, I have a message for you."

His eyebrows rose. "What is that?"

"Don't judge humans too harshly. We live short lives compared to your kind. Our wisdom has only a moment to spark before death snuffs it out. I'm to tell you to remember the kindness of the brotherhood who fostered you, of the free traders who saved you, and of the human woman who loves you. They're worth your patience, deserving of your affection, just as you are of theirs."

His heartbeat paused for a moment. Even the draga quieted. "And who gave you this message?"

Sunlight outlined Siora's frame in a shimmering luminescence as she stepped across the threshold. "You once defended the dead to your Halani and spoke for those whose voices the living choose not to hear. I offer you the gift of one voice, one message. Yain asks that you remember her fondly."

Malachus gasped, nearly dropping Asil. Siora stepped farther into the street, away from the door. By the time he remembered to breathe again and follow, she was gone, only the flutter of drying linens hinting at her passing.

CHAPTER TWENTY-FOUR

Siora's suggestions for taking a different route back to the free trader camp served him well. Malachus sped through the quieter side streets, Asil quiet in his arms as he carried her toward their destination. He kept a steady jog past houses and shops, moving farther and farther away from the palace, where a woman famous for her beauty and notorious for her brutality waited for him with the splinters of his mother-bond in her possession. Even with most of the artifact tucked against his skin and its sorcery surging through his blood, Malachus still felt the draw of the splinters.

He reached the free trader camp without incident. The camp was an anthill of activity, and the traders gathered around him, crying out Asil's name and touching her as if to assure themselves she was real. Their joy faded when she remained unresponsive to their greetings.

A worried frown darkened Saradeen's features. "You found her. Thank the gods." He glanced at Malachus's bloodstained trousers. "And had a hard time of it by the look of you." He turned to shout over his shoulder. "Hamod!"

The man Malachus had seen in the lightning when he first arrived on these shores appeared in the doorway of the wagon Malachus had shared with Halani the night before. He looked thinner and far more haggard than the wagon master in his vision, and his eyes rounded when he spotted Asil in Malachus's arms.

He leapt off the wagon, striding toward them, his demeanor becoming more aggressive the closer he got. The crowd of free traders parted before him, creating a path leading from him to Malachus.

His surprise at seeing his sister changed to a furious scowl, and he stopped short of plowing into the waiting Malachus with only a finger's length of space between them. "What did you do to her?" he bellowed before shoving Malachus in the shoulder.

Malachus didn't budge under Hamod's push. He turned, offering his burden to Saradeen, who took Asil gently into his arms. Hands free, Malachus returned Hamod's shove, sending the wagon master flying backward.

"Don't touch me," Malachus said in a low voice. "Ever." The free traders gaped at him before a pair of them moved to help a shaken Hamod to his feet. Malachus answered Hamod's question, ignoring the wagon master and addressing Saradeen instead. "She was like that when I found her. The woman who helped me said she's walking the Dream Road." His gaze flickered over the crowd, not seeing the one face he expected when he returned to the camp. Her notable absence sent a spike of icy dread down his spine. "Where's Halani?"

Saradeen gestured for a couple of the women in the group to join him. He set Asil on her feet, keeping a light grasp on her arms in case she couldn't stand. She stared past them. "Take her to your wagon, Anjul," he told the woman closest to him. "Get her cleaned and settled while we pack, and set someone to watch over her."

Anjul nodded, motioning for the other women to help guide Asil toward her wagon. "Come, love," she said softly. "A wash with my best soap and a cup of hot tea will have you well and good in no time."

Silence reigned among the group as they watched Anjul escort

Asil away. Malachus's fear for Halani threatened to consume him, yet a small part of him was glad she wasn't here to see her mother's current state. He turned his attention back to Saradeen and repeated his question. "Where is Halani?"

Saradeen ran a hand through his hair, his features haggard. "After you left, an Unknown delivered a message none of us could read. We sent him away. Another man returned, this time to tell us Gharek of Cabast had information about Asil. He wanted Halani to meet him on the Galdoka Bridge. Alone."

"And you let her go?" Malachus clenched his teeth against a bellow. He recalled the cat's-paw's seemingly throwaway comment when he demanded Asil's whereabouts.

Is that her name? Halani never said.

Saradeen snorted. "Despite what Hamod might like to think, no one among us is Halani's keeper. And this was Asil. Nothing short of nailing Halani's feet to a wagon floor would stop her from trying to get her mother back."

Halani's devotion to Asil was all encompassing. Malachus admired her for it, though in that moment, he wished it otherwise.

"Is Gharek still alive? Do you know if he has the draga bone?" Hamod stood out of reach, his weathered face stamped with dislike, his eyes bright with avarice.

Human greed, Malachus thought. It always came back to greed. Had Halani not taken possession of his heart and bound him to her body and soul, he'd walk away from them all. Even his sister's words, delivered by a woman who heard the voices of the dead, wouldn't keep him here. Only fair Halani with her somber gray eyes and the song of earth wrapped around her.

He eyed the wagon master, disdain curling his upper lip. "Gharek is still alive, and the empress has the artifact. You're no longer of any importance to them." His contempt deepened as relief and disappointment played across Hamod's face. If he was concerned for Halani's fate, he didn't show it.

Malachus, on the other hand, had to restrain himself from tearing out of the camp and racing for the palace in a blind rescue attempt, the impulse guaranteed to get him and Halani killed. Instead, he plied Saradeen for more information. "What happened with the second messenger?"

"She left with him." He pointed to a stripling lad on the verge of his first beard. "I sent Peleus after them to spy. Tell Malachus what you witnessed."

Peleus blushed at the attention suddenly cast on him. "I didn't get close enough to hear their conversation, but a man ran up to Gharek and whispered in his ear. He looked angry, afraid. He told one man to give the empress his message, then ran away. Three more men joined the one who had hold of Halani. I followed them as far as I could to the palace before a pair of guards chased me off."

"Gods," Malachus breathed, grappling with the confirmation of his worst fears. The empress not only had the tiny but important splinters of his mother-bond; she had Halani as well. His task had just become monumentally harder, and his chances of failing much greater.

Though Hamod was the wagon master and leader of this free trader band, Malachus disregarded the fact to work with the more reasonable Saradeen. "You can't stay here."

Undeterred by the shunning, Hamod interjected. "Why not? The empress isn't looking for me anymore, and we can use this as our planning point for rescuing Halani." He paled a little at Malachus's withering stare.

"Your machinations are why we're in this predicament. Halani needs help, just not yours."

Saradeen followed Malachus's lead. "We've already started packing the wagons for leaving and sent a messenger to meet Kursak on the road and warn him not to come to Domora. A few of us thought to remain here until you returned with Asil and then figure out a way to get Halani back."

No matter how well-meaning Saradeen and his plan were, an entourage was the last thing Malachus needed. "I can get inside the palace easier alone, but having a few of you wait in Domora will work in my favor. You can take Halani out of the city if I can't."

Hamod still refused to be shut out of their strategizing. "Why can you get in the palace without trouble?" he said, suspicion thick in his voice.

Malachus smirked. "Because the empress has all but invited me."

He refused to expound on his comment. Time was short, every passing moment decreasing his chance to pry Halani from the empress's clutches. He didn't dwell on the prospect that to save her, he'd have to die, or that for all their best-laid plans, she might be dead already.

He donned different garb, tied back his hair, and replenished his spent supply of quarrels for the borrowed crossbow. His changed look wasn't much of a disguise, but a cape and hood worn in summer would attract too much notice. His best strategy was to move fast, stay off the main streets, and avoid as much as possible the bands of soldiers filling the city. He agreed to Peleus accompanying him to the spot where he'd lost sight of Halani and her captors. "Don't linger while we're there," he warned the boy. "If you're caught, I can't save you." Peleus's enthusiastic nod assured Malachus he'd bolt back for what remained of the camp the moment Malachus gave the signal to do so.

Before he left, he exchanged a friendly arm clasp with Saradeen. "The woman who helped me find Asil said Gharek didn't abuse her. I think her abduction put her on the Dream Road. If the gods are kind, she'll travel back to us and do so before Halani returns."

If Halani returns. The dark flicker in Saradeen's eyes revealed his grim thought. He kept the words to himself, gripped Malachus's arm, and offered a nod of acknowledgment. "We'll do our best to wake her. May the gods keep you and Halani, and bring you both home to us."

Peleus, young and strong, kept pace with Malachus as they raced toward the palace, avoiding the crowded bridge where Halani had met Gharek. They paused twice, once for Peleus to point out the route where Gharek's henchmen had taken their charge, and once to duck out of sight from a battalion of Kraelian soldiers marching in formation toward some unknown destination. They reached the perimeter of the palace grounds as the shadows lengthened across manicured loggias and carefully tended gardens dotted with fountains and man-made ponds dug and filled for the royal court's pleasure.

"This is where the guards chased me away," Peleus said as they lingered at the edge of a hedgerow clipped into the shape of a turreted wall.

Malachus eyed its length, the spots where overhanging tree branches and the bend of shadows created alcoves in which to hide. If he was careful and navigated each of those sanctuaries, he could reach the palace itself without a confrontation. He turned to Peleus. "Go back to the camp and do as Saradeen bids you." He paused, reluctant to give voice to the unavoidable potential of failure in his quest. "Tell him if I don't come back with Halani by the small hours that he shouldn't wait any longer. Join the rest of your kind outside of Domora and get as far from the city and the empress as you can."

Peleus paled at his words but didn't argue. He echoed Saradeen's blessing and raced back the way they'd come. Malachus watched until the boy disappeared before once more eyeing the long wall of spiky hedge that created a green barrier behind the stone-and-mortar one surrounding the palace. He darted from shadow to shadow, working his way toward the more humble buildings built as part of the royal complex that served the numerous and unending needs of those it housed. A smithy, bakery, laundry, millhouse; a massive royal stable built to house hundreds of horses and all their tack.

Malachus had visited different palaces in his travels through Winosia for various reasons. Most were built on two principles—to impress the population surrounding it and to act as a defensible, unbreachable fortress in times of war. And every royal house kept a prison. If this palace were like other royal dwellings, he'd find a small door leading to a hive of cells filled with the condemned, the forgotten, the dying, and the dead. All overseen by an army of the brutal and inhumane. He discovered a prison entrance inset into the palace's thick walls adjacent to the provender building dedicated to the stables and guarded by a dozen soldiers, all milling about, either bored or drunk, or both.

Had he the luxury of time, he'd scout the palace's entire perimeter, hunt for another way in, even if he had to start from the topmost spire and work his way down. But Malachus didn't have time. He'd have to fight his way in and fight his way out, with the latter being the more difficult of the two. He didn't hold out much hope for surviving the endeavor, but if he could free Halani, he'd die content.

The guards didn't anticipate the silent whirlwind of demonic violence that suddenly erupted in their midst. Four lay dead before the rest even realized they were under attack, and by then they could do no more than swing wildly at their assailant before gasping out their last breath or choking on their own blood as they fell atop each other in front of the door.

Malachus tossed bodies aside until he found the man with the key ring, which held a disheartening number of keys. While his attack had relied on speed and surprise to succeed, the challenge of the door's lock required trial and error. He crouched to more closely inspect the keyhole, stopping several times to look over his shoulder and listen for any approaching footsteps. The mechanism's shape and size vaguely matched that of five keys on the heavy ring. He separated those from the rest, inserting the first into the keyhole. The gods didn't answer his prayer the first three tries, but on the fourth, the mechanism clicked, and the key rotated inside the keyhole.

He eased the door open, using the wood as a shield against anyone on the other side waiting to fire a round of arrows into him from a nocked bow. The door opened onto an empty corridor shrouded in shadow, with rows of barred cells cut into the rock foundation. Malachus closed the door behind him with a soft snick and crept into the palace's underworld.

Some of the cells were empty; others held ragged creatures who might once have been human tethered to the rock walls with chains. None of the cells held Halani.

He came to the end of the hallway and halted, staring at the endless corridors that branched off from this one, all lined with cells that stretched into a darkness occasionally broken by the far flicker of a torch. He'd be here for years looking for Halani if he explored every hallway and checked every cell.

The sound of marching feet forced him to dart into a corner out of sight, and he observed a small cadre of troops escorting one of their own, bound and beaten, down one of the hallways. Their footsteps echoed throughout the labyrinthine prison like distant drums.

Malachus stayed where he was for several moments after the troop passed, caught on an idea the percussion of their march had inspired. His magic was a risky thing to use. It depended on the draga within him to strengthen it. With the mother-bond so close and its pull so strong, his heritage writhed inside him like an angry serpent. Employing his magic only made it worse, but he might have a way to find Halani. She was worth every risk. He pressed his hands to the wall beside him, its damp, slimy surface cold under his palms. All his senses narrowed down to his fingers, to the bones of the earth beneath them. He opened himself to the deep, resonant hymn Halani claimed to hear in the back of her mind, one she manipulated to guide a caravan across flooded ground, one a creature of the fens had used to lure her into the mud and nearly drown her.

He was no earth witch, but he was draga, and his kind had known how to manipulate the elements long before men had even understood the uses of fire or the tilling of fields. Malachus sought and found the clear river of melody, letting his spirit ride its current until it slowed and finally pooled not far from where he hid now. It was no guarantee the hymn was clearer in that spot because Halani resided there, but it was his best hope. Surely, the prison wasn't teeming with earth witches.

Blood trickled from his nose, and smoke rose from his fingernails. He wiped away the blood and once more slinked through the prison's web of hallways, guided by the beacon of song. He found Halani in one of the cramped cells notched into a curving arch of wall. She huddled on a bed of filthy straw, curled in on herself, hands tucked close to her chest.

"Halani."

She jumped, a gasp echoing in the cell as she squinted at him in the half dark. "Malachus!" She reached for him through the gaps between the bars and he caught her hands, wrenching a strangled cry from her. He dropped her hands as if scalded.

"Where are you hurt?" Her agonized expression made him rattle the bars in a vain effort to tear them out of the stone in which they were anchored. Once more she tucked her hands close to her chest, but not before he got a glimpse at them. Her slender fingers looked the same, except for the smallest ones. Swollen and strangely bent, with bruising running their lengths and over the knuckle to her fourth fingers.

Rage exploded through him, and flames burst from his palms to race along the sides of his own fingers. He leapt away from the cell bars, fearful of harming Halani. She gaped at him, wide-eyed. The red haze descended over his vision for a few moments, and he breathed harder than a winded horse with the effort to suppress the draga's inevitable rise. When he could finally speak, and the fire in his hands was no more than the memory of smoke, he stared at his lover through the unyielding bars. "Who did this to you, Halani?" Two broken little fingers was no accident. Someone had tortured her.

"I did."

Malachus turned at the sound of a lilting voice addressing him from the opposite end of the corridor. A troop of soldiers blocked the exit to the main hall, every man armed, their weapons trained on him. At the head of their company, a blonde woman of extraordinary beauty stared at him with a raptor's gaze, blue eyes as brilliant and hard as sapphires. She wore an ornate gown of crimson silk, its bodice embroidered in a complicated design made of small precious stones and beads. The bell-like sleeves did a fine job of almost completely disguising the fact that one of them was empty.

Dalvila, the empress of the Krael Empire.

She strolled toward him, her self-assured demeanor bordering on arrogance. Either she had supreme confidence in her guards' ability to protect her, or she understood the value of her hostage to her adversary and his unwillingness to put her at greater risk.

The empress halted not far from him, out of his immediate reach but close enough that with a quick leap forward, he could snap her neck before one of her soldiers could lift his blade to defend her. It didn't matter if she stood close enough to tread on his feet. Two of the guards held drawn bows with nocked arrows trained on Halani. Malachus hardly dared breathe, much less attack.

Dalvila's gaze raked him, pausing at his shoulders, his midriff, his groin, the slash in his trousers. More bloodstains decorated his garb, enough that the one put there by Gharek's cut was no longer distinguishable. She ran a small red tongue across her lower lip. "Well. Not quite what I expected. Handsome enough but not very epic. What is your name? I asked your whore, but she refused to tell me, even after I broke fingers."

He answered promptly in case she took it as an invitation to break more of Halani's bones. "Malachus. And you are Dalvila, the Spider of Empire." He didn't bow, though he would if she demanded it. Whatever it took to keep Halani alive.

The empress's lush mouth curved into a delighted smile. "Is that what they call me? I like it."

She would. Even in far Winosia, everyone had heard rumors and tales of the Kraelian empress. A calculating predator of exceptional cunning. "I've heard you've searched all of the Empire for me," he told her. "So you know why I'm here."

One of her elegant eyebrows rose. "Do I? I have two things of value to you. Which one do you want most? The whore?" She nodded toward Halani before retrieving the false mother-bond from the cuff of her empty sleeve. "Or your mother-bond?"

Under his tunic, the real mother-bond pulsed hard, as if sensing that the bits and pieces taken from it were close. Were he here alone, he'd call the false bone to him and embrace the imperative of his heritage. In the throes of a transformation, he would be impervious to any puny human arrow. He'd destroy the empress, her guard, those suffering wrecks in their cells, and half the palace in the act, and good riddance to them all. He'd also kill Halani.

He answered Dalvila's question with one of his own. "What do you want of me?"

She laughed, a sound that made Malachus think of a barn snake swallowing hens' eggs with an unhinged jaw and throat muscles that flexed and crushed. "I want all of you, Malachus. Your blood, your bones, your meat. I'd take your soul if there was a way to capture it. Every part of you is valuable to me."

Foolish woman. For all her power, she was no different from most, fearing the one thing she couldn't control and which came for every living being at some point—death. "Very flattering," he countered. "But why would I willingly sacrifice myself to you?"

"Because if you don't, I will decapitate your whore in front of you." Her smile widened to a grin at the distressed sound Halani made.

This woman deserved the death she so greatly feared, and Malachus hoped when this was done, he'd be the one who dealt it. She played a game with him, her scrutiny sharp as any hawk's as she waited for his next expression, his next reply. He kept his features carefully blank. "She's no use to you alive once I'm dead. You'll kill her just to make space in the cell for the next prisoner."

The empress shrugged. "True, but what choice do you have?"

"More than you think. Without the mother-bond, I can't transform, and I must transform. If I don't, I will burn in a conflagration of my own making. My choice is to refuse the mother-bond and burn." Dalvila lost her satisfied smirk. "Keep it," he told her, playing a deadly game of bluff. "I will die as a man and do so in fire, so all that blood and bone and meat you so badly covet will be lost to you, and there will be nothing you can do to stop it."

And everything near me will burn to ash as well. He didn't say those words, didn't want to dwell on them, for Halani would die with him too. It was a fate he desperately wanted to avoid, but he wouldn't leave Halani to the empress's savagery.

The smile Dalvila bestowed on him was no longer so triumphant but far more calculating, even admiring. "What a shame you're worth more in pieces than whole. I think you'd do well as an ambassador for the Empire. You know how to negotiate without giving in, nor are you intimidated. A bargain, then, instead of a sacrifice. My people need a reminder that they live in the greatest empire that ever existed, ruled by the greatest monarch who ever lived. Kraelag's destruction was an aberration. The Savatar savages won the day; they didn't win the war they've started, nor will the Nunari enjoy their emancipation for long. I will have my revenge and recapture my territories. My armies are ready.

"With your blood, I will regain my arm, and your bones will replace those of Golnar lost in Kraelag's fires. Instead of hanging them from my ceiling, they will go before my armies, a reminder of the might and power of the Krael Empire. All will know that Empress Dalvila is unbroken, undefeated, the conqueror of men and dragas alike."

Malachus studied her, certain that this bargain of hers didn't just spring up in her mind in response to his threat. It reeked of a long game's manipulation, as if she'd set up this particular chessboard with many outcomes to consider. His threat to burn was just one, and she had a solution ready in case he used it. What else could he do but play it and see where it went?

"You still haven't said what would inspire me to contribute to your personal glory," he said.

Her delicate hand, with its manicured nails and unbroken fingers, fluttered in the air in a flirtatious gesture, as if they courted each other. In a way it was a courtship. Of the deadliest sort. "I want to host a celebration, a spectacle to entertain all of Domora. A replay of 'The Sun Maiden.' You will be Golnar trying to steal the Sun Maiden statue for yourself."

Both his stomach and his heart plummeted at her words, and the floor felt as if it dissolved beneath his feet so that he fell toward an abyss with no bottom and only the wind to follow him down. He would be forced to embrace his mother's fate, and he knew even before he asked who would embrace Yain's. "And where will you get your Sun Maiden?"

The sly gaze she sent Halani only verified his certainty. "I will put the Sun Maiden on the battlements. You'll have the chance to rescue her. If you can get her off the walls without dying beforehand, you can set her down outside them. She can then run away. I won't waste my soldiers chasing after her, though I can't guarantee a few enthusiastic townsmen won't try and capture her for their own purposes."

Torn apart by a mob frenzied with bloodlust. His own death would be more merciful simply because Dalvila would make certain his butchers took care with their cleavers. He'd have to find a way to live long enough for Halani to get free of the city and its citizens.

The empress was a cruel woman, but also an intelligent one. No doubt she had an answer for his next question, but he'd ask anyway.

Answers often revealed things not always intended. "And if I decide to just fly away once I transform?" A newly transformed draga didn't just flutter off like a starling, but Dalvila didn't yet know that.

"My sorcerers will see to it that you don't fly away. Leashes woven of magic that won't let you get too far. It's said that dragas can breathe fire, though Golnar didn't use his for some reason when he faced Kansi Yuv. If I see so much as a puff of smoke wisp out of your nostrils in my direction, your own Sun Maiden is dead, and I'll make sure the dying takes a very long time."

Malachus saw Halani shudder, though she kept silent as she listened to their negotiating. The empress's reptilian gaze gleamed in the muddied light of the flickering torches. *Golnar didn't use fire because she didn't want to immolate her own daughter, you vicious bitch,* he thought. "I thought magic was outlawed in the Krael Empire."

Dalvila stiffened. "I am the Empire. The law bends to my whim, not the other way around."

It was a demon's bargain, with almost no chance of getting Halani out of Dalvila's clutches alive and no chance whatsoever of him surviving. But for now there was no other way. To refuse her offer meant signing Halani's death warrant. At least by agreeing to the empress's terms, he'd buy a little time to find a way out of this disaster for both Halani and him. "I want to see her before you put her on the battlements and while you're putting her there so that I know it's her, and that she's alive and unmarked."

A diabolical triumph glittered in Dalvila's icy blue eyes, and her expression had lost all of its sardonic humor, leaving behind only a serpent's cold-blooded scrutiny. "Fair enough. I'll even bring her to you once it's time for you to transform. Do I have your agreement?"

He nodded. "You do." The empress would have her spectacle.

"Malachus." His name on Halani's lips might have been a prayer, an entreaty, a last mournful denial of this bargain he'd made.

He glanced at her, shaking his head to signal for her continued silence before turning back to Dalvila. "What do you require of me?"

"Follow me, and I'll show you."

Her soldiers made quick work of divesting him of his knives, the crossbow, and its quarrels. They patted him down in search of any other hidden weaponry, never finding the mother-bond, whose magic served to hide its presence from all others now that he was reunited with it. Satisfied he was no longer armed, they clapped his hands and legs in irons.

He didn't want to leave Halani in the dark, filthy cell, but he had no choice. He paused to stare at her, offering with his gaze what he dared not say out loud. *Trust me. I will alter the heavens to save you.* She nodded as if she heard him, and in her gaze he saw longing, fear, and unshakable faith.

His bonds forced him to shuffle, and the journey from the prison to the palace's upper floors was a long, slow one. Impatient with their progress, Dalvila left him behind, warning the soldiers not to injure him. "I want him whole and without a bruise on him. He can't do what I plan if he has broken bones and wounds."

A few of the men muttered their disappointment once she was out of earshot, but none defied her, and they reached a grand chamber with a soaring ceiling and polished marble floor with him uninjured.

Dalvila waited in the room's center, flanked by three men dressed in guild robes he recognized as those worn by sorcerers bound to an order existing in Winosia. The empress had imported her magicians. Obviously, the laws that applied to Kraelian citizens didn't apply to Dalvila. As she'd told him, she was the empress; therefore, she was the law.

Malachus noted that the chamber's floors were intricately carved with runes and sigils set in a colossal circle that took up most of the space. He recognized a few—binding runes and wards. The entire place hummed with power.

"The sigils were put there when sorcerers were far more powerful and served the will of the emperor," the empress said. "They used this circle to summon entities that made dragas seem fragile. You'll wait inside it for now while I prepare the city for our little spectacle."

She nodded, and his escort shoved him hard across the circle's rune perimeter so that he stumbled and fell to his knees, still fettered by the irons that shackled his wrists to his legs. More power, old and blood tainted, seized him in a suffocating embrace. He shook it off, breaking the invisible weave that sought to bind him as much as his shackles did. He staggered to his feet, unwilling to kneel long in the empress's presence.

She circumnavigated the circle's perimeter, reminding Malachus of his trip across the sea, when he'd seen the sharks course around the ship he was on, waiting for some unfortunate sailor to pitch from the deck into the waves. "I forgot to ask," she said. "Where is Gharek? Did you kill him?"

He didn't risk a lie. She might believe him, but if she didn't, Halani would pay for his attempted deception. "Your cat's-paw hoped to outmaneuver me. He lost."

Dalvila sniffed. "Ah well, he served his purpose. It doesn't matter now. You're here where I want you, and soon you'll provide Domora's citizens with the finest entertainment and me with the opportunity to gain back my arm and retain my youth."

If he wasn't sure disabusing her of such ridiculous notions would destroy any hope of rescuing Halani, he would have laughed. Instead, he walked to the circle's center and sat down, wondering how long it might be before she released the false mother-bond with its precious splinters to him so he could transform, and if he'd have the strength to hold down the draga much longer.

She watched him, puzzlement drawing her eyebrows together. "You find me dull, don't you?"

Malachus sensed she'd be amused by his unadorned answer. "I find you vile."

Dark laughter danced in her blue eyes. "Another draga, doomed to repeat Golnar's failure in trying to steal the Sun Maiden." The laughter vanished, leaving behind only the darkness. "You're going to die. You know that, don't you? You will never leave Domora still breathing."

There was really nothing subtle at all about this woman. "You're the Spider of Empire. No one believes in mercy from you."

"True, but mercy never raised empires and conquered kingdoms. To be loved or feared . . ." Dalvila clucked her tongue. "Neither matters to me as long as I'm obeyed."

He didn't bother arguing with her. He'd witnessed mercy and its sister compassion, been a recipient of both. They lived within a woman whose soul shone as bright as this creature's pulsed dark, and if the gods favored him, he'd see to it before he died that the first lived on in the world and the second did not.

CHAPTER TWENTY-FIVE

Halani pressed herself to the cell bars as the soldiers pushed Malachus through the corridor and out of sight. She'd wanted to cry out his name, ask why he was bloodied, had he found Asil, a million questions hovering on her lips that she dared not speak in front of the empress. That monstrous woman would lap up Halani's distress as if it were nectar.

Had she seen the last of her draga lover? She shied away from the bleak thought. She'd never been one to delude herself regarding difficult realities. The fact that she hadn't been raped yet while imprisoned didn't mean it wouldn't happen in the next few moments or the next few days. She'd been groped and leered at by those who'd brought her here before being tossed in this cell, but none had forced themselves on her. Not while her well-being had value as the lure to bring in the elusive, provocative prey that was a draga.

Without a window to see the outside world, she had no idea how much time had passed since Dalvila had taken Malachus, but the hours dragged before a pair of guards appeared, keys in hand. These men didn't work in the prison itself. They were too finely garbed in the livery of the palace's more gracious floors. Nor did they leer at her with the same feral lust she'd seen in the other guards.

One unlocked the cell door. "The empress says you're to attend her," he announced. He opened the door and ushered her out with an impatient gesture.

Unlike Malachus, who'd been trussed in heavy irons when they led him away, she remained unfettered as they navigated the prison's confusing maze of hallways, ascending several stairs before finally reaching doors that opened onto a guardroom manned by more of those dressed like her escort. They wrinkled their noses as she passed them.

Were she not a prisoner, she might have stood in awe of the palace's interior. The entire place was an architectural marvel—yet it was presided over by a sovereign who defiled the prison itself with her presence. Halani's guards didn't allow her to slow or linger but pushed her toward another pair of massive doors set in one side of the grand receiving room.

The space beyond was even grander. And peculiar. Halani sensed a strangeness about it even before she saw the cryptic symbols carved into the floor and embedded in the decorative designs painted on the walls. She swallowed back a cry when she spotted Malachus watching her from the center of a circle carved into the polished marble floor.

Dalvila stood nearby, a cluster of guards and men wearing robes embroidered in arcane symbols in attendance behind her. She glided toward Halani. Like those in the guardroom, she wrinkled her nose, and her lip curled into a sneer. "You stink," she declared. She pointed in Malachus's direction. "Make her stand there at the circle's edge," she instructed the guards. They leapt to do her bidding, yanking Halani toward the spot the empress had indicated.

While the guards' revulsion for her state hadn't fazed her, Dalvila's remark sent the heat of humiliation into Halani's face by virtue of the fact that she'd stated an obvious and unpleasant truth in front of Malachus. As if he understood the source of her embarrassment, his eyes warmed. "You're beautiful, Halani," he said. "That will never change."

Judging by the view revealed through the windows lining one wall, she'd been trapped in the cell for a day and a night, but that was all it took to smell like the reeking middens adjacent to the prison. She greedily soaked up the sight of Malachus with her eyes, relieved to see he bore no new wounds. Still, in the time since Dalvila had taken him from the prison, a noticeable change had descended over him. His breathing was labored and his skin had turned a sickly, jaundiced shade. Dark circles ringed his eyes, and smoke wreathed his frame, drifting even from his nostrils with every exhalation. "You look so ill," she told him.

Her alarm knew no bounds when he told her, "It's hard to control the draga now." He gave her a slow blink. "You should know," he said in a lethargic voice, "I found her. She's back home."

He didn't use a name, but Halani knew to whom he referred, and her joy in the news burst past the wall of her fear for a moment. He'd rescued Asil. She stepped closer to the circle's edge, stretching a hand toward her lover. Her palm collided with an invisible barrier that revealed itself only in a brief ripple of air and an odd vibration that coursed through her swollen hand and made her broken finger throb even more. "Thank you, Malachus," she said in fervent tones that offered him far more than gratitude. His pinched features softened, even as his eyes glittered with a banked anger at the sight of her injured hand.

Dalvila sidled up to the circle's edge, blue gaze avid as any raptor's. "I thought you might like to see what you've been fucking," she told Halani. "He can't break free, even without chains, even with draga strength."

Halani could only imagine what manner of cruelties must have taken place in this arcane, breathtaking chamber. She lowered her hand and stepped back from the circle to glare at the empress, reckless in her anger. "Then if he's trapped and not a danger to you, why not just give him the mother-bond? Do you enjoy the torture?"

"Halani, please." Malachus's plea begged caution.

Dalvila only laughed. "As a matter of fact, I do, but you're right." She raked Malachus with a sneering gaze. "He won't be much good to me if he burns himself into an ash heap." She gestured to the robed men, who stepped forward to stand at points outside the circle. One started the first notes of a droning chant and was soon joined by his compatriots. Gooseflesh pebbled Halani's skin, and the fine hairs at her nape stood up in warning. Spellwork. In the palace of a sovereign whose laws punished those accused of witchcraft and sorcery with pitiless efficiency, magic pulsed and swelled in the rise and fall of a cant. Cold light spooled out of the magicians' fingers, slithering past the perimeter's wards to wrap around Malachus's arms and legs like the iron shackles he still wore. These were shackles as well, forged from sorcery instead of metal but no less binding. Halani could only guess the purpose of these newest bonds. If the empress was involved, it could only be a dire one.

Satisfied with what their spellwork had wrought, the sorcerers ceased their chant and stepped back from the circle's edge. When the one who initiated the chant nodded to Dalvila, she tossed something into the circle that Halani hadn't seen since the day in the Goban market when she'd begged Hamod not to buy the artifact whose power had soaked into her skin. "Your trinket, draga."

The mother-bond tumbled across the circle's carved barrier,

and Malachus snatched it neatly from the air, fist closing protectively around it before pressing it against his chest. The effect of its touch was instantaneous.

Both Halani and Dalvila backed away from the circle's perimeter when he uttered a plaintive cry, back arching as if bent by an invisible hand intent on tying him into a knot. Halani would have charged into the circle if she could.

Malachus's ordeal worsened as the spell that trapped him in human form fractured and shattered. He contorted and convulsed in the throes of a transformation that seemed designed to extract every drop of agony from its victim before it finished.

She refused to close her eyes or look away when he fell to his knees, then his back, writhing and twisting in agony that robbed him of the ability to even scream. The sounds spilling from his throat were no more than guttural moans. Halani feared she'd retch when she glanced at the empress and saw the fevered lust in her face. The cruelty.

The ghostly smoke that had wafted off him earlier grew denser, darker, until it resembled a red fog that slowly filled the space within the circle, obscuring Malachus completely. Halani had assumed such a change entailed a gentler transition, complete with glowing light. How wrong she was. How foolish.

There was only pain and the bloody miasma that roiled and swirled within the circle's confines. It was more than a thick mist. It swelled and writhed, spitting whips of fire in every direction that bounced against the circle's wards with blinding flashes and waves of heat. The circle bulged against the force of so much contained magic, as if it fought to cage a burning sun.

The fiery smoke thickened even more, developing defined angles and curves, coalescing into a shape Halani had seen in paintings and sculptures, depicted on temple walls. She gazed in awe, staring up and up toward the expansive roof high above her.

Where a man had collapsed in agony, a creature of legend now stood, shaking off the last of his old form with a snort from arched nostrils and a ripple of bright scales. Colossal, with a head that nearly scraped the chamber's soaring ceiling, the draga defied any attempt to capture the scope of his size, his power, the sheer magnitude of his presence in the room. The imprisoning circle's invisible walls rippled, and the tethers woven by the sorcerers' spells stretched taut against powerful legs and the curved claws tipping a pair of membranous bronze wings.

Halani wept silent tears. The lover she'd held in her arms was gone. After centuries of waiting, the draga had come into its own, complete with scales, claws, teeth long as boar spears and ten times more lethal, eyes more fiery than the bloody sunrises that heralded a coming storm. Its wings lay tucked against a back wide enough to carry two free trader wagons side by side.

"Magnificent," Dalvila said, the awe in her voice the first thing Halani could empathize with. The notion made her slightly queasy.

The draga's great head swung on a serpentine neck, plummeting toward them, jaws partially open to reveal the awesome fangs and a long red tongue resting within his mouth. Dalvila backed away, despite her boasts that the circle's wards would hold anything inside its circumference. She needn't have worried. The draga's attention rested solely on Halani.

Halani stepped to the circle's edge, heart in her throat at being this close to something so enormous, so lethal. She lifted one hand to press it against the invisible shield a second time, once more experiencing the tiny shocks of sorcery darting through her hand, numbing her fingers. "Malachus?"

The pupil in one of his large, fiery eyes expanded at the sound of his name, and the draga bent his head even closer, finally pressing one scaly cheek to the ward shield where her hand rested. Jagged shards of sorcerous light arced across the wards at his touch.

Behind Halani, Dalvila celebrated and planned. "The people of Domora will be in raptures over the spectacle I have in store for them! Bards for generations will tell a new version of 'The Sun Maiden.' Instead of Golnar, it will be Malachus who will fulfill his role, and all shall praise my name for restoring the Empire's glory."

Halani ignored her, focused entirely on her transformed lover. A mistake she soon learned to her cost.

"Take her," Dalvila snapped. "Have her bathed, painted, and brought to the north wall." Halani whirled to face the empress and was instantly caught up in the guards' unyielding grip. She thrashed to get free, biting, kicking, and clawing until one of the guards cocked back a fist and struck her. Just before the world went black, a draga's roar shook the chamber's walls, and the floor shivered under Halani's feet.

Halani regained consciousness long enough to discover herself naked and half submerged in a bath. A woman's voice sounded above her. "She's awake. Let's get the elixir down her before she comes to enough to fight us."

Someone gripped her chin, forcing her mouth open even as they pinched her nostrils shut with their fingers. Halani gasped for air, then choked and gagged when someone else poured a bitter brew down her throat. The black shroud of oblivion fell over her again, wiping away all resistance.

* * *

Roused a second time, Halani raised her aching head at the dull roar of thousands of voices all around her. How long had she been senseless? Hours? Days even? A bright sun speared her eyes from the east, and she blinked several times in an effort to clear away the blurry fog obscuring her vision. To her horror, she found herself shackled to a pole on a dais set on the battlements high above Domora, her hands and ankles bound with rope. Her skin itched and burned, even as the effects of the narcotic she'd been force-fed threatened to pull her under once more. She glanced down, struggling to understand what she saw.

Gold. As bright as the sun and gleaming with a metallic sheen to dazzle the eye. Halani jerked hard on the ropes once her mind worked past the drug-induced confusion. They'd painted her in the stuff. Whoever had fed her the elixir had covered her nude body from head to foot in a thin layer of gold paint. Even her hair, scraped back from her face and clubbed at the nape, was lacquered in gold paint. From what she could see of herself, she resembled a statue. A golden statue of a woman. The Sun Maiden.

Terror blasted through her, obliterating the elixir's lingering effects. Halani lunged against the ropes, her movements evoking shouts and catcalls from the excited crowd gathered below on either side of the city's encircling wall.

She twisted against her bonds, looking to either side of her and then above for any sign of Malachus as the draga. The battlements were crowded. Aristocrats in their fine clothing shared space with soldiers armed with both longbows and crossbows, and at regular intervals, teams of soldiers grouped around ballistae parked on the wall, loading either stone shot or large bolts into the rails. The rhythmic clink of the winches and the creak of the torsion springs as the teams ratcheted the ballistae's bowstrings back rose above the crowd's noise, an awful sound in her ears disproportionate to the roar of the gathered audience. Halani's vision blurred with tears. She wanted to scream down curses on the heads of those who'd come to watch siege weapons tear apart the man—the draga—she loved, but she kept silent, refusing to offer them the entertainment of her sorrow.

Malachus was nowhere in sight, and Halani prayed she wouldn't spot him bound like her, waiting to be butchered in some brutal game to appease the audience's bloodlust. They gathered below her, cheering and chanting Dalvila's name as they waited for whatever their empress had in store to entertain them. Where was Malachus?

A sudden roar traveled through the crowd like a wave. Halani twisted in her bonds, turning just enough so she could see the source of such loud adulation: a palanquin carried by a half dozen bearers, three on either side of the horizontal support staves. They carefully set the sedan down at the bottom of a set of steps leading to the eastern parapet, where an awning had been erected to provide shade from the worst of the sun's blinding rays. The crowd roared again when the empress emerged from the palanquin and gracefully climbed the steps. An escort of soldiers surrounded her as she walked beneath the awning and stepped onto a more decorative dais than the one Halani occupied and raised her arm, silently demanding more cheering, louder voices, the roar of her name in the people's throats. They complied, deafening Halani.

"My people," Dalvila shouted, once the voices had died down. "Today I have a gift for you. A symbol of the Empire's endurance, its strength, despite the loss of Kraelag." She paused as a torrent of hisses and disapproving whistles rose from the crowd. When they faded, she continued. "We are not defeated, only inspired. We will crush the Savatar and make the Nunari pay for the insult of their betrayal. We will rebuild our garrisons in the east and overrun the Goban." She worked the crowd into a frenzy with her words, every last one of them ready to take up a sword and hack away at anyone they thought remotely resembled a steppe nomad. "How can we do this? Because we are Kraelians! We are powerful. Our armies are fearsome. And no pack of steppe dogs can stand against an Empire that can capture a draga!"

The crowd once more erupted into deafening cheers and applause, which soon changed to terrified screams when a monstrous black shape emerged from a place inside the city walls and took to the skies with the thunderous clap of giant wings.

"Malachus!" Halani shouted his name, her cry lost amid the cacophony rising from those on the ground.

The draga continued his ascent toward the clouds, his great wings concussing the air around them as if the wind had a heartbeat. Reassured by their sovereign's lack of fear as she watched the draga's flight, the crowd settled, pointing and exclaiming at the sight of a creature all had thought long extinct.

Dalvila continued seducing her audience, extolling her own powers in the most glorious light. "The beast does my bidding, succumbs to my will. And today, it will entertain you with a story much loved and oft told. I am descended from the great Kansi Yuv, and this draga is one of Golnar's kind. And once more, we have a Sun Maiden. Do you want a story?"

"Aye!" the crowd roared, itself a singular beast.

"Are you ready for a killing?"

"Aye!"

Angry sobs swelled Halani's throat when the draga beat his bat-like wings against the thick summer air and dove in a clumsy swoop toward the city walls. His massive shadow passed over Halani, and a blast of wind buffeted her when a wing flapped close enough to her to touch if her hands were free. "Fly away," she shouted as he passed her. "Please, Malachus, fly away!"

Surely he saw the ballistae rolled onto the wider parapets and perched on the loggia, manned by soldiers and loaded with arrows the length of a man's arm, their spiked tips guaranteed to punch a hole through anything they hit.

A hum of discordant earth magic surged through her as the draga flew past, the shimmering trail of the sorcerous tethers still bound to his legs and wings on one end, the other ends anchored to the earth. Dalvila's sorcerers had done their work well. The draga could fly high and far enough to give the crowd a good show, but he couldn't fly away, leashed to the ground by powerful earth magic.

Halani herself stood in the sights of loaded crossbows, a warning to the draga that if he tried to cheat the empress of her spectacle, Halani would pay the ultimate price.

Malachus burst skyward before making an abrupt dive. One of the ballista teams fired at him, the arrow spinning toward him in a death spiral. The draga executed his own midair spiral, and the arrow sailed harmlessly past him. The crowd bellowed its approval. Halani sagged in her bonds, her heart pounding so hard against her ribs, she was sure it would burst free from her chest at any moment.

A vicious game of cat and mouse played out between draga and ballista teams to the onlookers' excited encouragement, as Malachus dodged the arrows and stone shot fired upon him while attempting to snatch Halani from her place atop the platform. Twice Halani screamed his name in terror, the first time when a ballista bolt found its mark, slamming into the draga's flank hard enough to knock him out of the air. Malachus crashed to earth, wings flapping as he thrashed on the ground, and the terrified people gathered outside the walls fled in every direction. Injured but undefeated, he gained his feet and sprang skyward with a bellow and a gusting flap of his wings. Blood streamed down his flank, dripping off his claws to splatter some of the Kraelians below him.

Another hit from a different ballista prompted Halani's second cry, this one to Malachus's right wing by a round of stone shot. Shrapnel missed the elongated finger bones to which the wings were attached but tore through the membrane itself, once more sending the draga spiraling toward the ground. This time he recovered before he hit, wings beating hard to keep him airborne as he roared his fury and pain to the bright blue sky.

He banked toward her again and again, managing to avoid the kill shot from the numerous ballistae firing bolts and stones at him with increasing speed and accuracy. The ballista teams were learning his flight patterns, adjusting their aim. The sorcerous tethers made him an easier target. Even without those chains, Halani's presence trapped him here. She was Malachus's greatest vulnerability and the empress's most effective weapon against him. Better even than the most powerful ballista operated by the sharpest-eyed archer.

There had to be a way to break him free. Halani closed her eyes, turning inward, away from the crowd's screeching din, the percussive clap of giant wings, and the image of Dalvila's gloating, triumphant features. Away from the growing burn of the paint raising blisters on her skin. She stood on a platform high above the ground, and here, the earth's hymn was much more muted in her head. So faint Halani had to strain to hear it. It didn't matter. She didn't need her feet planted in soil to call on the magic of the earth. She was surrounded by gold, precious metal that was one blood among the many different bloods running through the earth's deep veins.

She imagined the sorcerous tethers, envisioned them in her mind as skeins of twisted ropes, much like the torsion springs on the ballistae, stretching taut every time Malachus flew toward the sun. Ropes broke. They also unraveled, and sometimes the anchors that held them gave way. Halani focused on the anchors, embedded into the earth by its magic. There were five, and they were strong, woven by those whose sorcery was far more powerful than her own. Such knowledge didn't deter her. Their magic was in service to a malice that rejected all the life-giving earth represented. Halani's was in service to a child of Pernu and Ninsurgha. Lightning might love the draga, but so did the earth.

Halani concentrated on one of the five anchors, using the metal paint covering her body to find the specific earth hymn bound up in the anchor.

Only silence greeted her questing at first. Then she heard it, a bass note reminiscent of a heartbeat. Unlike the sweet bell chime of the gold, but no less beautiful. And strong, ungodly strong.

Halani focused even harder on her vision of the anchor, imagining it wiggling free of the earth holding it, soil falling slowly away as it slipped toward the surface. A tickling pop teased the inside of her nostrils, and soon twin ribbons of warmth leaked from her nose to drip over her lips. The bass note in her head thrummed and thumped, swelling and contracting as she worked to break the magicians' spell. The gold covering her skin shifted, the paint tightening and hardening, blistering her skin even more.

She groaned at the sudden burst of agony inside her skull, and her stomach heaved in protest. The hymn halted with a snap, and in her vision the anchor ripped free of the earth, dissolving the rope to which it was attached. She didn't hesitate in turning her magic toward the remaining anchors, despite the fact that her stomach lodged in her throat, her head threatened to crack open, and her eyes bulged from their sockets. One by one, the anchors broke free, and the sorcerous chains fell away. Earth's hymn resounded in her ears, pulsating through every shard of bone, every vein flowing with blood, until she was Ninsurgha herself, who opened her hand and set her last child free. Blood no longer trickled over Halani's lips. It poured.

A roar trumpeted above her, and she opened her eyes in time to see Malachus swooping toward her once more, his wings flapping fast as he drew nearer, until he hovered dangerously close to her and the ballistae. Her gaze met his fiery one, his elliptical pupil dilating to dwarf the red iris.

The draga roared again as he dodged another bolt and shot toward the clouds, no longer leashed by earth magic. Sick, exhausted, with her vision blackening at the edges, Halani dragged her gaze to Dalvila, who watched Malachus's flight with an expression that changed from victorious to feral the higher he soared. Her red lips pulled back from her teeth in a snarl. She lunged from the couch, face a mask of hatred as she screeched at the ballista soldiers. "Bring him down!" she bellowed. Madness twisted her features as she turned toward Halani, the glitter of sunlight bouncing off the knife she clutched in her hand.

Halani watched, helpless, as death, dressed in colorful silks, raced toward her. Fear no longer plagued her. Her mother was safe and Malachus free. She relaxed against the pole to which she was bound and grinned at the furious Dalvila. "I win," she whispered.

CHAPTER TWENTY-SIX

Malachus trumpeted another victory call as he gained altitude in preparation for a dive. Resourceful Halani had found a way to break the empress's invisible shackles on him and allow him to break hers.

He arced toward the city walls far below him now. As a draga, he'd gained superior vision, even this high up. His great heart, pumping furiously to give his wings the strength they needed to power his bulk into the air and fly fast, seized at the sight of the empress herself sprinting toward bound Halani, a knife in her raised hand.

The roar he emitted cracked the sky as he tucked his wings tight against his body and dove hard for the battlements. He slammed, clawed feet first, into the ballista and its team nearest Halani, exploding wood shrapnel, body parts, and stone masonry in every direction. The crowd's raucous bellows turned to terrified screams as Malachus hurled pieces of the ballista into their midst. He raked a claw across the parapet where archers with their bows trained on Halani stood, flinging them off the wall to the ground and into the churning mob below.

Dalvila, slowed by the rush of people trying to escape the battlements, checked her headlong dash toward Halani, but only for a moment. Even the threat of being hurled off the battlements wasn't enough to stop her from wreaking her vengeance on Malachus for spoiling her plans. He launched into the air just in time to avoid a shot from the ballista positioned on the wall perpendicular to the one on which Halani stood. The bolt split the air with a whine before embedding itself in a section of wall, exploding a corona of mortar and stone across the panicked crowd.

This time he didn't go as high as before. He needed to reach Halani before the empress did. Bound to the pole, she wouldn't survive Dalvila's attack. The thought made his wings beat faster, and he turned once more, diving fast.

Ballista crews scattered like rats in every direction as Malachus whipped his tail against a ballista, slinging it behind the city walls and into the streets. He closed a claw around the pole to which the now-unconscious Halani was tethered, ripping it out of the ground with an effortless jerk.

People ran pell-mell across the battlements, looking for any escape route, screaming and praying for mercy. One voice rose above it all, nearly incoherent with rage.

"Shoot that fucking draga, you bunch of craven shit stains! *Shoot him now!*"

His own fury almost blinding him, Malachus gently grasped his precious cargo in his claws and swooped toward the raving empress, her once sublime features monstrous. She didn't run when he dove toward her, standing her ground to hurl every filthy epithet in existence at him. She didn't flinch when Malachus opened his mouth and snatched her from the wall into his jaws.

Nor did she make a sound when he bit down, shredding flesh and crushing bone as her blood burst hot and coppery across his tongue. What remained of the fleeing crowd screamed in unison at the sight, wailing their horror even louder when Malachus cocked his head back before lunging forward, spraying them all in a shower of gore, saliva, and the empress's remains.

He didn't return for another attack, desperate now to get as far away, as fast as possible, from Domora and the remaining ballistae. His leg throbbed from the bolt embedded in the scales and muscle there, and his torn wing burned. Worst of all, Halani hung limp in his clasp.

Malachus winged toward a forested part of the nearby foothills. He could land at the tree line and limp his way into the forest's wider spaces. It wasn't much of a hiding place, and he couldn't count on the shock of the empress's gruesome death to stop her army from immediately setting out to hunt him. At least half the city had witnessed him flying in this direction. He had a few hours at most before they reached this place.

The forest offered a cool, quiet sanctuary, its thick canopy a shield from the sun. Malachus landed lightly on one foot, folding his wings tight to his body. He hopped toward the trees, searching for the places where they grew tallest so that they concealed his height. He found a shady spot where the understory grew thin and lay Halani carefully down on a heap of dead leaves. He used one claw to sever her bonds from the pole. She crumpled before him. For a moment, terror seized him at the sight of her blood-smeared face. Had the magic she wielded to free him killed her? The thought rammed a ballista bolt straight through his soul. He could accept the idea of him dying for her, but not her for him.

Never that.

A low, rumbling growl traveled up his throat, relief and half-dead hope mixing together when her chest rose and fell on a slow breath. If he could change back into a man, he'd gather her in his arms, bury his face in her neck, and whisper her name over and over until he finally convinced himself she was alive and safe.

But he couldn't change back. Not like this, with injuries he could survive as a draga but not as a man. He barely understood the workings of this new, unfamiliar body. His inaugural flight possessed all the grace of a fledgling tossed out of the nest and nearly got him killed more than once. And if changing back to a man meant suffering through the same convulsions as changing into a draga, they, plus his wounds, would end him for certain.

His more sensitive hearing picked up Halani's faint sigh. She looked so small, lying there in the bed of leaves, no bigger than an infant to his draga eyes. Her eyelids fluttered before opening, revealing a gaze made demonic by burst blood vessels that turned the whites of her eyes red. She stared at him for a long, silent moment before her lips curved in a bloody smile. "You're so beautiful," she whispered. "And so big."

A bubble of laughter traveled up his throat, escaping between his teeth in a deep snort that shot a plume of smoke out of one nostril. Halani's bloodshot eyes rounded before she too gave a weak laugh. Malachus wanted to tell her he thought she was beautiful as well, and very gold, but the words wouldn't shape themselves within his draga mouth or on his draga tongue, and his teeth seemed enormous and more numerous than the trees in this forest.

Halani reached up to caress his snout, the flat bridge and wide, curving nostrils, the smaller, more flexible scales that covered his cheeks. "I can't believe you ate the empress," she said in a voice both wondering and aghast.

I didn't eat her, he wanted to say. *I just rearranged her before returning her to her admiring subjects.* Instead, he settled for another snort, this one conveying his disgust.

Her weak laughter held a trace of revulsion, though it seemed such revulsion was reserved for the fact that he actually had to bite down on such a foul specimen as the empress. "I'm sorry you had to experience that."

So was he. The woman tasted foul, but he was glad she was dead, and even more glad he'd been the one to kill her. The gods only knew who would take her place on the Kraelian throne, but surely they could be no worse than the Spider of Empire.

While Halani was alive and even able to laugh, she'd suffered her own ordeal and was far from well. Not only that; she was naked and painted gold, and as she became more conscious, her discomfort grew. "The paint," she said, grimacing. "I'm blistered from it, I think."

As a draga, Malachus was big, powerful, and pulsing with magic. He was also utterly useless in his ability to help her out of this predicament. Flying off with her to find a stream to wash in was too dangerous. He could lick the paint off her, bursting blisters and stripping off the first layer of her skin for his efforts.

Halani patted his snout at his frustrated rumble. "Don't fret. It's not so bad. I just need to rest for a moment, to sleep. We'll figure out what to do when I'm more awake. We'll find a way." She drifted asleep after that, sheltered within the tent he made of his wings.

In the end, the way found them. The crackle of leaves under a wary footfall alerted Malachus to the presence of others. He coiled around the still sleeping Halani, his body hiding her from view, and waited to see who emerged from the trees. His uninjured wing involuntarily snapped open at the sight of familiar faces, making the group who faced him leap away with frightened shouts.

Saradeen and four other free traders gaped at him, slack-jawed, their gazes passing over him in disbelieving awe. Saradeen was the first to recover his composure and gave Malachus a lopsided smile. "I bet you can eat a lot of sheep, Malachus."

Malachus's stomach rumbled at the notion. He hadn't eaten in days and had no doubt he could decimate a couple of flocks, either as a man or as a draga.

The old free trader gestured to the men with him. “We were outside the city and saw what happened. You’re damn lucky that Kostan here is part of our band. He grew up in this area and knows these forests like the back of his eyelids. He led us straight to you once you flew off with Halani.” He scowled. “Which means we can’t linger here. We’ve broken camp and left Domora. The city’s in chaos, and half the Kraelian army is looking for you two.” He glanced to the side of Malachus. “Where’s Halani?”

Malachus uncoiled his length to reveal Halani’s head and shoulders but not the rest of her. All of Domora had seen her unclothed on the battlements. It didn’t mean they had to keep seeing her that way.

Saradeen clucked. “Poor girl. She’s a brave one. Always has been. Kind, too. She didn’t deserve what Dalvila did to her.” Malachus nodded, buffeting the smaller humans with a gust of air from the movement. The trees around him rustled. The free trader reached inside a small pack he carried, pulling out a long overtunic. “She can wear this to cover up. There’s a stream not far from here. We can get her there to clean the paint off, certainly before Hamod sees her like that, or he might try to sell her.”

Malachus’s lips curved back from his teeth in a silent snarl. Every man uttered a prayer, except Saradeen, who flinched. “Sorry. Poor joke.”

At the sound of new voices, Halani woke a second time. She gasped her joy when she saw the free traders. “You found us!”

Saradeen grinned and offered her the tunic he held. “It wasn’t hard, thanks to Kostan, but that’s both a good and bad thing. If we found you, others will too.” He kept up a flow of light chatter, staring into the forest while Halani pulled on the borrowed garb. "We weren't sure how we'd get either of you out of there," he said, "but after Malachus ate the Spider of Empire, it didn't matter anymore."

I didn't eat the empress. Malachus was beginning to miss his human voice.

"How is Mama?" Halani's features held a yearning Malachus recognized. He still felt it for his mother, long dead but never forgotten.

Saradeen helped her clamber over Malachus's tail before he could shift it out of the way. "She's resting and eating well," the free trader said, adroitly sidestepping the fact that Asil walked the Dream Road. Malachus was grateful for the man's discretion.

A zephyr wind wrapped through the trees, carrying with it the scent of men, dogs, and horses. Malachus rose to his feet, towering over the humans, who once more gaped at him in awe, all except golden Halani. The hunt was on. They had to leave. Now.

Saradeen pointed to the bolt sticking out of Malachus's flank. "That's a deep wound," he said. "I don't think the four of us can pull it out, and I'd caution against it even if we could in case you bleed out."

Halani's small hand was cool on Malachus's scales, her painted features fearful, sorrowing. "What can we do to help you?"

There was nothing they could do except let him go, and escape the Kraelian hunters themselves. For a long time Malachus had searched the world for his birthright, eager to embrace it, become a draga and leave the guise of humanity behind, if not for good, then for a very long time. Now he wished he could be a man once more, even if it was just long enough to tell Halani those things he should have told her when the power of human speech was his to command. Instead he nudged her gently with his snout and half closed his eyes.

As if she read his earlier thoughts, she echoed them aloud. "You can't stay here. The Empire is no place for a man made into a draga, a wounded draga at that. You must fly away from here as soon as you can." Tears filled her eyes, turning them even redder. She clasped either side of his nose in her hands before leaning forward to press a light kiss to the tip, her lips as cool as her hands against his scales. "I've not lived an extraordinary life. Not until I met you. Until then I was asleep. You awakened me, and in you I see all that is noble and brave, and beautiful." She sniffed, letting the tears course freely down her cheeks. "Thank you for saving my mother. Thank you for saving me. I'm proud to have been your lover, privileged to have been your healer, blessed to have been your friend. And I will never forget you all the days of my life." She kissed him a final time, leaning her body into his scales for a far-too-brief moment. "I love you, Malachus. Don't forget me."

His claws dug trenches into the earth in the bid not to snatch her back to him and deal with the consequences of such a shortsighted decision later. Halani turned away to join the free traders, her back straight but her head bent.

Saradeen offered him a deep bow, one of a man before his sovereign. "Should you ever find yourself on the trade roads again, Malachus, know you'll always be welcomed in our band for as long as you choose."

The other men followed suit, offering bows and words of gratitude for the aid he'd rendered to them. Malachus barely heard them, his focus on Halani.

Saradeen motioned for the others to lead her out of the forest. She looked back once, a long gaze both accepting and grieving, before following them. Saradeen remained behind for a moment. "We'll split up," he told Malachus. "Two of us to get Halani to the stream, the other two to lead that hunting party off your scent long enough for you to fly off without being shot full of bolts." He glanced at Malachus's torn wing. "Can you still fly?" At Malachus's nod, the free trader brushed his palms together. "Then I bid you good luck and fair journey, draga. You've given me a lifetime of stories to tell my grandchildren. May you live long to do the same for others."

He left then, to join Halani and the others at the edge of the forest. Malachus rose, muffling a snarl at the pain shooting through his leg. A pain not nearly as awful as the one crushing his heart. Winosia called to him, those fair lands where dragas weren't hunted and harvested, where he might heal and learn how to live within this new form that was more natural to him than the human one he'd worn for as long as he could remember. Winosia, where snows fell on the mountain monasteries in a shroud of white, and the farmers in the fields constructed household shrines and lit votive candles in the names of ancient dragas. Winosia, where Halani, the light of his soul, was not.

EPILOGUE

Winter came to the hinterlands of the Krael Empire on an angry howl of wind that chased away the last days of fall in a single evening, casting a bitter cold across the territories. The cold didn't stop Kraelian noble families from slaughtering each other in a bid to claim Dalvila's throne for themselves, leaving the Empire teetering toward chaos.

Worried at the growing anarchy within the Empire's borders, Hamod had taken his free trader band and begged sanctuary for the winter within the Goban territories that bordered the Savatar pasture lands.

Even during the bitterest days, when breathing froze the lungs and everyone chipped the ice filmed over their washbowls just to reach the water in them, the mood in the camp was buoyant, and the free traders spent many nights swapping stories and dinner with the Goban farmers who lived nearby and reciprocated with invitations to every birth, wedding, and winter festival observed.

Halani adopted a cheery, smiling manner, especially when she was with Asil. Her mother had finally left the Dream Road and returned to the living world one autumn night while Marata told the story of the draga who attacked Domora. Most had proclaimed Asil's return a blessing of the gods. Halani fell to her knees every night, thanking every deity whose name she could remember for her mother's return. She thanked Malachus, too, his name soft on her lips when she said it, which was often.

She tried not to think of him too much, a fruitless endeavor, especially during the night's small hours, when the memory of Domora kept her awake, either from nightmares or from the ache of missing Malachus so much her bones hurt from it. Had he made it to Winosia safely? And if so, where did he convalesce? Was he still a draga, or had he once more assumed the guise of a man so he might walk among other men? Did he remember her? Miss her the way she missed him? So many what-ifs and no answers to them. Sometimes she thought she might go mad from their spinning in her brain.

Those who knew her best, besides Asil, weren't fooled, though they didn't push her to drop the jovial facade or spill her loneliness on their shoulders. The very idea of it made her shudder.

Several months and two seasons had passed since his departure, and he still occupied nearly all of her waking thoughts, and every one of her dreams. Even with her efforts at presenting a jocund front to the others, Asil sensed something was wrong. She'd always groomed Halani's hair and returned to the task with an enthusiasm that bordered on worship, stopping sometimes to silently hug her daughter and offer a comfort that was a balm to Halani's lonely soul.

The gray winter days with their bleak skies and anemic sun didn't help her mood, and the punishing cold only made her want to huddle in bed under the covers and not come out of the wagon until spring. But that was an indulgence granted only to the wealthy, who had armies of servants to attend them. Everyone in Hamod's camp had chores that kept them busy from sunrise to sunset. Cold weather didn't bring them to a halt; it just made the tasks more miserable.

Today, snow clouds had rolled in, bringing with them a white-out of fat flakes that caught and stuck on everything standing outside. The wagons, the livestock, the horse herd huddled together as they nibbled at the bits of brittle grass buried under a shroud of crystalline white. Halani stood in front of the horse trough, breaking up the newest layer of ice that had formed across the water's surface. A trio of horses stood on either side of her, waiting for her to complete the work, sometimes snorting and tossing their heads as if to encourage her to hurry it along. One of them was Batraza.

Except for a fuzzy winter coat, the easygoing mare looked no different from the first day she entered their camp and set the horses and other livestock to whinnying and stamping their feet in alarm at her nearness. Halani now knew why animals reacted so badly to Malachus and to Batraza, enchanted by his magic. He'd been forced to leave her behind, and Halani was grateful for one thing of his she could keep. Batraza became her mare, and she rode her every day, even if it was just an ambling walk around the camp's perimeter. The other animals still shunned Batraza, until one day they didn't, and Halani discovered the mare grazing contentedly amid their small herd as if she'd always belonged there and been accepted. Malachus's spell was broken. Happy for the mare, Halani still wept over the loss.

She paused in breaking up the ice to pat Batraza's withers. "Cold enough to freeze a brazier fire today, Batraza," she said.

Suddenly, the other horses bolted, galloping away from the camp as fast as they could. Batraza stayed, watching the fleeing pair with only a forward flick of her ears to show her interest. Startled by their surprising reactions, Halani accidentally dropped her stick in the frozen water. She braced herself to plunge her hand in the frigid water and fish it out but stopped when she noticed that not only the horses near her had spooked. Every animal had. The entire horse herd, the goats in their pens, even the stolid oxen. Halani spotted Kursak coming toward her, club in hand. "Wolves?" she asked, though that seemed unlikely. Winter's deprivation made the packs more aggressive, more desperate, but she'd never seen the bigger animals react this way to a hunting pack.

"I don't think so, but that kind of skittishness didn't spawn from a snowflake landing on someone's nose." He scanned the surrounding landscape, obscured by the heavy curtain of falling snow. "I don't like it. Gather up any children and get them to the wagons. If you pass one of the men, send them my way so we can round up what's run off."

"Where's Hamod?" Halani had just seen his favorite horse, Pippet, bolt toward a copse of winter-bare trees, two more mares following close behind her.

"Probably strapping on snowshoes to track down Pippet and bring her back."

He'd just finished speaking when an enormous dark shadow passed over the pristine pasture, blocking out what little of the weak sun still managed to break through the cloud cover. Those animals that hadn't spooked and fled with the first group did so now.

Hamod stomped toward Halani and Kursak in his snowshoes. "Everyone in the wagons now!" he ordered. His eyes narrowed on Halani. "Where's your mother?"

Halani's heart raced. "With Osun's boys and girl. Snowball fight." She scanned the heavy sky, blinking into the falling curtain of white. "Did you see what it was?"

"No. It might just have been a cloud, but something's spooked every animal in a quarter league of this camp. I may not trust men, but I trust a horse's instincts every time." He clopped past her. "I'll fetch Asil and the others."

He didn't get far before the same dark shadow suddenly pierced the heavy veil of clouds, diving fast toward the camp. People screamed and raced for the wagons. A few stood frozen in place, including Halani, Saradeen, and Kostan. Kursak nearly yanked her off her feet pulling her toward the nearest wagon. She jerked away, jarred out of the stupor that took hold of her at the sight of immense wings that stirred up the snow in a whirling shower as a familiar bronze-scaled draga landed in front of her. The snow was still settling when a vortex of bloody smoke consumed the creature, and in its place a black-haired man with unforgiving features and ink-dark eyes stared at her. Awed exclamations rose behind her, commands from one group to another to lower crossbows and put away swords. Not far from the stunned and disbelieving Halani, Saradeen casually brushed the snow off his clothes and addressed their visitor. "You'll have to go back where you came from and find some other monarch to eat," he called out, startling a laugh from Halani. "They still haven't chosen an emperor or empress to take the Kraelian throne."

"I'll never hear the end of it, will I, old man?" Malachus called back. "I didn't eat the empress."

His gazed again settled on Halani. He glided easily toward her through the snow, even without the benefit of snowshoes. His smile remained, but charged with an intensity that made Halani's breath stall in her chest. He stopped a few steps away from her.

Hardly daring to believe her eyes, she stood rooted in place, blinking away the snowflakes that gathered and melted on her eyelashes. "Did you forget something, Malachus?" Her voice warbled, and she cleared her throat. A thousand miserable years had passed since she'd seen him, or so it felt to her. He was flesh and blood and real instead of a dream born of yearning.

Malachus's smile faded. "No, I didn't. I couldn't, even had I tried. It's why I'm here. Did you forget me, Halani of the Lightning?"

"No," she said softly. "Never." Some might say their separation had made her fanciful, but she'd insist to anyone that he'd grown more handsome. "You returned home safely. I'm glad. I was worried."

A small frown creased a line between his eyebrows. "I returned to Winosia and to the monastery. The brotherhood took care of me while I healed and learned what it is to be draga." He closed the distance between them, tipping her chin up with his thumb to bring her face closer to his. "I'm still learning, but I didn't go home, Halani," he said. "I've come home. If you'll have me."

The euphoria bursting through every pore of her body made her shake. She clasped his wrist, remembering the heady warmth of his skin. "This is a dangerous place for a draga."

"It's a dangerous place for witches, yet you're here. It's the perfect place for this draga."

"You'll have to sit by Asil during storytelling. She'll insist on it."

He grinned. "I can do that."

"And sleep beside me every night. I'll insist on it."

The smile turned seductive. "I'm more than happy to share your bed. Is that all?"

She tapped a finger against her lip as if the question were a weighty one. "Take me flying one day." *What wonders might that hold,* she thought to herself. *See the world with a bird's-eye view from the back of a draga.* There was a story to tell.

Malachus gathered her into his arms, snow cascading off his shoulders. "Any day you wish."

"On the day you bond with me," she offered, holding her breath.

His eyes blazed bright. "That is a good day. The best of days." He kissed her then, telling her without words that he'd pined for her as much as she had for him. "My gods, woman," he said when they came up for air. "How I've missed you."

She cupped his face with her palms. "You will always have a place among us, a place beside me, in life and beyond death when the earth sings us to dust and tells the wind of how Halani of the Lightning loved a draga and he loved her in return."

ACKNOWLEDGMENTS

Writing is a solitary endeavor that takes place as much in the writer's head as it does via the keyboard. Creating a book is a team effort. Sincerest thanks to all those who put in the work to package this tale into a book. Special thanks to my editor Anne Sowards, whose editorial guidance continues to make me a better writer; to Mel Sanders for her brilliance and advice in all things writing related; to Jeffe Kennedy, who made me laugh in the middle of some serious mental exhaustion; and to Sarah Younger, my agent, whom I fondly call Agent Badass and who lives up to the name.

ABOUT THE AUTHOR

Grace Draven is a Louisiana native living in Texas with her husband, kids, and a big doofus dog. She is the winner of the RT Reviewers' Choice Award for Best Fantasy Romance of 2016 and a *USA Today* bestselling author.

CONNECT ONLINE

GraceDraven.com
GraceDravenAuthor
GraceDraven